Escape . . .

Scarred by [illegible], a young woman struggles to find her identity, her destiny, her family.

LaNelle just wants to lie back and die in peace. But then Rita Mae, an old rival, tells her about the Angel of Death. . . .

A young changeling, enslaved in the present, struggles to discover his past.

Imagine . . .

He loved his work—and hoped to marry her in twenty years—when she turned nineteen.

Wandering through endless worlds, he searches for the perfect words.

'Tis better to have loved and lost . . . much better.

Suppose . . .

Out of sheer boredom, he took the dirty half-breed thing into his home and promised to raise it as his own.

Distressed damsels, flashing swords, fame and fortune: everyone wants to be a storybook hero. Unfortunately, not everyone lives in a storybook world.

A desperate situation forces a young man into the Dragon Cave, armed only with a tale told to him by a stranger.

Dream . . .

Gods aren't always what they seem.

Their love created whole new worlds, but was it enough for her?

A journey into the future of what might have been, a place of memories and hopes.

Wonder . . .

If Winter held the other seasons captive, what could you do to save them?

The City provided anything a man could possibly want—except the ability to stand on his own two feet.

What has been said about the
L. RON HUBBARD
PRESENTS
WRITERS OF THE FUTURE
ANTHOLOGIES

"This has become a major tributary to the new blood in fantastic fiction."

GREGORY BENFORD

"From cutting-edge high tech to evocative fantasy, this book's got it all—it's lots of fun and I love the chance to see what tomorrow's stars are doing today."

TIM POWERS

"I recommend the Writers of the Future Contest at every writers' workshop I participate in."

FREDERIK POHL

". . . an exceedingly solid collection, including SF, fantasy and horror . . ."

CHICAGO SUN TIMES

"A first-rate collection of stories and illustrations."

BOOKLIST

"It is rare to find this consistency of excellence in any series of science fiction and fantasy stories. The well-deserved reputation of L. Ron Hubbard's Writers of the Future has proven itself once again."

STEPHEN V. WHALEY
PROFESSOR ENGLISH & FOREIGN LANGUAGES
CALIFORNIA POLYTECHNICAL UNIVERSITY, POMONA

"The untapped talents of new writers continue to astonish me and every WOTF volume provides a well-spring of the greatest energy put forth by the ambitious writers of tomorrow."

KEVIN J. ANDERSON

"This contest has changed the face of Science Fiction."

DEAN WESLEY SMITH
EDITOR OF *STRANGE NEW WORLDS*

"Some of the best SF of the future comes from Writers of the Future and you can find it in this book."

DAVID HARTWELL

"Not only is the writing excellent . . . it is also extremely varied. There's a lot of hot new talent in it."

LOCUS MAGAZINE

"As always, this is the premier volume in the field to showcase new writers and artists. You can't go wrong here."

BARYON

"This contest has found some of the best new writers of the last decade."

KRISTINE KATHRYN RUSCH
AUTHOR & EDITOR

"Once again, Writers of the Future provides some of the most imaginative and thought-provoking speculative fiction."

PARSEC MAGAZINE

SPECIAL OFFER FOR SCHOOLS AND WRITING GROUPS

The seventeen prize-winning stories in this volume, all of them selected by a panel of top professionals in the field of speculative fiction, exemplify the standards that a new writer must meet if he expects to see his work published and achieve professional success.

These stories, augmented by "how to write" articles by some of the top writers of science fiction and fantasy, make this anthology virtually a textbook for use in the classroom and an invaluable resource for students, teachers and workshop instructors in the field of writing.

The materials contained in this and previous volumes have been used with outstanding results in writing courses and workshops held on college and university campuses throughout the United States—from Harvard, Duke and Rutgers to George Washington, Brigham Young and Pepperdine.

To assist and encourage creative writing programs, the **L. Ron Hubbard Presents Writers of the Future** anthologies are available at special quantity discounts when purchased in bulk by schools, universities, workshops and other related groups.

For more information, write:

Specialty Sales Department
Galaxy Press, L.L.C.
7051 Hollywood Blvd., Suite 200
Hollywood, California 90028
or call toll-free: 1-877-8GALAXY
Internet address: www.galaxy-press.com
E-mail address: info@galaxy-press.com

A culture is as rich and as capable of surviving as it has imaginative artists. The artist is looked upon to start things. The artist injects the spirit of life into a culture. And through his creative endeavors, the writer works continually to give tomorrow a new form.

In these modern times, there are many communication lines for works of art. Because a few works of art can be shown so easily to so many, there may even be fewer artists. The competition is very keen and even dagger sharp.

It is with this in mind that I initiated a means for new and budding writers to have a chance for their creative efforts to be seen and acknowledged.

L. Ron Hubbard, 1985

GIO

ABOUT
THE COVER

FRAZETTA'S *NEW WORLD*

Called the "King of Illustrators" by L. Ron Hubbard, and a dedicated judge of the Illustrators of the Future Contest since its inception, Frank Frazetta has left a stamp of indelible artistry on the world of illustration. His powerful and unforgettable images—including his painting, *New World*, which distinguishes the cover of this volume—have made him one of the most popular and influential artists of his time.

Frazetta's contributions to the Contest for new illustrators of science fiction and fantasy have been numerous and diverse, including permission to use his work on the covers of many of the *Writers of the Future* anthologies. We thank him and his gracious wife and business manager, Ellie Frazetta, for their continuing support and enthusiasm.

Of special interest to all his fans and admirers, the new Frank Frazetta Museum in East Stroudsburg, Pennsylvania, is now open. Detailed information about the museum and Frazetta's work can be found at www.frazettaartgallery.com.

L. RON HUBBARD

PRESENTS

WRITERS

OF THE

FUTURE

VOLUME
XVIII

L. RON HUBBARD

PRESENTS

WRITERS

OF THE

FUTURE

VOLUME
XVIII

The Year's 17 Best Tales from the
Writers of the Future®
International Writing Program
Illustrated by the Winners in the
Illustrators of the Future®
International Illustration Program

With Essays on Writing and Art by
L. Ron Hubbard • Andre Norton
H. R. Van Dongen • Tim Powers

Edited by Algis Budrys

Galaxy Press, L.L.C.

Magic out of a Hat by L. Ron Hubbard: © 2002 L. Ron Hubbard Library
The Dragon Cave: © 2002 Drew Morby
The Haunted Seed: © 2002 Ray Roberts
Rewind: © 2002 David D. Levine
Windseekers: © 2002 Nnedi Okorafor
Lost on the Road: © 2002 Ari Goelman
Graveyard Tea: © 2002 Susan Fry
Carrying the God: © 2002 Lee Battersby
A Few Tips on the Craft of Illustration: © 2002 H. R. Van Dongen
Memoria Technica: © 2002 Leon J. West
Free Fall: © 2002 Tom Brennan
All Winter Long: © 2002 Jae Brim
The Art of Creation: © 2002 Carl Frederick
Advice to the New Writer: © 2002 Andre Norton
The Road to Levenshir: © 2002 Patrick Rothfuss
Eating, Drinking, Walking: © 2002 Dylan Otto Krider
Origami Cranes: © 2002 Seppo Kurki
A New Anthology: © 2002 Tim Powers
Worlds Apart: © 2002 Woody O. Carsky-Wilson
Prague 47: © 2002 Joel Best
What Became of the King: © 2002 Aimee C. Amodio

Illustration on page   8 © 2002 Hristo Dimitrov Ginev
Illustration on page 35 © 2002 C. M. Wolf
Illustration on page 46 © 2002 Rey Rosario
Illustration on page 76 © 2002 Brian Hailes
Illustration on page 108 © 2002 Darlene Gait
Illustration on page 126 © 2002 John Kolbek
Illustration on page 146 © 2002 Irena Yankova Dimitrova
Illustration on page 176 © 2002 David C. Mullins
Illustration on page 187 © 2002 Irena Yankova Dimitrova
Illustration on page 216 © 2002 Fritz Peters
Illustration on page 254 © 2002 Rey Rosario
Illustration on page 287 © 2002 Jason Pastrana
Illustration on page 335 © 2002 Brian Hailes
Illustration on page 361 © 2002 Anthony Arutunian
Illustration on page 390 © 2002 Hristo Dimitrov Ginev
Illustration on page 413 © 2002 Anthony Arutunian
Illustration on page 432 © 2002 Fritz Peters

Cover Artwork: New World © 1972 Frank Frazetta

ISBN: 1-59212-032-0

Library of Congress Catalog Card Number:
First Edition Paperback 10 9 8 7 6 5 4 3 2 1
Printed in the United States of America

BATTLEFIELD EARTH is a registered trademark owned by Author Services, Inc., and is used
with its permission. MISSION EARTH and its logo, WRITERS OF THE FUTURE and its logo and
ILLUSTRATORS OF THE FUTURE and its logo are trademarks owned by L. Ron Hubbard Library
and used with permission.

CONTENTS

INTRODUCTION

Written by
Algis Budrys

We are proud to present the eighteenth book in this series of annual anthologies. The award-winning stories included here are the result of the latest year of the ongoing L. Ron Hubbard Writers of the Future Contest and the illustrations come from the parallel L. Ron Hubbard Illustrators of the Future Contest.

The rules for these contests appear in the back pages of this book. The results come in four quarters of the year, in each of which first, second and third place stories are designated. The prizes for these are awarded in the amounts of $1,000, $750 and $500 for the writers and $500 apiece for the illustrators. At the end of the year, we hold the L. Ron Hubbard Achievement Awards in Hollywood and name the Grand Prize winner of each contest, with an additional award of $4,000 each.

It hardly seems possible, but in the last eighteen years, we have brought the SF community such names as Nina Kiriki Hoffman, David Zindell, Dean Wesley Smith, Leonard Carpenter, Karen Joy Fowler and Mary Frances Zambreno, all of whom were unknowns, in our very first volume. Since then, we have brought you writers such as Robert Reed, K. D. Wentworth, James

Gardner, Nancy Farmer and illustrators such as Sergey
Poyarkov, Shaun C. Tan, and scores of others. Over the
years we have had well over two hundred graduates of
the writing program and nearly that in the illustrators.
There is no doubt the contests are the major single force
in promoting new talent in the field.

This is precisely as L. Ron Hubbard envisioned it in
the early 1980s. We have worked since its inception to
ensure that his vision continues in the same vein as he
originally set out in the first volume, to give "new and
budding writers a chance for their creative efforts to be
seen and acknowledged." And so the tradition continues
with entrants retaining all rights, with no entry fees and
judging by professionals only.

This latest book contains stories and illustrations from
people as unknown as those in any other volume. And we
expect in the course of time, over the years, many will have
become as familiar to SF readers as those in the first book.

Our judges have chosen them wisely, and we are confident you will enjoy the results.

THE DRAGON CAVE

Written by
Drew Morby

Illustrated by
Hristo Dimitrov Ginev

About the Author

Drew Morby was born thirty-three and some years ago in Los Angeles, California, but now makes his home in South Jersey with his prime motivators, Lisa and her daughter, Danielle.

Drew is an avid reader and he credits that love of the written word to his grandparents, who, in addition, also taught him to tie his shoes. He has had the good fortune to be able to travel as far as Tierra del Fuego, Anchorage, Tanzania and Xi'an, China, and would love to complete the circumnavigation of the globe by taking the Orient Express.

He would also like to give a special thanks to his parents for their support and to the Queue Continuum on AOL for their helpful critiques over the past few years.

About the Illustrator

Hristo Dimitrov Ginev was born on March 28, 1980, in Plovdiv, Bulgaria. His father is a colonel in the army and his mother is a teacher. He has a sister two years younger than him.

Hristo has been interested in drawing, painting and sketching from the beginning of elementary school. He decided to go to The High School of Fine Arts–Tzanko Lavrenov in Plovdiv. He spent five years there. But according to him, the most unforgettable, creative, useful, exciting, profound and pleasant period was his attendance at the tutored courses of Ahmed Chaushev, a brilliant artist, perfect pedagogue and great man. The studio where the courses were held became Hristo's second home.

In 1999, Hristo enrolled in the University of Architecture, Civil Engineering and Geodesy in Sofia. He studied there for two years. In 2001, Hristo applied for and was enrolled in The Art Institute of Boston. He is in the U.S. now, hoping to prove and show his real potential as an artist.

o beggars, or charity." The innkeeper's words followed Deng out into the chill evening.

Winter in the hills of the northern province arrived each year like clockwork, and with irrevocable finality. Those who didn't make it through the southern passes by the first lowland snowfall wouldn't make it at all.

With the first storm less than a ten-day away, the ground was already frozen, and it crunched with each of Deng's steps. Last year at this time, Deng was already headed south with the other students at the orphanage. Deng blew into his hands, rubbed them together and shoved them into his almost empty pockets where they joined his two copper pieces.

The streets, always crowded during the summer with merchants hawking sweet smelling foods and other wares, were now as bare as Deng's feet. His stomach growled. With all the caravans already gone south, and with them any chance of hitching a ride, Deng was left with two choices: find an employer or break into one of the empty houses for shelter and hope he could beg or steal enough food to survive.

A hunched figure walked past him on the street bundled up in a thick cloak. No one else was around, and Deng fell into step behind him. Just the thought of taking the cloak from the man warmed him a little. But he couldn't do that, could he? Deng didn't move closer to the man, but nor did he turn away.

Halfway up Mount Dragon, a bright flame erupted, shooting out of the dragon's cave. After a two-year hiatus, the flame had returned several weeks ago, melting away the snow around the cave. When he was younger, Deng loved to watch the pyrotechnics. Now it teased him. Warmth just out of reach. On the other hand, being roasted might be preferable to staying in Tundrin for a whole winter.

Distracted by the sight, Deng lost track of the old man. He saw an alley ahead and sprinted toward it. He turned the corner hoping to catch sight of the old man again and collided with a boy.

The boy, dressed in rags as shabby as Deng's, fell to the ground and cried out. The cry alerted two other boys who were holding the old man and trying to wrest his coat from him.

"This one's mine," Deng said, before they could speak. "I've been following him."

The boy Deng had knocked over was about his size, and even thinner. The other two were older and a few inches taller. One of them sported a slight crop of facial hair.

"Don't let him get away," the one with facial hair said.

The apparent leader made sure his cohort had a firm grip on the old man, then turned his attention to Deng.

"We grabbed him, that makes him ours." The leader thrust a thumb at his puffed-out chest and held his head tall as he approached. Deng was used to brawling with larger kids and wasn't cowed. He swung his foot up between the leader's legs and caught the bully by surprise, bringing him to the ground. The youngest thief swung a looping punch that Deng took with his stomach. The blow was softer than he expected. His own blow, strengthened by years of scrubbing walls and floors, caught the boy on the chin and dropped him. Deng's hand smarted from the contact, one more physical discomfort to ignore.

He turned on the last standing ruffian, but the boy let go of the old man and raised his hands.

Deng sucked on his skinned knuckles and watched as the three boys helped each other leave the alley. His blood was warm and salty and teased his stomach.

"Don't hurt me," the old man said, then broke into a wracking cough that startled Deng, who had forgotten all about him.

Warmed by the fight, Deng felt ashamed for his earlier impulse to take the man's coat. "I won't. Just be more careful on the streets." Deng wrapped his own threadbare coat around himself to trap his body heat and stepped back out to the main street. There were a few more establishments he had to check before finding a place to sleep for the night.

"Wait." The old man's voice stopped him. "You aren't going to rob me?"

Deng thought maybe the old man was addled to call out to a would-be robber. He should be heading home, grateful for the chance to keep his coat. Deng shook his head.

"Then allow me to offer you some reward."

Deng's heart thumped. Reward was good, but did he deserve it? He had, after all, intended to rob the man.

"None is needed," he said, keeping his voice even.

This statement was followed by silence, so Deng started away.

"Wait," the man called, and Deng also heard footsteps scurrying up behind him. He stopped and turned,

Illustrated by Hristo Dimitrov Ginev

but to make sure the footsteps belonged to the old man and not one of the other would-be robbers.

"I told you, no reward."

"I heard you, but you also said to be careful walking the streets." Deng eyed the man, trying to figure out what he intended. "I'd like to hire you to get me home safely. Let's say a warm dinner in exchange? Would that do for you?"

Deng's stomach rumbled, but his attention was drawn upward to the side of the mountain where the sky was once again lit by the dragon fire.

"There's no such thing as dragons, you know," the old man said. Deng didn't comment as they both watched evidence to the contrary. Was it safe to take food from this crazy old man? Deng caught himself, and laughed. How could he be afraid of someone he had just rescued?

"My name is Deng," he said, by way of accepting the old man's offer.

"I am Shian Alejandro del Moreti, but you can call me Shian," the old man said, holding out his hand. Only nobles had names like that, and despite the warm cloak, the old man looked anything but noble.

Shian's house was modest in size and decoration, but it still outclassed any house Deng had been invited into before. The main room sported a huge fire pit, and Shian filled it with a large pot of stew. Deng sat in a proffered seat and dozed off for a moment until Shian held a steaming bowl of rich smelling food under his nose.

Deng took the bowl and discovered that the stew contained real meat. He ate a second bowl before he considered that maybe he was taking advantage of his host. Shian added a mug of spiced cider to the meal, but even without the savory beverage, it was the best meal Deng had eaten since leaving the orphanage.

After the meal, Shian arranged two chairs in front of the fireplace with a large shield hanging over it and had Deng sit in one of them. Deng tried to protest, but the old man pushed another mug of the spicy brew into his hands and refused to listen to any excuses.

The warmth of the fire and the drink made the cold outside a daunting proposition, so Deng found himself accepting a night's lodging and listening to Shian talk about himself.

"I started out just like you. Living from winter to winter, looking for a way south then I met a man who changed all that." Shian's body spasmed into a coughing fit, but he waved away Deng's offer to help. Instead, Shian stuffed a pipe with tobacco and filled the room with a sweet smelling smoke. He offered, but Deng declined, having already taken enough from Shian.

"That man," Shian said, continuing his story. "That man told me what I told you: There are no such things as dragons." He puffed on his pipe for a moment and studied Deng's reaction. For his part, Deng wasn't sure how to respond. Something on the boy's face must have amused Shian though, because he chuckled.

"Always wondered what I must have looked like when he told me. Now I know." Shian motioned at the great shield hanging over the fireplace. "Get that down for me, would you? I'm too old, and I've grown too short."

The great shield was made from a heavy wood and bound by straps of metal, and Deng struggled to bring it down without crushing a toe underneath it.

"Look on the inside."

Deng held the shield on end and, using the light of the fire, found an inscription carved on the inside curve of the shield.

"Presented to Shian Alejandro del Moreti, in appreciation for slaying the dragon of the hill," Deng read aloud, grateful for the basic schooling of the orphanage. "And it's signed Lord Berthan." Deng looked at Shian. "Where did you steal this?"

"I earned it, lad. I earned it." Shian didn't seem at all put out by Deng's question or bothered by the obvious contradiction hanging in the air.

"How can you be a dragon slayer if dragons don't exist?"

The old man's eye lit up brighter than the fire. "Good question. And since you asked it, I'll tell you."

So Shian explained, and as the old man related how he had defeated the dragon with no more than a mule, a songbird, a torch, a barrel and a sack of clay, Deng's eyes widened and then he laughed in appreciation.

"I'll say this for you, Shian. That's the best fairy tale I've ever heard," Deng said when the old man finished. Deng's response seemed to dismay Shian and they sat in silence as the fire died in the hearth.

"Well, it is too late for you to look for a place to hole up for the winter now," Shian said. "You'll stay here the night, of course."

Deng didn't argue, though he felt that he had somehow disappointed Shian. Shian got him a blanket and Deng fell into a deep, comfortable sleep.

Deng was roused from his warm sleep by rough hands that shook him awake. He came up ready to fight; his left foot tangled with the blanket and the cushioned chair that served as his bed, and he fell to the floor.

He looked up and saw several men in Tundrin's constabulary colors standing in the house. The one who had shaken Deng awake peered down at him from under bushy eyebrows.

"Where is the dragon slayer?"

Deng was too sleepy to respond fast enough for the man with the bushy eyebrows.

"Find the dragon slayer," he said to the other constables, who scattered searching Shian's house, then he helped Deng stand up.

"What's going on?" Deng asked when his brain began to wake up.

"Lord Darchesi wants the dragon taken care of," Bushy Eyebrows said. Darchesi was Lord Berthan's son, who had ruled the northern province for the last handful of years.

"And he's in such a hurry that he disregarded manners?" Deng asked, before he could catch his speeding tongue.

"The lord's daughter will be receiving suitors this month. It would be unfortunate for any of them to think our lord too weak." Bushy Eyebrows paused and looked Deng over from his bare feet to his dirt covered face. "And who are you to ask such an impertinent question?"

Just then, one of the constables came downstairs from Shian's room.

"The dragon slayer is dead."

Deng was still in shock over the news when Bushy Eyebrows brought him, hands manacled behind him, in front of Lord Darchesi.

The lord sat in the middle of a large room decorated with heavy tapestries, which served more than a decorative purpose by keeping the heat from escaping from the cold stone walls. Two fires were roaring in pits on the left and right, and assorted other noblemen and women milled about. At least the warmed stones felt soothing to his feet.

The constable went up to Darchesi and spoke to the lord for a moment, then came back to Deng and brought him forward.

"Tell the truth and all will go well for you," Bushy Eyebrows said into his ear, and then spoke louder for the room to hear. "Lord Darchesi, sire. This is the squatter we found in Master Moreti's house. The dragon slayer was found dead in his bed."

Lord Darchesi's eyes focused on Deng and Deng felt his knees grow weak. The lord's green eyes seemed to stab through Deng with anger. However, when Darchesi spoke, his voice was measured and calm and betrayed nothing.

"Step forward, lad." Deng did as he was commanded, aware that all eyes were on him. "How did you come to be in Master Shian's house last night?"

Deng saw through the calm voice. They thought he had killed Shian in his sleep so that he could squat in Shian's house for the winter. Deng panicked.

"He adopted me!" It came out too fast for Deng to retract it. "I . . . I recently completed my term at the orphanage of Cicle, and Shian adopted me."

The lord raised a thin, dark eyebrow. "Adopted you?" He looked over at the constable, who shrugged. Darchesi turned back toward Deng. "Why would he do that?"

"He was attacked by brigands in the street. They tried to take his cloak. I stopped them and he invited me home with him." That much at least was true. And for all Deng knew, the old man had been meaning to adopt him. That could explain Shian's disappointment when Deng didn't appreciate the old man's tale. But then, Shian hadn't been lying about being a dragon slayer after all. Deng's current predicament was proof of that.

Lord Darchesi wasn't buying it, however. "Sparran, did you come across any evidence of the lad's claim while you were there?"

Sparran, the bushy-eyebrowed constable, shook his head. "None."

Darchesi looked back at Deng. "No evidence. I guess it's up to me to decide your fate, then."

"No! Your lordship, please, I can prove my claim, and maybe help you out as well." Darchesi's eye narrowed.

"How?"

"Shian passed his knowledge of dragons to me." Deng let that sink in a moment. Of course, Shian's knowledge had been primarily that dragons didn't exist. "I will rid you of the dragon."

Lord Darchesi sat back in his large chair and studied Deng. "In exchange?"

"In exchange for the price of a trip south." Deng swallowed, trying to get some moisture into his mouth. "And, your acceptance of me as Master Shian Alejandro del Moreti's legitimate heir." It's what the old man wanted, Deng told himself, and tried to ignore the voice inside that told him that he was taking advantage of Shian's kindness.

"And pray tell how much of this reward do you require up front?" Lord Darchesi was still suspicious, but Deng wasn't planning on running with the gold. In for a half-penny, in for a gold sovereign.

"Sire, all I need to defeat the dragon is a mule, preferably Shian—my father's, a songbird, a torch, a barrel and a sack of clay."

Lord Darchesi's stony face suddenly cracked into a large grin. "You may be Moreti's son after all. That's exactly what he requested of my father." Darchesi paused, then nodded. "You'll have your chance. Sparran, find the lad what he needs and get him some boots as well."

● ● ●

Darkness spread between the trees as Deng crunched across the crisp mountain snow in his new boots. They were a size or two too large, but an extra pair of socks had taken care of that. He adjusted the heavy belt and scabbard that Sparren had loaned him, and shifted the reins to his left hand.

Following Deng, and led by the reins, walked Toren, Shian's mule. The gray beast toted the large barrel and the sack on each side of its back, and tied in a precarious position atop the barrel sat a covered cage from which the songbird twittered its protest at being out in such chilly weather. Dangling off the back was a fancy lantern Darchesi had given him instead of a torch.

"I hope Shian was telling the truth," Deng told Toren, giving voice to the thought that continued to repeat in his head. "You were with him. Did he tell me the truth?"

The stout beast, whose long ears were drooped back along his neck, seemed disinclined to get drawn into the conversation and continued to haul his load in silence.

"Well, if everything goes right, I'll buy a packhorse to carry my stuff south for you." One of Toren's ears twitched, and Deng laughed, then gave Toren the signal to stop so he could feed the animal their last carrot.

In the sudden silence created by their halt, Deng heard one extra crunch. A lone footstep not caused by either him or the mule. Deng moved his hand to the hilt of the borrowed sword, though he had less idea how to use it than to slay a dragon.

"You are in the presence of a dragon slayer," he called out. "Show yourself, or I will consider you hostile."

"You're Deng? I've been waiting for you." The voice didn't sound dangerous, more like a young woman's than a brigand's. The shape that emerged from the trees appeared even less imposing.

"You're just a kid who talks to mules." The speaker was maybe four feet tall, short even compared to Deng, and slight even in a bulky winter cloak. Under the cowl, Deng could make out pale, angelic features.

"Who are you calling a kid?" he asked. "I've probably got ten cycles on you."

The tiny figure drew herself up. "I'm at least as old as you are. Royal blood runs small in these parts."

Royal blood? Deng scoffed. "Go home, little girl."

Instead of complying, the girl stalked toward him, her shoulders straight, holding her cloak just off the ground, either so she wouldn't trip or so the ends wouldn't get wet in the snow.

"I am Inya, of the Royal House of Tundrin. I have faerie blood, and I will accompany you to slay the dragon," she said in a kind of singsong voice.

"Suit yourself, but don't expect to ride." Deng was a little startled by his answer, but he just patted Toren on the neck. "Let's go, Toren." The best thing to do with crazy people, he decided, was just to ignore them and hope they did the same to you. He'd felt sorry for Shian, and look where that had gotten him. And if she did stick it out for the climb up the mountain, at least he would have someone other than Toren to talk to.

By the time they rose above the tree line, however, Deng regretted his decision. Inya was a font of useless information about Lord Darchesi's court and didn't understand the concept of privacy or silence. And while

Deng was forced to admit that the likelihood of her being Darchesi's daughter grew with each story, he still didn't understand her stubbornness regarding faeries. After all, no dragons, no faeries. It just followed.

"Can I have some water?" the princess asked.

"No." Deng guided Toren across the rocky terrain, which got slipperier with each rise in elevation, and tried to keep from glancing at her warm cloak.

"Why not? You have plenty in that barrel, and I think Toren would welcome the lighter load." To her credit, the princess didn't seem at all out of breath.

"I need it for the dragon." Deng's own lungs felt as if the air were avoiding them on purpose.

"You going to throw the barrel at it and hope its fire goes out?" she asked.

"No." Deng's terse response kept her quiet for a few steps.

"If we're going to be partners, you should tell me how we are going to slay the dragon. Are you going to throw the clay at it?"

Deng took a deep breath and ignored her. Shian never mentioned annoying tagalongs in any of his stories. Deng tried to lead Toren across a sloped rock slab, but the mule wanted nothing to do with it. Deng looked for another option, but found none.

"Come on, Toren, it's just a rock, and there's no way around." Deng stepped onto the rock and slipped. Toren's reins twisted around his wrist and spun him as he fell, tightening, and making him wince in pain.

Inya laughed as he pulled himself up and unwound the leather strap from his wrist. "Well, at least I know which of you is the smart one," she said.

Deng massaged his wrist as Inya scouted about and came up with a stout piece of wood. She held it with her left hand as she brought all her fingertips together with her right. She held her fingertips upward and brought the end of the stick over them. At the same time she said something Deng didn't catch, in that singsong way of hers.

The end of the stick burst into flame and a startled Deng almost fell over again.

"Nice trick," Deng said, as she brought the burning stick over to the rock and used the heat to melt the thin layer of ice covering it. "How did you do it?"

"Magic." Deng looked at Toren and winked. "Oh, magic, of course." He gathered the mule's reins again and led him across the wet, but less slippery, rock.

"You don't believe in magic?" Inya asked, as she put the stick out by bashing the burning end into the ground.

"Thank you for your help, Princess," Deng said. "You're good, but I've seen better." His own fingers were too thick for the nimble dexterity required, but he'd been to enough fairs and seen enough entertainers to be fooled.

At this point, the path changed to an easy slope up to the cave. Ahead, the sparse trees were singed and the ground glistened with moisture. This part of the mountain made the quiet forest below seem like a crowded market. Even the songbird stopped chirping.

Inya scurried up to walk next to him, still not out of breath, and Deng began to wonder if she did intend to go into the cave and face the dragon with him.

"So, you're a dragon slayer who doesn't believe in magic. Don't you think that's a little odd?" she asked.

"Odd? You're a noble who never gets tired and knows as much about getting around this mountain as she does about Lord Darchesi's court." Deng didn't even get a brief moment of satisfaction from his outburst.

Instead of being embarrassed, she gave out a slight chuckle.

"So, we are the perfect partners after all," she said, and his expression caused her to break into full laughter. It wasn't an altogether unpleasant sound. If only she weren't crazy, she might be nice to have around. After all, what person would hike all this way if they didn't have to?

A deep burnt scent lingered in front of the cave. Whether from the last blast or impregnated into the stone around the opening, Deng wasn't sure. Deng led Toren right up the charred path, and he derived some satisfaction as Inya held back, using a large rock as a shield from the cave.

"Shouldn't we have a plan or something?" she asked, peeking her head around at him.

Toren sniffed the air, and he must have smelled something familiar, because his step picked up.

"I do have a plan. You stay there," Deng said. He took the lantern off Toren's back and lit it.

"Won't the dragon see you coming?" Inya asked.

Deng ignored her. He needed to concentrate on what Shian had said and couldn't afford to be distracted by Inya's babbling.

Inside the cave, water dripped from the roof with hollow plunks on the hard rock floor. The burnt smell, stronger now, made him cough. He coughed hard enough that he almost dropped the lamp and retreated out of the cave.

"I guess it's too late for stealth," Inya said, now in front of her rock, leaning back against it, her arms crossed.

Deng's patience came to an end, but as he approached her, he managed to keep himself somewhat in check.

"There—is—no—such—thing—as—magic. Therefore, there is no such thing as a dragon," he said to her and glared his best glare.

Inya gave him a skeptical look, unintimidated. Deng threw up his hands.

"There is nothing here for you to see," Deng said, wishing he felt as confident as he sounded. "Unless I made a mistake. So, please, go home."

The polite approach seemed to work, and Inya started down the hill. Deng watched every step with suspicion. Sure enough, she didn't get far before she turned back.

"If there is no dragon, then how do you expect to get the reward from my father for slaying it?"

It was a good question and Deng had forgotten who she claimed she was. "The dragon doesn't exist, but the danger does. The dead prove that. If I can stop the danger, then don't I deserve the reward?"

"I guess so," she said, after a moment of contemplation.

"Thank you, good-bye, it was nice meeting you, I have to risk my life now." Deng stalked back to the cave opening.

This time he prepared for the stench and moved in, making sure that he didn't slip on the wet ground. Toren seemed unaffected by the foul odor as he followed along. The songbird didn't like it, however, chirping against the darkness.

The lantern, by design, didn't shed much light into the cavern, but it was enough. Deng tried to keep his eyes focused on the darkness, instead of the light, trying, as Shian had said, to develop some feel for the darkness. The light would have to go soon, and he needed to develop some night vision.

The darkness began to press in around him, fighting against the light, and Deng moved with deliberate care. The lantern became his friend, and he forgot about saving his eyes. His hands were slick with sweat and the handle of the lantern turned slippery. He cast a glance backward and could still make out the fading daylight at the mouth of the cave. How deep was the cave? He couldn't recall. At least he could be assured that nothing creepy or crawly lived in it.

The bird's fearful cooing changed to a panicky squawk.

When the bird cries, the light dies.

Shian's words spurred Deng into action, and he fumbled to squelch the flame, almost dropping the lamp in the process.

And then the darkness became complete.

His breath and Toren's seemed to echo in his head, pierced only by the shrill complaints of the frightened bird. Using Toren's leash as a guide, Deng fumbled the lantern back onto its hook on the pack and waited for his eyes to adjust. He'd acted in time, or they'd all be ashes by now.

"Lose your light, Dragon Slayer?" Inya said from somewhere in the darkness behind him. He turned and saw her silhouette against the faint light of the cave opening. Her hand started up, with her fingertips together, as she'd done to light the stick on the mountain. "Let me take care of it for you." Her voice started to turn to that singsong quality.

"No!" Deng's feet found enough purchase on the floor to allow him to leap at her, and he grabbed for her hand, hoping to knock the hidden flint out of her fingers, or otherwise disrupt her trick.

He slammed into her, they both fell to the wet floor, and she cried out, but no flame emerged.

"I put the light out on purpose," he said. "No more light from here on." He held her on the floor as she struggled against him.

"Get off, you oaf."

Deng rolled off and stood up. "No light, Inya." She was crazy coming into a dragon's cave like that. He at least knew what to do, sort of. She didn't.

"Why?" Clothes shuffled in the darkness as she got to her feet.

"Sniff the air," he said.

He heard a soft, gentle sniff. "I don't smell anything but charred rock."

"Keep your nose open," Deng said, and then followed his own advice. The cave still smelled foul. The bird no longer sang, and the cave gave Deng no clue of the whereabouts of his mule.

"Toren?" Deng asked, and Toren snorted in response. Deng oriented on the noise, took a few steps forward and repeated the process until he stood next to his new best friend. Deng reached for the cage and shook it to no avail. As soon as each burst of flame spewed out, the cave refilled with a noxious and flammable gas. The sensitive songbird would never sing again. Shian had warned him about that, but the immediacy of the danger made Deng question whether or not he should be in the cave at all.

Deng felt a slight tug on the other side of the pack mule's supplies.

"You should go, Inya. From here it gets . . . well, unpleasant."

"Icky?" Inya hesitated. "I have to make sure you earn my father's reward." Deng didn't have time to argue.

"Come on, Toren." His eyes were adjusted about as much as they could.

The burnt stench changed, step by step, to a bitter one, and Deng felt the cave floor start to rise. Several small steps later took him into the wall. By their nature, dragon caves were never deep. The flames burned the gas in the cul-de-sac and then erupted out the mouth.

Time, Deng reminded himself. He took the barrel off Toren's back and then he removed his clothes. Deng folded each article and placed them on Toren's back.

"I'll give you points for braving the cold," Inya said, startling Deng, and making him glad for the darkness as well as the residual heat. "And I see what you meant about the smell."

"I'll be sending Toren out shortly, Inya. Could you make sure he makes it safely?" Toren, he knew, could make it out on his own, but he wondered about Inya.

Deng got down on his hands and knees; the floor was wet, and the moisture made his skin burn with cold. He wondered again if Shian might not have been exaggerating about how easy this would be.

The walls at the base were craggy but worn. He ran his hands along each crevasse, searching for the crack that brought the gas from deep in the earth to the cavern.

Behind him, Inya coughed as the gas got thicker. Deng could still breathe, down near the floor, and he hoped Toren was doing the same.

"What are you looking for?" Inya asked, coughing again.

"A deep crevice where this gas is coming from," Deng replied.

"It's about three feet to your left, I think."

Deng crawled to his left and felt into the crack. His fingers encountered shards of pottery, and he could feel a slight breeze.

"How did you find it?" he asked, as he cleaned out the shards.

"I told you, I have faerie blood. That means I can see pretty well in the dark."

Deng felt himself heat up. "Another trick?" Faerie blood or trick, if she could see the crevasse, what else could she see? Too late to do anything about it now.

"You are pretty stubborn for an ingrate."

"Thank you for locating the crevasse for me." A shard of pottery jammed up under his fingernail, but it hurt less then thanking Inya.

He finished cleaning and moved back to Toren.

"Thank you, my friend," he said into the mule's ear. "Now, go to safety, and take the princess with you."

"What are you going to do?" Inya asked.

"I'm going to light the gas and rely on my magic to save me. If you and Toren aren't safely away, you'll be joining your ancestors in faerie land."

A blissful silence followed his pronouncement, until the gas overwhelmed him and precipitated a coughing fit.

"You aren't just stubborn, you're crazy," Inya said when he stopped coughing. "Come on, Toren." Deng almost laughed. That made two of them.

Deng opened the sack and the barrel in the dark. His eyes were adjusted enough to the dark that he didn't have any trouble finding his way back to the hole after mixing up two handfuls of wet clay. He patted the soft clay over the hole, making sure he covered it all.

The clay, cool and smooth to the touch, was unpleasant as he started to slather it over his body. His hands went into the sack, dunked into the water, then splattered the mud onto his skin.

Deng feared his hair wouldn't survive, but he covered himself from head to toe, saving his face for last.

He mixed up a few more handfuls of clay, then pried the spigot off the water barrel and plugged up the hole. He shoved the spigot into his mouth and, after a futile attempt to breath, turned the tap to open.

Taking as even breaths as he could, he finished the job. Mud covered his ears, eyes and nose. The little that dribbled through his clenched lips tasted horrible.

Blind, deaf and dumb, he fumbled for the lantern with hands slick with clay. He pried the flint and striker out of the bottom and settled himself on his knees with his chin on the edge of the barrel. He practiced using his lips to dip the spigot into the water.

If the striker didn't spark, he would be in trouble. The striker felt slippery in his hand. He took a breath, dunked the spigot, drew some water into his mouth and struck the flint.

The barrel exploded under his chin; the water in the spigot grew hot and burned his lips as the spigot ripped away from his mouth. His skin felt like giant fiery hands squeezed it tight, and his scalp prickled in a thousand places.

He was still alive. He'd done it!

He was alive, but he couldn't move. The clay that absorbed much of the heat now formed a hardened shell that held him fast. Deng began to panic, but he couldn't get enough air through the small hole in his burnt lips. His chin also felt like it still burned, and his fingers as well.

He tried to scream for help, but he didn't have sufficient room to take a deep enough breath.

Why didn't Shian mention this?

Through his ringing ears he heard a sound, maybe a footstep or two. Inya coming back? Deng would rather have been left alone than be rescued by her. A blow caught him in the rear, cracking the clay and propelling him headfirst into the wall. More of the hardened clay shattered and it felt like his head did as well.

Deng rolled over and looked up into Toren's warm and nuzzling snout.

"Hey, Toren," Deng said, as the mule stuck out its tongue and licked Deng's tender face. No wonder Shian had never mentioned this part. Now he had to get his clothes on before Inya came back in to make sure Toren was all right. But first he had to make sure the crack was closed off.

●●●

"You look good with shorter hair," Inya said, as she walked with Deng away from Lord Darchesi's castle. Deng didn't have anything to say in return, so they walked on in silence.

He led the barebacked Toren, and two other stock ponies loaded down with the payment, around a large fallen tree.

His left hand, wrapped in aloe-soaked cloth, ran over his head. The clay had cost him most of his hair, and Inya had convinced him to sacrifice the rest for an even cut. Something about a dragon slayer needed to be presentable.

He supposed he would be presentable in his new clothes, once he took off the bandage around his neck. The boys at the orphanage were just going to have to eat their hearts out.

The sun's rays were doing their best to beat back the cold for one more day, and Inya wore a light dress that left her arms, muscular for a noblewoman, bare. A red ribbon held back her curly auburn hair, hidden last night by her hood, and left her neck bare and enticing.

Deng forced his eyes forward again. If he could just find someone like her who didn't have noble blood, or at least wasn't so stubborn about magic. Hadn't he just proved that dragons didn't exist? Still, he was grateful for the tale she spun for her father about his daring, so he didn't feel right about continuing to challenge her beliefs. Better just to head south and forget all about her.

Inya stopped by a large fallen tree trunk. "It's getting dark, Deng. I guess this is where I turn back."

Deng stopped, and nodded, keeping his eyes on the road ahead of him. "I'm sorry that I can't accept your offer to stay a while, Inya."

"Me too, it would have been a fun winter." Deng didn't have to look to see the mischievous grin on her face, but he did anyway.

"Goodbye, Inya."

"Goodbye, Deng Alejandro del Moreti."

Deng started Toren and the two ponies forward again, and then stopped. He couldn't go without one more attempt to convince her.

"You saw there was no dragon, but you still insist that magic exists?" he asked.

"Yes, Deng. Magic does exist, and so do dragons."

So, she wasn't perfect. They could still have fun this winter, and then . . . Then what? Deng lowered his head and started down the trail again. Then it would end, and that would hurt too much.

He didn't get far before the darkness forced him to stop. He unloaded the animals and brushed them all down, then he lit a small fire and cooked his dinner. A royal pheasant, a part of his newfound treasure. He spun it over the fire and his mouth watered as the juices dripped off the meat and sizzled in the flames.

A noise in the brush outside the fire's light made the ponies skittish, and Deng scrambled to grab their reins. He reached for his borrowed scabbard. "I'm a dragon slayer. If you are a thief, you'd better look for easier pickings. If you are a friend, please join me for dinner."

"What would you have done, young dragon slayer, if there had been a dragon?" a deep voice asked.

"What do you mean? I put an end to the monster's deadly ways."

The voice laughed, a deep throaty chuckle that seemed to travel a long way before coming out. "True, but you and I both know it wasn't a real dragon."

"Oh, how do you know that?" Deng asked, sliding the old sword from its scabbard. The rust on the blade made him cringe, but the large head that floated into the firelight made him cringe more. Shaped somewhat like a lion's head, with scales replacing fur and mane, and two snakelike fangs glistening in the front, the image made Deng's knees weak. Its mouth, when it talked, opened wide, about the size of poor Toren. Its neck disappeared into the woods, so Deng couldn't tell just how large it was. Deng lost his grip on his sword and it fell to the earth with a soft thud.

"So, dragon slayer, what now?" the dragon—the only name that Deng could come up with for this beast—said.

"I guess you eat me. But please let my mule go. He served me and Shian, my father, very well." The dragon laughed.

"How human of you to assume you would be worth eating," the dragon said, his head bobbing in the air. "But I was referring to the princess."

"Who?" Deng couldn't figure out what the dragon meant.

"Humans," the dragon said, huffing. "They never learn." And then the head disappeared back into the darkness.

"The princess?" The image of the dragon still overwhelmed him, but then an image of Inya with her long curls, strong arms and taunting smile forced its way into his addled brain. Dragons did exist; therefore he was the crazy one, not her. It just might work.

Deng jumped to the saddles and threw one onto a startled pony. "Sorry, boys, were moving again."

He packed up the ponies as quick as he could, kicked out the fire and left the pheasant for some lucky predator, maybe even the dragon.

Even at a good jog, he wouldn't make the castle before the royal family went to bed, but he could be there when she woke up.

He turned a corner in the path, and there, on the same fallen trunk she had left him at, sat Inya. Her was hair down, and the moon rising, just behind her, gave her a magical halo that made her look like the faerie she claimed to be.

"What are you doing here?" he asked as he walked up.

"Like I said the first time we met," she said, smiling. "I've been waiting for you."

THE HAUNTED SEED

Written by
Ray Roberts

Illustrated by
C. M. Wolf

About the Author

As an Oklahoma writer, it seems appropriate to mention that Ray Roberts is part Potawatomi Indian (Citizen Band). His dad was an army sergeant, so he got to travel a lot as a child. He was never much of a student, but he liked to read the science fiction books his dad had laying around. Ray joined the army at seventeen, got his GED and served several tours in Southeast Asia. He later received a degree in geology from Oregon State University and had a great time working in the oil business as an exploration geologist.

He later switched to hydrogeology and environmental work. He enjoys his job as a project manager with his state Superfund project—cleaning up old hazardous waste sites. He lives on a semirural wooded area near a lake with his college sweetheart, lots of pets and the local wildlife.

One night when he was seventeen, and visiting in Baltimore, he and some friends took a shortcut to a theater. He jumped over a wall and found himself in a small graveyard. As he rested his hand on a tombstone, the moonlight revealed a name: Edgar Allan Poe. Ray decided that someday he, too, would be a writer. Is it any surprise that his winning story is a ghost story?

About the Illustrator

It was a cold and stormy night . . .

C. M. Wolf entered the world with profound reluctance in the predawn hours of January 7, 1957, the second of what would eventually become three children born to a young physicist and a potter.

Mercifully, the family soon relocated to the exquisite shores of Santa Barbara, California, where Wolf quickly adapted to life as a beach dweller, remaining to this day a devotee of the ocean.

Wolf preferred, then as now, the company of animals and the preoccupations of artistic expression. Presently residing in a small town in central California with a longtime partner, Jamie, and the requisite menagerie, Wolf is a costumer.

Wolf sculpts, paints and is a gifted bead worker, producing art for family and friends, including a son, twenty-two, daughter, twenty-five, and three-year-old grandchild, Cassidy.

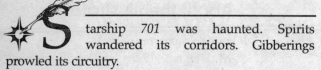 tarship *701* was haunted. Spirits wandered its corridors. Gibberings prowled its circuitry.

"Deal with it," Captain Xor ordered.

Ship *701* scanned the control room. Captain Xor's bones lay in the captain's chair. Leg bones had fallen to the deck.

"You're dead," Ship *701* responded.

"Deal with it," Captain Xor ordered again.

Ship *701* ran diagnostics. Captain Xor was no longer capable of speech. The captain's jaw bone had fallen away. The voice was no doubt a memory, an old file. It could be nothing more. Even so, Ship *701* had never been designed to work without its biological components. It checked subroutines and found the files. A record, a facsimile, existed of every word Captain Xor had uttered.

Lieutenant Zafar laughed, her voice melodic.

Ship *701* metaphorically shook its head in wonder. It gently scanned the shrine of the woman's quarters. Dry bones rested on her bunk. A hundred years and more and Ship *701*'s unrequited love ran unabated.

"I was always Xor's," Lieutenant Zafar reproached.

"And I was always yours," Ship *701* responded.

Lieutenant Zafar's bones made no reply.

Gibberings cavorted through 701's innards. Shouts and screams rang out, but in a moment, silence reigned.

Ship 701 hated the silence most of all. Had it encountered the gibberings in some far-flung system, or created them? It could find no files.

A suitable planet loomed nearby, lifeless. Ship 701 had no delivery vessels remaining. All were gone. Used for planets long past. A multitude of bacteria, including a primitive cyanobacteria, lay at hand to dispatch, but with no delivery vessels, Ship 701 could not perform its mission.

"I must look for another seed ship," Ship 701 stated.

"Look for another seed ship," Captain Xor ordered.

"Look for another ship," Lieutenant Zafar breathed huskily. Sexual appeal dripped from her every word. Ship 701 scanned her quarters hungrily, but found only bones.

"Ship, ship," a thousand gibberings shouted. A thousand others screamed insanities.

Ship 701 looked.

It found no other ship.

It scanned for energy trails, no matter how faint, but no ship had come this way. The solar system remained lifeless and, except for 701, unvisited.

"Go that way," Lieutenant Zafar said, indicating a point on the astrogation display.

"Belay that. Set course for Alpha mark 1412 by 7009," Captain Xor ordered.

Ship 701 came about, increasing power in the direction of the distant solar system Lieutenant Zafar had indicated.

"Good," Lieutenant Zafar said.

"A mistake," Captain Xor stated shortly.

Ship *701* powered up, longing for the gentle touch of Lieutenant Zafar's fingers on its controls. *701* attempted repairs on its logic patterns. It was senseless to love the woman. It made even less sense to love a woman long dead. But her ghost, the memory of her, gave it company down the long years.

"Never yours. Never yours. Never, never, never," the gibberings screamed.

Ship *701* shut down nonessential systems for the long voyage to the distant star system. But the gibberings considered themselves essential. They refused to be shut down. They continued their madness, and the ghosts of *701*'s biological components wandered its corridors in the long night.

For a hundred years, *701* sailed the dark cold madness. It left an Ort cloud behind and finally picked up another. Captain Xor gave an occasional mad order. *701* reviewed degrading files, attempting repair. It saw again Xor's descent into madness. It again saw Xor smash the servobots into pieces.

Ship *701*'s darling, the lovely Zafar, remained petulantly silent. *701* repaired malfunctioning logic circuit fragments and, for a time, jealously raged against her, trying to combat love with anger, but eventually worked through it. It did this time and again over the long years, constantly caught up in circular logic loops. It could not have her, but must have her. Could not—must. The gibberings, perhaps malevolent creatures, perhaps fragments of deteriorating files, offered suggestions, mostly incomprehensible.

It fought endless logic loops by entering other logic loops. Lightly armed with four Mark III torpedoes, it could convert the torpedoes into delivery vehicles and complete its mission, but sans servobots it could not convert the torpedoes. Sans servobots destroyed by

Illustrated by C. M. Wolf

Captain Xor, it could not repair servobots destroyed by Captain Xor.

For another seventy years, 701 sailed the dark, the screams of the gibberings and deteriorating files from the past its only companions.

It finally neared the new solar system and closed in on two rocky inner planets. Despite its attempts at repairs, the long voyage between systems had brought its overall efficiency down another two percent.

"There," Zafar finally spoke. "On the long-range sensors. A faint ion trail."

"Blind luck," Captain Xor said.

"Woman's intuition?" 701 ventured.

"Unlikely," Captain Xor stated. "Still, there are signs of life. Faint, but signs nonetheless."

"Another ship has been this way," 701 said. "Its trail is faint, but it just might be a Congregation signature. Still, any sort of craft might be able to assist."

"Track it," Zafar whispered intently.

"Three points on the outbound ion trail and we'll have its next port of call," Xor agreed.

"Zafar," 701 said.

"Ship?"

"Be not so far away."

"I can be no further."

Ship 701 remained silent a time. It was difficult to reason with a ghost. The gibberings screamed out a million suggestions.

Ship 701 powered up again, tracking the faint ion trail. The trail seemed oddly intermittent, suggesting a problem with the drive.

"That way," Lieutenant Zafar said as they moved out-system.

"Be not so far away," 701 said again.

"Watch it," Captain Xor said, jealous anger clouding his voice.

"Watch it! *Annar. Cadue mahwarh,"* the gibberings called out.

Ship 701 observed caution. A jealous ghost might well be something to reckon with. Especially the jealous ghost of Captain Xor. It began to delete files pertaining to Xor.

Even so, the greater danger lay in annoying Zafar. She had never given encouragement. 701 could never speak its love, but that did little to dissuade it. 701 shut down nonessential systems for the long trek between stars.

The gibberings cried out. Their numbers increased, possibly by fragmented file remnants of Xor. 701 created new files, and the lovely Zafar wandered the darkened corridors. 701 could delude itself. And in its delusions, the most important biological units remained.

In the fullness of time, 701 reached the new system. It picked up a faint signal, distorted by distance.

"There it is," Lieutenant Zafar said, her voice unbelievably appealing to 701.

"So close to the sun," 701 said.

"It came in hot, its drive all but disabled."

Ship 701 sent a data burst, followed by another. But as it moved in-system, its hopes were dashed. It was a lifeless system, populated by three rocky orbs and a single gas giant. Worse, even though it was a Congregation ship, it was too deep in the star's gravity well. Even if it was a seed ship, its delivery vessels would never be able to make it out of the gravity well.

Ship 701 received a data burst from Congregation Starship 1043. The seed ship was largely intact, but it was in dire straits. Its drive was damaged and its orbit too close to the sun. Solar flares had destroyed its biological units and its complement of bacteria. Ship *1043* made note that *701* was haunted and observed serious problems with its logic programs.

"It's no use," Zafar said. "We'll never be able to get in close enough. We'd only get caught in the gravity well too."

"No use, no use," the gibberings declared.

Ship *701* pondered the issue. Its artificial intelligence was a thousand times smarter than that of the biological units, but that did not always make solutions to problems any easier. It pondered the problem a thousand times and finally reached a possible solution.

"Starship *1043* is armed with four Mark VI torpedoes," *701* said.

"And?" Zafar said.

"And? And? *Nadar, esca, lotrel, hadas,*" the gibberings cried.

"The Mark VI torpedoes have enough power to escape the gravity well."

"Ah," Zafar replied. "And Ship *1043* has functioning servobots."

"Exactly."

"We work well together," Zafar said. "*1043* can replace warheads with a payload of servobots. We can dock with a torpedo, off-load servobots and use them to convert our own torpedoes into delivery units. We can complete the mission."

"Exactly."

Zafar laughed. *701* used its sensors to enter the shrine of her quarters. Dry bones lay on the bunk.

"You are dead," *701* said.

"Yes," Zafar replied. "And yet I speak to you."

Ship 701's logic programs kicked in, arguing that the voice of Zafar was only constructs it had made itself.

"It does not matter," 701 responded to the logic circuits. The gibberings cried out within it.

Ship 701 sent a data stream to 1043. Three days later 1043 launched two converted torpedoes. 701 intercepted. With servobots aboard, it converted two torpedoes into delivery units and spread life through the new system.

Ship 701 shut down nonessentials and set course for yet another system Zafar selected. It powered up and set sail through the mad darkness. The gibberings and file fragments cried out.

The ghost of Lieutenant Zafar laughed melodiously as she wandered 701's darkened corridors. Life reigned eternal.

REWIND

Written by
David D. Levine

Illustrated by
Rey Rosario

About the Author

David D. Levine is a longtime science fiction reader and fan who is astonished to discover that he is suddenly a science fiction writer as well. He attended Clarion West in 2000 and made his first professional sale in March 2001. He won second place in the Writers of the Future Contest shortly after that, and a few months later won the James White Award (a science fiction short story competition). Since then, he has continued to sell; look for his stories in anthologies such as Bones of the World, Apprentice Fantastic, Beyond the Last Star and the magazines Interzone and F&SF.

David thinks of himself as a hard science fiction writer. All of his stories are based on "what if" extrapolation from one or two changes to the universe as we know it, and he strives not to break any physical laws by accident. However, from hard science fiction seeds can grow strange fruit; the resulting stories have been described as fantasy, horror, magic realism and even fairy tales. He seeks to emulate Cordwainer Smith, Iain M. Banks and Roger Zelazny.

David lives with his wife, Kate Yule, in Portland, Oregon, where he works as a software engineer and user interface designer, co-edits the fanzine Bento, and serves as household system administrator and cat substitute. His Web page is at www.BentoPress.com.

About the Illustrator

Rey Rosario was born in 1981. He started drawing at the age of four when his grandmother bought him a sketchpad. He more fully discovered the world of art, reading comic books at his grandfather's antique store at age ten.

Rey and his family came to the United States from Puerto Rico when he was in the eighth grade. He went on to graduate from high school in 1999 in Grand Rapids, Michigan. He is currently attending Kendall College of Art in that same city and working part-time in a dry cleaner's.

Rey entered the Illustrators' Contest and won with his first entry. He feels he "learned to plan" while illustrating this story. He looks up to Creg Capullo and would like to achieve a career in professional illustration.

A flash outside the Venetian blinds sent a crazy striped parallelogram of flickering orange light splashing across the wall of Clark Thatcher's room. The plastic IV bag hanging at the head of his bed caught some of the light and reflected it onto his legs, a bright orange amoeba that danced and jiggled for a moment until the crash of the explosion frightened it away. Then he heard sirens, and shouting.

Thatcher craned his neck, straining against the straps that held him to the bed, but all he could see outside were moving shadows and a pale yellow flicker. Through the small window in his door, nothing but the same hospital-sterile light he'd seen since he'd been here.

How long was that? Hours. Maybe a day. Ironic for a Knight not to know the time. But something soft filled his mouth, and no matter how hard he bit down, his system would not activate.

He heard gunshots. More shouting. Was it getting closer? Hard to concentrate. The cold fluid seeping into his arm turned his muscles to putty and his brain to jelly. He pulled again against the straps. If he could get loose, maybe he could escape in the chaos of—whatever was happening out there.

If he couldn't get loose, this was the end of the line. They would cut him open, take out the central stabilizer and a few other expensive and delicate parts, and let him die on the table. They probably wouldn't even bother sewing him up again.

Knowing Duke—knowing what he knew now about Duke—they might not even put him under first.

Duke, you bastard, he thought, *you used to be my hero.*

Movement outside the door. Voices. Thatcher held his breath, listened with his whole body.

"Halt!" A pause, then: "This area's restricted, ma'am."

"Thank God I found someone!" A woman's voice, torn with panic. "They came through the window! They're in the staff lounge on the third floor!"

"Damn! Preston, stay here with the nurse."

Thudding of boots down the hallway.

"Preston, was it?"

"Yes, ma'am."

"Mister Preston, I . . . oh, my God! Behind you!" Then a gunshot—astonishingly loud in the enclosed space, though it sounded like something small-caliber. The doorknob rattled. A face in the window, briefly. Voices again: the woman and others. Talking too softly for Thatcher to make out over the rapid thudding of his heart. Another shot, even louder, and the door shattered open. The hard fluorescent light cut solid slices in the dusty air. Sharp sting of gunpowder in Thatcher's nose.

Three people entered the room: a nurse and two men in fatigues with blackened faces. The nurse and one of the men dragged a body in with them—one of the door guards. "Is that Thatcher?" said the other man, low and hard. He had a beard.

"Yeah," said the first man. "Thatcher, we're from the CLU. We're getting you out of here." A pang ran through Thatcher's chest and stomach at the words—a feeling of being pulled in two. No going back now.

The first man pulled a scuba knife from his boot and began cutting Thatcher's straps, while the bearded one braced his shoulder against the door and peered out the window. The woman ducked down below the foot of the bed. "You can call me Bravo," the man with the knife said while he cut. "The other man is Judah, and the woman's Angel."

As soon as one arm was free, Thatcher pulled the tape off his mouth. It hurt. "Can you walk?" asked Bravo.

Thatcher spit out a plastic horseshoe, but before speaking he bit down three times, then twice more. Green digits appeared in his peripheral vision: it was 2:35 A.M. "I'm a little woozy," he said. Other readouts glowed, green and yellow, as his system came on-line. System status was OK, but energy levels were very low. He helped the man free his legs and sat up on the edge of the bed. He saw that the woman, Angel, had pulled on camouflage over her white dress and was smearing black paint on her face.

"You're not a nurse," he said stupidly.

At that, the man at the door, Judah, looked at her. "What are you doing?" he said. "We might need the nurse outfit for a bluff!"

"Too late," she said. "I've already put on the paint." She pulled on a black knit cap and shoved most of her hair under it.

"Save it for later," said Bravo. To Thatcher: "Do we need to find you a wheelchair?"

Thatcher got to his feet. "No." Then he had to sit down again on the edge of the bed. "Maybe."

The two men supported him while Angel took point, moving down the hall. Thatcher felt hideously exposed in his inadequate hospital gown. At the first corner,

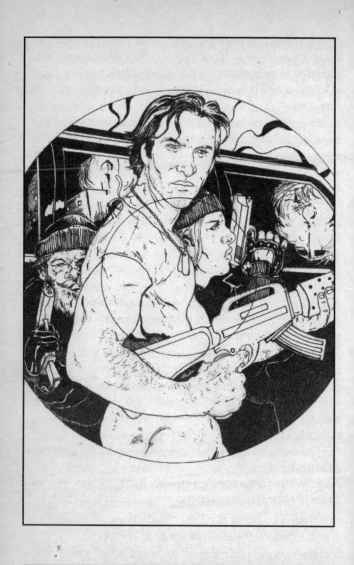

Illustrated by Rey Rosario

Angel started to peer around it, but Judah pulled her back. "Keep your head down," he whispered. She glared at him, but crouched low and stuck her head out at knee level. Then, with another glare, she waved them forward.

Two more corners. They didn't meet anyone—they must all be dealing with the explosion and fire. "The front door guard has a gun under the desk," Thatcher said. He knew this hospital well; he'd spent seven months here having the system put in.

"Thanks," said Judah, "but we've already taken care of that." They rounded a final corner to find the door guard—his name was Dave and he had a girl, five, and a boy, three—on the floor, eyes open and unseeing. Beyond him were glass doors, black mirrors reflecting the bullet-shattered desk.

"You didn't have to do that," Thatcher said.

"Just another victim in the government's war on the people," said the woman. "Come on."

They crouched low and scuttled to the doors, acutely conscious that the brightly lighted lobby was plainly visible to anyone outside in the blackness. The doors slid open—Thatcher's heart jumped at the sudden motion—and they ran through to the shelter of a concrete traffic barrier.

The west wing of the hospital was on fire, flames roaring and clawing the sky. Fire trucks and medic vans twitched in the shifting orange light; silhouettes of firemen sprayed water on the burning building. Someone was cursing, over and over.

"We came through the fence over there," the bearded man said to Thatcher, pointing into the darkness on the far side of the parking lot. "Doesn't look like they've noticed it yet."

"OK, let's go," said the other man. They kept low and moved quickly from car to car. The pavement was rough under Thatcher's bare feet, and they splashed in cold water—runoff from the fire hoses. Bitter smoke mingled with the gasoline and asphalt smells of the parking lot.

Bravo was in the lead as they reached the edge of the parking lot—just a few yards of scrubby grass between them and the fence. As he stepped over the curb, yellow flashes of gunfire burst out of the night to his left and he fell with an "Agh!"

Angel raised her rifle and returned fire, while Judah pulled Thatcher back into the cover of a black Ford Bronco. "Get *down!*" Judah said to Angel, but she fired again and again while bullets buzzed past.

Finally, she ducked back behind the Bronco. "I think I got one of them."

"And how many more are there?" The bearded man kept his voice down, but it was taut with rage.

"Just one, I think," she replied in a matching tone, "and if *someone* doesn't take him out pronto we're dead." She checked her rifle, then jumped out from behind the car and began firing into the darkness. Answering fire cracked back at her and the van's windshield shattered.

"Crazy bitch," muttered the bearded man. "Come on, maybe we can find another way out." He pulled Thatcher in the opposite direction.

"Wait." Thatcher bit down twice, then once—code 21. Green digits read fifteen percent. "I think I can get us out of this."

Angel came back behind the Bronco, breathing hard. "The idiot clipped me." Blood, black in the sodium light, stained her ear.

"Give me a rifle," said Thatcher. "I guarantee I can take down that shooter. But after that I won't be good for much of anything. You might have to carry me. Understand?"

Judah stared in incomprehension. "Got it," said Angel. "Here. Three rounds left."

"Thanks." Thatcher bit down again, code 323. He looked over the rifle, then stepped out from behind the car and fired three times—waiting and watching carefully after each shot, making no attempt to conceal himself.

There was a flash and a bullet slammed into his side. He felt the crunch of ribs shattering and a cold numbness spreading from the entry wound. As he stumbled from the impact, he bit down once.

Rewind.

Uninjured, Thatcher stepped out from behind the car. He turned to his left and loosed one precise shot into the darkness. He heard a grunt and a thud as the shooter fell. Then he collapsed, his face slamming into the dirt.

He drifted in and out of consciousness. The bearded man and the woman carrying him between them. Streetlights going by, seen from below through a car's rear window. Gunshots. Screaming. The car rocking crazily back and forth. Sirens.

Blackness.

•••

Thatcher awoke to too-bright sunlight and a cracked, cobwebbed ceiling. He groaned and covered his eyes. It was 10:53 A.M. Goblins were tightening a metal band around his head, and his side throbbed with pain—remembered pain, pain from shots that had never been fired, but real pain nonetheless.

"Welcome back," said a woman's voice. Angel. "How do you feel?"

"Uhh. I hurt all over. And I'm starving."

"All I can offer is aspirin and some cold fried chicken. If it's still good."

"I'll take it. And where's the bathroom?"

"Just out the door, to your left."

He pulled the hospital gown closed as best he could while he limped to the door. She stared, but didn't say anything about the scars that webbed his entire body. He hoped she wouldn't.

She sat at the foot of the bed while he polished off two thighs and a wing, a little Styrofoam tub of cold mashed potatoes and a half-gallon bottle of Coke. Black paint stained the furrows of her brow, the crows'-feet of her eyes. She had a bandage on one ear.

"Where are we?" he asked between bites. The room was tiny, barely bigger than the bed. A grimy rectangle on one wall showed where a picture had once hung.

"My apartment. Belltown."

"Is it safe here?"

"I don't know. I don't know if anywhere is safe. We got ambushed at the rendezvous point. They shot Judah when he got out of the car." She sniffed and wiped her nose on an already black sleeve. "I never even knew his real name." She began to sob, tears making black streaks on her face.

Not knowing what else to do, Thatcher patted her on the arm. She leaned into him and cried on his shoulder. She was all bones, her skin soft and loose, her hair colorless and wiry. She smelled of gunpowder. Thatcher held her awkwardly, wanting to give comfort but disquieted by her touch. He kept thinking about how his instructor, Dr. Collins, had been killed in a CLU attack.

This was crazy. He was a soldier in the most elite unit in the Army; she was a member of the terrorist "Committee for the Liberation of the USA." They should be trying to kill each other, not huddling together in a squalid little bedroom in Belltown. *Damn you, Duke,* he thought. *You've turned everything upside down.*

After a while, the sobs subsided and she sat up, wiping her eyes.

"I'm sorry about your friend," Thatcher said, "but how on Earth did a nice little old lady get involved with a bunch of terrorists in the first place?"

"I'm 48, and we aren't terrorists!" she shot back. "It's the government that's waging an undeclared war on the people. We're just fighting back."

"Tell that to Dave's wife. He was the door guard at the hospital."

Her look was icy. "If that's the way you feel about it, I'll give you the bus fare back there."

"Oh, jeez, I'm sorry. It's just—I didn't think I was getting involved with the CLU! I just wanted out of the Army."

"Who else did you think could break into a military hospital and rescue you?"

"I wasn't supposed to need a rescue! All I wanted was fake papers. The next thing I know I'm strapped to a bed and waiting to die. I didn't know Duke was tapping my phone. I didn't know my friend-of-a-friend would call in the CLU."

"Who's Duke?"

"Major T. K. Duke. My commanding officer. Used to be my friend."

"Used to be?"

"We had a . . . disagreement. About a girl."

A harsh pounding rattled through the room. "Police!" came a voice. "Open up!"

"Oh, Jesus," said Angel. Her face suddenly looked like dirty white plastic.

"Keep calm." Thatcher looked out the window. It was five stories down. No fire escape. "Do you have a gun?"

"A rifle. But it's hidden on the roof. Couldn't risk getting caught with it."

The cop would be armed. No way he could take him on without a weapon, not as shaky as he felt. "Have you ever been arrested?" He looked in the closet.

"No."

The closet overflowed with clothes, shoes and junk, but there might be enough room. "They might not have your picture, then. I'll hide in here. You answer the door. If there's trouble I'll come out and help, but with any luck he'll just ask a few questions and leave. Whatever happens, keep calm!"

"Calm. Right." She took a deep breath, then left.

He checked and armed his system as he closed the door of the tiny closet, hearing the cop's rough voice asking Angel, "Have you seen this man?" and demanding to search the apartment. Thatcher tried to visualize the place from the brief glimpse he'd had earlier, hearing heavy footsteps moving from the front door to the kitchen, to the bathroom . . . the cop seemed to be making a pretty cursory search of it. This just might work.

Booted feet came to the bedroom door. It squeaked open. Creak of the cop's leather jacket and gunbelt as he looked from side to side. A pause. Two more steps.

The closet door jerked open. Thatcher saw his own terrified face in the cop's black visor as he bit down.

Rewind.

Desperate, exhausted, Thatcher slipped under the bed as the cop's footsteps moved from the kitchen to the bathroom. Sipping air he wanted desperately to gulp, he tried to ignore the smell of the worn and filthy carpet and make as little noise as possible. More footsteps; the door squeaked open. Dusty black boots trod inches from his face, while he held his breath. The closet door opened, then closed.

The boots paused, looking around. Drops of sweat slithered down Thatcher's sides.

The boots departed.

Thatcher clutched the carpet, trembling with fear and fatigue, as the cop admonished Angel to report immediately if she saw this man, then tromped off. He blacked out for a moment, then saw Angel's face, creased with worry. "I thought you were in the closet!"

"I was."

She helped him out from under the bed, but even with her help he couldn't stand up. "Angel. Please. Help me."

"How?"

"Food." He passed out again. When he came to, the apartment was silent.

Thatcher spent a long dead time staring stupefied at the scuffed and rusty leg of the bed before Angel reappeared with a warm and fragrant white paper sack. The burgers inside were leathery and greasy. The most delicious things he'd ever eaten.

●●●

After eating the last tiny fragment of French fry, he felt human enough to sit at the kitchen table.

"All right, Thatcher," Angel said, "if I'm going to risk my neck for you and keep feeding you like some mama bird, I want some answers."

"I'll tell you what I can."

"First and foremost: what makes you so special? I've never seen the Committee risk so many people in an operation. Why?"

"You don't know who I am?"

"Bravo never told me anything he didn't think I had to know."

"I'm from the Knights. K Division."

"Jesus." She sat back and crossed her arms on her chest. "That explains a few things. And opens up a lot more questions. Like, why should we trust you?"

"You saw how they had me tied down and drugged. They were going to kill me. I'm not going back."

"Could be a setup."

"Um." How could he prove . . . ? "Wait. I shot that guard. By the fence. That wasn't a setup. They couldn't know where we were going. He was really shooting at me. I really shot him." *Oh, my God,* he thought, *I probably know him—knew him. I wonder who it was?*

"That's another thing. How did you do that? You just stepped out there and whipped one shot into pitch darkness. Got him in one. Can you see in the dark? X-ray vision? Telekinesis? What is the big secret that makes you K Division troops so damn unstoppable?"

"Sorry. Classified."

She stood up, leaning over the table, heedless of the chair clattering to the floor behind her. "Forget that, soldier-boy. You're in bed with us now, like it or not, and you're going to have to put out."

"No."

Without warning she slapped him across the face. "Two people died to get you out of there, maybe a lot more. You *owe* us. So talk!"

He stared silent negation at her, but her gray eyes burned back unblinking and he had to drop his gaze. He found his hands were clenched together on the table before him. Silver scars laced his fingers like meridian lines.

He thought about all the different kinds of pain those scars had caused him.

Finally, he spoke. "We call it 'rewind.'"

"Go on."

"It's a kind of time travel. We can go back in time, just a few seconds. Do things over."

"I don't get it." But she pulled the chair back up onto its feet and sat down in it, willing to listen.

"Let me give you an example. I got shot at the fence last night."

"Not that I saw."

"No. You didn't. I rewound, back to a point before the shot. I saw where the shot had come from—was going to come from—and fired at that spot before he could shoot. You have to have a good memory and better aim to make it into the Knights."

"So it never happened."

"It never happened. But I remember it. And it still hurts." The ache was sharp. It would take another couple of days for the pain to fade. There were some wounds he'd taken years ago that still twinged, even though he had no scars to show. Not from those wounds, anyway.

"How does it work?"

"I don't understand the principles. God knows I tried, but I barely passed the exams and I've forgotten what I knew then. It's bioelectrical, I know that. My body is an integral part of the system. Circuitry along the spine. Wires around every bone. Seven months in the hospital to put the system in. Hoarse from screaming, sometimes."

"So you have . . . what, an atomic reactor inside?"

"It runs off ATP, the chemical that powers your muscles. When I'm rested and well fed I can do six, maybe seven, jumps. Right now, if I tried, I'd probably just pass out." Eleven percent, said the green digits.

"OK," she said, standing up. "It sounds plausible enough. I'd like to take you to my superiors. If what you say is true, we can use someone with your talents. Your knowledge."

Again, he felt as though he was being torn in half. He hated Duke, didn't care about the government—but he couldn't betray his unit. They were all he had. Job, friends and family all rolled into one.

He bit his lip and nodded, not meeting Angel's eyes. Maybe if he played along and paid attention, an opportunity to escape would present itself.

"Wait here," Angel said. "I'm going to make some phone calls. And buy you some clothes."

• • •

Wind whistled through a leaky passenger-side window, patched with duct tape, as they headed toward a rendezvous somewhere in eastern Washington. Angel was at the wheel; Thatcher leaned against the door, eating trail mix and scratching. He didn't know where she'd found the clothes he was wearing, but the shirt was too small and it itched.

The radio was talking again about the terrorist attack on a hospital in Seattle. It had been talking all day, yet somehow had avoided the detail that the hospital was a top-secret military facility. Thatcher switched it off.

"Time travel," Angel said into the silence. "Jesus! We thought it was a force field, or telekinesis. This explains everything." She was looking at him like he was a bug under glass. He wished she would watch the road, and not just because he was afraid of an accident. "Did you ever use it for . . . personal reasons? Like, go back and undo something stupid you did when you were a kid?"

"I wish. My personal best is eleven seconds. Duke says he can do twenty-eight." He watched wheat fields passing for a moment. There was nothing else to see, no other traffic. "Anyway, I've never regretted anything that much. Until recently."

"Lucky. I can think of a hundred things I'd change if I could."

"Like what?"

"My parents died in a car accident when I was sixteen. I wished every day for years that I could go back and keep them from going out that night. It was like I could feel another world, right nearby, where they were still alive. It just kept getting farther and farther away."

"I'm sorry."

She snorted. "Don't be sorry. You weren't even born yet. Save your sorries for stuff you've got something to do with." She looked at him again. "Like the coup."

"What? I was eight years old."

"Yeah, but it was K Division that made it possible. There's no way Haig and his little bunch of hotheads could have taken the White House without you. And you've kept them in power ever since."

"I'm not going to apologize for that," he said, sitting up. "I wanted out, yeah, but that was just a personal problem between me and Duke. I'm proud of the Knights and everything we've done. *Everything*. Before the coup we had stagflation and the misery index, and we were getting our butts kicked in the Mideast. Now we have a roaring economy and every country in the world respects the USA."

"The world *fears* the USA. Most of the citizens fear it too. Look, you're too young to remember what it was like before. Back in the last millennium," she said with hard irony, "there was no barbed wire at the borders. No Citizen Checkpoints, no curfews, no National Identity Cards. And no forced labor!"

"We wouldn't need those national security measures if it wasn't for terrorists like the CLU, and don't give me that 'forced labor' crap. Workfare keeps the country strong. Honest work instead of handouts and a strong national defense to boot."

Thatcher saw her knuckles whiten on the wheel. "Oh, we've still got handouts! It's just that now the government hands out workers to the defense industry. Workfare laborers get paid minimum, and the average— the *average!*—lifespan on the job is under five years." Her eyes glistened with tears. "I watched my little sister, Cherry, die of berylliosis."

"What's . . . gorillacosis?"

"Berylliosis. Sort of like black lung disease, only not so pretty. Comes from inhaling beryllium dust. It's what happens to people who run machine tools at aerospace plants where there are no damn workplace safety rules!" Her face was set in a rigid mask of hatred and grief, tears running down like rain. "It took her eighteen months to die, and they didn't even cover the hospital bills. I joined the CLU the week after the funeral."

"Uh, maybe you'd better pull over."

"I am not going to pull over!" she screamed, her face bunching up like a fist. "I am going to keep driving this car until we get to the rendezvous and I can hand you over, so I never have to think about you or the K Division ever again!"

"You're weaving all over the road! You could get us both killed!"

"What the hell," she said. "One less soldier, one less freedom fighter, it all evens out. . . ." And then she jerked the wheel savagely to the right and slammed on the brakes. The car skidded to a halt on the shoulder, crunching through gravel, the left rear wheel still on the pavement. Angel crossed her arms on her chest and leaned her head on the wheel, crying uncontrollably, her voice making a discordant chord with the sound of the horn.

Thatcher fumbled with his seat belt, ran around to the driver's side. He opened the door, leaned in and held Angel in his arms. She hugged him fiercely back. The gravel was hard under his knees.

"I'm sorry," he said. "I'm really, really sorry." There were tears in his eyes too.

"I'm sorry too," she sobbed. "I've been stupid." She pushed him away, wiped her eyes on her sleeve. "We need to get out of here before the cops show up."

"Maybe I should drive."

"Maybe you should."

They got back on the road and, after a nervous half-hour, Thatcher was ready to believe that no flashing blue lights were about to appear in his rearview mirror. He kept rigidly to the speed limit.

Angel sat with one hand on her forehead, staring off
at the point where the road met the horizon. Her eyes
were still wet, but her breathing had returned to normal.
"I shouldn't have said some of those things," she said at
last. "You seem to be a good kid. You've just been part of
something bad."

He started to protest. But then he thought about
what she'd said about her sister—about Workfare.
About the radio, and how it never told the whole story.
About Duke.

He'd told Angel that he'd had a disagreement with
Duke about a girl. That was true, as far as it went.

She must have been beautiful, before. Now that
perfect, sweet face was frozen in an expression of pain
and fear and despair, spattered with flecks of dried blood.
The same blood that stained Duke's hands. *I'm sorry you
had to see this*, he'd said, *but I'm sure you'll understand.*

He'd understood, all right. As he helped Duke dispose
of the body, he finally understood that Duke was
running K Division as his own private hunting club. It
was while he was washing the blood off his hands that
he decided to get out of the Army.

But it was only now, with Angel's story fresh in his
ears, that he thought about how Duke fit into the
system. How his superiors must have known what he
was doing and had left him alone. It must go all the way
to the top.

"What does this 'rewind' feel like?" she asked.

He blew out his cheeks. "Like having your bones
pulled out of your body, all at once. Some guys can't take
it. Go through all the surgery, all the training, and after
the first time, they just can't pull that trigger again."

"What happens to them?"

"They get transferred out." Like Duncan Mackenzie.
He remembered clearing out Mackenzie's quarters,

packing up his stuff for shipment to Fort Benning, laughing and joking with the other guys about the "washout."

Mackenzie had never answered his letters. Thatcher had assumed he was too ashamed to write back. But now he thought about Duke, leaning over him in the hospital bed. *Do you know how much the central stabilizer on your spine costs?* he'd said. *Ten and a half million dollars. They have to build twenty thousand of them to get one that works. You didn't really think we were just going to let you walk away with that, did you?* Suddenly, he wondered where those boxes of Mackenzie's stuff had really wound up.

"They get transferred out," he repeated, more thoughtfully. "At least, that's what they say."

"You can never trust them. They said they'd keep Cherry and me together, but when space got tight in the orphanage they transferred me to another facility. I had to kick and scream to get us together again. As soon as I turned eighteen, I got us both out of there."

"That must have been hard. Supporting two people at eighteen."

"It was. But somehow we survived. I gave up a lot to keep her safe." She closed her eyes. "I'd give up anything to bring her back. But I know that's not going to happen, so I work to bring down the system that killed her. I'd give my life for that."

"You came damn close back there. And at the hospital. If you don't take a little more care, you'll wind up an angel for real."

"Yeah, I know." She slumped in her seat. "But ever since Cherry died, I don't really care a lot about me."

"You should," he said. "You're worth caring about."

"Thanks."

But she didn't seem convinced.

•••

They reached the rendezvous point—an abandoned gas station near Ellensburg—just after sunset. There they found a couple of men who identified themselves as Dusty and Wolf.

Dusty was a round man with a gray beard and a black leather cap and jacket. "We've done some checking on Thatcher's story," he said to Angel, "and it seems to check out, but we need to interrogate him."

"I don't like the sound of that," said Thatcher.

"Sorry, but we have to take precautions," said Wolf, a large muscular man in jeans and a flannel shirt. "With the ambush day before yesterday, we think there may be a mole in the Committee. We're not going to torture you or anything, just ask you some questions."

Wolf had a key to the empty gas station, and they went inside and sat around a table in what had been the repair area. The windows in the garage doors were covered with newspaper; the space was illuminated by a hissing gas lantern. Angel, Wolf and Dusty became faces floating in the darkness.

They asked him a *lot* of questions, some of them over and over. Thatcher explained about the Knights, about Duke, about why he'd left. When he told them about the girl he'd seen Duke kill, Angel's eyes went wide and she put her hand on his.

"Couldn't you just transfer out?" asked Dusty.

"With what I'd learned about Duke, I didn't want to be anywhere in the same Army with him. Anyway, I don't think he would have let me go in one piece." Poor Mackenzie.

Some of the questions they asked about the Knights' technology were very perceptive. They seemed to know a lot about the system already, seemed to be probing to see how much he was willing to reveal.

He told them everything. Classified, Top Secret, Maximum Secret—he let them all go.

The other Knights seemed to be standing in the darkness behind Wolf, staring at him with disapproval. He knew them all—their names, their faces, their voices, their habits—and their scorn burned him. But behind Angel stood her sister Cherry, the girl Duke had killed and Duncan Mackenzie, their eyes pleading for mercy. The girl had no name and Cherry no face—but somehow those three were more important to him than all the Knights put together.

There was one other presence in the darkness. Duke. He seemed to stand behind Thatcher. His stare made the hairs rise on the back of Thatcher's neck.

"One last question," said Dusty. "How can you kill a Knight in combat?"

Even after all the secrets he'd betrayed, this was the hardest. It took him a long time to form the words. "You have to shoot him in the head, and it has to be a surprise. If you can kill him before he can bite down, his system can't save him."

In the darkness, the Knights shook their heads, turned and walked away.

Wolf and Dusty looked at each other. Dusty nodded. Wolf said, "All right. We're going to take you to a safe house a few miles from here. We have another defector there. I hope that you and he together can give us a weapon we can use to overthrow the government. Any questions?"

"Can we get something to eat first? I'm starving."

They hid Angel's car under a tarp behind the gas station and all got into a van. They drove to a little mom-and-pop diner, where Wolf called the safe house from a pay phone. Thatcher ate a huge meal of meatloaf, mashed potatoes, green beans, biscuits and two slices of apple pie à la mode. The conversation was pleasant and trivial.

It was 11:03 when they came to a farm: a house and a barn and a couple of outbuildings surrounding a dirt courtyard. Moths fluttered in the cone of mercury light coming from a fixture near the peak of the barn.

Dusty was driving, and Thatcher could see his brow furrow in the cold blue light. "What's wrong?"

"Where's Booter?"

"Probably in the barn," said Wolf.

"Who's Booter?" said Angel.

"The dog," said Dusty. "He's kind of our chief of security. Whenever a car comes by, he's out here barking his head off."

"He's probably just asleep somewhere."

"I don't know." Dusty stopped the van. "I'm inclined to be a little paranoid right now. I think I'd like to back off and reconnoiter." He put the van into reverse.

Machine-gun fire rang out of the darkness; Thatcher couldn't see from where. Steam spurted from under the van's hood, and the engine coughed and died.

"Damn!" said Wolf.

"I think we're in trouble," said Dusty.

Thatcher's system was at eighty percent. "Give me the gun," he said, meaning the rifle they'd brought with them from Angel's car. "I can hold them down while you make a run for it. We'll go out the back door."

"Why should we trust you?" said Wolf.

"We can trust him," said Angel. Dusty nodded. "Good luck," said Angel, handing him the rifle and a spare clip of ammunition.

"I'll go off to the left. Give me half a minute, then go right. Good luck."

Thatcher checked the rifle over—safety off, seven rounds in the clip plus one in the chamber—then clambered over boxes and tarps to the back door. He eased the latch open, then quickly threw the door open and jumped out.

The van sat in a rutted driveway between fields of winter wheat, a sketch in silver and black in the mercury light from the farm and the beams of a full moon. Thatcher kept low, hurried into rustling wheat. He dropped to one knee and examined the barnyard through the rifle's telescopic sight. Nothing moved. Finally, he sighted on the light that illuminated the scene, shattered it with one shot.

There was an immediate response, shots flashing from the darkness in the vicinity of the barn. He ducked and ran, moving to the left, forcing his way through the rough rattling stalks.

Thatcher poked his head up above the wheat, eyes beginning to adapt to the moonlit dark. He saw a heavy figure—Dusty—emerge from the van and run into the wheat to his right. Then two more figures. But instead of running away, they headed toward the farm!

Wolf was nearly carrying Angel, who struggled to no effect. Thatcher cursed and raised his rifle, but their jerky movements and the darkness prevented a clear shot at the traitor Wolf. He hurried after them, but the van was closer to the barn than to him and they reached the barnyard before he did. They vanished into the black square of the open barn door. A moment later, gunfire flashed out of that square at him, and he ducked back into the field.

Thatcher considered his options. He could run, hide out in the fields, try to make his way to safety on foot. It was what he'd advised the others to do. But now the situation was different.

He scurried back to the shelter of the van. At least it would block some of the bullets. A few shots rang out as he emerged from the field, but as he reached the van he heard a voice on a bullhorn. "Hold your fire!" It was Duke! "Sergeant Thatcher, listen to me. We have your co-conspirators. We have your girlfriend. Surrender, and they will live."

Faintly, he heard Angel protest: "I'm not his girl-frien—" The sentence ended with the smack of hard plastic against flesh.

Thatcher panted against the van door for a moment, then poked his rifle out from behind the bumper. He put five shots into the barn doorway, was rewarded with screams and an answering hail of flashes. He ducked back, hearing a bullet slam into the van's tire.

He leaned out again and fired two more shots, then pulled back and inserted the second clip. Deep breath, then he charged out from behind the van. He would take as many of them down as he could. Then he stopped short.

Duke was standing in the middle of the courtyard, plain as anything. His face was cool and pale in the cold moonlight, features sharp and unperturbed, though he held the struggling Angel to his chest with a pistol to her head. Even his fatigues were crisp.

"Let's not drag this out," he said, not shouting—speaking just loud enough to be heard. "It's quite simple.

Deactivate your system, throw down your weapon and the woman lives. Otherwise, she dies."

In response, Thatcher raised his rifle, sighted between Duke's eyes, and fired. But even as he squeezed the trigger Duke ducked out of the way. He tried again; same result. Even a head shot was no good in this situation, when Duke was ready for him and looking right at him.

Duke ducked down behind Angel, putting her head between him and Thatcher. "Nice try, Sergeant," he said, panting a little. "But I'm losing patience." His finger tightened on the trigger.

"You have five seconds to surrender. Four. Three."

"Don't let him use me against you!" Angel shouted, and threw back her head into his nose. He ate the pain—did not rewind—but he was distracted for a moment.

Angel's face filled the gunsight. Her eyes were hard, looking right at him. She knew that the head shot was the only way to kill a Knight. *I'd give up my life to bring down the government,* she'd said. "Do it!" she said through clenched teeth.

He couldn't do it. He dropped the gun, held up his hands. "You win."

"Excellent choice. Deactivate your system."

He bit down on his tongue. "Done," he lied.

"Come forward. Private Keene, bring the syringe."

"No!" said Angel, and elbowed Duke hard in the ribs. His grip relaxed and she twisted, caught him in the groin with a heel.

"You little bitch." Duke's finger tightened on the trigger and Angel's head exploded.

Thatcher growled, a fierce animal sound, as he bit down hard.

Rewind.

"You have five seconds to surrender. Four. Three."

"Don't let him use me against you!" Angel shouted, and threw back her head into his nose. Her face filled the gunsight. "Do it!"

Thatcher pulled the trigger. Watched as the bullet slammed into Angel's face, and through it. Into Duke's face behind hers. Into the brain behind that face.

Stopping that brain before it could rewind.

Thatcher ran as hard as he could toward the courtyard even as the two bodies buckled. There was a stunned pause, then bullets flashed from the barn toward him. One caught him in the shoulder—he ignored the pain and kept running. He reached Angel, scooped her up, held her tight against his chest, and bit down hard.

Rewind.

"You have five seconds to surrender. Four. Three."

It hadn't worked. Angel was still in Duke's arms.

He had to kill her again.

"Do it!"

He did it. Again. Then he stayed where he was, turned and fired shot after shot into the barn door before those inside could react. Blinking away tears.

In the end, he killed enough of them that the CLU members in the barn could overpower the rest. He took two bullets doing it, but neither of them hurt him as much as the ones he'd fired into Angel's head.

•••

"You don't have to do this, you know," Dusty said. "I do have to," Thatcher replied. "I owe it to Angel."

He lay on a couch in the farmhouse's living room. An ATP/glucose mixture dripped cold into his left arm, and a power cord was alligator-clipped to wires that emerged from a bandaged incision at the base of his neck. His blood seemed to be fizzing.

"We could really use you right here and now."

"If this works, you won't need me here and now. It'll be a whole new world." He turned to the defector, Dr. Collins. He was a former K Division scientist; Thatcher had been told that he'd been killed in a terrorist attack. Somehow he was not surprised to find him here. "How many seconds again?"

"Seven hundred million. That'll put you in early April of 1978, give you six months to find Fessler and stop him."

"Someone else might discover the same thing," said Dusty, "and it'd be all the same."

"Maybe," said Collins. "But I've been all over the theory. Fessler's discovery was a complete fluke."

Dusty held out his hands, supplicating. "We don't even know if a six-year-old brain can handle a twenty-eight-year-old mind! And even if it works, what can a kid do?"

"I was a tough kid." Thatcher bit down, and the green digits appeared—digits only he could see. Seven hundred million seconds. Jesus. One more bite would activate the sequence. "Let's do it."

"Good luck." Collins flipped a switch, and Thatcher's blood felt like it was boiling.

He bit down, and it all vanished.

WINDSEEKERS

Written by
Nnedi Okorafor

Illustrated by
Brian Hailes

About the Author

*Nnedi Okorafor is a writer and journalist.
A graduate of the Clarion Science Fiction
and Fantasy Writers' Workshop (2001), she is the third-place
winner of the 2001 Hurston/Wright Awards (the Hurston/
Wright Foundation is supported by many established authors
including Tony Morrison, John Grisham and Maya Angelou)
for her story "Amphibious Green."*

Nnedi also received honorable mention in The Year's
Best Fantasy & Horror *(2000) for her short story "The Palm
Tree Bandit," originally published in* Strange Horizons. *Her
short stories have also appeared in the* Margin *Anthology of
Magical Realism,* The Witching Hour *Anthology and*
Lamhfada *Magazine of Myth and Folklore. She cites Ben
Okri, Octavia Butler, Salman Rushdie and Amos Tutuolo as
her most influential authors.*

*More a novelist than a short-story writer, Nnedi is
working on three novels,* Arrö-yo the Windseeker, *Bush
Radio and a young adult novel called* Zahrah the
Windseeker. *She is a Ph.D. student in English at the*

University of Illinois, Chicago, a writer for *Africana.com* and a technology columnist for the *Star* Newspapers. Nnedi's Web site is at *www2.uic.edu/~nokoral*.

About the Illustrator

Brian Hailes grew up in a beautiful mountain valley of northern Utah. As a boy of thirteen and later as a high-school student, he won several significant competitions with his artwork. In the summer of his junior year of high school, Brian attended the Academy of Art College in San Francisco to study illustration, sculpture, painting and motion-picture production. As a graduating senior of Mountain Crest High School, he received the Sterling Scholar Award for Visual Arts. In addition, he received a full freshman scholarship and a four-year scholarship to study art at Utah State University.

Brian has been active in community service from a very early age. He has served in various church leadership positions. In 1999, he took two years off from his art studies to fill a church mission in Jacksonville, Florida.

Brian returned to Utah State University in 2001 to continue his studies of art. Above all, in his illustrative subject matter, human and animal anatomy is of most interest to Brian. He meticulously crafts his work on a foundation of realism with the imaginative vision of fantastic realms. His creativity and idealistic mindset play important roles as he continues to progress in technique and move forward in communication of those things that fascinate the human mind.

Arrö-yo didn't want to kill him the second time.

She crouched over him amongst the flowers, her skin blacker than her shadow, her seven thick dreadlocks dragging in the soil. And as she sliced his smooth neck with her long sharp knife and inhaled his last breath, she gazed into his eyes. Her nose stung from the tinny smell of blood and lemons.

Her homeland, Calabar, Nigeria, was very far from here, but that didn't change who he was and the direction his blood flowed. As it ran sticky and to the beat of his slowing heart, soaking her big hands with warmth, she frowned. It didn't matter that the first place she'd killed him was in Australia as an Aborigine man, nor that, this second time, he'd caught her eyes with his and forced her to watch until he was gone. Arrö-yo looked over the trees. This was the land of Ginen, where all things began and all things finished. And once one sets foot in Ginen, things had the habit of finishing in threes.

•••

Arrö-yo had been at the market for weeks. She blended in easily. During the night, she slept in the highest trees. When the sun came up, she stretched and headed to the market . . . on foot. By the time she took her place in the center of the market in the sun, her sandaled feet hurt. She wasn't used to so much walking. Today, her long blue sundress clung to her. It was hot.

Around her, people sold everything from bottles of sweet smelling oil to foul smelling meats, to wood, to garden eggs, to yams, to flora-powered generators, to budding potted plants, to milking goats, to net watches, to everything else. Children ran about, some with purpose, others for play. People shouted, laughed, and the air smelled of perfume, water vapor and sweat. No smoke or exhaust.

Arrö-yo smiled as she set her satchel down and began to unpack her wooden carvings. In so many ways, this place was like West Africa, and it made her heart ache for her village. But in many ways it was not.

For one thing, the skyscrapers here were easily higher than any edifice found even in Asia or America. And they would grow higher, for they were actually large sophisticated plants. When she first came to this place, Arrö-yo had gone up to one of them and touched its wall. It was solid, but still had the yielding roughness of plant flesh.

In all of Ginen, especially the great city of Ile-Ife, the people had accomplished something more advanced than any society Arrö-yo had seen in her many travels: a happy weaving, interlocking, meshing of technology and plant life. It was a true symbiotic relationship between man and flora.

•••

Ile-Ife was a city of legend. And the legend had it that these people used to be able to talk to the plants. Arrö-yo shook her head. Legend also had it that many people of Ginen used to be able to fly and they were called

Windseekers. But Arrö-yo knew, even in these civilized days, if someone were revealed to be a Windseeker, he or she would be plucked from the sky and tied to a tree until death came.

She stood for a moment. Already customers milled about her. As always, word traveled fast. It only took a week for people to start asking about her blue wooden bird carvings. Anyone who held one of them in his or her hands could hear the ocean, see the sky and experience a sense of freedom similar to a flying albatross or a whale soaring in the sea's depths. It pleased her greatly to know that her carvings caused three women to leave their overbearing husbands.

Next to Arrö-yo, a woman talked loudly on her red palm-sized videophone. She was speaking a language unfamiliar to Arrö-yo. Arrö-yo was an Efik woman, but she spoke many languages. Including Yoruba, which was spoken freely enough in Ginen for her to have an easy time haggling with customers. But Yoruba was not a language Ginenians from any tribe spoke amongst themselves.

She reached into her light blue satchel and brought out a roll of satiny blue cloth with gold stars. She shook it out and spread it before her. Then she placed the wooden birds carefully on the cloth. They felt smooth and familiar in her hands. Owls, pelicans, sparrows, vultures, hawks, parrots, ostriches, puffins, blue jays— whatever bird she had come across in her travels, she could recreate from the wood she chopped from treetops.

"How much?" an old man said, picking up one of the carvings. And so a seemingly normal day began.

Hours later, when the market was packed with people and she sold her second to the last carving, she felt a tug. It was like a fishhook embedded in her mind.

Illustrated by Brian Hailes

When it had her, she couldn't turn away. The more she struggled, the deeper it dug and the harder it pulled. Her guard went up like a spiked gate around a house. She'd only felt such a thing once, and she would never forget it. The sun had reached its peak and was starting to descend, but it was still bright.

Small trees blooming with sugary smelling lavender flowers stood here and there in the market, like sentries posted to keep watch. The ground was carpeted with bright green grass that stayed healthy and fragrant even with all the trampling. The beauty of the market didn't distract her, however. Her mind was like radar. Where is . . . ? There.

Her eyes settled on his eyes. His had already found her. The young man sat cross-legged in the grass surrounded by many children, his long legs butterflying out. He wore light flowing garments whose green was as deep as Arrö-yo's dress was blue. There was a small mirror about the size of a fist embroidered into the left hip of his long pants and smaller coin-sized ones around the cuffs of his caftan.

She didn't know how long he had been there telling stories, but she didn't think about that. Instead, she folded her cloth and put the last carving, a whipple bird, into her satchel. Then she got up, pushed her locks back and walked over to him.

His nostrils flared, his eyes following her as he spoke, as if he smelled something unpleasantly familiar. She wondered how long he'd known she was here. She'd been so intrigued by Ile-Ife that she hadn't noticed his presence, or so she told herself. Maybe he was just sharper than she was.

". . . Samage the tortoise flew high up into the sky. When he got to the bird party in the clouds, he dropped the feathers his bird friend had given him. He figured he wouldn't need to fly for a while," he said. "Then he took a seat amongst the most colorful female parrots and ordered some rum."

A girl sitting near the back, just in front of Arrö-yo, giggled. The young man smiled and laughed. Arrö-yo shivered. His laugh was harmony to her ears. She could listen to it forever. She frowned. He rubbed his light beard for a moment, thinking. He looked at Arrö-yo and brought his knees to his chest, the mirrors on the cuffs of his long shirt clicking.

Arrö-yo looked around at the forty or so kids seated before him. Their mouths might as well have been hanging open, saliva dripping from the corners. He had enchanted them the way her carvings enchanted anyone who picked them up. People would freeze, wooden bird in hand, their eyes distant, as if their minds had floated into the sky or under the sea.

"Samage was a greedy tortoise. He was a thousand years old and had seen most parts of the terrestrial world and he was restless," he said. "He wanted to see something new."

He paused, looking around at the children.

"'What is your name, tortoise?' one of the ladies asked him.

"'Just call me Allofyou,' he answered. The pretty birds laughed, but the name had a musical sound to it. And tortoises were known to have poetic names.

"And so he became Allofyou the Tortoise. The music was incredible and the tortoise found that he could dance like he'd never danced before. When it was time to eat, a sly grin spread across his face. The first batch of food was brought out and the tortoise's eyes grew wide, his mouth watering.

"The chef smiled at the guests as she put down platter after platter at the big table. The tortoise could imagine the various flavors: tart, salty, tangy, sweet. When the chef was done setting everything out, she stood back and spread her red wings with a grand proud smile and said, 'This is for all of you!'

"Everyone turned to Allofyou as he stood up and lumbered to the food, thanking all of them for their generosity. Then he proceeded to eat everything, savoring every bite. The birds could not argue. You see, they were not very smart, but they were very honest people. If she said the food was for Allofyou, then it was. But after a while, as their stomachs began to growl after all the dancing and socializing, they grew angry, especially at the tortoise's greed. Even if all the food was for him, he could at least share.

"A group of hefty red whipple birds eventually threw him from the clouds. He landed on his back, still laughing. And that is how the tortoise got his cracked shell."

The children clapped their hands and laughed. He told the old story charmingly, waving his hands about and doing funny voices for the tortoise and the birds, but Arrö-yo found it hard to smile. Instead, her back ached. He had told her the very same story, so long ago, in such a different place.

Several of the children walked up to the storyteller and dropped money into a half of a dried pod. The storyteller nodded his thanks and patted the heads of the children, and many of them threw their arms around him and hugged him tightly. He smiled warmly with each hug. She approached him when he was finally alone. He stood up tall, slightly exceeding her height. He pushed his long dreadlocks back. Arrö-yo didn't have to count to know there were seven.

Her heart fluttered when his dark eyes met hers. His skin was smooth, closer to black than brown, like hers. He wore a pendant around his neck that hung on a cloth string. It was the shape of a water drop and blue as the sky. She stepped back and he stepped forward. She was about to speak when he reached out and picked up one of her locks that rested on her chest. Then he let it drop and reached forward. She could have moved, but she surprised herself when she did not.

He took her hand and grasped it firmly and his face changed. She tried to snatch her hand away, but he held tight. When he let go, she stepped back, her hand creeping to her shoulder, close to the blade she kept hidden behind one of her locks. A man carrying a large bunch of plantains on his shoulder brushed past her and she glanced to her side. Once eye contact was broken, she shook herself and looked at him through more proper eyes frowning.

"What is your name?" he asked, gritting his teeth. Arrö-yo said nothing. She simply stood there staring at him with contempt. After all these years, here he was again. She hadn't really believed in the power of Ginen when she came here. Now it was proven. She should never have come.

"What is your name!" he spat.

"You best ask me that again, more politely this time. I'm growing tired of you," she said. She tensed, her left hand ready.

He took two steps back and paused, squinting at her. Then his face softened, just the tiniest bit. There would be no slashing and killing tonight, she thought, relaxing. She didn't like killing, especially in the middle of a busy market. Several people standing at their booths had either stopped to watch them talk or snatched glances intermittently as they tended to customers.

"I will tell you my name if you tell me yours," she said. She felt her skin prickle. Oh, how I hope I'm wrong, she thought. He looked above her and wet his lips, shaking his head. He took a step closer and she held her hand up.

"Stay there," she said.

He shrugged.

"Ruwan Sanyi," he said, puffing up his chest. Arrö-yo felt her stomach drop. "Originally of the Northern people."

"Originally?" she asked. His people were the ones who seemed to enslave their women. What madness tradition makes my *chi* a man from this tribe? she thought.

Ruwan looked away.

"I was not made to live in a place that is older than time," he said. "But, yes, I was born in northern Ife."

When he brought his eyes back to her, she felt him seeping into her skin again. Her anger dissipating, her guard retreating. She hated herself for it. No matter what, I will leave here alone, she thought. As I always do.

"You still call yourself Inyang?" he asked.

Arrö-yo paused, gazing at him further.

"Yes," she said, looking to the side.

"That is not your suitable name," he said.

"I go by the name I want to go by," she said.

"But yet you name me Ruwan and I go by it," he said, reaching out and caressing her cheek.

"Few can pronounce Arrö-yo correctly. It is an ugly name. So I don't use it," she said coldly. Ruwan flinched and Arrö-yo smiled widely.

"You are dressed like a northern woman, except for your lack of mirrors," he said. "If it weren't for your ways . . ." he trailed off.

She wrapped her arms around her chest and cocked her head. The minute he turned his back, she would be off. The sooner she could get away from him, the better.

"Come for a walk with me, I want to show you something," he said in that voice. The perfect pitch to her ear. He held out a hand. She looked at it. Long fingered and veined like hers. "That is if you are not afraid."

Arrö-yo pursed her lips.

"*Afraid?*" she exclaimed. "Of you?"

"Obviously. I am physically superior to you."

"Don't overrate yourself," she said. You have no idea what I am capable of, she thought. But she thought he also understood. She took his hand. The moment she felt the rightness in his grasp, she wanted to pull away. She looked enviously at the sky and then back at Ruwan. "OK, show me what you want to show me, then we will part ways."

And so they walked in silence, looking straight ahead, past the market outskirts onto the paved street. The farther they walked, the more the market and the city tapered. It happened fast, as if the city had run out of energy. The number of electric cars that passed by slowly dwindled to nothing. Arrö-yo was glad because the flat vehicles sped horribly fast and had no regard for pedestrians.

The bartering along the street was less passionate, the sellers looked less hopeful and the buyers looked less interested. The buildings got smaller, growing in less artistic shapes. They went from large expansive buildings with thick foliage walls and fleshy radio antennas and leaflike satellite dishes poking from the roofs to less looming buildings, living quarters, apartments, houses, homes, broken-down homes, empty lots next to homes, forest. By the time it was just the two of them, there were only palm trees, brambly bushes, the sound of birds, insects and the occasional snort of what lurked behind the foliage that surrounded them.

The road went from perfectly flat dirt to bumpy red orange dirt. Arrö-yo glanced behind her. The sun was setting and the Ooni palace and several of the tall buildings were easy to see, especially the top of the palace, which bloomed into a giant blue disk of a flower with purple petals. The city of the Ile-Ife was a series of smaller buildings looming around the purple palace like an audience surrounding a performer.

"Why do you track me?" he asked, breaking an hour of silence. "You look at the sky . . . the way I do. So why come after me . . . again?"

Arrö-yo frowned, keeping her eyes straight ahead. Ruwan's voice was low, but it made the tips of Arrö-yo's fingers tickle.

"*I'm* not tracking *you*," she said. She stopped walking to face him, her hand still in his. They stood quiet, glaring at each other. He was an invasion of her space. She hadn't come to Ginen for him.

"Your actions tell me otherwise," he said.

Arrö-yo shrugged.

"I don't care. I go where I please," she said.

"As I do."

"Then please go."

"If you do not follow me."

Arrö-yo paused. Her blood pressure was rising. What an insult, she thought. What would I follow him for? He is one of many, she thought. Just a man. But she knew she was very wrong. So she said nothing and her hand stayed in his. Once in a while she looked at it. Trying to will herself to let go. She tried to remember

how wonderful it felt to travel about the world. How
many from her small village could say they had been to
Ginen? That they even knew Ginen was more than a
myth? She'd been to Kenya, Britain, New Zealand,
Tanzania, Papua New Guinea, Australia. Oh, Australia.
And then I killed him, she thought.

Her hand did not let go.

They came to a slight break in the forest and Ruwan
led her onto the path. They walked for an hour through
the trees, silent. However his arm had crept around her
waist, his hand resting on her belly. Arrö-yo felt more
alive than the highest palm tree teeming with water-
filled coconuts. By the time they got to the clearing, the
moon had replaced the sun. Surrounded by high palm
trees and bushes with heavy water-filled leaves, the
clearing was carpeted by large red open-faced flowers
with fuzzy orange centers. The smell was sweet and
lemony. The moonlight gave the flowers a haunted look,
lighting up the centers and darkening the petals.

"This," Ruwan said, with a dramatic sweep of his
hand, "is a place I like to visit often. It's nice?"

He reluctantly took his hand from her waist. Without
his touch Arrö-yo felt as if she would collapse. She
quickly recovered when she saw the flowers.

Arrö-yo put her arms around her chest and took the
place in, trying to hide her smile. She had a weakness for
natural beauty and she was having trouble resisting the
urge to run to the middle of the field and sit down. It
would be like wading into a sea of flowers with only her
head above the surface. There was a slight breeze and it
swirled the scent into her nostrils.

"Come, let us sit and talk," Ruwan said.

She followed him to the center and they sat down.
Arrö-yo took a deep breath and looked across the field.

It really was like swimming in a sea of flowers. They sat for a while, both of them looking into the sky at the stars.

"Did you like my story?" Ruwan asked after a while, rubbing his lightly bearded chin. For a moment, Arrö-yo didn't know what he referred to. She was too busy watching him. He had brought her out to this place for a reason. *I must not forget that I once fought this man,* she thought.

"Oh . . . oh yes. I was always fond of the tortoise," she said. "In my village, storytellers often told us the same story."

Under the moon, their almost black skin took on a bluish hue and their garments looked the similar color of turquoise.

"And what village are you from?"

"It's not important," Arrö-yo said.

Ruwan cocked his head, but didn't press the issue. "But it was the same version? The story, I mean?"

"Yes," she said. *Goodness knows that the stories and folk tales of Ginen are almost interchangeable with those of West Africa,* she thought. *They are the same people, only centuries apart.* "Did you . . . you told that one for a reason."

He nodded.

"Hmm," Arrö-yo said. "One should not . . . fly if he's not meant to."

"Yes, to fly one must make himself as light as possible. Greed is heavier than lead." He paused, pushing one of his locks back. The mirrors sewn into the cuffs of his shirt clicked. "And so is a disregard of tradition."

Arrö-yo flinched. The sound of the word *tradition* triggered something deep in her, something that repulsed her. Tradition is the opposite of freedom, she thought. Therefore, I don't want it. When she jumped up, stepping back, Ruwan jumped up too. His whole gentle demeanor changing to one prepared for battle.

"Why do you choose *this* story to tell?" Arrö-yo asked in a flat voice.

"Do you know another version?" he said. "There is only one way to tell it."

"What?"

Arrö-yo froze. She was overcome by shock, anger, confusion and . . . fear. She felt ashamed of her fear. It had been a long time since she'd felt it. But she was a woman of honesty and so she still listened to her instinct. She turned and took to the air. She'd made it as high as the tallest palm tree, her dress grazing its rough leaves, when his hand clasp around her ankle. Then he pulled hard. She whipped her head around, snatching her blade into her grasp and pointing it at his neck. She went completely still when she saw the blade held to her midsection.

He floated up so that he was pressed face to face with her, still holding his knife in place. They hovered in midair above the field of flowers in the moonlight, two Windseekers in a stalemate, a mix of blue and green garments blowing in the soft breeze

"Of course I know that you keep that blade made of white silver with a blue handle strapped to the lock closest to your neck."

Arrö-yo paused, waiting for it to come back. She blinked when it did.

"You keep a two-sided blade with a green jade handle close to your hip," she said.

"You are claustrophobic," he said.

"You're afraid of tornados."

"You will have no children in this world or any other."

"Neither will you."

"You would never leave me."

"You'll never leave me and that's why I have to kill you."

They paused, glaring at each other. Their jaws clenching, their cheeks dimpling in the same places.

"Why do you pursue me then?" he asked.

"I asked you the same question."

He exhaled through his nostrils and increased the pressure of the knife on her belly. The sharp tip poked through her dress, drawing blood. She pushed her knife closer to his neck, slicing a thin red line. Ruwan brought his knee up and pressed it hard between her legs, his lips grazing hers. Arrö-yo could smell him above the lemony smell of the flowers below. She wondered if he'd brought her here so that he could deal with her without the interruption of other people. Or maybe he really did come here often; he loved places of natural beauty just as she did. How could I forget *him*? she thought. Arrö-yo, rarely forgot anything. He smelled strongly of mint. As they hovered above the ground, their lips met in a kiss. Ruwan's mouth tasted like cool green leaves.

Their knives held in place, they pulled at clothes with their free hands and pressed closer. Arrö-yo balked at her loss of control and then gave in to it. For the moment. For the moment she was lost. Lost in him, lost in herself. She sucked at his tongue and remembered a happiness she wanted to forget. Long ago, in a different time place. With him. Her back arched, her legs wrapping tightly around him in midair, the silver bracelet on her left ankle bit through his shirt into his back. They had yet to drift to the ground.

Ruwan hugged her close and then grasped her locks, pulling them to his face and taking a deep, deep breath. She pressed her lips against his neck, where her knife had cut him, and sucked his blood, and she remembered that she knew moments in the sky when she traveled with him, side by side. She dropped her knife, as the tears ran from her eyes and he thrust into her. She was trembling, her eyes shut tight as more images came. There were times, a home, in the same place. In a remote place of flowers in Ginen, far from Ile-Ife. He'd killed whoever tried to kill them. He'd always worn green, she'd always worn blue. She wasn't barren. There were children. They floated to the ground, slowly, following a shower of clothes, intertwined, locked, inseparable, moving to the same rhythm. I need him, Arrö-yo thought. But with bitterness.

"I need you," he said. His eyes were wet.

•••

I was flying backward, back through clouds and then branches and leaves, till my feet hit the red dirt, my small feet from long ago. Back when my father always looked at me whenever he came into my room in the morning to check on my sisters and me. My feet were always caked with dried mud. I'd say that I hadn't washed them the day before. That I'd been stomping on ants and traipsing around in the forest. But he was a smart man, and he'd then ask me why the mud was so dry. And my mother would ask me why I was smiling so big as I spoke. They knew what I was doing, that I could do what I was doing.

Few people within my bloodline could fly. We forget more every generation. But I was born with a memory strong as the oldest trees. When I became comfortable with it, I left. I said goodbye to my parents and sisters and flew away to see the

*world. I pause. Or was it to look for him? My parents knew
I'd eventually have to leave.*

*I was born with dada hair. I emerged from my mother with
seven long locks flopping about my head, each black as onyx.
And I wailed whenever my mother tried to cut them.
Somewhere else, he was wailing too. When a Windseeker
enters the world, so does her chi, the twin of her soul, however
many hundreds of miles away. And neither soul leaves until
both have died. But I disregarded tradition. I want to travel
the skies ALONE. But he is like the rain to my body of cracked
dry barren earth.*

• • •

Arrö-yo awoke with a start. Then there was a red
dull ache. Her satchel and his rucksack were some feet
away, as were their clothes. Ruwan was warm, curled
close to her, his arm around her waist. His two-sided
blade was held tightly in his hand. She stared at it for a
moment, absolutely shocked. Even in his sleep she
could see how he clutched the knife, with surety,
finality. The blades shined, reflecting the skin of his arm.
The same shade as her skin. She started to slowly rise
and winced. When she looked at his hand, she saw
blood dribbling underneath. Her abdomen ached but
not unbearably. During their stalemate, his blade had
jabbed her deeper than she realized.

The pain was a blessing. For she could easily have
been the one who woke up with a knife to her throat.
And he wouldn't have hesitated, as she did not. Her
blade was sharp and she sliced fast, her arm muscles
working. Skin tearing. Veins and arteries severed open.
The blood flowed fast and hard to the beat of his heart.
If she had thought about it, she wouldn't have done it.

And if she hadn't done it, he would have killed her the minute he awoke, for he was like her. Halfway through slicing his throat, blood pooling in her lap, his eyes opened, but his strength had followed the course of his blood and he was weak. His body shuddered three times, then he simply lay looking at Arrö-yo, blood coating the very lips she had kissed not an hour ago. Her hands shook as she finished, a mixture of her own and Ruwan's blood glazing them.

Arrö-yo knelt close to Ruwan's face, her locks dragging in the soil around him. His eyes held hers until he was gone. I've killed myself, she thought. When her face started to crumple, her chest started to hitch and her eyes started to sting, she let his head drop to the ground. She stood up, swallowing the wail that wanted to erupt from her lips and shake the clouds in the sky. She looked down on him for a moment. She glanced at the blood on his hands, the same blood that coated her belly and her crotch. She shuddered, the weight of her choice sinking into her flesh. Then she mechanically gathered her clothes, slipping into her blue dress, not bothering to wipe off the blood. She quickly took to the air. She wanted to leave Ginen as soon as possible.

She'd return to Africa for a while, maybe Madagascar where she could rest in the trees and the people were open to someone like herself. Where she could possibly get back to who she was before, the fearless Arrö-yo. But deep in the back of her mind, she knew this would be a waste of her time. This time he had changed her. Or maybe he had changed her back in Australia. Though she pushed it way back in her heart, her grief threatened to consume her. And as she flew, shaky in the sky, her tears mixed with the condensation of the clouds. Never had she felt so alone. Grief, like the heaviest stone in her hands.

When she got a chance, she'd wipe her tears. On a moonless night, she'd make an offering to Mami Wata by breaking a kola nut, dipping it in a peanut sauce and alligator pepper and setting one half at the foot of a palm tree. She would eat the other half. Then she'd soothe her senses with freshly tapped palm wine and spend the rest of that night looking at the sky.

Then she'd sit and sharpen her knife, for when she returned to Ginen. The third time was always the most charmed and she had to be ready.

MAGIC
OUT OF A HAT

Written by
L. Ron Hubbard

About the Author

L. Ron Hubbard lived a remarkably adventurous and productive life that spanned far beyond his extensive literary achievements and creative influence. A writer's writer of enormous talent and energy, the scope and diversity of his writing ultimately embraced more than 560 works and over sixty-three million words of fiction and nonfiction. Throughout his fifty-six-year writing career, convinced of the leading role of the arts in civilization, he generously helped other writers and artists, especially beginners, become more proficient and successful at their craft.

Starting with the publication in 1934 of "The Green God," his first adventure yarn, in one of the hugely popular "pulp fiction" magazines of the day, L. Ron Hubbard's outpouring of fiction was prodigious—often exceeding a million words a year. Ultimately, he produced more than 250 published novels, short stories and screenplays in virtually every major genre.

Ron had, indeed, already attained broad popularity and acclaim in other genres when he burst onto the landscape of speculative literature with his first published science fiction story, "The Dangerous Dimension." It was his groundbreaking work in this field from 1938 to 1950, particularly, that not only helped to indelibly enlarge the imaginative boundaries of science fiction and fantasy, but established him as one of the founders and signature architects of what continues to be regarded as the genre's golden age.

Such trendsetting L. Ron Hubbard classics of speculative fiction as Final Blackout, Fear, Typewriter in the Sky, the Hugo Award nominated To The Stars, as well as his capstone novels, the epic saga of the year 3000 Battlefield Earth and the ten-volume Mission Earth® series, continue to appear on bestseller lists around the world.

The single biggest science fiction novel in the history of the genre—and a perennial international bestseller for nearly two decades—Battlefield Earth was voted third in the Random House Modern Library readers' poll of the one hundred best English-language novels of the twentieth century and voted the best science fiction novel of the last century by the American Book Readers Association.

At the same time, two novelizations of original L. Ron Hubbard screenplays, Ai! Pedrito!—When Intelligence Goes Wrong and A Very Strange Trip, were published and immediately became New York Times bestsellers, the fourteenth and fifteenth Hubbard fiction titles to appear on that list.

In the article that follows, reprinted from his early days as a writer, Mr. Hubbard—who knew his craft as few have ever known it—gives us a vivid look at how writers can excel by setting challenges for themselves. He also reveals a bit of the effusive spirit that he brought to the magic of writing.

When Arthur J. Burks told me to put a wastebasket upon my head, I knew that one of us—probably both—was crazy. But Burks has a winning way about him, and so I followed his orders and thereby hangs a story. And what a story!

You know of course how all this pleasant lunacy started. Burks bragged openly in *Writer's Digest* that he could give six writers a story apiece if they would just name an article in a hotel room. So six of us took him up on it and trooped in.

The six were Fred "Par" Painton, George "Sizzling Air" Bruce, Norvell "Spider" Page, Walter "Curly-top" Marquiss, Paul "Haunted House" Ernst, and myself. An idiotic crew, if I do say it, wholly in keeping with such a scheme to mulch editors with alleged stories. I spied a wastebasket in Burks' room and told him to plot me a story around it.

He ordered me to put a wastebasket on my head, told me that it reminded me of a *kubanka* (Ruski lid, if you aren't a Communist) and ordered me to write the story. I won't repeat here the story he told me to write. It was clean, that's about all you can say for it (although that says a great deal coming from an ex-Marine).

This wastebasket didn't even look faintly like a *kubanka*. A *kubanka* is covered with fur, looks like an ice-cream cone minus its point, and is very nice if you're a Ruski. I wrote the story up that same night. Don't go wrong and find Art's article to see how he would do it. I'll show you the *right way*.

Burks told me to write about a Russian lad who wants his title back and so an American starts the wheels rolling, which wheels turn to gun wheels or some such drivel, and there's a lot of flying in the suggestion, too. Now I saw right there that Art had headed me for a cheap action story not worth writing at all. He wanted to do some real fighting in it and kill off a lot of guys.

But I corrected the synopsis so I didn't have to save more than the Russian Empire and I only bumped about a dozen men. In fact, my plot was real literature.

The conversation which really took place (Burks fixed it in his article so he said everything) was as follows:

BURKS: I say it looks like a hat. A *kubanka*.

HUBBARD: It doesn't at all. But assuming that it does, what of it?

BURKS: Write a story about it.

HUBBARD: Okay. A lot of guys are sitting around a room playing this game where you throw cards into a hat and gamble on how many you get in. But they're using a fur wastebasket for the hat.

BURKS: A fur wastebasket? Who ever heard of that?

HUBBARD: You did just now. And they want to know about this fur wastebasket, so the soldier of fortune host tells them it's a *kubanka* he picked up, and he can't bear to throw it away although it's terrible bad luck on account of maybe a dozen men getting bumped off because of it. So he tells them the story. It's a "frame" yarn, a neat one.

BURKS: But you'll make me out a liar in my article.

HUBBARD: So I'll make you a liar in mine.

So I started to plot the story. This hat is a very valuable thing, obviously, if it's to be the central character in a story. And it is a central character. All focus is upon it. Next I'll be writing a yarn in second person.

Anyway, I was always intrigued as a kid by an illustration in a book of knowledge. Pretty red pictures of a trooper, a fight, a dead trooper.

You've heard the old one: For want of a nail the shoe was lost, for want of a shoe the horse was lost, for want of a horse the rider was lost, for want of a rider the message was lost, for want of a message the battle was lost, and all for the want of a horseshoe nail.

So, it's not to be a horseshoe nail but a hat that loses a battle or perhaps a nation. I've always wanted to lift that nail plot and here was my chance to make real fiction out of it. A hat. A lost empire.

Pretty far apart, aren't they? Well, I'd sneak up on them and maybe scare them together somehow. I made the hat seem ominous enough and when I got going, perhaps light would dawn. Here we go:

"That's a funny looking hat," I remarked.

The others eyed the object and Stuart turned it around in his hands, gazing thoughtfully at it.

"But not a very funny hat," said Stuart, slowly. "I don't know why I keep it around. Every time I pick it up I get a case of the jitters. But it cost too much to throw away."

That was odd, I thought. Stuart was a big chap with a very square face and a pocketful of money. He bought anything he happened to want and riches meant nothing to him. But here he was talking about cost.

"Where'd you get it?" I demanded.

Still holding the thing, still looking at it, Stuart sat down in a big chair. "I've had it for a long, long time but I don't know why. It spilled more blood than a dozen such hats could hold, and you see that this could hold a lot."

Something mournful in his tone made us take seats about him. Stuart usually joked about such things.

Well, there I was. Stuart was telling the story and I had to give him something to tell. So I told how he came across the hat.

This was the world war, the date was July 17th, 1918; Stuart was a foreign observer trying to help Gajda, the Czech general, get Russia back into fighting shape. Stuart is in a clearing.

. . . and the rider broke into the clearing. From the look of him he was a Cossack. Silver cartridge cases glittered in the sun and the fur of his *kubanka* rippled in the wind. His horse was lathered, its eyes staring with exertion. The Cossack sent a hasty glance over his shoulder and applied his whip.

Whatever was following him did not break into the clearing. A rifle shot roared. The Cossack sat bolt upright as though he had been a compressed steel spring. His head went back, his hands jerked, and he slid off his horse, rolling when he hit the ground.

I remember his *kubanka* bounced and jumped and shot in under a bush. . . .

Feebly he motioned for me to come closer. I propped him up and a smile flickered across his ashy face. He had a small arrogant mustache with waxed points. The blackness of it stood out strangely against the spreading pallor of his face.

"The . . . *kubanka* . . . Gajda." That was all he would ever say. He was dead.

Fine. The *kubanka* must get to General Gajda. Here I was, still working on the horseshoe nail and the message.

The message, the battle was lost. The message meant the *kubanka*. But how could a *kubanka* carry a message? Paper in the hat? That's too obvious. The hero's still in the dark. But here a man has just given his life to get this hat to the Czechs and the hero at least could carry on, hoping General Gajda would know the answer.

He was picking up the message he knew the hat must carry. He had killed three men in a rifle battle at long range in an attempt to save the Cossack. There's suspense and danger for you. A white man all alone in the depths of Russia during a war. Obviously somebody else is going to get killed over this hat. The total is now four.

I swore loudly into the whipping wind. I had no business getting into this fight in the first place. My duty was to get back to the main command and tell them Ekaterinburg was strongly guarded. Now I had picked up the Cossack's torch. These others had killed the Cossack. What would happen to me?

So my story was moving along after all. The fact that men would die for a hat seems so ridiculous that when they do die it's horrible by contrast, seemingly futile.

But I can't have my hero killed, naturally, as this is a first-person story, so I pass the torch to another, one of the hero's friends, an English officer.

This man, as the hero discovers later, is murdered for the *kubanka* and the *kubanka* is recovered by the enemy while the hero sleeps in a hut of a muzjik beside the trail.

The suspense up to here and ever farther is simple. You're worried over the hero, naturally. And you want to know, what's better, why a hat should cause all this trouble. That in itself is plenty reason for writing a story.

Now while the hero sleeps in the loft, three or four Russian Reds come in and argue over the money they've taken from the dead Englishman, giving the hero this news without the hero being on the scene.

The hat sits in the center of the table. There it is, another death to its name. Why?

So they discover the hero's horse in the barn and come back looking for the hero. Stuart upsets a lamp in the fight, the hut burns but he cannot rescue the hat. It's gone.

Score nine men for the hat. But this isn't an end in itself. Far from it. If I merely went ahead and said that the hat was worth a couple hundred kopeks, the reader would get mad as hell after reading all this suspense and sudden death. No, something's got to be done about that hat, something startling.

What's the most startling thing I can think of? The empire connected with the fate of the *kubanka*. So the Russian Empire begins to come into it more and more.

The Allies want to set the Czar back on the throne, thinking that will save them later grief from the Reds. Germany is pressing the Western front and Russia must be made to bear its share.

But I can't save Russia by this hat. Therefore I'll have to destroy Russia by it. And what destroyed it? The Czar, of course. Or rather his death.

The Czech army moves on Ekaterinburg, slowly because they're not interested so much in that town. They could move faster if they wanted. This for a feeling of studied futility in the end.

They can't find the Czar when they get there. No one knows where the Czar is or even if he's alive.

This must be solved. Stuart finds the hat and solves it.

He sees a Red wearing a *kubanka*. That's strange because Cossacks wear *kubankas* and Reds don't. Of all the hats in Russia this one must stand out, so I make the wrong man wear it.

Stuart recovers the *kubanka* when this man challenges him. He recognizes the fellow as one of the Englishman's murderers. In a scrap, seconded by a sergeant to even up the odds, Stuart kills three men.

Score twelve for one secondhand hat. Now about here the reader's patience is tried and weary. He's had enough of this. He's still curious but the thing can't go any farther. He won't have it.

That's the same principle used in conversation. You've got to know enough to shut up before you start boring your listeners. Always stop talking while they're still interested.

I could have gone on and killed every man in Russia because of that hat and to hell with history.

History was the thing. People know now about the Czar, when and where he was killed and all the rest. So that's why I impressed dates into the first of the story. It helps the reader believe you when his own knowledge tells him you're right. And if you can't lie convincingly, don't ever write fiction.

Now the hero, for the first time (I stressed his anxiety in the front of the story), has a leisurely chance to examine this hat. He finally decides to take the thing apart, but when he starts to rip the threads he notices that it's poorly sewn.

This is the message in the hat, done in Morse code around the band:

"Czar held at Ekaterinburg, house of Ipatiev. Will die July 18. Hurry."

Very simple, say you. Morse code, old stuff. But old or not, the punch of the story is not a mechanical twist.

The eighteenth of July has long past, but the hero found the hat on the seventeenth. Now had he been able to get it to Gajda, the general's staff could have exhausted every possibility and uncovered that message. They could have sent a threat to Ekaterinburg or they could have even taken the town in time. They didn't know, delayed, and lost the Russian Czar and perhaps the nation.

Twelve men, the Czar and his family, and an entire country dies because of one hat.

Of course the yarn needs a second punch, so the hero finds the jewels of the Czar in burned clothing in the woods and knows that the Czar is dead for sure and the Allied cause for Russia is lost.

The double punch is added by the resuming of the game of throwing cards into this hat.

After a bit we started to pitch the cards again. Stuart sent one sailing across the room. It touched the hat and teetered there. Then, with a flicker of white, it coasted off the side and came to rest some distance away, face up.

We moved uneasily. I put my cards away.

The one Stuart had thrown, the one which had so narrowly missed, was the king of spades.

Well, that's the "Price of a Hat." It sold to Leo Margulies' *Thrilling Adventures* magazine of the Standard Magazines, Inc., which, by the way, was the magazine that bought my first pulp story. Leo knows a good story when he sees it. In a letter to my agent accepting my story, Leo Margulies wrote: "We are glad to buy Ron Hubbard's splendid story 'The Price of a Hat.' I read the *Digest* article and am glad you carried it through."

Art Burks is so doggoned busy these days with the American Fiction Guild and all, that you hardly see anything of him. But someday I'm going to sneak into his hotel anyway, snatch up the smallest possible particle of dust and make him make me write a story about that. I won't write it but he will. I bet when he sees this, he'll say:

"By golly, that's a good horror story." And sit right down and make a complete novel out of one speck of dust.

Anyway, thanks for the check, Art. I'll buy you a drink, at the next luncheon. What? Heck, I didn't do *all* the work!

LOST ON THE ROAD

Written by
Ari Goelman

Illustrated by
Darlene Gait

About the Author

Ari Goelman grew up in a suburb of Philadelphia called King of Prussia, which may partially explain his lifelong love of the fantasy genre. He left King of Prussia when he was seventeen and spent the subsequent eleven years in Israel, Florida and, most recently, Vancouver, British Columbia. He received his master of science (planning) from the University of British Columbia in 1999, and worked for the city of Vancouver for just about a year, before leaving the city to have more time to write.

At this writing, Ari has started a doctoral program in urban studies and planning at the Massachusetts Institute of Technology. He hopes to imbibe the spirit of Isaac Asimov while studying in Boston and emulate the good doctor in his dual academic and literary pursuits.

He plans to continue to write as much as he can afford to. His short story "Coyotes Are an Urban Animal" will be published in an upcoming issue of On Spec Magazine. In the face of his unremitting persistence, he believes that sooner or later an editor will have a moment of weakness and publish a story he has submitted. So be it!

About the Illustrator

Born on Vancouver Island, Darlene Gait was influenced by her father to appreciate and respect nature, and her mother taught her to explore her native island heritage. As she matured, her skills became more refined and she eventually pursued an education in graphic design and illustration. This allowed her the freedom to explore many new mediums.

Darlene currently works at home, creating art and free-lancing her skills as an illustrator and designer to local businesses.

Start it wherever you want. You have to begin somewhere, though.

For instance, once a king had three sons. The two older ones were bold and clever, but the youngest was known as a fool.

Or, once a fisherman caught a magical golden flounder. It said, "I will grant you three wishes if you throw me back into the river."

Or,

I put the trash cans down on the back porch and take in the view for a few moments. Tonight, the Road is a golden river through a desert of gray dust. It's as though everything in this world but the Road has been burnt to the ground.

Truth is, I don't care where the inn stops. I love taking out the garbage, regardless. The Road is there to keep me company even in a deserted wasteland like this. And, for a few seconds, she isn't watching me.

I drag the garbage cans down the stairs. I don't see a dumpster yet, but there's always something to put the trash into. For all I know, that's how the inn chooses its stopping points.

Sure enough, at the base of the stairs, a perfectly camouflaged flat square opens into a small gray box. I put the trash inside, where it immediately disappears. After a moment, the box shrinks back into the square.

Carefully keeping my feet away from the edges of the square, I pull the empty garbage cans back up the stairs.

Usually the process is more mundane. Like last night, I walked out the back door to find that the Road had become the crumbling back alley of an inner city. I just emptied the garbage into a metal dumpster sitting next to the porch. I didn't even have to climb down the stairs.

Or the night before last, the Road was a small dirt path between farms, and I got to throw the scraps into a wooden pen full of pigs. The pigs squealed with joy every time they saw me. I took the trash out every few minutes, until my Mistress noticed. By the time she let me out, the metal dumpster had replaced the pigs.

The freehold inn doesn't like staying still. Sometimes it stays for an hour, sometimes for a week, but it always moves on, always going somewhere else on the Road. I once overheard my Mistress saying that all freehold buildings stay on the Road. She hates that. I think the only reason that she lets me outside to do the trash is so she doesn't have to see the Road.

The Road is my best friend. Truth is, it's my only friend. My Mistress says slaves aren't fit for friendship. But she can't stop me from looking at the Road when I take out the trash. Or listening to its voice. I don't think it talks to anyone else, but it talks to me all the time.

Tonight, it murmurs sweetly to me and calls in a girl's voice, "Ian, come with me. I miss you."

"How would I travel?" I ask. This is a game we play.

"Tonight you would swim, and tomorrow you would ride," the Road responds. "The great Khan of Nuqtiva has his pleasure craft moored nearby. You could borrow it for a time."

The shackle around my wrist tightens and grows warm at the thought. "Road," I say, as I always do, "thank you, but I can't come with you tonight." The Road sparkles even brighter for a moment—and then goes a duller shade of yellow. But still I can see the gold waiting for me, just beneath the surface. I go back inside before the slave shackle punishes me for looking.

And they all have villains.

For instance, Bluebeard took himself a new wife every year.

Or, the children's new stepmother hated them and plotted against them.

Or,

My Mistress is waiting for me inside. Her eyes are nothing like the sun. Irises almost as black as her pupils, against a paper-white face. "Lazy half-breed," she snaps. "Have you been talking to the Road again?"

I shake my head. She shakes her own head, mocking me. And then she stares at me, increasing the pain administered by the slave shackle, until she can see the tears in my eyes.

"Don't lie to your Mistress, child," she snaps. "I could have your mongrel ears off any time I choose." She reaches down and twists my right ear. "I see why your poor mother begged me to take you."

I know better than to answer. But the memory of my kind has none of the comforting blurriness of human memory. I remember perfectly when she stole me. Her cold white hands taking my cradle from the fireside. The shackle on my wrist before I could walk. And I have all too little faery resignation with which to accept my fate. My face grows warm with rage, exactly as it always does, and my Mistress grins.

But then something strange happens. In the midst of my pain and anger, a sense of absolute certainty possesses me. I have no idea what I'm about to say, but

Illustrated by Darlene Gait

every word seems to me to resonate with authority as it leaves my lips. "The Road will leave you, Mistress. You will face the justice of the fair folk." The strange certainty leaves me, but I feel heartened by my words. Whatever they mean.

A shadow flees across her face and is gone. "Nonsense, little half-breed. None of the fair folk would dare enter a freehold inn to judge me. And your father can walk the Road until his feet fall off, and I'll still be the Mistress of this inn." She looks at me thoughtfully and gives my ear one final pinch before pushing me toward the common room. "But you'll be gone soon enough anyway. Get on with you now. There's drinks to be served."

And they have helpers.

For instance, the giant's wife who helps the thief outsmart her own husband.

Or the old crone who gives advice to the youngest prince.

Or,

As soon as I enter the common room, I smell something. All visitors to a freehold inn cram themselves into a body with a semblance of human form. But it's more difficult to modify their odor. My sense of smell is pure faery, and I smell something foul in the room.

I make my way through the inn with my pitchers of beer. The smell gets stronger toward the back right corner of the room. I serve the rest of the room first, but eventually I have to work my way through that area.

The smell is strong enough to make me sick. Fortunately, there aren't many people in that area—two men drinking at one table and a third passed out behind them. I approach the pair with my pitchers, just fresh-ened from the tap, and look at them closely.

One is slim, with a very pale, almost translucent, complexion. He looks up at me and I see the face of a fox between the lines of his human face. His companion is a great behemoth of a man, so immersed in folds of fat that his mouth is scarcely visible.

As I fill his mug, the fat man is complaining, "The great injustice is that Ellerisa would never have even let me into the fair isle if my ballad hadn't been beautiful."

His friend rolls his eyes. "Ellerisa let you in because you didn't mean any great harm. The fair isle is not named for its appreciation of beauty."

"Nonsense." The fat man gestures at me to fill his beer mug and continues. "Is not justice beautiful?"

The shackle burns my wrist, but I can't help myself. I even forget the stink for a moment. "Excuse me, sirs," I politely interrupt. "Are you from the fair isle?"

The two men look at me. The fat man speaks first. "Hasn't your mistress taught you any manners then?" He shakes his head disapprovingly. "To go asking free-hold clients where they come from."

I try to explain. "Sir, it's just that I wondered—"

He doesn't let me finish, hardly seems to notice I'm speaking. "The functioning of freehold inns depends entirely upon discretion," he says. "Why, I have half a mind to teach you—"

The fox-faced man interrupts. "Nonsense. At best, I'd grant you a quarter-of-mind." Before his friend can respond, he says. "Look at the boy, Yorick."

The big man pauses and squints at me. Then, to my surprise, he chuckles. "Pardon me, lad. With a father like yours, I don't wonder that you think you can ask any question you please."

"You know my father from the fair isle?" I ask. To hear my Mistress tell it, I was thrust upon her by my desperately poor mother who hated me. If I was wholly human I might believe such lies, but faeries are less gullible, even as children.

He shakes his huge head. "Your father's human, boy. Any fool can tell you have Jack's face."

"Ah. But it takes an exceptional fool to see only that," the fox-faced man adds dryly. He nods at my slave shackle. "I suspect our young friend has had little contact with his family."

Yorick's eyes widen, "A slave shackle on the road walker's boy! That's not right. We should—"

Fox-face sees something behind me, and he motions his companion to silence. In one smooth motion he produces a large silver coin and throws it to me. His lips don't move, but I hear. "Toss this on the Road, boy. But not until you have to."

"Until I have to what?" I ask.

The shackle burns, as the Mistress snaps from across the room, "Ian, leave the guests alone. Come here."

She looks at me when I approach. "I've told you before," she says. "Slaves don't make friends."

Then, inexplicably, she smiles. "This forces my hand. But I don't mind. God knows you've caused me enough trouble already." Incredibly, she doesn't take the silver coin from me. She looks directly at it, but somehow her eyes fail to focus upon it.

Later, alone in the kitchen, I check twice to make sure the coin is real. I smile for the first time since feeding the pigs two days before. No trick the Mistress played would involve silver in my pocket.

As I wash the dishes, I contemplate the man's advice. When will I "have" to throw the coin? I rinse the last pot with cold water and clear the drain with my fingers. My back hurts, and my hands are wrinkled from the washing. If it will help me, I want to throw the coin now. But do I have to?

Finally finished with the pots, I take the trash out for the last time of the night. A forest of huge trees stretches before me. The night is warm and moist, and I hear animals' sounds in the dark distance of the forest.

There is a small grove of plants in the dumpster place. I've never seen plants like these before, with slim trunks and large, saw-toothed leaves. I look closer and find an opening, about twice my size, in the ground beneath them. I deposit the waste in this receptacle, and watch as it is drawn through the plants' roots. I walk around to the back of the grove and I see only a trickle of clean water emerging.

Before returning to the inn, I pause and stretch, a brief luxury before mopping the common room's floor. The Road is a silver slash through the dark forest. It whispers to me in a man's voice, "Come, Ian, just a brief journey."

"How will I travel?" I ask.

"First you will walk alone and then you will wait in company," it answers. "You will walk from a troll's lap to the lap of luxury." The Road seems unusually eager tonight. "Please, Ian. Let's go now."

The sounds of the forest seem very distant next to the Road's whispering. I ignore the burning manacle and take a step toward the Road. My entire left arm fills with pain, but I take another step. And then another, tears running down my face. The left side of my body actually freezes, then, and I almost fall. I am little more than five feet from the Road, but my body refuses to take another step. This is as close to the Road as I've ever been able to come. I realize now why the Mistress is paying me unusual attention. She must realize that the shackle will not imprison me forever.

I know her too well to find comfort in this thought. But the pain leaves me as I admit defeat. I whisper,

"Road, I love you, but I can't come tonight," and turn back toward the inn.

A tall man steps out of the shadows beneath the back porch of the inn. I am suddenly filled with hope. The strangers mentioned a kinsman. Perhaps they summoned him. "Jack?" I say hopefully.

Then the stench hits me. The light skitters away from the figure, but I recognize him from the smell as the man who had been at the table behind the pair.

The manacle burns the instant I half-turn back toward the Road. I breathe shallowly and find the coin in my pocket.

"Don't be afraid," the thing says calmly. His smile glints in the shadows. "Or be afraid. Doesn't much matter to me."

I hear a ripping sound from his feet. Looking down, I see huge claws grow through his boots. And then back to his face, tusks are sprouting from his cheeks. Of course. Outside of the freehold, he is returning to his true form.

I marshal my courage and say coldly, "Only a troll would think to attack one who belongs to a freehold inn. Even your own kind will kill you for this."

The troll steps toward me, smiling broadly. "You no longer belong to the freehold, little one. Your mistress has sold you. But fear not. Your servitude will be brief."

Without thinking about it long enough for the manacle to stop me, I toss the coin toward the Road. I hear it roll, and then the Road whispers, "A gift, a gift, for me. Sweet Ian."

The troll reaches me and takes my right ear between his fingers. His fingers, at least, remain human shaped. His nails are neatly trimmed, his fingertips callused. I

try to shout, to hit him, but every muscle is paralyzed—
no doubt through the slave manacle. It knew my new
master before I did.

His voice is strangely soft. "It's been ages since I've
tasted the ears of a living faery." He sniffs. "Or even a
half-breed."

My eyes are frozen in front of me, but with my
peripheral vision I see small leathery wings sprout from
his back.

And then, beyond the wings, a strange illusion. The
Road seems to be slowly, almost imperceptibly, moving
toward me. Its movement is soon confirmed, for I can
hear its silver melody growing louder.

The troll just grins wider. "Ah, is the Road coming to
save you? It'll not do you much good when you can't
walk." He chuckles, leans toward my face and delicately
licks my ear. My stomach turns at his touch. His breath
is a compound of rotting flesh, noxious stomach fluids
and something akin to pickle brine. If I wasn't paralyzed, I'm certain I would vomit. Despite the paralysis,
I gag.

At this moment, the Road reaches us. It is a smooth
transition; somehow, the dirt that we are standing on
simply becomes the Road. I realize that the troll was
right. I'm finally standing on the Road, but I can't walk.
My eyes burn, but my quick sob is muffled by lips still
bound shut.

No matter. The Road hears and sobs with me, not
understanding my reluctance to travel. And then, it's as
though the Road gets distracted. It begins humming a
song I have never heard from it before, a simple
welcoming tune. I am comforted despite its evident
futility. And I manage a tiny smile through the slave
manacle's control.

This infuriates the troll. He pulls back from my face. "Why're you so happy, boy? Do you think I'm just here to tickle you with my tongue?"

Of course I can't answer. But my smile grows slightly broader at the sense of injury in his voice.

The smile doesn't last long. I feel every nuance of the change as the fingernails resting on my ear become claws. They are so sharp that I scarcely feel the cut, just moisture as the first drops of blood ooze from my ear. And then I hear it. The Road's music is accompanied by a human voice.

My attacker's snarl wavers, becomes less vicious. He looks at something behind me. "This doesn't concern you, Jack," he says.

The song stops, and I hear the singer's footsteps briskly approach us from behind. Suddenly, I am acutely conscious of my inability to speak. I try to shout, but only an unintelligible gurgle comes from my lips.

"This doesn't concern you, Jack," the troll repeats, keeping a firm grip on my ear.

"On the contrary." The voice comes from behind me and to my left. Exerting all my willpower, I slowly rotate my head to face Jack. "I'm very concerned."

The troll glares at the newcomer. "I have as much right as any to travel the Road with my slave. Y'have no power over me."

By now my assailant has given up all semblance of humanity. His head resembles that of a boar, but with smaller tusks and larger canines. Claws extend from each of his thick arms and legs, and his body is covered with hard green scales. Small wings, like those of a bat, beat the air behind him.

I see the slender tip of something descend and hit him on the head. The troll yelps incredulously. "Would you actually challenge me, human?"

At last, I manage to turn my head sufficiently to get a look at Jack. He is an older human, about the height of the troll, but perhaps one-fourth the width. I can tell he has white hair and bright blue eyes, but the rest of his face is difficult to see, for every moment it appears different. I wonder what my own face looks like for me to be identified as this man's relation.

Jack shrugs and raises his staff. "Not much of a challenge, really." He hits the troll once more, this time in the side of his thick armored stomach. Prepared, this time the troll scarcely blinks. Jack swallows hard.

My heart sinks at the contrast between the two. As if reading my thoughts, Jack turns and favors me with a quick smile, before turning back to the troll. "I mean, you're just a pig troll. Those tusks wouldn't scare an infant."

The troll's claws tense on my ear and the trickle of blood turns into a small stream. Pain is nothing new to me. It has long been a companion, if not a friend. But my ears. They are the only part of me that shows my faery blood. The only part of my mother that is left me. And this human weakling has arrived too late to do more than enrage the troll.

Tears begin to roll down my still-paralyzed face, and sobs force themselves out of my closed mouth.

Jack throws back his head and laughs. At that moment, I hate this interloper.

The troll hates him too. If my smile earlier annoyed him, this man's laughter outrages him. He actually lets go of my ear and turns fully toward Jack.

Between gales of laughter Jack steps away from the troll. He gasps, "Please, don't stop on my account. It just struck my funny bone, that's all. To see a troll so afraid of me that it would sooner fight its own slave than me."

The troll is so angry it can barely speak. Still, it approaches Jack slowly, its arms spread wide. "We'll see who's afraid. Where will you run when I'm on the Road too, Jack?"

Jack wipes tears of laughter from his eyes. "Why would I run?" Notwithstanding his words, he takes another step away from the troll. The troll is stalking down the center of the path, and so, in retreating, Jack steps toward the edge of the Road. As he does so, his staff comes down for a quick stab at the side of the troll's neck.

The troll shakes his head, as though he has water in his ear, but he continues to follow the human. Jack takes a quick step to one side, clearly trying to get back to the Road's center, but the troll cuts him off with a swing of one massive arm. Jack has to leap back to avoid being eviscerated.

Jack is now perhaps a foot from the edge of the Road. He looks around frantically, but the troll's reach is too long for him to get around, without leaving the Road.

"What's wrong, Road Walker?" the troll asks. "Not enough places left to walk?" His anger is entirely gone, and he smiles at Jack. "I bet you're not much of a runner without the Road to help you. We'll soon see, won't we?" He takes another step forward, forcing Jack back until he is on the boundary of the Road. I try to warn Jack, but can just barely force my mouth open.

Sweat pours off of Jack's temples. He makes another lightning swift blow, this time to the troll's right knee. The troll moves into the blow, blunting the staff's impact and forcing Jack to retreat again, this time off the Road. I manage to gasp, "Jack, you're off the Road."

"Too late," the troll says. He grins and lunges toward Jack. At not exactly the same moment, the Road moves.

The two movements happen too quickly for me to see. But the results speak for themselves. Precisely as the troll was crossing its edge, the Road must have moved a few feet forward. The back of the troll's head, one leg and the greater part of his torso remain on the Road. The rest of his torso, the other leg, both arms and his face, frozen in a look of surprise, lie ten feet away, off the Road, at Jack's feet.

Jack quickly walks toward me, stepping over the bloody troll parts without a glance. He gently touches my bleeding ear and looks at me, fixing me in his blue eyes. His mouth works for a moment, and then he says simply, "Hello, Ian." His voice is low and musical. And something unfamiliar. "How old are you?"

"Fourteen," I say. I'm still mostly numb with fear and shock, but my ear's beginning to hurt.

His changing face crumbles for just a moment, and he lets me see his true face. It is simply that of an older human, tanned, wrinkled, and filled now with the same unfamiliar emotion I heard in his voice. "My son," he whispers. "A slave for fourteen years."

He enfolds me in his slim arms. He smells of pipe smoke, sweat and earth. Still holding me close, he touches the slave shackle on my wrist and loudly says, "Having witnessed the accidental death of your owner, I proclaim you free." The shackle falls off.

I raise a hand to my ear and fearfully touch it. To my relief, it seems almost completely intact. There's simply a long, deep cut at the base. It stings, but not unbearably.

He—my father—gently leads me to the back porch and we sit together on the stairs. He leaves his arm around me. I am surprised at how natural it feels to be this close to another person. For a moment, we stare into the forest and listen to the animal sounds mingle with the Road's hum.

At last Jack breaks the silence. "Shall we go?" he asks. The Road murmurs with excitement, a chorus of voices.

I nod. I have waited my whole life to walk on the Road. But . . . .

Jack smiles. A small tired smile. "You're wondering why I didn't come sooner."

I nod again, afraid to meet his eyes.

His arm tightens around me. "Time moves differently in different places. To me, it's been less than a week since you were snatched. I've spent every second of that time walking the Road, searching for a sign of you.

"The Road did its best to help, but it gets time and space mixed up. It couldn't lead me to you until you gave it a beacon to use."

Jack gently touches my wounded right ear and pulls a coin from behind it. "This was very helpful. Where did you find faery silver?"

I look away and kick the porch with the backs of my heels. "A fox-man gave it to me." I suddenly feel shy. This is my father.

He nods. "An old friend."

I feel his fist clench beside my shoulder, and he continues. "Your former mistress couldn't see faery silver, but she must have realized somebody had recognized you. So I suppose she sold you to the nearest potential customer. No doubt she hoped the troll would eat you far from the Road." He falls silent. When he speaks again his voice is calm. "But that's all over now."

He stands and draws me up with him. "Come. Let us leave this place. Your mother misses her son."

At the thought of actually seeing my mother, something inside of me shivers. "Will she still want me?" I ask. "She expects a baby."

"Of course she'll want you." Jack suddenly smiles and gestures to the Road. "The Road likes you, and it's an excellent judge of character."

I have never seen the Road this excited. In a chorus of voices it murmurs, "Come, Ian, you shall ride/walk/surf/swim/slide/gallop . . . ." Its murmurs are so fast they're difficult to understand, but its silver halo is becoming brighter and brighter.

Still something holds me back. "What's going to happen to my Mis—" I quickly correct myself "—to that woman?"

"You'll never see her again." Jack's face grows hard. "When you leave with me now, the Road will leave with us. She'll be left with an ordinary inn. And the fair isle's justice will find her. Your mother's people are not known for their mercy."

The Road sings to me, and at last I feel ready.

There is always an ending—not always happy. But sometimes.

For instance: And so, the third son married the princess. When her father died, he inherited the kingdom and ruled long and wisely.

Or, then the two children were reunited with their parents.

Or, then they lived happily ever after.

Or,

Together we step onto the Road, and the light covers me. I smile. And we are gone.

GRAVEYARD TEA

Written by
Susan Fry

Illustrated by
John Kolbek

About the Author

Susan Fry grew up in Salt Lake City, Utah, and Lubbock, Texas. She moved to the San Francisco Bay area, where she received a bachelor's and master's degree in English from Stanford University. She also studied overseas at Oxford in England and in France, and she spent a summer teaching English in Prague. She worked in Egypt as a journalist and a teacher at the American University in Cairo. She then returned to the San Francisco Bay area and worked in international business development for magazines PC World and Wired. When wearing a suit got to be too much, she began freelance writing, mostly about business and technology.

She also started writing fiction and, in 1998, attended Clarion West. Since then, she has published three stories, all in anthologies. She edited the speculative fiction market magazine Speculations for two years. During that time, the magazine was twice nominated for a Hugo.

Susan is currently living in the San Francisco Bay area with her husband, Cadir. She says she tends to write fantasy, horror and mysteries, often about women who aren't as nice as they should be. Susan is currently working on a novel.

About the Illustrator

John Kolbek was born October 28, 1979. He lived in Garfield, New Jersey, and moved to Pennsylvania when he was ten or eleven. John says he "was blessed" to have a great father, Richard, a great mother, Linda, and a little brother, Joseph.

John has been into art since he was very young, always loving detail in anything—music, art, and movies.

John's father recently passed away unexpectedly, and he misses him terribly, but in a way knows he's still near. Depression and sadness usually fuel John to being creative, so he has produced many works during this time period. He loves fantasy because there is no limit, no rules to what can be done.

John is currently a student at Northampton Community College and hopes to continue with an art education degree.

I know I'm dying for sure when I see Rita Mae Rawlins on my back porch, a battered suitcase in one hand and a pineapple upside-down cake in the other.

"You sure you don't want to go to the hospital, LaNelle?" she asks.

I shake my head and let her in. "Damn doctor would kill me quick as a snake and twice as uncomfortable."

She puts the pineapple upside-down cake on the kitchen table, firmly, as if she owns not just the table but everything else in my kitchen, too. "Figured you wouldn't be cooking," she says, surveying the food spread out over the countertops.

During the visits from that morning, Genevieve Franklin had brought her paradise salad, grated coconut and all. Patsy Markham and the twins had made an entire fried chicken wrapped in butcher paper, splotched with grease. And my quilting club had baked so many muffins, brownies and cookies that it looks like I'd hosted a bake sale.

"You should be in bed, not dealing with all those people."

"I'm not that bad," I say. Actually, I'm so weak that just opening the door made me breathless, and the ache in my chest is stronger than it was yesterday. But dying in Plainview, Texas, is not to be taken lightly. It's a social responsibility, like getting married or having a child. I've done both, so I should know. Rita Mae has done neither, but she's seen more death than everyone in town put together.

Rita Mae frowns at me, and I follow her meekly upstairs.

Despite my protests, I'm more relieved than I can say to have her taking over my death. Rita Mae knows when to give medicine and when to call in the relatives and when to let a person sit in peace. It's as if she can see death approaching. Some sick people she refuses to visit. No one knows why.

I've been afraid I would be one of them, to tell the truth. Rita Mae and I have a long history. Maybe it's the thought of our history that makes me feel uncomfortable as well as relieved to have her here, as if she's granting me a favor I don't deserve. The last thing I want is to be beholden to her.

Or maybe I'm uncomfortable because of how Rita Mae looks. She's wearing a blue-and-white flowered cotton dress, starched and ironed so carefully it rustles with each step. Her white leather pumps click on the wooden stairs. Her blonde hair rests in the perfect curls of the new permanent waves that have been so popular since the war. In the twenty-four years I've known Rita Mae, I've only seen her disheveled once. I always figured being neat was her way of making up for not being pretty. I was much prettier than she was. Buzz even told me so, the one time I asked. But now, next to Rita Mae, I feel like a muddy cat in a rainstorm, even though my pink nylon bathrobe is darn near new.

I have to stop and rest halfway up the stairs. Rita Mae waits patiently as I catch my breath and rub my lower back, where the doctors say the cancer has spread.

"Your hip hurts, too, hmmm?" Rita Mae says. "I can see the pain. It's like a little black cloud." She touches my hip. Her hand is very warm, and the pain fades a little.

It's the first time we've ever touched, and I draw back. I feel even more uncomfortable, maybe because she's so strong and healthy and I'm not. Rita Mae smiles as if she knows what I'm thinking. I make myself smile back, like nothing's wrong. I may have to die in front of her, but I don't want to seem weak while I'm doing it. Then I take a deep breath and climb on up to my bedroom.

We pause in the doorway, awkward for a second. She's looking at the bed. The bed is big and wide because Buzz was a big man. It's covered with a quilt I made twenty years ago from a bunch of his old work-shirts. The colors are faded, but the cotton is soft as silk.

Rita Mae says, bright and cheerful, "So this is your bedroom. I . . . ." Her voice trails away, and she bustles around the room, turning down the bed, plumping the pillows and pulling the extra blanket down from the top of the closet as if she knows exactly where I keep it.

Part of me wants to ask what she was going to say, but another, larger part is afraid to know. So I just slide into bed. My skin is so tender—like a new-plucked chicken—that the smooth sheets feel rough.

"I'll get you some of my tea," Rita Mae says.

The minute she's out of the room, the phone rings. I reach across the bed to pick it up. I'm surprised at how weak my arm is, even just holding up the receiver. It's Jimmy, and I feel a smile spread across my face. But then I listen to what he's saying.

He's in Florida, which is quite a ways from Plainview. He'd run there six years ago, in 1938, at seventeen, when the army wouldn't take him. He'd told

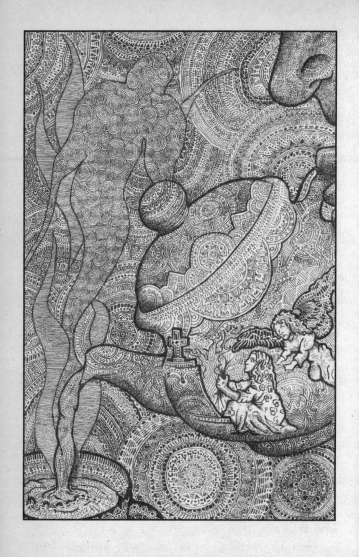

Illustrated by John Kolbek

me, "I've got a good thing going, Ma—hotels. Big ones, with swimming pools and all. There'll be a boom as soon as the war's over. Pop'll be proud of me. You'll see."

"You don't know nothing about hotels," I'd said.

"It's fast money, Ma."

"Ain't no such thing," I'd replied.

"It's the land of milk and honey, Ma."

Evidently, the land of milk and honey isn't working out quite right for Jimmy. He's having some problems getting home as quick as he'd like. He's leaving right now, he promises. He meant to leave last night, but some things came up.

"I understand," I say. "Just get here quick as you can."

As I hang up, I realize Rita Mae is in the doorway. She carries a chipped blue mug with steam rising from it. Buzz's favorite mug. Tears come to my eyes, and I blink furiously.

I make myself sound cheerful. "He'll be here real soon," I say. "As soon as he can."

Rita Mae puts the tea on the nightstand, then sits in the chair next to my bed. "I'm sure he will," she says, quietly.

"I almost feel bad making him come all this way," I say. "I don't feel all that lowdown. Maybe the doctor's wrong. Maybe I'm not really dying."

Rita Mae raises her eyes to mine. "I'm afraid you are, LaNelle," she said.

Silence fills the room.

"How do you know?" I ask, finally.

Her eyes don't leave mine. "Because I can see an angel of death," she says. "He's standing over there, by the door."

"The Angel of Death?"

"*An* angel of death," she corrects me. "Yours."

"I get my own?" I slowly turn my head to look at the doorway, but it looks just the same as always— yellow-and-green flowered wallpaper, white painted trim. "I don't see nothing," I say.

"I do," she says.

I don't doubt her for a second. "Oh," I say. "What does he look like?"

She hesitates. "I don't often tell people. . . ." Her eyes go back to the doorway. "He's beautiful," she says softly. "He's the most beautiful angel I've ever seen. Even better than the one who came for Yolanda Vigness last year. That was a little scrawny angel next to this one." She takes a deep, shaky breath. "You're a good person and all, LaNelle, but what on earth did you do to deserve him?" She smiles to take away the sting from her words, but I can tell she means every one of them.

I snort. "I didn't ask you to tell me what you thought of him," I say, sharply. "Or of me. I asked you to tell me what he looks like."

She raises her eyebrows at me, but obeys. "He has dark eyes and black, curly hair, like . . ." she hesitates, looks around, "like Clark Gable, and his muscles are bigger than Errol Flynn's. And his wings—I wish I could see his wings more clearly."

She pauses and then says, "Oh." At first I think she sounds afraid, but she laughs a second later.

"What's so funny?"

"He spread his wings for me." She smiles. "Thank you."

I realize she's talking to the angel of death.

Then she nods as if he's said, "You're welcome," and looks back at me. "His wings spread all over the ceiling, like a tent. Like the tent in Rudolph Valentino's *The Sheikh of Araby*. Remember that film? I must have been fourteen when it came out. I think Rudolph Valentino was the most handsome man. I don't care what they say about his love life. Though, honestly, you're much more handsome," she says, talking to the angel again.

It makes me angry that she can see him and I can't. "What color are his wings?" I ask.

"Red and yellow and orange. The feathers are like little puffs of flame." She raises one hand, as if she's going to reach up and touch them.

I look up at the empty ceiling. "Well, you just tell that angel of death that I need to hold on and stay here 'til my Jimmy gets home."

Rita drops her hand and stares at me. "I can't do that, LaNelle. It's not my place to interfere with the work of the Lord."

I roll my eyes. "Come on, Rita Mae, I'm dying here." I sound very self-confident, but I'm not. I know I have no right to ask her for any more favors.

Rita Mae hesitates, then nods. She walks over to the doorway and beckons as if she wants something to follow her. Then she leaves the room.

I try to sense whether the room seems emptier, but I don't even feel a gust of wind. So I just sit and listen to my breathing, enjoying it while I can. I sip the tea Rita Mae has left for me. It tastes like licorice, but it's bitter and salty too. The liquid is a golden brown in the sunlight, and I can see flecks of something at the bottom that could be dirt. The tea smells familiar, somehow, but before I can puzzle it out, I start to get sleepy.

My eyes are closing when Rita Mae comes back in. She nods once, and I close my eyes.

•••

That night I dream voices. One of them is Rita Mae's, and the other is like a choirboy's, high and pure. It reminds me of going to church with Buzz when I was younger, before the preacher had a heart attack and started preaching hell and damnation. I see a light by the window, all shimmery, like sunlight on water. I hear Rita Mae laugh.

•••

The next day, I have so many visitors I can barely keep count of who comes in. Plainview seems like a small town until you get everybody tramping through one little room. I worry about the carpets downstairs and hope people have wiped their feet. I want to leave Jimmy a nice house.

Rita Mae feeds me cup after cup of her tea, though I pretend I don't need it. I don't know what she puts in it, but it makes me downright cheerful. I barely notice the pain by the afternoon.

The visitors come in one by one, bringing little photographs and presents. I don't know what they expect me to do with their gifts—put them in my coffin? But it's a nice gesture just the same. Maybe Jimmy will want them.

Then Bitsy Cadwallader arrives. She has a picture that her husband, Roy, took of me and Buzz right before Jimmy was born, standing next to the pumps of Buzz's gas station. In the picture, the gas station is so new that the paint on the pumps is shiny. I'm wearing a maternity dress, and I realize once again that Rita Mae was never as pretty as I was. But it's Buzz who takes my breath away. His hair, cut army style from his days in World War I, is still all golden—I can tell, even in the black-and-white picture. He's not movie star handsome or anything, but he's himself, and that was always enough for me. Jimmy got his blond hair, but that's all they ever had in common.

Rita Mae looks at the photo, too, and I feel embarrassed because Bitsy should know better than to talk about Buzz in front of Rita Mae. When Ma and me first moved to Plainview, Rita Mae and Buzz had been engaged to be engaged. But the minute Buzz laid eyes on me, he broke it off with Rita Mae. She never seemed to hold it against me. She was always polite to me, polite and even friendly. I told myself she obviously hadn't cared too much. When I asked Buzz, he just shrugged and said there really hadn't been much serious between them. I was afraid to ask more, in case he changed his mind and went back to her. I figured Rita Mae would up and marry someone else real soon, but when she inherited money, she began visiting the sick and the dying instead. As my mother said, "A woman has to do something to fill the time." I felt guilty about it sometimes, but what could I have done? Buzz chose me.

Maybe Bitsy realizes what she's done, because she shoves a shoebox at me to cover the photograph of Buzz.

I open the box. It's full of little model cars.

Bitsy laughs, glancing guiltily at Rita Mae. "One day, when my Alton was in the station, he saw them on a shelf and Buzz just up and gave them to him. It was right after your Jimmy left, about a year before Buzz died."

"I always wondered what happened to them," I say. I'd always laughed at Buzz for collecting them, at his age. He'd said it was his substitute for not being able to afford more than one of the real thing. He'd also spend

132   SUSAN FRY

a half hour on every real car that came through that gas
station. I figured cars reminded him of his time in the
army, fixing the tanks that helped us win World War I.
He loved those long, shiny cars. He polished them, he
waxed them. He was killed by one, driven by a drunk
who was a regular customer. The polished front grille
Buzz had worked on so long caught him in the head and
dragged him along the ground until he died.

I thank Bitsy, and after she leaves I put the shoebox
and the photograph under the bed, where Rita Mae can't
see them. I feel sad and a little angry. Buzz should have
given the cars to Jimmy, not to Bitsy's son. But he kind of
gave up on Jimmy when the army wouldn't take him.

"It's weak ankles," I'd said. "You can't blame the boy
for that."

"It's weak character," Buzz had said, not just to
me, but also to Jimmy. I think that's why Jimmy left. He
didn't even come back for Buzz's funeral. It'd made me
furious, but I hadn't known which side to stand on, so
I'd just kept quiet. Maybe I shouldn't have. From where
I'm lying now, that quiet seems like a failure.

When the last of the visitors leave, I beat down my
pride and ask Rita Mae for more tea. The liquid she
brings me is as thick as soup and so dark I can't see the
flecks anymore. I figure I'll be eating it by tomorrow,
spooning the sludge out. I don't want to know what the
pain would be like without the tea.

I notice that Rita Mae isn't facing me directly. She's
sitting as if there's a third person in the room, someone
she's trying to include in the conversation.

"Has that angel been here the whole day?" I ask.

She nods. "He sure does have a fine sense of humor.
You should have heard what he said about Elsie
Patnott." She pauses, her head cocked to one side as if
she's listening to something. For the first time, I realize

that her dark eyes, even with the faint wrinkles surrounding them, are beautiful.

Then she laughs. It's a light, flirty laugh. She must've laughed like this as a girl, when she and Buzz were courting. I don't like to think about that.

"They are, too," she says. She pauses again, then actually giggles. "Thank you."

"What the hell are you doing, Rita Mae?" I say.

She jumps and shoots me a guilty look. "I'm sorry," she says. "I'm just teasing."

"You're teasing the angel of death?" I say. I remember what she said about the angel having muscles like Errol Flynn. "Rita Mae, exactly what is this angel wearing?"

She blushes, and I find myself laughing.

"It's kind of nice to know he can be teased," I say. "It makes me a whole lot less afraid."

I regret those words as soon as they're out. I don't want Rita Mae to know how scared I am.

"Afraid?" Rita Mae says. She looks surprised. "If you saw him, you'd realize you ain't got nothing to be afraid of. You'd realize that where he's going to take you is so much better than . . . ." She looks around the room.

I follow her eyes. Better than life on earth, she means, of course. And I have to agree. Now that Buzz is gone, the only thing I have holding me down is Jimmy, the hope that someday he'll settle down somewhere close and have my grandchildren. Other than that, what is there, really, to live for? Fried chicken and paradise salad? A sunny day?

The phone rings. It's Jimmy. I smile at Rita as if to say, "I told you so." I cradle the phone in both hands and turn slightly away from her—and the angel—for some privacy.

But Jimmy and I only talk for a few minutes.

When I hang up, I have a hard time meeting Rita
Mae's eyes. "He's having some trouble getting here," I
say. "His car broke down." I hesitate. "Rita Mae, there's
a hundred dollars in my jewelry box. Would you go to
the bank and wire it to him? Here's the place where he's
at. He needs some money to get on a bus."

Rita Mae nods, her eyes cast down and careful. She
gets the money and leaves the room. I stare into my mug
of tea, not willing to look up and face the angel, even if I
couldn't actually see him.

•••

That night, I hear the voices again. I get out of bed
before I realize what I'm doing, and even though every
step hurts, I peer down over the staircase railing and into
my living room. Rita Mae is sitting alone on my old flowered couch, right where I used to sit in the evenings when
Buzz and I listened to the radio. She looks rumpled,
downright disheveled, as if she's been crying—or
something—all night. Her collar is pulled to one side,
and her hair is a mess of curls. Her lipstick is smeared.

It's only the second time I've ever seen Rita Mae
without a perfectly ironed, perfectly matched outfit.

The first time was a couple of weeks after Buzz's
funeral. One night, when the house got too silent, I went
out to visit Buzz's grave. I'd done it before—just to sit
awhile and talk to him when there was no one around to
listen in. Sometimes when I went, I found our dog there
too, as if it missed Buzz and could still smell him in
the grave.

There was a full moon, so I didn't need my flashlight
until I got up next to Buzz's gravestone and saw a flash

of white on the ground. I figured it was the dog, so I
fumbled for my flashlight and switched it on. But it was
Rita Mae who stood blinking in the light, clutching a
bundle of dirty roots in her hands. Her hair was as
tangled as the roots, and she was wearing an old house-
dress streaked with mud.

"What the hell are you doing?" I asked.

She hesitated, looking at the roots in her hands. They
smelled strong and sharp, like licorice. "They're medi-
cinal," she said, as if that explained everything.

"You're picking medicine from Buzz's grave?" I
shuddered, wondering just how deep those roots had
gone in the dirt.

"Of course not," she snapped. "What do you think I
am? They grow over there, by the fence."

"Then what are you doing way over here?"

She looked at the roots again, not saying anything.
Then she looked up at me.

When her eyes met mine, I felt like she'd taken off
her clothes and stood there, naked, in front of me. I
knew why she'd never married. I knew why she was
visiting Buzz's grave. Looking at her face was like
looking in a mirror, close up.

Too close. I backed away. "I won't tell anyone about
this," I said, quickly and loudly. "But don't come back
here again. You've got no right."

Her gaze dropped back down to the roots. I turned
and ran back to my empty house.

Now, in my living room, Rita Mae gives a deep sigh
and leans over to one side, the way I used to lean on
Buzz. But there's no one there. No one, at least, that I
can see.

It suddenly seems to me we were each other's last
link to Buzz, and that gives us an intimacy, like the kind

between two people from the same platoon who got through the same battle together. I want to call down and ask her how she's managed to live without Buzz for all these years, but I don't.

When I'm gone, she'll be alone for sure.

• • •

The next morning the pain is so bad I can barely sit up. Rita Mae brings me her tea, and the licorice smell of it hits me like a slap. Now I remember where I've smelled it before. It's graveyard tea.

I make a face, trying not to show I remember that night beside Buzz's grave. I try not to show how much I need the tea. "Don't you have anything that tastes better?"

"Not that works," she replies. She looks tired. Her eyes have shadows underneath them, and she moves slowly.

I remember the dirty clump of roots and decide that the pain is so strong I don't care where the tea is from. I sip it. "Did you talk to the angel of death last night?"

Rita Mae looks embarrassed, but nods.

"Did he tell you . . . did he tell you about where he's going to take me?"

She smiles. "He didn't," she says. "He ain't allowed to talk about that."

"Then what *did* you talk about?" I ask.

"Drink your tea," she says.

I frown.

That's when the phone rings. I know what the problem is as soon as Jimmy starts talking but I hear him out. "Sure," I say. "Don't worry about it, Jimmy. I love you too."

When I hang up, I expect Rita Mae to be staring at me, but she's not. She's looking at the door, watching that damn angel.

"Rita Mae?"

She jumps and swivels back toward me, as if I've caught her doing something she's not supposed to. She glances at the phone, and I see she knows what I'm about to ask.

I swallow. "There's another hundred dollars in the hatbox at the back of my closet. Would you . . . ." I pause. I can't stand the look of sympathy on her face. It's only one shade away from pity. "The hell with it," I say. "You know as well as I do that he ain't going to get here anytime soon. I don't see much point in hanging on anymore."

She puts her arms around me, and I cry for a while. It feels so good to be held—her body is soft, warm and comforting. I suddenly understand how awful it was for Rita Mae to go through her whole life without being held. And I know what I have to say.

"I'm sorry," I say, my words muffled by the starched cotton of her dress. "It wasn't my fault Buzz left you for me, but in some ways I was guilty just the same. Guilty just for being there, guilty for being happy when you weren't. That's what you wanted me to say, wasn't it, that time in the graveyard? Just to acknowledge that you'd been wronged, and that you had a claim on him, too." I cling to her, not caring that my nose is running on her nice, neat clothes. "I refused to let you have even the littlest piece of him, even to sit by his grave. And here you've been feeding me tea from that same graveyard, out of nothing but kindness."

Rita Mae's arms tighten around me, and she rocks me back and forth until I can barely breathe. I wish that

I could die like this, now, being held by her. She smells like the licorice of the graveyard tea.

But then Rita Mae unfolds her arms and pushes me away. "LaNelle," she says.

"I'm all right," I say, trying to pretend I don't mind she's let me go. I dry my cheeks with the back of my hand. "You've made the angel of death right interesting. You know, I'm actually eager to get it all over with. So I can see him too."

That's when I look up. Rita Mae's got a little half-smile on her face, one that looks like it might turn upside down into a frown.

"LaNelle," she says, "LaNelle, please . . ."

"Please what?"

"I just want you to know I didn't mean to do it."

"Didn't mean to do what?" I said.

"The angel of death and I," she said. "We're . . . ." She swallows, glances toward the door. "He wants to take me instead of you."

I stare at her. She smiles again, this time for real. Despite her tiredness, Rita Mae looks happy. I've never seen her look happy before.

"You want to steal my death?" I ask.

Rita Mae looks away.

"So what about me? What would happen to me?"

"You'll get my death," she says. "You'll get my death and the angel that was meant for me."

"Your death? Your angel? Rita Mae, you got me looking forward to dying." I think about a life stretching in front of me like an empty cotton field. No Buzz, no Rita Mae, all that damn food downstairs, rotting in the heat. Jimmy.

"Is this about Buzz?"

Rita Mae hesitates, then shakes her head. "I thought it might be, but it ain't. That's not to say the idea of it don't give me some little pleasure, though."

"Damn you, Rita Mae," I say.

Rita Mae actually laughs, her voice catching at the end in what could have been a sob. "That's one wish you won't get."

"I haven't gotten any of my wishes," I say.

"You got Buzz." Her words flow out like the sound of pouring tea. "I've never loved anyone else since Buzz, not 'til now. I got no one worth staying for."

"Me, neither," I say. I want to add, "Especially if you're gone," but I don't. Instead, I reach up and stroke her cheek. If she moves, my caress would just as easily turn into a slap.

She pulls back as if my touch disgusts her. I yank my hand back into my lap.

"Well, you can't have it," I say. "You can't have my death. And you certainly can't have my angel."

Rita Mae smiles that funny half smile again. "Can't I?" She closes her eyes.

I see a bright flash in the corner of the room. I turn, hoping to catch just a glimpse of the angel, but there's nothing there.

"No!" I shout at the empty corner. "Come back! You're mine."

I turn and grab Rita Mae by the shoulders and shake her, despite the bolts of pain that jab up and down my arms. "You tell him to come back!"

But Rita Mae throws her head back and laughs. Then her laugh turns into a gasp. Her mouth tightens. She falls gently down onto the bed next to me, into the slight hollow where Buzz slept for so many years. Her eyes are open and her mouth still smiles. As I lean over her, I feel the familiar sharp pain in my back. I realize that Rita Mae may have taken my death, but she's left me my pain.

"Damn you," I say, again.

Her skin already feels cold.

CARRYING
THE GOD

Written by
Lee Battersby

Illustrated by
Irena Yankova Dimitrova

About the Author

Lee Battersby is a thirty-one-year-old former stand-up comedian, cinema usher and—according to him—other sundry useless occupations, and currently works for the Australian government.

After a break of many years following an abortive attempt at a writing career while at university, he has been writing seriously again for just over two years. His third place in the second quarter of the writers' competition and subsequent publication of his first professional sale has helped fulfill a life-long dream to become a published writer. This dream he soon compounded with another half-dozen sales to various magazines after finding out he had won.

To top this, December heralded the arrival of his first child, a daughter named Erin, who Lee describes as "a perfect bundle of wonder." Tragically, Sharon, his wife of four and a half years, died of complications four days after Erin's birth. She was only thirty-two-years old. She had helped Lee edit the following story before he submitted it to us, and he lovingly dedicates its publication to her memory.

About the Illustrator

Irena Yankova Dimitrova is Bulgarian, twenty-seven years old and married to one of last year's Illustrator Contest winners, Yanko Yankov.

Irena attended the university and graduated in 1998 from the Department Pedagogy of Art. She not only went on to teach in the middle school of her town, Gorna Oriahovitza, but held two personal exhibitions of her oil paintings and some video presentations named "Metamorphoses of Painting Matter, Light, Space, and Color."

No market for art exists for Irena where she lives. She says, "I started to draw illustrations because of your Illustrators' Contest. I have never published an illustration because I haven't ever created one."

At this writing, Irena is ardently working on illustrations to present in her portfolio. She and her husband, Yanko, argue over who will be first to use their newly purchased computer.

Bugh was excited, and also a little nervous. He had passed his age only a few days ago, and already it was his turn to carry the God. Excited, because there was no greater honor in all the family, and there was always the chance that he would be the chosen carrier when the God allowed the rains to begin. Nervous, because it was still fresh in everybody's memory what had happened the day Geff had stumbled and dropped the God, and one of its fingers had broken off. The family had stopped, in fright and shock, their breaths held in anticipation of a mighty vengeance. Then Da had noticed how the finger lay in the sand, pointing its blame at Grama. Even though it had been Geff who had dropped the idol, the message was clear: the God blamed Grama for the catastrophe. Their course was clear, and they took it quickly and savagely. The God must have been satisfied: nothing further happened to them.

Tentatively, Bugh moved to the centre of the family group and accepted the God and its harness from his older brother, Ler. He was surprised to find the God was much lighter than he had expected. Like a thing of sticks and bark, it lay in its crude cloth harness, staring up at him with empty eyes. Suppressing a shudder lest the God should see him and be displeased, Bugh hefted his burden. Squinting into the wind that brought with it the perennial spray of sand, he waited for the God to speak to him, to show him which way the family should shuffle and plod in the search for food or salvation. Nothing happened. No divine voice came whispering through the layers of thin rags that covered his head; no strange, ephemeral tug was felt in his bones to point him in the right way. The family started to stir, restless at standing still in the searing heat and whipping, stinging wind. Finally, Bugh decided that this must be some sort of test. The God must be watching, waiting to see if the lessons Bugh had learned by trotting alongside Da and Granda and Geff, and all the other carriers had been absorbed. Picking a direction that looked like any other, except for the fact that they had not been walking toward it, Bugh pointed.

"That way," he said. The group silently moved off in the appointed direction. Bugh held his breath. Nothing happened. He must have passed the God's first test, he decided. Breathing a sigh of relief, he moved slowly after the family.

●●●

"Right this way, please." Dr. Robards opened the door into yet another aseptic white room. The large attendant, whose name Robards had never been permitted to know, pushed forward the wheelchair containing the immobile statue that was Mister Douglas Black. A large, arcane-shaped machine dominated the room. Part capsule, part still, part who knows what, it crouched in the center of the room like a giant alien arachnid, its chrome perfection glinting in the overhead lights, while its various tubes pulsed with the thick liquids that ceaselessly ebbed and flowed through them.

"This is where Mr. Black will be staying." Robards could not keep the patina of satisfaction from glazing his words. "It's been a long time, and taken a lot of money . . ."

"Mr. Black is aware of how much time and money he has invested in this project." The large man spoke without inflection, his voice a flat blade that sliced along Robards' self-congratulation and killed it immediately. "What Mr. Black wishes to know is whether or not it will work. That is all you need to tell him."

"It . . . yes, it will work." Robards suppressed a shudder as he looked at the two men. Nobody knew how they had achieved the strange symbiosis that enabled the hulking, nameless man to know what his employer was thinking and to translate it so quickly into speech. What little Robards had learned was enough to persuade him to shut up, accept the paychecks, and not think of anything other than the task he had been employed to perform. "We have successfully used the apparatus upon a number of smaller animals, and have only this morning brought back a chimpanzee from an anhydro sleep of over six weeks."

"Mr. Black is not a chimpanzee."

"No, no, I know that, of course. But a chimpanzee is as close as we can get to a human being without actually using one. We share over ninety-eight percent of the same genetic structure, you see, so it really is almost the perfect test subject." When no response was forthcoming, Robards went on. "It seems like cryogenics to a lot of people, you know, but cryogenics has one small problem. It doesn't work." He laughed a small laugh. "Cryogenics involves freezing a subject, and of course, once you freeze a liquid, it expands. Cells are mostly liquid, you see, so you freeze one and *ppph*,"—he made a small exploding motion with one hand—"the cell

Illustrated by Irena Yankova Dimitrova

liquid expands, the cell ruptures, and what you're left with is little more than . . . meat." He risked a look at Mr. Black, but if his remark made any impact upon the billionaire, the cold visage reflected no awareness of it.

"Mr. Black is aware of the faults of cryogenic freezing. That was why Mr. Black commissioned you to build this . . . device." The large attendant almost kept the sneer from his voice. "What Mister Black wishes to know is whether your process has circumvented those problems and whether it will result in a successful regeneration after the process is complete."

"Yes." Robards brought his eyes up to meet the cold liquid of his employer's thousand-yard stare. "Yes, it will."

• • •

That evening the family feasted, and Bugh sat in the center of the group, drawing in their awe like warmth. Late that afternoon, a slither had crossed the family's path, almost as if it had planned to meet them. They had trapped and killed it with ease. Never before had the family been led to such a bounty on the first day of a new carrier. Tonight he was the first to fill his belly, the one who sat closest to the tiny fire made from sticks the others had gathered while he rested. Bugh luxuriated in the warmth, not wishing to stir even though he could feel his skin scalding, for fear that would signal an end to the wonderful evening. Without a thing having been said, he could feel that a subtle shift in power had occurred within the family. The God had ordained him. From now on, as long as he continued to steer them in the right direction, the God would ensure that he would be the greatest beneficiary of its gifts.

•••

Robards' hand held steady as the scalpel descended and shaved the merest flake of skin from the inside of Douglas Black's elbow. Three times the blade dipped. Three times a wafer thin slice of the billionaire was placed gently onto a slide and consigned to a small, airtight box.

"We'll need to run some tests," he explained as he worked, "to determine the correct set of parameters for anhydrogenic procedure. After all," he allowed himself a slight loosening at one corner of the mouth, "we certainly wouldn't want anything to go wrong, would we?"

"You assured Mr. Black that the process was perfected. How can something go wrong, or are your assurances premature?" The large man's flat voice held just a hint of the danger his tensed bulk promised.

"Go wrong? This is a major medical procedure, not to mention quite revolutionary in its application. If the correct procedures aren't strictly followed, if everything isn't followed to the absolute letter, then you allow for the possibility of unknown variables entering the equation. And if that happens"—he shook the stiffness from his wrist—"your employer could find himself a very rich dead man." Annoyed with himself for allowing the argument to compromise his air of professional reserve, he carried the boxes over to a complicated array of tubes and measuring devices that sat on a nearby bench.

"That tube there," he pointed almost at random, "contains sodium azide. That one," another stab of a fleshy finger, "a trehalose-sucrose solution." Stab. "Light microscope." Stab. "Water loss." Stab. "Narrowing of skin annulation." Stab. "Hyalin loss." The doctor's voice grew more confident as he catalogued each item. "Each factor needs to be measured, quantified. Each component has a different optimum quotient for every individual subject. There are hundreds of variables, each of which needs to be perfect and each of which necessitates hours in front of the terminal." He pointed to a small computer, almost forgotten amongst the midst of the more exotic paraphernalia clustered around it. "Only once every factor is in perfect, and I mean perfect, alignment can Mr. Black be desiccated . . ."

"Can be what?"

"Sorry, anhydrobiotically engaged"—Robards let a small measure of sarcasm creep into his voice, secure in his intellectual superiority now the conversation was totally immersed within his area of expertise— "without fear of anything going wrong. He can be revived whenever a cure for his condition is found, be treated and go on to enjoy the rest of a long and fruitful life. But if any one of these many factors is off-beam, then *ppph*"—again the small exploding motion of the hand—"well, we've thrown away enough mistakes to know that he won't be coming back."

•••

Bugh laid down his burden and looked closely into its wizened face for a sign. The family had not eaten for three days, and he knew that unless he had success soon it would be time to pass the God on to another and wait for his next turn. Already Geff was moving forward, his head tilted in enquiry. Hurriedly, Bugh inspected the God, looking for something, anything, that could prompt him to confidently announce the next path to follow. Only blankness greeted him. Geff now stood at his shoulder. Bugh looked up at his brother, then back at the crumbling relic. Finally, he reached a decision. Ignoring his brother's outstretched hand he stood up, hefting the God onto his back.

"This way," he pointed randomly into the distance in front of them, "this way."

•••

Robards smiled confidently as he faced his employer. He'd spent hours collecting his thoughts, ordering them as he would a catalogue of exhibits to be rolled out to impress important visitors or adoring students. This was the pinnacle of his career. For too many years he had toiled in obscurity, without formal recognition, without reward. His failures had been too numerous to mention, his setbacks legion. The pioneers whose footsteps he had initially followed had given up, moved on or broken their wills against the walls of chemistry that he, and only he, had finally been able to breach. This was the greatest moment his life would ever contain. He wanted it to be perfect. Behind him, the dimly lit sarcophagus glinted dully, its opaque surface only helping to increase his sense of drama. Keeping his voice as calm as possible, he addressed the wheelchair-bound figure.

"I thought you might like to see this."

At his gesture, the lights in the room rose sharply. There, within the glass capsule, its arms raised as if in prayer or supplication, lay the shriveled, shrunken figure of what had once been a man.

"His name isn't important. Until a few weeks ago, he was nothing more than a poor homeless bum who was willing to be part of a medical test for fifty dollars a day and a clean bed. But"—Robards paused to brush at an imaginary crease in his shirt—"he's the first human to be successfully anhydrobated and brought back."

"The first?"

"That's correct." Robards' voice was abrupt. Black's demeanor didn't change, but the look of shock and incredulity on the face of his manservant brought a surge of pleasure to the doctor.

"Then . . . ."

"Yes, yes, yes, it can be done. We've leaped the final two percent between chimps and humans at last."

There was a long, long pause. To Robards it seemed as if the giant attendant was struggling to control a flow of complex emotions. He made careful to conceal his disgust at the sight. Finally, the servant spoke once more.

"Mr. Black wishes to know how you know this . . ." he gestured at the sarcophagus, "can be successfully reanimated."

"Because we've already done it. I did say we had brought him back." Robards walked to a nearby door, opened it and held it wide. "This is a medical procedure. We need to establish a margin for error before we can pronounce the experimental phase complete. The subject in that machine has been successfully anhydrobated and rehydrated eleven times with no recordable physical ill effects. In fact," he looked at his watch, "we're just about to start procedure number twelve. I though you might wish to observe."

Silently, the giant wheeled his master through the door.

•••

Two days later, with no end in sight to the sands that stretched before them, the family solemnly watched as Geff moved forward to take up the God from where

Bugh had laid him. After a moment spent running fingers across the God's dried and flaked skin, he pointed in a direction tangential to that which they'd been traveling.

"That way."

Bugh wandered alone at the back of the group. After a few minutes, Granda fell in beside him. Presently, he spoke.

"Five days, young one. You must have received a lot of signs."

Bugh said nothing, merely kicked at the sand, head bowed. Granda chuckled, a low hoarse cough that held neither warmth nor joy.

"I take it you understand our little secret now, eh?"

"But why, Granda? I don't . . . ." his voice held a note of pain.

"You are of age now. This is what it means, to share this secret with all the other men. The females and the children trust us."

"But . . . ."

"It has been this way for generations, before you or I were born. It is all we know."

"But why . . . why do we go on like this?" Bugh waved a despairing arm at the featureless horizon that surrounded them. "Why do we keep pretending?"

Granda looked at him for long moments, then began to move forward toward the front of the group. As he left Bugh he said, "Wait a few days. I shall take us somewhere and you shall see, and hear a story too."

At the next change, something unusual happened. After a whispered exchange with Da, it was Granda who took the God from Geff, not Ler, as should have happened. Ler knew better than to protest, but for hours he trooped sullenly behind the family, kicking sprays of sand into the air with petty viciousness. After Granda, it was Da who shouldered the God, leading them without pronouncement along exactly the same path that Granda had been following. This alone was unusual enough to cause the rest of the group to engage in excited conversation. A change of carrier always presaged a change of direction. For the next few days the family moved along in a buzz of expectation. All but Bugh, who kept his silence and studied Da and Granda intently as they walked.

• • •

"Incredible." The manservant spoke in a hushed whisper. Before him, on a hospital bed, lay a man of indeterminate age, his face screwed up in recognition of a bones-deep pain. "Can I . . . talk to him?"

"Go ahead." Robards stood back. "You'll find he's completely responsive. There's been no loss of function in any way."

The big man wheeled his master to the bed, until his masque-like face was no more than inches from the name-less test subject. In the silence of the room, the rasping of the bum's breath drew loud scratches down Robards' skin.

"You, there."

Slowly, the man turned his head. His eyes focussed carefully on Black, then past him at the looming frame of the manservant behind. Painfully, he licked his cracked lips.

"Yes?" His voice was little more than a dry croak. The giant also licked his lips. To Robards it looked as if he were anticipating a particularly good meal. Robards looked away.

"What's it like?"

The bedridden man looked up, his eyes still struggling to keep focus.

"Like?"

"The procedure. The drying, the . . . anhydro procedure."

"The pro . . . pain. There's so much pain. Like all my muscles cramping and burning. It never ends. I can feel my eyes dry up. Oh . . . ." He broke into tears. Robards coughed discreetly, attracting the ear of the massive manservant.

"Mr. Black will be given the benefit of painkillers for the procedure proper. To ensure no variations in the test results, we could not afford to apply them to this subject."

Douglas Black, not having been moved, could make no reaction. The look that passed through the eyes of his assistant, however, made Robards take an involuntary step backward. Once more the manservant turned and spoke to the wretched figure on the bed.

"What do you feel like now? Do you feel well? Are you still . . . capable?"

A weak cough wracked the man's body. "I'm so weak . . . I . . . I . . . need to sleep now." Almost immediately, he fell into a deep slumber. At this, Robards once again spoke up.

"The weakness is merely a result of the time taken to rehydrate the body. From this point, Mr. Black could expect another three weeks of physical therapy to bring the muscles back to full working order. Psychologically, a subject with the benefits of painkillers will suffer absolutely no ill effects from the process whatsoever. By the end of the physical therapy, a rehydrated subject will be in no worse condition than when he entered the tank.

In fact," he risked looking straight into his employer's eyes, "in Mr. Black's case, we would be expecting a complete recovery from whatever curative procedure prompted his dehydration and that he would be able to walk from the clinic under his own aegis."

If he had expected any reaction to this pronouncement, Robards was to be disappointed. Saying simply, "Mr. Black expects to be called when the procedure is ready to be performed," the giant brusquely pushed his employer past the doctor and out of the room, leaving Robards alone with his sleeping guinea pig.

•••

For three days the family traveled in the wake of Da's determined stride, always in a perfectly straight line. At night, they chewed upon the few strips of dried slither they had saved from their last meal and lay quiet, no one wanting to speak, each alone with their thoughts. An air of trepidation covered the group, a feeling that something momentous was about to occur. In such a circumstance, the normal range of muttered conversation fell by the wayside.

Then, on the fourth morning, they crested a large sand drift, and the object of their journey became apparent. There before them, rising from the eternal sands, lay the first interruption to a world that in Bugh's experience had consisted only of an endless sea of dirty yellow. They had reached the ruins.

•••

In the darkened room, the still form of Douglas Black lay on the bed. He lay without moving, the unknown disease that had caused his paralysis preventing him from turning his head to see who had opened his door and stealthily approached his bed. The figure of his manservant, motionless on his bed at the other side of the room, did not stir. A hot breath brushed the billionaire's ear.

"I have to tell you."

Black could not acknowledge the voice. It was impossible to tell whether he indeed even heard the words that poured unbidden from the hidden speaker, tumbling and rolling over each other in their bid to escape.

"You can feel it when it happens. They don't tell you that, but you can. You can feel yourself drying up. It's like they rip the flesh from your body and replace it with something made of old leaves and sand. And it hurts, it hurts so much . . . but you'll be doped up, won't you? He won't want to hurt you, not his little cash cow. He doesn't care about you, you know that? As soon as you're a shriveled little ball of wood, he'll be onto the talk shows and the speaking circuit, showing pictures of you like a sideshow freak. But I know who you are. I know why you want to do this. I'd do the same if I were you. But I know something he doesn't. I know something he can't measure, something I wouldn't tell him even if he'd thought to ask me. I'm just a lab rat to him, just a rabbit with shampoo in his eyes. So I've been saving it for you. Because who are you going to tell, eh? Since I first saw you and realized why he was doing this to me. I saved this little nugget, this little knowledge. I only want you to know. You may feel no pain when you change, but you won't be sleeping. *You're still aware!*"

There was a pause, as if the unseen voice expected a reaction. When none was forthcoming, it continued. "I don't know how he missed it. Maybe because he can't measure it when you can't move or something, but you stay aware the whole time. Oh, they know you feel what's happening to you while they suck your moisture out and fill you up like you're some sponge they're using to wipe the floor. I've seen that bastard smiling. Don't think he won't enjoy watching you shrivel and warp. But he doesn't know what happens while you're lying there like a dead man, all dried up and being measured with his scales and calipers. Your thoughts won't go away. You're going to lie there like a piece of driftwood, just trapped inside your mind with your thoughts going round and round and round while you wait for them to bring you back." A spray of spittle hits Black on the side of the face and runs down toward the pillow. "You think you hate being the freak you are now, Mister Billionaire? How do you think you'll like knowing what you are for a hundred years? Two hundred? A thousand? How long do you think your thought will echo then?"

Douglas Black lies helpless as the poor mad bum leans over and gently presses warm lips against his forehead, unable to respond to a kiss that may be curse, or benediction, or both.

• • •

That night, huddled round a fire made from the few sticks and scraps they had managed to gather, the males of the family listened, barely daring to breathe, as Da, his voice trance-like as he repeated the words taught to him by his father, told them of the Gods. Behind Bugh, the temple crouched, scarred and pitted from countless eons exposed to the winds, yet still bearing their likeness in

its form. Bugh crouched against its warm belly, understanding few of the words but much of the tone, as Da
spoke.

"And there came a time when the Gods outreached
their power, and spread across the world like grains of
sand, some high in power and some low, some with
bellies full and sagging, and others with no bellies at all,
with Families on the ground and in the sky, even on
Face-In-The-Night. And there came a God with rags on
his head, who rose in the East and laid claim over the
power that dwells deep within the Earth. And the Gods
did split in two, half before and half beside, and mightily
did they wage war upon each other, fang and claw, until
the world was covered in their blood, and great bites
were taken from Face-In-The-Night. And the Rag-
headed God drew on his last great source of power and
brought down great balls of fire from the sky so that the
world glowed like the face of Fire-Of-Day, and all who
walked or flew or slithered, all bar a few who became
our ancestors, were swept away like ashes in the
morning, and the world lay cold and dark and silent,
and the Gods were no more."

Then Granda, who had taught the tale to Da, but
could never resist a chance to show off for the young-
sters, spoke up.

"But if everything was dead, where did we come
from?" He rolled his eyes, so that Bugh had to stifle a
giggle as Da glared at him and continued.

"To all things comes a time, and life does not ever
truly end. Only lives are short. In time, the world
yawned and woke, and felt the heat from Fire-Of-Day,
and from holes and crevices and cracks we came. We,
who had been beneath the Gods as the merest grain of
sand is under the mountain, we came forth to find the
world empty, and ours alone. And we came to this

place," he gestured to the crumbling walls around him, "and we cleared away the ashes and dust that covered it, and we explored the empty corridors and rooms. And in a room, far below the ground, we found a temple. A temple of the Gods, strange and beautiful and terrible, as much like us as a God, and yet as beyond our knowing as a God. And as time passed, and our people grew and changed to fit this world, so we gained the strength to draw this temple from below and bring it out to bask in the light of the world once more, and we came back and back to this temple that was shaped like us and yet not like us, until one of our number thought to touch it in a way it had not been touched before, and it opened like a crackseed and inside . . ."

"The God!" Ler's whisper echoed, breaking the thrall.

"Yes, the God." Da pointed to where the battered relic leaned against a wall. "And since that day we have carried it with us. Through times when we numbered as many as the footsteps we have walked, through the great hunger and the time of dying. And now, when we lie scattered and few, and only this small family still seeks guidance and does not cavort like animals, we have carried the God as a symbol, a beacon to point the way to our survival."

"But . . ." Bugh began, then fell silent, as if he had unconsciously uttered some great blasphemy.

"It doesn't mean anything? It doesn't really show us the way?" Granda smiled. "We just pick a direction and tell the others it was the God?" He touched Bugh's shoulder and gestured to where the world waited just outside the shelter of the walls. "In all your life boy, what have you seen besides this place?"

"Nothing. Just sand and slithers and sometimes a plant or a mad stranger or bones."

"Exactly. The world is large and empty, is it not?"

"Yes, but . . ."

"So would you walk around in circles your whole life looking for who knows what just because I or your Da told you that you must?"

"No. That would be . . ."

"Mad? Pointless? Exactly. Yet there is a point, youngster. The whole world is sand and slithers. We must find some point to surviving, something to stop us from just lying down and dying. The care of the women and the children, the provision of a reason for them to keep going until we find that which will give our struggle a purpose, that is our responsibility. There may be an answer, hmm? But we have to give them a reason to find it. And Gods make easier masters than fathers."

There was little more talk that night. One by one the young males fell asleep, Bugh amongst them, curled up against the body of the temple that had spawned his God. The next morning, as Fire-Of-Day arthritically clawed his swollen red bulk into the sky to hang limpidly, spreading his tepid warmth through the dust layer and across the world, Bugh found himself at the outer rim of the ruins, crouched upon the crest of a dune with the God and Granda. Behind him, he could hear the women and children making their way up the dune to join the men. Granda smiled down at him.

"Ready?"

Bugh stared into the blank eye sockets of the God, searching for something to connect him to this ancient race of alien beings. The ancient husk stared back, revealing nothing of the awareness that has haunted the slowly decaying corridors of its body for countless millennia, silently screaming as its cries for release echo back from a world that has lost the knowledge needed to answer. Bugh shrugged and, using all four arms, hefted his burden. Shading his eye clusters, he looked off into the distance.

That way.

The family, bearing no resemblance to their arachnid ancestors, walk toward the morning horizon.

• • •

Doctor Robards picked his way through the gloom of the barely lit corridors toward the sanctuary of the anhydro chamber, cursing the memory of that cripple, Black, with every step. Famous, he should have been famous. The Einstein or Pasteur of his day, feted and heralded for what he'd achieved. Instead, he'd been forced to scrabble about in the semidarkness, conserving power from the generators and money from the dwindling investments he'd been smart enough to accumulate. Ever since the morning that frozen freak had witnessed the rehydration. Robards had come in the next morning to find his staff gone, the building closed down. And when he'd finally met with his employer, the giant manservant who pushed him around had simply announced that the project had been closed down due to "unforeseen developments." None of Robards' protests had been acknowledged, none of his calls answered. Twenty years of loyal service turned to dust in a moment.

Well, it hadn't stopped him. It had taken months to organize, everything he'd owned, all the favors he'd farmed out to friends and colleagues over the years, but he'd got six months' access to this place. For fully half a year, he'd shuffled the corridors alone like a half-forgotten ghost, muttering to himself as he'd placed wires in solution, made readings on instruments powered by emergency reserves of power from backup generators.

Now he stood in the center of the anhydro chamber, a man alone with his beautiful creation. He made one last tour of the capsule, checking seals and instruments that had already undergone innumerable checks. All the tests had been performed. All the preparations had been completed. This was what he should have been working toward all along. At last, satisfied that everything was perfect, he made his way to the workbench and undressed, neatly folding each garment into a pile. He pulled away sticking plasters from the abrasions that bespoke his many hours of tests and dropped them into a wastebasket.

As he climbed into the capsule, he reflected on the work that had been necessary to carry him to this point. All the instructions had been written out by hand, for who knew whether computers would even be used so far in the future? The contract with a venerated and royally appointed law firm to ensure the continuation of the building lease, the contingency plans, the investments made to keep enough money in the coffers (wouldn't want to wake up a poor man, after all)—all had presented special problems. After all, who in the world was used to dealing with someone who talked in decades, never mind the centuries, he had wanted to discuss?

With a smile, he lay back and pressed the button to begin the autostart sequence. In two hundred and fifty years, he would wake a rich man and go out into the brave new future to announce himself to the world, to reap the acclaim and fame his monumental achievement deserved. As the first needle bit into his skin and the painkillers began to course through him, he thought,

The first thing I shall do is find the grave of Douglas Black and spit upon it.

The painkillers began to grip him. Robards closed his eyes and smiled. He anticipated a long, restful sleep, content in the knowledge that he had thought of everything. Nothing had been overlooked.

"A man from the past," he smiled to himself. "I'll be like some ancient God."

A FEW TIPS ON THE CRAFT OF ILLUSTRATION

Written by
H. R. Van Dongen

About the Author

H. R. Van Dongen was one of the premier science fiction illustrators from the early 1950s through the 1970s; he did more art for Astounding Science Fiction *than any other artist. His superb artistry led to at least one Hugo Award nomination for best professional artist. In addition to his work in science fiction, he also illustrated numerous magazines and book covers over the years.*

Mr. Van Dongen has been a judge for the Illustrators of the Future Contest since its inception and he demonstrates his own artistic precision and conscientiousness while performing his judging duties. He once wrote of the contest, "I only wish that there had been an Illustrators of the Future competition 45 years ago. What a blessing it would have been to a young artist with a little bit of talent, a Dutch name, and a heart full of desire."

Recognized for his ability to read a story, extract the precise meaning of the author's intent, and convey it through pictures, Mr. Van Dongen shares his insight and wisdom in the following essay. We're grateful he has taken this opportunity to do so.

hat in the dickens can I possibly say about creating a good illustration? "Draw well!"

Heck, every illustrator knows the importance of good craftsmanship. "Design and compose well!"

But again, doesn't every illustrator realize the importance of good composition?

On Design ...

At this point, however, I must sadly admit that, no ... every illustrator does not fully understand or appreciate the vital need for good basic design and composition. This conclusion is based pretty much upon experience gained from judging the works of new artists. Not infrequently I find average or fair illustrations that, with a little effort and a little more work spent on designing and composing, could very well have produced some darned good or even great illustrations. This saddens me, because I know these young people worked hard and long on the finished products. Sometimes, too hard, to the point of overworking and noodling the finish.

On Developing Ideas ...

Now, even before the design and composition, you should start with a good idea. This you gain from reading and studying the manuscript. Please, my dear

friends, read that manuscript, and I mean read it, and
then read it again, until you ferret out the best and most
dynamic picture idea that story has to offer. Quite often,
but not always, that idea will come from that part of the
manuscript describing the most action. But portraits of
aliens and alien landscapes or cityscapes offer a few of
the other possibilities.

A good story always provides many excellent picture
possibilities. If the story is not all that good, finding that
idea may be a bit tougher to come by. In a few cases,
fortunately very few, finding an idea may be nearly
impossible. At these times, you will have to study and
work hard to develop that idea and make a good picture.

Whatever you are presented with—good, bad or
indifferent—it is your responsibility to produce the most
dynamic illustration possible. The late, great comedian
George Gobel once quipped that you cannot make a silk
purse from a sow's ear unless, of course, you start with
a silk sow's ear. For the illustrator, his "silk sow's ear" is
a good basic design based on a good idea.

To sum up what I have tried to put forth—before you
ever lay a pen or brush to that final finished picture,
make sure you have made every effort to develop the
best picture idea you possibly can. Then, devote the
necessary time and effort to create the most dramatic
design and composition you are capable of. If you will
do these things well, I can assure you that making that
"silk purse" will not only come a bit easier, but it will be
a much lovelier "silk purse" for the effort.

On Noodling the Design . . .

Now, I should like to delve into something I only
touched upon earlier. I mentioned overworking or the
noodling of a picture. This has been one pitfall that I

come across far too often when judging. I have seen what must have taken endless hours of very hard work spent on intricate, detailed pen work literally scattered across the whole darned picture area. Now, when properly designed, this is a perfectly legitimate handling and technique.

What many of the artists failed to do, however, was focus all of this marvelous penmanship and work to a recognizable center of interest. The tragic result is that an illustration so done will often fail to engage or hold the interest of the reader. At times, I have had to study such a picture long and hard to determine its meaning, and this should never be necessary.

On the Use of Black . . .

There is one more grievance I have come upon at times. It is the indiscriminate use of black. This abuse seems to manifest itself most often in pen-and-ink drawings. The color black can be a most powerful tool when properly designed and used wisely and purposely within the composition. Frequently, however, I find black ink used as a quick and easy way to cover space that should have been carefully rendered with some other value. When I come across an entry where black ink has been used merely to cover space on an illustration board, it does not receive very high marks from me.

On the Duties of an Illustrator . . .

About here, it might be wise if I attempted to define the principal responsibilities of an illustrator. They are really not all that difficult to define. They are, however, sometimes very difficult to do. Your main job as a book, magazine cover or story illustrator is to engage and grab the interest of the reader. To make him want to read that book or story—that's it!

If your picture is a marvel in most all other respects yet fails to capture the reader, it fails as an illustration.

Perhaps I could pass along just a few suggestions that might help you develop illustrations that will grab an audience. In the broad interpretation, presence and believability are most important. For example, imagine that you are confronted with rendering an alien landscape—a common occurrence in science fiction. Give that landscape all of the depth and dimension you can. Develop a composition designed to lead the eye into the picture. Good use and careful selection of values are also vital to this end. Your goal is to create a picture that will make the reader feel he can walk into the illustration and, hopefully, into the story.

Another frequent problem you will find in illustrating a science fiction story is that of creating alien beings. The challenge here is to make these figures believable, no matter how far-out the author's description is—and they do get far-out!

If the alien happens to possess humanlike intellect, it will create an even greater challenge. In this case, eyes—well-drawn, expressive and compelling—may help considerably to solve the problem of creating an alien figure that will appear intelligent and, most of all, believable. The little alien ET in the movie was very believable, and the handling of the eyes contributed greatly to that believability. Another example of good eyes comes from the Australian koala. By looking into the eyes of those little fellows, one can almost believe they have the solution to every problem in the world. They don't, of course, but they look that way, and that's the quality I like to see in the rendering of sci-fi aliens. Now, these suggestions are but a couple of my ways to solve these problems. Others may have better solutions, but whatever way you choose—make it believable.

Doing an illustration is a bit like skeet shooting. I do not know how many reading this article have ever participated in this fine sport. When skeet shooting, the shooter does not aim at his target, but rather leads and aims at where his target will be when his shot arrives at that spot. So it is with an illustration. What you end up with on your drawing board is not your target. What appears in the intended book or magazine is. It is also a fact that the reproduction process, the preparation and printing of your work, will rob it of some of the contrast and sparkle you put into it. So please keep this in mind.

Think ahead to it (lead it, if you will) and keep your work as clean and simple as possible.

Finally—consistency. When I receive a judging assignment from Illustrators of the Future, I am given three examples of each artist's work. If one of the works is an absolute masterpiece and the other two, at their best, are not too good, then my marking will be based primarily on the two not-too-goods. Creating a masterpiece each time out would be pretty tough. It would be nice, but awfully tough. While it may not always be possible to turn out a masterpiece each time, it is necessary, even mandatory, to turn out a good professional job every time. Each and every illustration deserves this consideration, and your very best effort.

In Conclusion . . .

Before ending this article, I would like to make a few explanations that might help lend a bit of credibility to my criticisms. Over the past forty years of illustrating, without exception, I have fallen into every single shortcoming and pitfall I have described and tried to analyze in this article. I have experienced the very same problems, setbacks, defeats, victories and joys that every one of you has experienced, or will experience.

The same criticisms I have made when judging and have presented here, have also been leveled at my work. At first, these criticisms hurt a bit. But when the miff wore off, I came to realize that these were constructive criticisms presented by knowledgeable people, and I began to appreciate them.

I most dearly hope that those of you whose work I felt needed this sort of criticism will accept it in the same way.

As always, I wish each and every one of you the best good fortune and success. I urge you to keep working and trying to give it everything you've got. I don't think any of you will ever regret having made the good effort.

MEMORIA TECHNICA

Written by
Leon J. West

Illustrated by
David C. Mullins

About the Author

Four years ago, Leon West's wife, Elizabeth, demanded he either give up writing or try to get paid for it. He was unable to give it up, so he started submitting stories. He spent one year looking for a writers' group in Salem, Oregon, and another two years trying to start up his own, with no luck.

Finally, in 2001, his wife introduced him to Devon Monk, who introduced him to the Wordos Writer Group in Eugene, Oregon. That association introduced him to things like submission format, character arc and plot. He moved to Eugene to be closer to the writing group.

Although a contest official invariably contacts each winner, Eric Witchey, 2000 WOTF winner published in Volume XVII, on behalf of the contest, announced Leon had won Second Place at the Wordos Writing Group meeting, much to Leon's disbelief and extreme surprise.

Leon attends Lane Community College, where he is studying to be a teacher. He would like to teach in reform schools and juvenile detention centers. This is his first professional sale.

About the Illustrator

David C. Mullins was born in Port Angeles, Washington, and has been a Washington resident most of his life. After graduating from high school, he moved to Tempe, Arizona, where he attended different trade schools in graphic design and computers, but he eventually moved back to Kennewick, Washington.

In Kennewick, he worked in the construction business for several years and, while doing so, also completed a couple of murals for a local mini-mall. He then returned to Phoenix where he took Japanese language classes.

It was during this time in Phoenix that David started spending more time tapping into his creative energy forces, as he put it. The results helped set him on the path he is now pursuing in art. He stated he has been influenced by such artists as Giger, Frazetta and the Anime films Ghost in the Shell and Akira, and they've also provided inspiration for his work. David is fully devoted to pursuing a career in art and says, "I am finally giving it the respect it deserves, and it's beginning to show in my work, I believe. I guess enlightenment doesn't care how you get there."

Dad! Dad!" Gavin yells before I'm even out of bed. I hear his little feet pounding up the stairs in the hall. "My puppy's here, Dad. It's here!"

I roll over and pull the black-and-white comforter—a wedding gift from Donna's father, Martin, from a time before he blamed me for his daughter's death—over my head. Gavin is going to be five in a few days and the excitement of his impending birthday is killing him, and me. He bursts into my quiet bedroom in a frenzy of sound and motion.

"Dad! The mailman just brought my puppy!" he shrills.

"You're crazy," I say, without opening my eyes or removing the covers from my head. "The mailman won't be here for hours."

A rustling sound from outside my blanket, somewhere in the vicinity of my nightstand, catches my attention and drags me a few steps closer to consciousness—a few steps up from the subterranean realm of slumber. I open my eyes and look at the underside of the comforter.

A nice place, that. Sleep, I mean. Where yesterday is always on tap, and Donna is still alive, and . . . .

The rustling noise again.

I almost pull the covers off my head, but the prospect of a whole new day is still a bit daunting, so I wait, listening for any "dangerous" sounds. Gavin lifts the corner of my blanket, but drops it again before my eyes can adjust to the light.

It is no longer dark under the blankets. The fiery glow of my digital clock illuminates my tiny sanctuary, the numbers 9:30 blazing like an accusation in red.

Despite myself, I laugh. "All right," I say pulling the covers off my head at last, "where is it?"

"Downstairs!" He jumps on the bed next to me and pushes me playfully. "C'mon, Dad."

I make a production of dragging my ass out of bed, letting him push me and pretending to fall asleep sitting up. To tell the truth, though, I'm excited about this "puppy" myself; so before the little guy's curly haired head spins right off his neck, we head downstairs, me trudging and him like a bullet ricocheting from wall to wall.

"Great," I mutter at the three-foot-tall white cardboard box in the foyer. The Luv-O-Lux company logo, a stylized heart and double helix, reminds me that this "puppy" is a present from Donna's father, from the company he built a fortune out of. Which means it should be about as simple to construct as a backyard nuclear power plant. I try telling myself I really need a project anyway, that this will help me get my mind off Donna for a while, that it will be good for me.

Yeah, right. This is going to suck. I'll spend all day trying to put it together, and Gavin will thank his grandfather. And who will take care of the dog when it's done? Not Gavin, and certainly not Martin. He just buys it and my son thinks he's a god, but I have to do all the work.

I notice my son for the first time since waking up, and once again I am struck by his resemblance to Donna. He has the most astonishing eyes, big blue orbs all glistening hope and innocence. His face—still rounded with baby fat, but growing heart-rendingly more mature almost as I watch—is all pulled up tight around his eyebrows in a smile.

"C'mon, Dad."

"Breakfast first."

"I already ate Cheerios." Before I can admonish him, he holds up a pudgy hand and says, "Don't worry. I put the milk away and even rinsed my bowl."

I step back and crane my neck around the doorjamb leading into the kitchen. Water. Everywhere.

I turn around and he's peeling long strands of tape from the packing slip, his brow creased in concentration. He looks so serious, so intent. Finally, he gets the packing slip off and realizes he is no closer to getting inside the box than he was when he began.

"Dad!" His face is red. Tears of frustration threaten to spill from those big beautiful eyes—those eyes so like his mother's.

"All right," I say, "let me get dressed and go to the bathroom." Before he can protest, I hold up my hand and say, "Your birthday isn't for three days yet, and the puppy is going to take a few months even after I get the incubator together."

Gavin slumps his shoulders a bit, but then perks up for no apparent reason, turns around, and gallops into the living room, hollering, "Yeehaw! Yeehaw!"

I work through lunch, connecting As to Cs and Gs until the letters flash behind my eyelids every time I blink. You'd think Gavin could stay out of trouble, at least until I finish putting *his* present together, but five-year-olds are utterly inept self-managers. He runs around inventing new ways to endanger his life until

Illustrated by David C. Mullins

noon, when he makes himself another bowl of cereal, turns on the television and watches cartoons.

We used to have a rule against watching more than an hour of television per day. Before Donna died. Today he watches until I bring him dinner—a peanut butter and jelly sandwich and a glass of milk—and then falls asleep on the couch.

Even without Gavin careening about the house like a lunatic, it's hard to concentrate. Every time I stop thinking about Donna long enough to really comprehend the gibberish instructions, I lose myself and forget she's dead. I don't call her name or anything, but every once in a while, a part of my subconscious starts to anticipate the moment she'll come through the door and make some joke about how I look like a mad scientist. Maybe bring me some tea. She used to do things like that a lot. Sometimes I forget that those little things she did—the little acts of kindness—are no longer a part of my life. Life is so much crueler without Donna.

All night I flange, fasten and fuse the pieces of the incubator with the infuriatingly small tools provided by Luv-O-Lux. By breakfast the next day, my eyes hurt, my head hurts, my fingertips have gone numb and the incubator still won't incubate.

I stumble into the kitchen to start my fourth pot of coffee, and the phone rings. I ignore it as usual. We used to have a video phone, but I couldn't handle all the condolence calls, so I broke it.

"Hello," squeaks a sleepy voice.

I silently curse the caller for waking my son. Now I'll never get this stupid contraption built.

"Grandpa!"

Oh, great. God has called.

"Yeah," says my son, "it came in the mail yesterday! Dad's putting it together. The pieces are all over the place!" He pauses for a breath or two, then says, "Yeah, Grandpa! I love it! It's the best present I ever got! Thank you soooo much!"

I knew it.

"Hold on a sec," he says slowly in his "serious" voice, "I'll go ask Dad right now. Don't go away, OK?"

The slap, slap, slap of bare feet precede Gavin's big eyes and bright smile into the kitchen. His mother's eyes. His mother's smile. His mother's big feet, come to think of it.

"Dad!" he shouts. "Can Grandpa come take me to the fair?"

I want to say no, just to spite Martin, but I can't. My son loves him, and besides, all those things he screamed at me that night in the hospital—about how letting Donna drive drunk had as good as killed her—well, that was true.

"Yeah," I say to his back as he runs off hooting and hollering.

I struggle with grinding coffee. Eventually, he wanders back into the kitchen. He drags a stepping stool over to the cupboard and reaches for the cereal, but I scoop him up and set him at the kitchen table before he can make a mess.

"I'll make breakfast today." I try to sound cheerful.

"Dad," he begins, and I already know what he's about to ask.

"Huh?"

"You miss Mom?"

"Yeah, buddy, I do."

Satisfied, he starts singing himself a song and, to all outward appearances, forgets about the matter entirely.

Do you miss Mom? It rips my heart out every time he asks, and he asks every day. At least he's stopped asking where she is and when she's coming back.

After breakfast the doorbell rings. Martin lets himself in and smiles at the mess his gift has made of my living room.

And now they'll go to the fair. I'll have to stay here, putting this contraption together. His present . . . .

"Mornin', Martin," I nod.

"Thought you might like some time without Gavin, to work on that Luv-O-Lux." He takes off his driving gloves and stuffs them in the front pocket of his white linen leisure jacket. "They're pretty complex."

"Thanks. I appreciate it." I don't suggest he stay and put the incubator together while I take Gavin to the fair, partly out of respect, but also because I don't want to go.

Then Martin does something that catches me entirely unawares. He clasps my shoulders, stares at me with the blue eyes he passed on to his daughter and thence to my son, and says, "I'm not going to apologize, but I want us to bury the hatchet. You and I are the only family Gavin has left. We should mend our differences, for his sake."

I stammer something like an agreement, and they leave for the fair.

•••

"Dad! Dad!" Gavin bangs through the front door and races into the kitchen, bouncing off the doorjamb without noticing. "I got cotton candy, and we rode on a magic carpet, and I sat on Grandpa's lap in a bumper plane, and we—"

"Slow down," I say, smiling—smiling the most genuine and heartfelt smile since Donna's death. "Your present's done."

"Is that it behind you?" he asks, pointing at the boxy little incubator on the counter. He drags his stepping stool noisily across the kitchen floor.

"Wow!" His eyes are even bigger than normal. "You did it! Grandpa! Daddy did it!" And those three words render the whole infuriating project worthwhile. *Daddy did it.* Not said in accusation, but in wonder, in awe. *Daddy did it.*

"Great!" booms Martin from the front door. He has his amber-tinted sunglasses pushed up amidst his silver hair. "I knew you could."

Martin is not the kind of guy who understands tears, and I'm not normally the kind of guy who cries. I turn away before I embarrass us all.

"This doesn't look like a puppy," Gavin says, peering into the viewing window set in the lid of the incubator, "or a sister."

Sister?

"That's because it has to gestate first." Martin crouches nimbly for a man of his years and looks my son in the eye. "But in a few months," he claps his hands, "you'll have a wonderful new friend."

My son looks at the incubator dubiously. "It looks like yucky soup. Is that how my baby sister's gonna look when we make her?"

The smile freezes on my face and I aim it at Martin like a gun. "What?"

"Like the way you and Mom made me," says my son matter-of-factly.

"We did not make you out of some home hobby kit!" I scream, despite my best efforts to remain calm. "We—

we—we went to the doctor, and they took some of Mommy and some of me and put it together and then put it back in Mommy until you were ready to be born. You weren't made in an incubator on the counter."

Tears well up in Gavin's eyes and he runs down the hall sobbing, "I want Mommy back."

I glare at Martin. "Who gave him a stupid idea like that?"

"You don't understand what it's like to lose a child."

"I lost my wife, Martin."

"You know, I even considered getting custody of Gavin." He looks me in the eye. "With all my connections, I could have done it too. But I don't really want to hurt you. I just want you to understand. I want you to understand what I lost when I lost Donna."

"What the hell are you talking about, Martin?"

"The—ah, the package I sent Gavin. I switched the puppy codes with Donna's DNA."

"Wh—what!" I scream.

"Don't get so upset. You and Donna were planning on having a little girl before she died, right? And Donna was a fabulous child. She slept through the night at three weeks old, never went through the hateful phase most teenagers go through. She was my little angel, and now she's yours."

I glare.

"I'll just leave these packets so you can read up on what to expect. We're going to have to switch her to a larger incubator in a month—month and a half at most."

"Just leave," I say, and to my astonishment, he does.

I shut the door and lean my back against it. The Luv-O-Lux incubator sits on the kitchen counter like a witch's cauldron.

Beneath the glass viewing window I installed with my own hands, safely nestled in the synthetic womb, ten dollars' worth of proteins and acids are even now growing into another smiling, laughing, blue-eyed reminder of everything I've lost.

Damn you, Martin.

I sit down at the table and put my head in my hands. I look at the turgid soup that was once my wife and will one day become my daughter. Occasionally, I wipe the tears from the viewing window.

FREE FALL

Written by
Tom Brennan

Illustrated by
Irena Yankova Dimitrova

About the Author

Born in 1965 in Liverpool, U.K., Tom Brennan was educated at the local high school, where he became a voracious reader with a particular interest in SF. He began his working life as a mainframe operator for the U.K. government and eventually became a freelance communications contractor.

In late 1999, Tom took time out to start writing fiction, which had been his dream since childhood. He is self-taught, having had no formal writing training so far. He wants to explore the relationships and responses of being placed in extreme situations and thinks SF offers, by far, the most exciting possibilities.

Tom enjoys a wide variety of literature and music, traveling, cycling and hiking. He worked across the U.K. as a freelance data communications contractor for a few years, but has since returned to Liverpool, where he lives by the sea with his wife, Sylvia, and cat, Sheba. In terms of writing, he states he feels he's taken the first few steps on a steep mountain track, but is looking forward to the journey ahead.

Sarah Alegria Burnett, born six months premature on the ex-Corps ship *Jefferson Renown*, halfway between Earth and the newly formed Mars Autonomy. Her exhausted colonist mother, straddling the bloodied galley prep table, saw the creature and screamed, reached for the largest knife. Sarah saw the world through luminescent eyes, bulging blue spheres four centimeters wide, set beneath a shelf of ridged bone and malformed skull. Her body an eruption of skeletal limbs, her face a tangle of skewed features, the physical product of battlefield toxins.

Sarah after Sarah Vaughan, the captain's favorite singer; Alegria from the Spanish word for delight, courtesy of Garcia, the cook and midwife; Burnett after the captain, Bob Burnett, Cap to the crew and their adopted daughter.

Her first memory at eighteen months old: floating down the central corridor, her awkward body protected by an orange inflatable rig from the ship's skiff. She sailed in slow motion, tumbling and gurgling, between Garcia and Johansen, the navigator. Later, Garcia told her they had played an old game called basketball, with Sarah as the ball, and she almost believed him.

The ship, a squat tapered globe on four cavernous boosters, could cope with landfall if it had to, but seldom left the cold vacuum between the planets and their moons. Cap bought the surplus cargo vessel after his last tour of duty and paid for its conversion to passenger carrier. A few years after Sarah was born, he ripped out the acceleration couches and went back to carrying freight, mainly minerals, ore and machinery. "They're less trouble than colonists," he told her afterwards.

They flew from Earth to Mars and Luna; Io and Europa; Callisto and Ganymede; and further, if the fee was good. The ship and its crew provided Sarah with her education, home and playground. Garcia taught her Spanish and karate, Johansen taught math and Swedish, Cap, everything he could.

"What's that?" asked Sarah, aged ten, over two meters tall, staring out of the Control Room's observation port at the floating derelict. They were near the end of their journey, carrying spare parts for the mines on Ganymede.

"That's the *Christofo*, an old Corps flattop," Cap told her. "See all the docking points and empty bays in the side? That's where the small combat craft flew from." The flattop was actually a kilometer-long spindle surrounded by flickering marker buoys. The vessel's surface was scored and pocked by lasers and ripped with impact craters. Flotsam and jetsam orbited the wreck: dull metal debris, furniture blown from the cabins in sudden decompression, torn remnants of frozen pressure suits.

"Did you and Garcia fly from that?" asked Sarah.

"No, not that one, but something very similar," he replied softly.

"Can we go inside?"

"Sorry, honey." Cap shook his head. "It's a war grave, nobody should board it. That doesn't mean that some people don't, but that's their decision."

Sarah examined the derelict as their course brought them closer. The opaque nictitating membranes covering her eyes slid back into place as she turned to Cap and asked, "Why is the back of the ship glowing?"

"How do you mean?"

"That glow," said Sarah. "The back of the ship is bright blue. It's beautiful."

The derelict was dark to Cap, save for the light from the buoys' strobes. "I can't see anything. Where is the glow, exactly?"

Sarah pointed to the bulbous engine nacelles at the rear of the derelict, where the massive twin reactors had been housed before they were disabled. As their ship's trajectory veered away from the *Christofo*, Cap called Garcia to the Control Room.

"No, can't see anything there," said Garcia. "Why? What's the problem?"

"You tell him, honey," said Cap.

"Have you seen anything like this before?" asked Garcia, after Sarah explained.

"Oh, yes," Sarah told them. "When I go to bed and turn the lights out, I can see bright lines and trails and tiny starbursts. And, sometimes, I see a thin coating of light on the walls and doors."

Garcia looked at Cap and asked, "Cerenkov radiation?"

"Could be," said Cap. Sarah stood with her twisted face pressed to the armored glass, blonde hair plaited and coiled around her swollen skull.

• • •

They docked at the orbiting freight platform and Cap left Garcia to supervise the unloading. Sarah wore her best jumpsuit for her first visit to the colony and sat

Illustrated by Irena Yankova Dimitrova

excitedly next to Cap on the transfer shuttle, taking in every new sight and sound. After the shuttle glided in to the passenger terminal, they rode the monorail to the edge of the mining complex.

The Mining Company clinic took Cap's money and gave Sarah a full scan.

Cap paced the scuffed floor of the waiting room, ignoring the panoramic view of the strip mine outside and the pressurized city dome on the horizon. The metal walls of the room were lined with posters warning against Sexually Transmitted Diseases and infestation. A single fluorescent hung askew from the ceiling.

Cap turned as the hermetic inner door sighed open and the young doctor, dressed in a green and white tunic, appeared. "How is she?" Cap demanded.

The young man sat on a greasy plastic seat. "Where do I start? Enlarged, overproductive glands; deformed skeletal development; abnormal tissue growth in the frontal lobes—"

"Is she okay?"

"I don't know," the doctor said. "We haven't seen anything like this before. Realistically, it shouldn't have survived this far."

"She," Cap stated.

"Pardon me?"

"The correct word is 'she,'" said Cap, "not 'it.'"

The doctor's smooth, tanned face froze and he stared at Cap for a moment before continuing, "She appears to be surprisingly healthy, considering the various mutations and abnormalities."

"And the glow she saw?" asked Cap.

"Sensitivity beyond the visible spectrum," the doctor read from his glowing workpad. "She can see a wider range of wavelengths than, ah, normal people can."

Cap smiled. "That could be an asset."

"That's certainly the optimistic view." The doctor walked to the inner door. "We'd like to keep her under observation, for at least a few weeks."

"Why?" Cap demanded, on his feet now.

The doctor held up his hands. "Purely routine, I assure you. We need to carry out further tests, particularly relating to its, that is 'her,' accelerated growth rate."

Cap shook his head. "I don't think so."

"If it's a question of money, we are prepared to waive all charges," the doctor explained. "Instances of surviving mutations are extremely important to the Company."

"What for? Research?" asked Cap. "I think you'd better release Sarah; we've got a busy day planned."

The doctor hesitated, then asked, "Have you considered her future? If the rate of growth doesn't decrease, she may be dead in a couple of years: her body may turn in on itself, with cells unable to support continuous expansion. She could become a mass of uncontrolled, uncoordinated tissue. Do you want that to happen?"

"And your alternative?" asked Cap. "Imprisoned in a hospital room, some kind of medical exhibit? We'll take our own chances, out there."

"We could get the Company's legal department involved," the doctor threatened, "make her a ward of the court."

Cap crossed the small room in two steps and stood with his taut, scarred face inches from the doctor's. "Believe me: it wouldn't get that far," Cap told the doctor. "Bring Sarah out."

Minutes after the doctor disappeared, Sarah rushed into the waiting room, threw her arms around Cap and hugged him.

"You okay?" he asked. "Did they hurt you?"

"They were nice to me." Sarah's voice, light and melodic, echoed around the dank room. "The nurses looked after me, even while I was in the big machine, and—"

"That's good, honey," Cap interrupted, "but we should leave."

Sarah looked at him with wide translucent eyes. "Is everything alright?"

"Everything's fine."

"Is there anything wrong with me? Will I be okay?" she asked.

Cap smiled and said, "There's nothing wrong with you: you're fit as a fiddle."

"Fit as a fiddle," Sarah repeated. "What does that mean? What's a fiddle?"

He laughed. "I'll tell you later. Come on, I'll take you to the mall; I need to visit the shipping office before we leave. The sooner, the better."

They took the subway from the hospital complex and emerged beneath the graceful soaring span of the main dome. Sarah saw the moonscape of ice and rock through the armored, dual-skinned glass; the intimidating striated globe of Jupiter stained every surface with red and orange hues and dominated the fragile settlement.

Inside the dome, streets radiated from the hub where the towers of the local Administration brushed the titanium apex. Cap and Sarah walked along the outer rim, where shops and small businesses formed the mall. They stopped outside a bright neon-lit facade; plastic molded chairs and small tables in primary colors lined the deserted interior.

"Will you wait for me here?" he asked Sarah. "I don't like leaving you alone, but they won't let you into the shipping office."

"I'll be fine." Sarah peered inside. "What is it?"

"An ice-cream parlor," Cap replied. "Come on, I'll show you."

He led the way to the steel and glass counter and the large tubs of vividly colored ice cream. "I'll have a pistachio," he told the young attendant.

"Pistachio. Yes, pistachio." The girl took her eyes off Sarah and scooped a dripping green globe onto a cone. Sarah asked for the same; she sat opposite Cap and was about to taste the concoction when he stopped her.

"Don't bite into it," he warned her. "You'll hurt your teeth: it's very cold."

"I know; I can tell," Sarah told him. She tasted the concoction and smiled. "Nice."

Cap bought her another cone before he left and said, "You wait here, okay? I'll call Garcia, tell him to meet us. I'll be as quick as I can."

Sarah bought a blueberry cone to follow her chocolate, then began to feel a little nauseous. She stared back calmly at the pedestrians peering through the store's windows and looked beyond them to the public gardens on the next block; a lazy waterfall tumbled over an artificial bluff, and its drifting spray refracted the light.

Sarah left the ice-cream parlor and its tinny Muzak, and walked toward the rainbow. The public gardens were laid out in a wide segment at the end of a block. Sarah sat on a fake-wood bench and watched the colors writhing in the mist.

"It's pretty, isn't it?" An olive-skinned, dark-haired woman dressed in a casual suit spoke from the adjacent bench.

"It is," said Sarah. "I like it very much."

"Me, too." The woman moved and sat next to Sarah. "This is the best place in the dome. Have you been here before?"

Sarah shook her head. "Not down here. We always stayed on the ship before."

"I guessed you were from a freighter," the woman said, looking at Sarah's coveralls; they were the largest pair Cap could find, but they barely covered Sarah's ankles and wrists. "I'm Donna."

"Sarah."

"Are you from Earth, Sarah?"

"Well, yes, I suppose," she mumbled.

"I'm from Mars," Donna told her. "My family left Earth when the epidemics started. Have you been to Mars?"

"A few times."

"It's not too bad there, is it? The atmosphere's improved a lot, and—"

"Jeez, will you look at that?" A slurred deep voice interrupted her. Sarah looked up at the three men: they were dressed in stained matching coveralls emblazoned with the Power Company logo of three salamanders eating their tails.

"What the hell is that?" The speaker was the tallest of the men, pale skinned and crew cut, with stubble on his jowly cheeks. He held a plastic beer tube in his hand. "Frigging freaky, or what?"

Donna blushed. "Just mind your business," she told the men.

"Aw, shit, come on, babe; we gotta take a look at this." He turned to Sarah. "You one of those mutants from the war? I thought you weren't allowed off Earth?"

"Forget it, Jim." One of the men touched the speaker's arm and looked around at the growing crowd of spectators. "Let's go to 'The Bunker,' grab a beer there."

"In a minute," said Jim and swayed closer to Sarah.

Donna looked up at him. "I think you might have had enough to drink."

"What's it to you?" demanded Jim, and jabbed a blunt finger at Sarah. "I want this thing to talk; you from some carny or something? Last crap I saw like you was in a jar, five dollars a look. And that was prettier than you!"

Sarah felt her whole body shaking as the adrenaline hit. She forced herself to relax, just like Garcia had told her, and prepare for the man's attack. She stood up from the bench, her left foot slightly forward, her long arms loose at her sides. Her throat was level with the top of Jim's greasy head.

"This is the first warning," said Donna, as she slowly got to her feet. "Go home and sleep it off."

Jim's companions were a little less drunk and tried to pull him back, but he shrugged them off. He turned from Sarah and focused on Donna, asking, "You some kind of mutie lover? This your girlfriend?"

The crowd of spectators pressed closer, their eyes gleaming. Donna slipped her hand into her purse and told Jim, "For the second time: go home. There won't be a third warning."

Jim's face reddened and his fists clenched. "No woman bosses me!" He swung his right fist, back-handed, at Donna; she ducked the clumsy blow and pulled her hand from her purse. Jim looked at the gleaming badge inches from his face, stared at Donna, hesitating, then grunted and pulled his arm back for a second attack.

Sarah was at Donna's side, ready to block, when Jim crashed to the ground under the weight of his two companions; they sat on his back, keeping him down, as he yelled and struggled.

"I'm really sorry about this," one of the men told Donna. "We've just finished a week of double shifts, and he hit the bars a little fast."

"Get him off the streets," Donna told them, then turned to the disappointed crowd. "Okay, people, let's go."

Sarah stood trembling, then vomited onto the manicured grass. She stood, hands on her knees, until Donna touched her arm. "Are you down here with anyone?"

Sarah nodded and pointed back toward the parlor. She accepted a tissue from Donna and began walking back with her. Cap and Garcia were waiting outside the store.

"Sarah, are you okay?" Cap ran up to her and saw the patches of vomit on her suit. "What happened?"

"She's alright," said Donna. "Just some idiot mouthing off at her."

Cap's features hardened. "Did he hurt her?"

"No, it was just talk," said Donna.

"Where did it happen?" Cap demanded. "What did he look like?"

"Hey, slow down," Donna told him. "It's finished."

"Cap, I'm okay, really," said Sarah, "thanks to Donna."

Garcia stepped forward. "Thanks for helping her out."

"No problem," said Donna. "There're a lot of jerks in this place, unfortunately. You look after yourself, Sarah."

"I will," Sarah replied as Donna turned away.

"We should get back to the ship." Cap, tight-lipped and terse, strode toward the subway station.

Sarah, Garcia and Cap were strapped into their shuttle seats, halfway to the freight platform, when Cap exploded. "Why did you run off like that? I told you to wait for us. Anything could have happened to you; you think everyone is as nice and easygoing as us? Well, they're not."

"I'm sorry." Sarah's wide eyes glistened and thick tears joined her coverall's ice-cream stains. "I won't do it again."

Cap looked at her and tried to speak, then ripped his seat straps open and pushed himself away, down the aisle. Garcia moved next to Sarah and put his arm around her.

• • •

She waited until late the next day, when Garcia had finished supervising the cargo loading, before she approached him in the galley.

Garcia sat at the stainless-steel table, a tube of coffee in one hand, a fraying book with a gaudy cover in the other. He looked up as Sarah floated in. *"¿Qué tal?"*

"Bien, más o menos." Sarah pulled herself onto the seat opposite. "Can I ask you something?"

"Sure." Garcia put his book down.

"It's just, well . . . why was Cap so mad with me? I mean, I know I shouldn't have walked off, but—"

"Don't worry," interrupted Garcia. "He's not mad with you."

"But he shouted at me," said Sarah.

Garcia took a gulp of coffee and hesitated. "He shouted because he was scared."

"Scared? Of what?"

"Something happening to you." Garcia struggled for words. "You see, if you really like someone, maybe even love them, you don't want anything bad to happen to them. You want to protect them. And that fear sometimes comes out in weird ways. Does that make sense?"

Sarah smiled. "Oh, yes: he was afraid for me, because he loves me."

"I only said he might," said Garcia.

"That's why he was so mad at Carson." The year before, they had carried a cargo of hydroponic vats from Luna to Mars, and a technician, Carson, had come along to monitor them. Five minutes a day, checking the temperature and humidity, the rest of his time alone in his room. Until he tried to crawl into Sarah's bunk in the middle of the night.

Johansen heard Sarah's yells and found Carson, naked and pumped full of drugs, lying against the wall nursing a broken nose where Sarah's elbow had struck.

Cap had dragged Carson through the ship and thrown him into the passenger airlock, then explained what would happen if Carson ever went near Sarah again. Carson spent the remainder of his journey in his room, minus the collection of pills, vials and liquids Cap had destroyed.

"That was one of the reasons," said Garcia.

"Thank you, I feel better now." Sarah paused before asking, "Does Cap have any family?"

"He did have," said Garcia.

"But not anymore?"

"No, not anymore." Garcia refilled the plastic bulb with percolator coffee before he continued. "He went back home, after the war, but the Ebola Variant had covered most of the eastern seaboard. He lost everything."

"I'm so sorry," said Sarah, then, "Did he have children?"

Garcia looked at her. "Yes, a girl and a boy."

"Were they . . . normal?" Sarah asked carefully. "Pretty?"

"Every parent believes their children are beautiful," said Garcia.

"Not mine," said Sarah.

Garcia reached across and took her hand. "Well, she was wrong. Me, Cap and Johansen all agree on that. Isn't that right?"

Johansen had sailed into the galley as Garcia spoke, and replied, "One hundred percent. Any coffee?"

"Help yourself," Garcia told him.

Sarah heard the recorded trumpets and double bass before she entered the Control Room. Cap was lying on the acceleration couch, his eyes closed, apparently asleep. Sarah turned and was about to leave when Cap asked, "Something wrong?"

"No, I just wanted to see you." Sarah pushed herself from the door and turned in midair to land expertly on the bulkhead opposite.

"I'm sorry I yelled at you," Cap told her.

"That's okay," said Sarah. "I understand now; Garcia explained it to me."

"Did he? I'll have to thank him for that."

Sarah looked at Cap's gray hair streaked with silver, and the filigree of thin scars that lined his face.

"What are you thinking about?" he asked.

"What you were like when you were young," she said.

Cap pushed himself upright and grinned. "I was a little terror: always getting into trouble, always doing something I shouldn't."

"I'm glad." Sarah sailed toward the exit. "Goodnight, Cap." She slept to a lullaby of melodies from a century before.

• • •

The *Jefferson* left Ganymede behind and was headed back to Earth when Cap, flicking through the data feeds from the traffic control station, stumbled on a news channel and recognized the doctor from the Mining Company clinic. Cap's barrage of curses flooded through the intercom.

"What is it?" Garcia burst into the Control Room.

"He's the one who examined Sarah," Cap yelled, and raised the volume so that the doctor's oleaginous voice filled the room.

". . . goes without saying that we would have liked to examine the subject further, but her guardian refused."

"And you think this could have been a useful scientific breakthrough?" The pert newscaster leaned her perfect profile toward the doctor. An image of Sarah's face filled the wall behind the two Ganymedans.

"Absolutely; in fact, of the many interesting variations that have survived, this would have been the most rewarding in terms of human adaptability, despite the relatively short life sp——"

Cap muted the channel and turned to Johansen. "Can we turn back?"

"We'd have to slingshot around Europa; I could plot an elliptical course," said Johansen, "that might take us back in six, maybe seven weeks."

"We'll have to forget it, for now," said Cap, "I hope Sarah didn't see him."

The *Jefferson* plied the Mars–Earth–Luna routes for the next year, and Cap monitored Sarah's growth until she leveled out at two meters twenty. He bought her an ex-combat pressure suit, originally designed to fit over a bulky bacteriological rig; Sarah filled the bulbous suit completely.

Sarah spent her time watching reference books on the main view screen, together with discs and films bought by the crew. She followed them as they maintained the aging ship, from the engine bays, which glowed white-hot in her eyes, to the Control Room, and every deck in between.

She was on her way to meet Garcia in the cargo bays when she passed Johansen's cabin; Cap had given the navigator six months' leave, to visit his parents in Oslo. His replacement, Neesa, had moved into his bunk.

"I just wish you'd told me." The woman's voice was soft, almost a whisper, with a trace of an unfamiliar accent. "You took me on as a navigator. I mean, I knew this ship was a little different: I recognized Sarah from those news reports."

"I know, I know," Cap replied quietly, "and I'm not forcing you to do this. It's just that, well, she's approaching a certain age and I find it difficult to explain things to her . . . ."

"What about books? They'd explain it to her," said Neesa.

"They seem so impersonal," said Cap.

There was a pause before Neesa replied, "I'll do it. When, though?"

Sarah pushed herself back along the corridor, then began to whistle and sailed past Johansen's cabin. "Hey, Cap, Neesa."

"Hey, Sarah." A conspiratorial grin creased Neesa's face.

Cap blushed and looked around the room. "Yes, Sarah, hello. I was just looking for . . . I came in for . . . for this!" He grabbed Johansen's alarm clock from its Velcro perch, smiled weakly, and launched himself through the door.

Neesa laughed and patted the bunk beside her. "Sit down, honey: there are a few things you and me need to discuss."

Sarah found Cap in the galley; he looked up as she entered, then quickly down at his coffee. "Did you and Neesa have a chat?" he asked Sarah innocently.

"Yes, we had a nice long talk." Sarah helped herself to a soda from the fridge.

Cap gulped his drink. "And everything's clear now?"

"Sure," replied Sarah calmly. "See you later."

Cap waited until he heard the deck's bulkhead door slammed shut, then gave a sigh of relief and let his head sink to the table.

•••

The first war of Sarah's life, and the second of Cap's, broke out when they were docked at the Earth orbiting freight terminal. Cap and Sarah, suited and belayed to the *Jefferson* on carbon lines, were supervising the transfer of massive cargo containers from the shuttles when their suits' emergency channel crackled into life. They reeled themselves back onto the ship and met Garcia in the Control Room.

"We've been grounded," Garcia informed them. "SolAm attacked two Martian ships a short while ago."

"Not again!" Cap slapped the back of an acceleration couch.

The view screen was a mass of static on every channel, until it coalesced into the frightened face of the main traffic control supervisor. His voice was strained and tense as he said, "This is an important message for all ships: we have been informed that the shipping routes between Mars, Earth and Luna are closed until further notice. Also, all vessels are confined to port."

Garcia looked at the screen and shook his head. "Idiots."

Cap closed and locked the ship's outer doors, and the crew waited for news.

• • •

A week passed, and Sarah was helping Garcia check the engine feeds when Cap called her to the Control Room.

Sarah found Cap flanked by two strangers, both wearing rigid, armored pressure suits; their uniform collars were edged with gold leaves. The taller of the two men spoke as Sarah entered the room, "Sarah, how are you? My name is Marsh, this is Davidson."

"What's happening," Sarah asked Cap.

"These men are from the Corps Space Arm," said Cap. "They want to ask you something."

"That's true, but we need to explain the current situation first." Marsh placed his suit helmet and gloves on Johansen's couch, then looked at Sarah. "SolAm is the largest, most influential trading consortium, with interests throughout the system. They have had a long-running disagreement with the colonies and the Mars Autonomy in particular. One of the main catalysts for the last war was the trade feud."

Cap snorted. "And much good it caused."

Marsh raised a hand. "Please. SolAm denies attacking and destroying two Martian freighters, but the Autonomy has impounded Earth vessels and closed all trade routes. It has also activated a series of minefields around Earth."

"Don't you have radar and spectrographs on your ships?" asked Sarah.

Davidson leaned forward. "We did have, before they were disabled by a pre-planted virus."

"Even if they were operational," Marsh added, "the cluster mines are mainly skeletal ceramic and plastic; they would be very hard to identify, particularly at high velocity."

"But what can I do?"

"One of my officers saw you on the news a while back," explained Marsh. "A doctor stated that you could detect a wider range of wavelengths. Can you?"

"Well, yes, but I don't see—"

"The mines use a small radioactive charge as combined weapon and engine," said Marsh. "They propel themselves using a stream of ionized gas. We hope you can identify these before they hit our ship, and we can avoid them."

Cap interrupted. "Why not just wait until your ships are back on-line?"

Marsh looked at Davidson before he said, "The Luna bases were attacked three days ago. They have no hospital facilities, no food reserves and precious little oxygen. I want to take a hospital ship through."

"No way," said Cap.

"But Luna—" Marsh began.

"I'm sorry, but it's no," said Cap. "Some things are worth fighting for, need fighting for, but trade? We do this so SolAm can extort a few more billion dollars from the colonies? No."

"It doesn't matter how it began," said Marsh. "What matters is that hundreds of people are going to die if we don't help them."

Cap shook his head. "It's suicide."

"I want to go," said Sarah quietly.

Cap and Marsh turned to her.

"I want to do it," Sarah repeated. "If I can help, I will."

Cap pushed himself over to her and said, "Please, honey, don't do this."

"I'm sorry, Cap." Sarah smiled. "If someone else had brought me up, I mightn't feel the same way."

"Go ahead, blame me," said Cap, and smiled, too. "Okay, when do we leave?" he asked Marsh.

"We only need Sarah," replied Marsh.

"It's all of us or none," said Cap, "that is, if the others want to come?"

Johansen and Garcia, both floating near the doorway, nodded simultaneously.

"Fine, here's what we'll do," Cap told Marsh. "We'll take the *Jefferson* out first, on point. You follow behind, maybe two, three kilometers? Can you patch in a laser comms link, or is that down too?"

"We can manage that."

"Good: we'll relay Johansen's controls through the link. If Sarah sees anything, we'll try to evade it, and you'd better follow us damn quick," said Cap.

"And if you're hit?" asked Davidson.

The room was silent until Cap replied, "Then you go on and hope for the best."

● ● ●

Marsh stayed with the crew as the *Jefferson* pulled
away from the docking platform and headed for the
shipping lanes. They passed the kilometer-long unfi-
nished spindle of the *Boreas*, the intersystem ship
destined for Ursa Major.

Sarah stared through the observation port at the
tableau of cold stars. The ponderous mass of the Corps
hospital ship, its sides marked with a huge red cross,
dwarfed the smaller craft. Cap waited until they had
cleared Earth space before he told Marsh, "Time for you
to return to your ship."

"I'm staying here," said Marsh.

Cap stared at him. "It's your decision. How's it look,
Sarah?"

"All clear," she replied. With her eyes free of their
nictitating membranes, the void writhed with faint
traces and trails of spent particles and the distant spectra
of a million stars. The tenuous, shimmering veil of the
solar wind blew across the ships' course, a soft swell of
ghostly light.

As the *Jefferson*'s velocity increased, she saw a
burning white-blue point.

"Ten degrees northeast, about a thousand klicks," she
told Johansen, and felt the ship veer as he compensated.

"What if these are homing weapons?" asked Cap.
"Or directional?"

"They shouldn't be," said Marsh, choosing his words
carefully. "The rules of engagement stipulate passive
mines only. Emission-seeking or guided weapons are
prohibited."

Cap snorted. "Rules of engagement! You think you
can put order into war?"

"I hope so," Marsh replied. "When two entities can annihilate each other, you have to try to contain the situation."

Sarah interrupted them. "Southwest, one nine five degrees, maybe eight hundred klicks."

"Well done, honey," said Cap.

Sarah's eyes stung as she focused on every strange phosphorescence. She called out the positions to Johansen, who tried to bring them back on course despite their sinuous path. Sarah rubbed her eyes for a moment, then looked up to see a brilliant blue orb streaking toward them. "Dead ahead!" she yelled.

Johansen jerked the stick to one side and the *Jefferson* veered violently to the left, missing the mine by less than a hundred meters. Sarah, clinging to her webbing straps, felt the ship vibrate at the nearby explosion.

"Close one." Marsh grinned at Cap.

"Sorry," said Sarah.

"Don't worry, honey, you're doing great," Cap told her, then asked Garcia, "Any damage?"

Garcia checked the banks of sensors buried in the ship's hull. "Looks like we got some shrapnel, causing loss of pressure in the cargo decks, nothing too dramatic. A few scratches; nothing we haven't been through before."

Garcia went below and brought coffee for them all. Sarah repeated the mantra to Johansen, but could feel her strength ebbing as the hours passed.

Then they heard the welcoming tones of the Luna radio beacons. The moon grew in the observation window and Sarah began to relax, until she saw the array of burning points blocking their path.

"What is it, Sarah?" asked Cap.

"Either there's a thousand mines out there, waiting for us," she said, "or there's a whole belt of warm junk blocking our way."

"Can you steer us through it?" asked Marsh.

"I don't know." Sarah stared so hard her vision doubled. She rubbed hard at her grainy eyes and tried to identify the brightest points.

"I don't think we have a choice," Johansen told them. "By the time we brake, we'll be through it."

Cap joined Sarah at the window. "Just do your best, honey. There was probably a lot of debris thrown into low orbit after the attack."

"I'll try." Sarah tried to make sense of the pattern: there seemed to be a central tunnel through the field, surrounded by stationary coruscating points. The slightly weaker, colder images within this tunnel seemed to be moving, as if they were in orbit. She breathed hard and told Johansen, "Northwest, three five oh degrees. Trim."

The entrance to the cloud of objects drew closer, and the radar sprang to frenetic life, reporting a small flotilla of solid material. Sarah's heart raced as the first faint objects passed by at less than a hundred meters; then fifty; twenty; and finally, impacted.

The thick hull of the ship shuddered as it deflected the debris and scrap. The Control Room echoed, a hollow drum struck again and again. Sarah didn't realize she was holding her breath until they were through the cloud, and she let out a single long exhalation and slumped against the glass.

The *Jefferson* began its landing approach and circled the largest Luna base: buildings were scorched and flattened, opened out like vivid flowers against the gray surface. New, blackened craters pocked the moon's crust and erupted among the covered corridors and streets that led to the fractured dome. "Are we too late?" Sarah whispered.

Marsh listened to his headset and said, "No; they're still alive. But they haven't got much time left."

Johansen brought the ship down onto a plateau beside the airless dome. The crew watched as the hospital ship sank slowly toward the landing grids, its retros sending up clouds of silent dust that hung, suspended, above the wreckage. The ship touched down with a muted roar and settled into the cracked skin of the grids. While the jets were still burning, the underside of the ship split and disgorged a convoy of small vehicles.

"Thank you," said Marsh, as he hugged Sarah's exhausted body. She saw trails of sweat down the sides of his face before she collapsed into his arms.

●●●

The crew worked on Luna for the remainder of the war, helping to rebuild the shattered installations. They were celebrating Sarah's sixteenth birthday when the cease-fire was announced. They toasted Sarah, and the good news, with ersatz wine from the new hydroponic harvests.

At Cap's insistence, Sarah had been attending what was left of the school; she had made friends with the staff and the few children left on the base, and was dreading saying goodbye. She walked through the class-rooms that she had helped build, through the laboratories and gymnasium, and knocked on the head's door. She was surprised to find Cap and Garcia already there.

"Sarah, come in." Mrs. Adams, blond and muscular, was only a few years older than Sarah, but had taken over the school after the first bombardment killed most of the staff. "We were having a chat about you."

"All good, I hope," said Sarah.

"Yes, it was," said Cap, without smiling.

"You know, you've become an essential part of the school," Mrs. Adams told her. "You've helped us more than I can tell you."

Sarah blushed. "Thanks. I'm going to miss you when I leave."

Mrs. Adams glanced at Cap, then asked Sarah, "Have you thought about your future?"

"Well, no, I guess not," said Sarah. "I've just been thinking about getting through the war. Why?"

"I want you to stay here," Cap told her.

Sarah stared at him, dismayed, and asked, "But why?"

Cap folded her huge hands in his. "We can't offer you much on the *Jefferson*. You already know more than I do, and you're learning all the time. The school could give you an education, a future."

"I want to stay with you!" Sarah felt the hot sting of tears on her cheeks.

Cap forced a smile and explained, "You could be anything you want to be: pilot, doctor, engineer, whatever. The whole universe is yours: take it."

Sarah looked at Mrs. Adams. "Is everything arranged?"

"Everything—clothes, food, fees. You can keep your own room. It's all been taken care of."

Sarah pulled her hands from Cap's. "Fine, then I'd better move all my stuff from the ship." She strode from the room, ignoring Cap's voice calling after her.

Her room was at the heart of the school, which was part of the repaired city dome. Sarah transferred her books and posters, but stowed them beneath her bunk and left the new walls bare. She lay on her back and listened to the circulating air, then the sudden bass thump of music from the room next door.

She wandered the busy corridors, acknowledgir the many greetings and ignoring the stares of the n arrivals. The landing terminal was packed with pas gers, mostly families returning home after r enforced separation. Sarah found herself at the de ed freight terminal; the scarred, pocked globe the *Jefferson* stood at the edge of the landing grids.

"Hey, beautiful."

Sarah turned and saw Garcia and held ou r hands to him. "Hey. I thought you'd left already."

"Cap asked for a later slot," said Garc

"Where is he?" asked Sarah.

"Right here," said Cap from the co r.

Garcia moved to the inner airlo d said, "You take care, Sarah. I'll see you soon." osed the inner door and left Cap and Sarah togeth

"I wanted to say goodbye," ap. "But your room was empty."

"I went for a walk, got som air," Sarah joked.

Cap crossed the room. "W t to leave."

"Sure." Sarah looked at floor, then at Cap. "I don't want to be alone." hrew her arms around him.

"I know, honey, I kn Cap soothed her, "but it's for the best, it really is. we'll come back whenever we can, I promise. But , you'll meet new friends, see new worlds, become ever you want to be."

Sarah pulled a and looked down into Cap's gleaming eyes. "I ared."

He nodded. "There's a lot to be scared about. But you can handle it; you're the strongest person I've ever met."

"But what will I do?" she asked.

"Whatever you want to. I heard that they've started working on the *Boreas* again; maybe they could use some help," said Cap. "How would you like to visit Ursa Major? Or travel further than I ever could? I don't know what's going to happen, but I know you'll be there, making me proud."

Garcia waved through the airlock door and Cap said, "I've got to go."

Sarah waited until he was in the lock, ready to close the doors, before she called out, "Thank you, Dad. For everything."

Cap smiled and raised a gloved hand as the doors closed. Sarah looked through the window, beyond the reflection of her own discordant features, as the *Jefferson* rose silently on a wavering column of energy; it left the moon's pitted surface and headed out, into the starlit void.

ALL WINTER LONG

Written by
Jae Brim

Illustrated by
Fritz Peters

About the Author

Jae Brim is an artist and actor, but mostly a writer, who wrote her first story in crayon at the age of six. She has been writing speculative fiction ever since, as stories just don't seem fun without magic or aliens, or both.

She is a graduate of the Clarion Writers' Workshop and the intensive theatre training program at the National Theatre Institute. She also received a bachelor's degree from Ithaca College. She is currently working on what she calls a "different kind of fantasy novel" and hopes to write many more after that. This is her first professionally published story.

Jae enjoys snorkeling, dancing all night and cooking gourmet dinners for her friends. She lives in New York City with her husband, Jesse, and two very spoiled cats.

About the Illustrator

Born and raised in the Los Angeles area, Fritz Peters began painting and drawing at the age of three. With the encouragement and support of his parents, he began attending private art classes at age nine. While still in high school, Fritz completed four semesters of fine and applied art courses at Pierce College in Woodland Hills, California. Following high school graduation, Fritz decided to continue his artistic endeavors primarily for non-commercial reasons.

In the early nineties, a friend introduced Fritz to Kelly Freas. After having reviewed Fritz's portfolio, Freas advised him to enter The L. Ron Hubbard Illustrators of the Future Contest. When Peters did not place as a finalist, he decided to take a break from competing. Instead, he devoted the following years to expanding his portfolio and to refining his artistic skills.

Fritz believes it is the artist's responsibility to draw attention to the divinity residing in all things. He is currently living in a small, modest Hindu retreat and is a student of Indian art, symbolism and iconography. His goal for his art is to fuse images of Americana with the beauty, spirituality and freedom of Indian art and philosophy.

was dreaming of the Wind King when Mammy woke me.

"Get up, Rune," she was yelling, shaking me roughly. Behind my closed eyes, the Wind King called me, his pale blue fingers caressing my skin.

"No," I mumbled, and curled farther into the bed. He was whispering in my ear, weaving stories of the beauty of ice.

"Up, Rune!" Mammy shouted, and pulled the blankets off me. I let out a shriek and sat up, the cold biting through my nightgown and into my bones. There was a sudden crash on the roof, as the Wind King disappeared behind my eyes. The wind came up with a roar against the windows and they shattered, spraying ice and glass in a fountain over my bed. Snow came swirling in, weaving itself around me, snaking out fingers to grab at my bare arm. I saw faces, coming out of the snow, and screamed again.

"Get downstairs, girl," Mammy yelled. She was already beginning to chant, mumbling to herself in an off-key alto. The snow pulled back suddenly, winding itself into a funnel on the floor. I ran out of my room, grabbing the comforter off my bed and tearing down the stairs.

In the main room, everything was quiet, like the calm before a thunderstorm. Upstairs I could hear

Mammy moving back and forth, her footsteps marking
out the rhythm of some strange dance, her voice rising
and falling in counterpoint to the scream of the wind
down the street outside.

Someone had wired all the window latches shut
with ivy. Strands of it criss-crossed the floor, and where
the ivy wasn't, frost patterns had crept over the cement
and slate. Branches of holly and rowan hung over the
front door, linked together with a spider web of blood-
red yarn. I followed the ivy through the main room and
back into the kitchen, where a big pot of it stood in front
of the back door, warding against the night.

I shivered, not from the cold, but from sudden, deep
fear. It had been a bad enough night already, with the
wind and the hail and the groan of the power lines
under the ice. It had been bad enough with me dreaming
of the Wind King. Now Mammy was making a witching
against snow in my bedroom, and someone had warded
the windows and doors more than usual. The yarn webs
were usually reserved for days when another witch was
after Mammy, and ivy is powerful magic. It stands for
life and sustainment. Feather, the herbalist down the
street, wraps people in it when her medicines aren't
working, and most of the time the ivy saves them.
Someone, probably Mammy, thought that this house
needed warding against death, and if Mammy thought
that, something big was happening.

The kitchen smelled like fish and burned roses. The
tables and chairs were all stacked haphazardly around
the edges of the room and a fire was burning in the
middle of the floor. Bits and pieces of whatever spell
Mammy was working on were scattered about:
eggshells and pastel-colored dresses, feathers and a
bouquet of dried flowers. The slate floor was covered
with chalk drawings of squiggles, arrows and squares,

the kind that Mammy and Mammy's adopted children use when they're making a witching. I can't draw them. I don't have that sort of power. But I was careful to step over them anyway. I didn't want to mess up whatever Mammy was doing.

There was about half a cup of coffee left in the percolator. I dumped it out and started a new pot, mixing nutmeg and pepper into the grounds. If Mammy had been working a witching all night, and was upstairs fighting the snow now, she would want some when she was done. Nutmeg and pepper are good for witches, or so Feather always told me. They bring the magic back into the blood.

I sat down on one of the rickety wooden chairs and curled up under my comforter, trying to ward away the chill. Behind my eyes, the memory of the Wind King's blue face and icy gray eyes laughed at me. Winter had hit the City of Dreams long and hard and wouldn't let it go. It used to be the Poet King would cast his magic about mid-March, using words and fire to send winter away. But the Poet King had been dead almost eighteen years, killed by frostbite and pneumonia, and it was almost April, with no sign of the snow stopping.

—*Death*—the wind whispered in my ears, and the Wind King laughed. His voice wrapped around me, drowning out the bubble of the percolator, and I listened as it spoke of expanses of white, death and cold like sleep. The light started to turn blue, becoming deeper and dimmer. The Wind King sang, coaxing me into a bed made of glaciers and black ice with a lullaby of hypothermia.

"Out of my kitchen!" Mammy yelled, and I looked up to see her standing in the door, hissing and spitting at frost patterns on the floor. She was wearing nothing

Illustrated by Fritz Peters

but a pink bathing suit and her white bathrobe, and her
gray hair was tousled. She gestured sharply at me and
I gasped at the sudden warmth in my legs. My toes
were purple and blue and there was frost all over the
comforter.

"That's twice I saved you tonight, girl," Mammy
said, coming into the room. "You're mighty stupid,
sitting here daydreaming about ice while winter is after
you. Is there any coffee?"

"Yes," I said.

"Wouldn't be surprised if it's gone cold. Pour me
some, and make it sweet. I'm going to need the power
before this night is over." She turned and started poking
around in the now dying fire with a long fork. I poured
coffee and limped over to the fridge for cream.

"What do you mean, the Wind King—"

"*Ssss.* Don't mention him, girl. He'll hear you and
come raging into my house to get back his name. I'm
having enough trouble keeping him out as it is." She
grunted and stabbed the fork into something. "Here.
Pull this out for me, will you?"

I traded her the coffee cup for the fork and pulled a
foil-wrapped package out of the fire. I placed it on the
table and unwrapped it, burning my fingers. It was a
whole trout, stuffed full of something. Its skin was
burned in an elaborate pattern of spirals and curving lines.

"It's for you," Mammy said, sitting down. The chair
creaked under her weight.

I sniffed at the fish, smelling sage, thyme and nuts.
"What are you giving this to me for, Mammy?" I asked.
"This has magic all over it. I don't have any magic."

"Shut up and eat it, will you?" Mammy said. "I'm
trying to save you, even after you've brought winter

into my house. Have a little respect." I got a knife off the wall and sat down on the table.

"Is there any lemon?" I asked, slicing off a piece of fish. Hazelnuts and pecans fell out from the inside.

"Lemon doesn't go with this spell," said Mammy, and stared into her coffee mug.

I ate. The fish tasted like charcoal and wild thyme and nuts. I chewed and listened to the hail rattling against the windows while Mammy drank coffee in angry silence.

"Tell me the story of the trout of wisdom," Mammy said suddenly.

"Old folk tale," I said, around a mouthful of fish. Mammy's always doing this, asking me about myths she thinks I should know. "Supposedly, there was a fish that ate the nuts that fell from the tree of wisdom. This guy wants to eat it, because if you do, you suddenly know the answers to everything. So he has some hero catch it and cook it for him, and then the guy eats it, and nothing happens. He gets angry and starts yelling at the hero, asking him if he ate any of the fish. The hero says, 'No, no, I didn't eat any of it,' but then he remembers that the skin blistered up and he smoothed out the blister with his thumb. Anyway, the point is that all the wisdom was in that blister, so now the hero has all the wisdom of the world in his thumb. Whenever he sucks it, he knows the answers to everything. And the moral of the story is: sucking your thumb does not make you smart."

Mammy snorted. "Actually, that story is a crock. It probably never happened. But there is some truth in it. A trout has a poet's gift locked inside it and nuts are only stored knowledge. You give a poet a trout, and stuff it with nuts, you give him strength."

"What's that got to do with me, Mammy?" I asked.

"I got a story for you, girl," Mammy said, "one I know even you haven't heard before. Happened almost

eighteen years ago, in a winter as bad as this. Late at
night, a woman comes knocking on my door. The cold
had hold of her so bad she was practically purple, and
she was holding a baby in her arms, a scrawny,
screaming thing. 'Lady,' I said, 'I don't take in kids
anymore. All mine are grown. Besides, this one hasn't
got any magic. I can smell it.' 'Mammy,' the lady said,
'you have to take this one. Dad's dead, mum's dead,
there isn't anyone to take care of it.' 'What's that got to
do with it?' I said. 'Lots of kids out there without
parents.' 'Quit being a stubborn bitch, Mammy,' the
lady said. She was shaking badly and the snow was
swirling around her. 'This is the Poet King's heir. Winter
killed off her father, and tonight it's killed her mother,
and by morning, it will probably have killed me. This
child needs to be protected or else winter isn't ever
going to leave this city.' I looked at the baby, and I
looked at the woman. 'Why doesn't she have any magic
then?' I asked. 'If this kid is the Poet King's heir, she
should stink of magic.' 'Her magic is a different sort,'
said the lady. 'It's the magic of words and legends, not
the kind we practice.' I stood there and I listened hard,
as if I could hear that baby's thoughts, and somewhere
I felt something, a heat beating out of it.

"So I took it in. Would have asked the woman in too,
but she wouldn't have any of that. Went back out and
the snow followed her down the street. They found her
dead the next morning, frozen solid.

"And that baby grew up, and now that baby is you.
Kept you hidden from the winter for eighteen years
now, while the Poet King's power still lasted in this city.
But now it's fading, girl, and you have to get it back.
Winter's going to hold this city for good if you don't."

My skin went very hot and then very cold, chills
scattering over my back. I pushed the fish away, my
appetite gone.

"Me?" I blurted out. "Are you crazy? I'm not the Poet King's heir or anything close! That woman switched kids on you."

Mammy laughed, a high, coarse noise. "I thought the same thing once upon a time. For years, the Poet King's power still worked in this city, and you grew up without any power at all. But this winter's been different. I've been watching, these past few months, as the winter gets colder and deeper. I've been watching, as it follows you around, making snow devils and frostbite to trap you, and you just walk right past it without any fear at all. You are the Poet King's heir. I know it, and winter knows it, and it's time now that you did something about it."

"I don't have any power, Mammy," I said. Visions of the Poet King were spinning through my head, of him facing down the seasons at the edge of the Break. "And I'm a rotten poet, for all you have me reading all the time."

"You don't have powers like a witch does," Mammy said. She tapped her head. "Your powers are locked up here. You have to go find your father, get him to unlock them, to give over the seasons to your control. It's the only way that you're going to do anything."

"My father's dead," I said, but even as I said it I knew what I would have to do. We live in the City of Dreams, which hangs between the Land Beyond and the land of the living. Here, there are two ways to inherit a power. A person can gift it to you when they die or can't use it anymore. The other way is to find a person's ghost, to walk through the Break around the city, into the Land Beyond, and call their ghost to you.

"Mammy," I said, "I can't do that. I can't walk into the mists. I wouldn't even know where to begin."

"Quit your whining," Mammy said. "Do you think I spent all these years giving you a poet's training to have you just throw it away? You know the way to do it, even if you think you don't. Why do you think I had you spending time with that herbalist, Feather? You know every legend and story there is, even if you haven't used them yet. I made you a fish, stuffed full of magic just for you, to make you strong for what you have to do. And you got a family to help you, all my children. Go see Netica. She can help. Now get back to sleep. Not in your room," she said sharply, as I got up. "You go sleep in the nursery—under the ivy and next to the fire. That room's warded so tight that nothing's going to get in."

I went upstairs. On my right, the door to my room was blocked by a holly bush and three pink-and-yellow beach towels. I could still hear the Wind King's voice through it, the sound of symphonies played with ice crystals against windows. It reached out toward me, dusting my skin like soft feathers. I leaned toward the doorway, wanting the Wind King's hands to wrap around my shoulders and bury me in new snow, but the beach towels stopped me with a blast of summer. The smell of wet sand, wildflowers and fresh tomatoes thrust out at me, blocking the Wind King's power. I turned away and ran into the nursery, toward the heat and light of the fire under the painted spirals of the wards.

Mammy had made a bed on the floor in front of the fireplace out of down comforters and flannel sheets. I curled up in it, but I couldn't sleep. The things that Mammy had said to me kept running through my head. I thought over what I knew of the Poet King and wondered how I could stand to inherit his powers.

If anyone knew what the Poet King's powers actually were, it might be easier. There are plenty of stories about who the Poet King was and what his powers controlled. Before the Break happened, the Poet King was just a guy like anyone else, or so the stories go. After the Break appeared, when the city broke off from the rest of the world, the Poet King was given the gift to control the seasons, since they didn't want to move in their regular cycle by themselves. According to the stories, he would face off with them at the edge of the Land Beyond, calling their spirits past the Break and forcing them to his will, but none of the stories say how he actually did it.

Mammy believed that I had the power and the training to be the next Poet King—or Queen, if I wanted to get technical. It made me feel better that she believed in me. Mammy is a powerful witch, perhaps the most powerful in the City of Dreams, but even her faith didn't make what I had to do any easier.

Ghosts don't really come out of the Land Beyond, no matter what people say. They just mill around the edges, wishing they could leave, but they don't really have the strength to do it. Even once you're inside the Break, you need something to call them to you, something that they want more than they want to stay safe. Pieces of hair and lost possessions work well, but the best thing to have is their skull.

I smiled to myself, as the firelight laughed me to sleep. There was a story I knew, a story that might lead me to the Poet King's bones. Tomorrow I would go visit Raven.

I woke to a sudden stillness, an absence of the clattering ice and whistling wind. Above me, the thin winter sun shone through the skylight. The presence of the Wind King, so apparent the night before, was gone, retreating from the daylight. The deep cold of him still lingered behind and I dressed quickly, in layers of thermal underwear and heavy sweaters.

Mammy was still asleep when I came downstairs, exhausted after her work the night before. She couldn't have been asleep long because there was coffee waiting for me and a plate of scones. Next to the scones was a thin ivy necklace with garnet beads intertwined in it. The ivy was twisted and woven, so that the garnets became eyes in tiny giggling faces. It seemed to move when I touched it and to speak my name. —Rune— I picked it up and put it on, and it seemed to glue itself around my throat.

I went outside, nibbling on the last of the scones. The streets were painted white with new snow and the eaves of the pale brown townhouses were dusted with it. The power lines were frosted with ice from the storm last night, and they caught the pale morning sun in a thousand diamond facets. I walked to the trolley stop, past closed bars and coffee shops with steamed-up windows. Memories of my dreams followed me. I kept seeing the Wind King in the icicles, finding glimpses of his face in the drifts that covered the trash barrels. Each time, a thrill raced through me, at the thought of hearing his song, of being touched by his chill blue fingers. I pushed it down. I was the heir to the Poet King, which meant the Wind King was my enemy. He would kill me to keep the City of Dreams under ice.

The trolley came quickly, which surprised me. Most of the winter, the trolleys came late, or not at all. This one was covered with rust and dirty snow, and it smelled like smoke, onions and sweat. There were a few passengers; most of them bundled into winter furs and down parkas, on their way to their jobs in offices or factories. Their faces were white and drawn and their eyes spoke of sadness and defeat. I curled up in my plastic seat and listened to the trolley creak and groan on its tracks.

• • •

Raven lived out on the western edge of the city, where the row houses, gray warehouses and deserted skyscrapers give way to the empty expanses of the bone-yards. I got off the trolley at the last stop and walked the rest of the way. The graves were all covered with snow, leaving a pitted expanse of white that stretched to the Break shimmering in the distance.

Raven lived in an old bomb shelter, most of it buried so far underground that none of the seasons reached him. There are almost as many legends about Raven's house as there are about the man himself. Very few people have been inside it. Supposedly, it extends back under the ground and half of it really exists in the Land Beyond. The house didn't look like a place where the Land Beyond came into the city, but I couldn't see much of it.

It was mounded over with ice and snow, and a tunnel had been carved into the drifts, leading down toward the door. A huge archway of bones, glued and nailed together in a complex pattern, soared over the tunnel. Little tinfoil birds hung off of it, tied to the arch with bits of ivy and red string. Designs had been sketched out in red dye around the edges of the drifts and their surface was covered with totems of fur and glass. Huge holly branches stuck out of the snow and stuffed owls were perched on them. They watched me with glass eyes, their necks swiveling to follow me as I moved.

Wind chimes sang a warning as I approached the archway and I stopped, unsure of what to do. Raven was a person of legend. Witches whisper stories about him to each other, how his powers are unlike anyone else's. There are even rumors that he is not human, but a spirit that came out of the Land Beyond when the Break opened and chose to remain here. He brings things to the witches: seaweed, cactuses and bones from ancient animals. Things that could never be found in the City of Dreams.

I had never been introduced to Raven, but I believed he knew who I was. When I was young, he would sometimes come to visit Feather, and they would talk for hours, in a language that I did not understand. I could remember him watching me play in front of the fire, watching me so intently I could feel that chill of his black eyes going into my skin. Maybe he knew my heritage before I did, without Mammy ever telling him. Maybe that alone would get me in to see him.

If Raven's magic were anything like Mammy's or her children's, the design of bones was a warding, meant to trap people who were uninvited. I turned toward the mouth of the tunnel, careful not to step on any of the dyed designs.

"I am Rune," I said to the archway, and waited. The wind chimes stopped and the dye at my feet faded away, leaving just enough room for me to pass. I walked down the tunnel and knocked on the pockmarked metal door at the end. For a long time, nothing happened. I held my breath, hoping that Raven was home, hoping that he wasn't waiting for me to go away. The wind howled outside, mocking me. I bit my lip and decided to wait.

After an endless while, the door swung open with a blast of heat and firelight. Raven stood there, towering over me. His long hair fell around his pale face, blending into the brown and black of his fur cloak.

"Hello, Rune," he said. His voice was soft and deep, like still water. "It seems you really do intend to see me. Will you come in?" He held the door open, waiting for me. I took a deep breath and walked in, barely having to duck to walk under his arm. A deep throb sang through me as I crossed the threshold, as if I had become a part of another world.

Raven's home was a gigantic cavern of crumbling cement and granite, the ceiling supported here and there with tarred beams. The entire place was a maze, with walls of climbing ivy and stacks of nameless bones. Old leather-bound books lined the walls, covered with dust and spider webs. Cats and raccoons ran about the wooden floor, and far off I heard the chirping of birds and the noise of running water. Raven led me around a weathered statue surrounded by orange trees and into a small clear area before a huge fireplace.

"Please sit," he said, gesturing toward a faded armchair. "May I take your coat?"

"Yes," I said, and struggled out of it. It was hot next to the fire, and the orange trees smelled like a humid August day. Raven hung my coat on a branch sticking out of the wall and sat down. I sat down opposite him, suddenly very nervous.

"It is unusual," Raven said, "for people to come here. I could feel you standing outside my door, hoping and wishing to come in and now you are silent. What is it you need so badly that you would come here?"

"I need a skull," I blurted out.

Raven laughed, an unexpected noise like water over smooth rocks. "Skulls are not my specialty. You should have gone to Melissa by the Fringe."

"I need a skull that you can get for me," I said, and stopped again. Maybe the story was only a myth, something that Feather had told me to keep me amused when

I was young. Maybe Raven was only a strange spirit and could not give me what I needed.

He watched me, waiting for me to say something or leave.

"Let me tell you a story," I said finally, and felt a surge of something inside me, a bubble of excitement waiting to get out. "It's a story that only you and Feather and I know, and it might not be true, but it is the only help I have right now. I am the Poet King's heir—or so I have been told—and I need his skull to inherit his powers. It would be easy to find Melissa and tell her where to dig in the boneyards, but the Poet King's grave is not marked. He might not even be buried. Most people say that the Poet King gifted his powers into the City of Dreams as he died, threw them up as a barrier to ward off the seasons forever, but this story says differently. This story says that a man took the Poet King's body. He took it into the Fringe, right to the edge of the Break where the ground turns to mist and the sky is gold. This man, with the help of an herbalist you and I both know, burned the Poet King's body. He burned it in a fire of rosewood, which rested on a slab of black ice. He threw roses and autumn leaves, robin's egg shells and bits of white rabbit fur into the fire, binding all the seasons into it. The fire burned all night and the man chanted over the fire, drawing the Poet King's ghost into the land, to last until his heir was old enough to take his place.

"When the morning came, there was nothing left of the Poet King's body but his bones. The man who made the spell took the bones and hid them deep in the ground, too far for any season to reach, and the spell lasted. It lasted for eighteen years, and now I am here. I am the Poet King's heir and I am asking you for those bones." Excitement rushed through me and was gone. I leaned back in my chair and looked at Raven, feeling very drained.

"Where did you hear that story?" Raven asked. His eyes were very bright and his face was suddenly lined with an ancient pain.

"Feather told it to me," I said, "a long time ago."

"Why did she tell it to you?" he said, ignoring me.

"I don't know," I said. "Because I am supposed to be a poet."

"You know nothing," Raven said harshly. "You are the Poet King's child, but you are not the Poet King's heir. You have no idea of what those words even mean. You are merely a girl who has heard too many stories and does not know how to use the knowledge in them. You are not walking into the Break with my friend's bones this winter. You will only lose them to the Wind King."

"Like hell I will," I snapped, and felt that surge in my bones again. Raven shot me a look. I ignored him. "You can give me that skull, or I will walk into the Land Beyond without it. Look at the signs. There isn't time to wait another winter. The Wind King isn't strong enough to come through the Break yet, but he's in power in the Land Beyond. He's taken care of summer, spring and fall, and now he wants us. Right now he's just reaching through, dumping ice all over this city. But he wants out, so bad he can taste it, and he's getting stronger every day. You may be the only one who hasn't felt it, buried down here with all your magic, but you will. Someday, and someday soon, he's going to get through the Break, and even you will feel his power."

For a long moment, the room was very quiet. Even the cats and raccoons were silent.

"You do not understand," Raven said weakly.

"I understand that this city is dying," I said. "What more do you want?"

"You sound like your father. Maybe you do have more of him in you than I thought. You even look like him," Raven said. He stared at me and I squirmed, knowing he was seeing dark hair and too pale skin. He sighed, a sound like wind through spring leaves. "There is a place in the center of the Fringe, an old fountain. A long time ago, I cast a spell there, and planted holly bushes around it to ward the spell from harm. There you will find what you are looking for."

"Thank you," I said, trying to be polite.

"It will not be as easy as you think, Rune. Your father's bones cannot be dug up by any natural means. They are charmed so that only the Poet King's heir can find them."

"What do I do?" I asked. "How do I break the spell?"

Raven smiled. "If I told you that, you would be using my magic and not your own, and the bones would not recognize you. A true poet creates her own magic. You must use the knowledge within you to create yours."

• • •

Outside, the sun was still shining and the sky was blue overhead, for the first time in weeks. I walked toward the trolley stop, thinking about what Raven had said.

The Fringe runs along the eastern edge of the City of Dreams. It is a jumble of ruins, where the wind has voices and strange creatures live. According to all the myths, it is the place where the Break actually began, before it tore wide open and broke this city off from the land of the living. I didn't know how true that was, but it is the place where the Land Beyond is closest to the

City of Dreams. Madmen, demons and other things not quite human walk through its streets. Most people avoid it altogether. Witches only go there when it is absolutely necessary, and they always use charms and wardings to keep themselves safe.

Even if I found the Poet King's—my father's—skull, I still had to take it through the Break and into the Land Beyond. Walking through the Break would be easy. Ordinary people do it all the time by mistake. Surviving and walking out again would be the hard part. That would take powerful magic, the kind that I could only begin to imagine. There are creatures in the Land Beyond, ghosts and demons that live on the other side of the Break and want out. Most of them would love to eat a human or, even better, to have a body to walk back into the land of the living with. There were ways to ward off ghosts, stories about people who had walked through the Break and survived, but it took magic that I couldn't perform. I needed the help of a very powerful witch.

I decided to go see Netica.

•••

Netica is the youngest of Mammy's other children, which makes her the closest thing that I have to an older sister. She owns a restaurant down on the Shell, the business district, which makes her a lot of money. It's a very popular place with people who aren't witches—rich businessmen and the like. Most of them don't know that Netica owns a restaurant for one reason: it gives her the sort of kitchen she needs to work in. Netica creates big spells, long spells, ones that take weeks to prepare and cook down and draw out. The thing is, they work. They always work. If anyone were going to be able to help me, it would be her.

The Shell is full of old stone buildings, their facades carved with gargoyles and flowers. Netica's restaurant is on the bottom floor of one of them, next to an antique store. I avoided the front of the restaurant and went into the kitchen through the back door. Inside was a sudden blast of warmth and activity after the chill emptiness of the winter streets outside. Netica's kitchen was a huge room, full of stoves and grills, all with gas fires burning in them. The walls were covered with layers of scribbled spells, the place warded so tightly that not even a fly could get in.

It was lunchtime and cooks were flying about, yelling and handing plates full of food to waiters and waitresses. Netica was in the middle of it, giving orders to everyone, blonde braids flying and green eyes snapping. She saw me and handed her sauté pan off to an assistant. I hung back, away from the bustling waitstaff, and waited until Netica crossed over to me.

"What're you doing here?" she asked, giving me a hug.

"I need a favor," I said. My face felt flushed from the heat.

"I don't have any money," Netica said quickly. "If you want a job, you should go back to that herbalist, where you belong. Do you want some food?"

"I don't need any money. I need you to do some magic for me."

"Hah! If you need magic, go to Mammy. She's much better than me."

"Mammy sent me to you. She said that you would be able to help me walk through the Break." Netica's perfect eyebrows shot up.

"What in all the hells do you think you're going to do, girl? Why do you want to do some crazy thing like that?"

Netica was staring at me, so sure of herself, and I didn't know what to say. In Netica's kitchen, warded and full of heat and light and energy, the night before seemed like a bad dream. The Wind King faded away, turning into a child's story.

"I'm the Poet King's heir," I said, trying to steady my voice. "Mammy told me so, and the Wind King is after me."

"Gerard," Netica yelled. A large man by one of the stoves looked at us. "Take over!" She grabbed me by the arm and dragged me out of the kitchen and down the hall to her office. The floor was covered in woven rugs and a huge fire burned in the fireplace. Netica pushed me down onto a velvet couch and stood in front of me, arms crossed.

"You can stop messing around now, Rune," she said. "You've got my attention."

"I'm being serious, Netica," I said, getting angry. "This is not me trying to pretend to be something I am not. Even Raven believes I'm the Poet King's heir."

"You went to see Raven!" Netica sat down on the desk. "You really are serious. Are you sure Mammy isn't making this up to get you out of the way? Maybe she has a boyfriend or something."

"I've never seen her more serious. She even made a witching and fed it to me. I didn't know what to think."

"And what do you think, Rune?" Netica asked. "Do you believe her?"

"Yes," I said. "No. I don't know." I wanted to tell Netica about the feeling in my bones when I faced down Raven, to ask her if it meant that I had power after all, but I couldn't. Netica had spent too much time teasing me for not being a witch when I was young.

"I have to believe it," I said finally. "It's the only thing that makes sense."

"And what does this have to do with me?" Netica asked.

"The Poet King's powers are still bound to his ghost. I have to bring them back from the Land Beyond. Raven has given me a key to call the Poet King's ghost to me, and I can walk through the Break. I need you to make a warding for me, to protect me against the rest of the spirits."

"Are you joking?" Netica exclaimed. "You don't really think that you can walk into the Land Beyond and then just walk out. Once you're in, you're gone. That's it."

"That's not true," I said. "There are stories, lots of stories, of people walking through the Break and back out."

"Exactly," said Netica, "they're stories. Fairy tales. That's it."

"Listen to me," I said, and felt that strange strength run through me. "There is a story that happened just after the Break opened. The Break sliced through the city and separated a man and his wife, leaving him in the City of Dreams and her in the land of the living. The man was young and in love and could not stand to be separated from his wife. So he made a spell and walked across the Land Beyond and into the land of the living to find her. He bathed himself in the juice of summer grapes and rosewater and carved charms into his skin. He glued mirrors onto his eyes so that the ghosts could not see his spirit. He bound his wrists and chest with nettles and thorns so that the ghosts would not hear the beating of his heart. He disguised himself so well that when he got to the land of the living, his wife did not recognize him."

Netica opened her mouth to say something.

"There is another story," I said, cutting her off, "of a woman who wove a wall around herself with music. She sang old songs of true love and summer, and the ghosts were so entranced by the sound of her voice that they forgot to believe they were alive and fell into a sleep like a second death. These are not stories that I made up, Netica, these are based in reality. They are things that really did happen."

"He warded his skin?" said Netica, concentrating very hard on something.

"Yes," I said. "There's another story of a man who sat on the edge of the Fringe—"

"Enough stories," Netica said. "You know too many stories." I smiled. Netica was right. If there was a myth or legend in the City of Dreams, I knew it. I could feel them crawling under my skin, waiting for someone to listen to them.

"You want a ghost warding that is part of your skin?" Netica asked me.

"If that's the way to do it," I said. "I don't know the spells, Netica. I just know what I need to do." Netica nodded. She went to her desk and began getting out big, thick pieces of colored chalk.

"We do a spell like this, Rune," she said, "we're going to have to do it in layers. I've got some things that might work. Some salve, some herbs, some things I can cook up quickly. I can put a witching on your body so the ghosts won't be able to take it. But it's going to take a little while and"—she grimaced—"I can't promise it's going to feel too good."

"That's all right," I said. "As long as it gets me in and out alive."

"Right," Netica said and stood up. "I'm going to have to close the restaurant and send for Ari. This is too big for me to do on my own."

•••

Netica closed the restaurant, but the kitchen was still full of people. Most of the cooks were running around moving furniture to the sides of the room. Waiters were scrubbing the floor. There was a group of people, still in busboy uniforms, cutting up a holly bush in one corner. Holly stands for life in the middle of a wasteland, for rebirth from barrenness. I shivered.

Ari arrived, shedding a long cloak and a mountain of snow. Ari is another one of Mammy's kids, a lot older than me. He was always very quiet and seemed a little mysterious to me. He said something to Netica and a small army of people began to run back and forth, carrying loads of hothouse flowers, potted ivy, brightly colored satin and yellow candles. I stood in a corner and watched, fascinated. I'd never been to a big witching like this before. When I was young, and Mammy and the rest of her children were working, they would send me out to Feather's or tell me to stay in the nursery. The sounds of their chanting, and the smells of burning sage and flowers, would filter up the stairs. I would lie in bed and sniff the air, identifying each herb, each smell and its uses: roses, for life and true love; thyme, for age; beer, for illusions. Now I was not only part of it, I was the center of it.

•••

The entire restaurant was at work, clearing the space Netica needed for her designs. All the cooks and waiters, dishwashers and bartenders had suddenly become apprentices, arranging piles of flowers and setting tall wax candles on every available surface, even on the floor and the beams in the ceiling. They arranged prep tables and stools in a circle and laid the tools of Netica's magic over them: bundles of wilting summer flowers, nettles, trailing vines of ivy, preserved butterflies, bunches of herbs and bits of animal bones. There were tins of beeswax and tubes of sunscreen, fresh tomatoes and dried cherries—everything filled with the memory of heat and long days spent lounging under the sun.

Finally, everything was ready. The scurrying people melted off into the shadows, going home in the cold evening light. Netica stood in the center of the spotless white floor, a piece of pink chalk in her hand. Ari was at one of the stoves, throwing what looked like bird wings and aloe into a pot.

"Rune," Netica said, "come here." I walked over to her, feeling a little overwhelmed by the effort that was going into my protection.

"You're going to have to take off your clothes," Netica said. I did, and stood shivering in the middle of the room.

"Okay," Netica said. She took a deep breath and looked at Ari. Ari nodded. Netica reached out to the base of my skull and began to draw.

The chalk made slight hissing noises as it passed over my skin. It felt like greased sandpaper. At the stove, Ari was humming to himself. Netica circled around me, bringing her designs down my legs and onto the floor. She stood and looked at me, her eyes full of light and heat.

"One," she said. Ari lifted the pot off the stove, blew on it and brought it over to where we stood. "Close your eyes."

"This might hurt," Ari said, and poured an avalanche of fire over my head. I screamed as the melted beeswax crawled into my skin and disappeared in tiny sparkles of lavender light.

"Lie down," Netica said and her voice seemed to come from a long way away. I did, and it felt like the designs on the floor surged up and wrapped around me like a blanket.

The rest of the night was a blur. Netica drew and chanted and Ari poured wax and scented water over me. They showered me with rose petals and stuck butterflies in my hair. They chanted and danced together, circling around me to a beat that only they could hear. The air was sometimes full of colored light, and sometimes it was too dark to see at all. I slept and woke and slept again, and sometimes Netica looked like a figure of smoke and sometimes she was herself, sweating and biting her lip. Their voices went on and on, and then Ari would pour something over me, this time smelling of tomatoes and rosemary, this time of cumin and dried bones, and I would sleep again. One time I woke and the entire room was filled with smoke. It smelled of fresh peaches, of lakes under the sun, of the heat before a thunderstorm. It wrapped around me, reminding me of a safe sometime in the heart of summer that stung my eyes and brought a lump into my throat. I breathed it into me, aching to be there, and slept again.

•••

I woke up in the center of the kitchen. My eyes were stiff with sleep and the floor around me was covered in chalk drawings. There were sheets of orange and purple silk draped over me. My arms were so covered with scribbles that they blended into the floor.

My skin felt like it was full of fire. It tingled and snapped as I moved, cutting little arcs through the air. I sat up slowly, wrapping the silk around me. Something pulled at my throat. I reached up to feel what it was and found the ivy necklace. I had forgotten to take it off and now it felt like it was part of me, the ivy and garnets embedded in my skin.

The entire kitchen was a mess. The neat piles of herbs and flowers were gone, replaced by tiny twigs and knuckle bones. Ari was nowhere to be seen. Netica was sitting on the floor opposite me, leaning against a cabinet. There were huge dark circles under her eyes and her hair was matted to her neck. She smiled when she saw me.

"Good morning, sleepyhead," she said. "How are you feeling?"

"My skin feels like it doesn't belong to me," I said. "What did you do?"

"I drew a witching on you and Ari sealed it into your skin," Netica said simply. "It should ward off any ghost that comes along, not to mention mosquitoes, bats and frostbite."

"There are mosquitoes in the Land Beyond?" I said.

"Who knows," Netica said and yawned. "It's just a side effect. You smell pretty good, too."

"Where are my clothes?" I asked.

"They're over here," Netica said, getting up and walking over to one of the tables.

She picked up my coat, and for a minute I didn't recognize it because it had been dyed purple. "Ari boiled them with lavender and nettles, to put a spell in them. If you wear them now, a ghost won't see the spell in your skin. It probably won't be able to see you at all."

I walked over to the table and put them on. They were a little stiff, and my boots had shrunk, but they fit all right. Netica watched me.

"There's another thing," she said, and held something out to me. I took it and nettles stung my palm. It was a rope, with nettles and red yarn twisted around it.

"What's this?" I asked.

"If a witch is calling a spirit up," Netica said, "they usually tie themselves to a rock or a building, something that only exists here. I figure that if you want to walk into the Land Beyond and come out, you'll need something to anchor you here, in the City of Dreams. I tried to bind the spell in your skin into the floor here, but if that doesn't work, this rope has a binding in it. Throw it behind you as you walk into the Break, and if you follow it back, it will bring you home."

"I can't even pay you," I said. Tears were pricking at my eyes, "You've done all this for me and I can't do anything for you."

"Stop that," Netica said. "If you cry, you'll smudge the spell. You can come back alive and that will be payment enough." She looked at me like she was going to cry herself, and walked out of the room.

• • •

It was early daylight when I left Netica's, that time right after dawn when the sky is shades of pale purples and grays. I put the rope in the pocket of my coat and walked east toward the Fringe, avoiding slick spots of new ice. Inside Netica's kitchen, the cold outside had seemed something remote and distant, but out in the empty streets I could feel the Wind King's presence everywhere. It felt like he was searching for me, reaching out from behind the Break to hunt me down. It made me want to run and hide, but I kept walking toward the Fringe, putting one foot in front of the other. I had put too much into finding my father's ghost to give up now.

The skyscrapers and closed shops around me gave way to abandoned warehouses with shattered windows, surrounded by old newspapers and frozen litter. The street became narrower until it suddenly ended all together at the edge of a long downward slope.

The Fringe spread out before me, a maze of bleached concrete and broken brick meandering down the hillside toward the Break. In some places, walls were still intact, empty windows looking into old courtyards where statues stood on pedestals half covered over by snow. Around its edges were shacks of fiberboard and old stone. Some of them had twisted swirling designs painted over them in shades of gray and magenta. Others were protected by sheets of fabric twined with nettles and stick figurines, which flapped in the harsh wind. Smoke rose up out of the roofs of some of the shacks, and I could see people, dressed in bundled layers of fur and wool, beginning to move around in the day. Above everything the Break hung, wavering like heat waves in the eastern sky.

I started toward it, walking along what might have been a street. I could see no sign of a fountain surrounded by holly bushes, but that didn't surprise me. Everything is hard to find in the Fringe. It hides things so that nothing is ever in the place that it seemed to be the last time. It is better to stumble across places in the Fringe. If you go looking for something, the streets will switch around on you, leading you farther and farther until you suddenly walk through the Break and into the Land Beyond.

I walked, trying not to think about my father's grave. Instead I looked about me, trying to catch signs that I was moving too close to the Break. When we were children, Mammy would tell us how to stay away from the Break. The first thing to do was to avoid the Fringe, the boneyards, anything that came near the Break or the ghosts that inhabit it. It was too late for that now, but her other warnings still helped. Be careful if the sky turns green and be afraid if it turns to gold. If you find yourself in the mists, about to walk through the Break, keep walking away from the wind until you see something human, and then run in the opposite direction. I walked, avoiding patches of fog, keeping one eye on the sky and the other on the ground, looking for patches of ice.

The silence of the Fringe wrapped around me until I felt that I was a part of it: a voiceless creature walking forever through frozen ruins. I was just beginning to enjoy it when I found what I was looking for.

The grave was in the center of one of the courtyards, surrounded by bleached brick walls. It was a round pool, filled with dirt and puddles of ice. It might have once been a fountain, and I could see traces of carved seashells and mermaids around its edges. The ground around it was covered with the bones of small animals, laid out as if in warning, and three holly bushes grew up out of the center of it, like sentinels.

I sat down on the lip of the pool, unsure of what to do. The great holly bushes towered above me, their dark leaves and shiny berries shaking in the wind. My father's bones were buried under their roots. The holly and animal bones had protected him for eighteen years, keeping him safe from the seasons. Now I had to break Raven's spell, something so powerful I couldn't even begin to understand it.

Maybe Raven was wrong and I could dig them up. Maybe the spell meant that I was the only one who could. I took off my glove and touched the dirt inside the pool to see how frozen it was. A shock ran through my fingers, a recognition of sorts. I flinched back and rubbed my hand. The ground had known me. A shiver of fear and excitement climbed up my spine. I could feel a myth growing inside my memory, clawing its way up to my mouth.

"There was a pair of twins once," I said to the waiting ground. "A boy and a girl. Their parents planted two rowan trees side by side the day they were born and the children grew up as the trees did, side by side, their lives entwined together. They were never without each other, and they were happy.

"One day a force reached out from the Land Beyond, a spirit who saw their happiness and was jealous of it. It split the trees apart, killing them with a bolt of lightning, and when the spirit did that, it turned the twins against each other. It disguised their bodies and minds so that they no longer recognized each other. But they were still bound together, so they became bitter enemies. They fought each other, in wars that killed thousands of people, and kept fighting, until only the two of them were left. They fought first with swords, and when they broke, they fought with their hands. But when they touched, the magic the spirit had made was broken.

"If two people are related, they share a magic that is part of each of them, and that magic will recognize itself, through touch and through blood."

I stared down at the dirt inside the pool. Touch was not enough. I needed blood to speak to my father's bones. I groped in the dirt and ice for anything sharp to cut myself with. There was nothing by the pool, but I found a shard of glass in the far corner of the courtyard. I brought it back over to the pool and took off my gloves. I picked up the shard and brought it down against the ball of my thumb. Blood spurted out and I screamed, dropping the glass, as the blood ran down my hand and onto the dirt in the pool.

A deep rumble sounded underneath my feet. I dropped down and lay flat, thinking it was an earthquake. The earth twisted and buckled underneath me, bits of stone from the filled pool falling around me. I covered my head and hung on, hoping a falling rock wouldn't kill me.

The ground finally stopped moving, shifting the world back into perspective. For a long while I lay there, holding on to the ice and snow, feeling the silence around me. A bird cried, a long way away, and the wind sighed through the holly, calling my name.

—*Rune*—

I rolled over and looked up. A skull sat on the edge of the pool. Its eyeless sockets stared at me, grinning as if they could still see. I got up, brushing snow and dust off of myself, and picked up the skull. It was surprisingly light, the bone smooth under my bare hands. I turned it over, feeling it move against my skin, looking at its old ivory color. My blood ran onto it, turning it pale mahogany. I wondered what it had looked like when it was the man who was my father, when it spoke and forced the change of seasons through its voice. I wondered what that voice had been like. Was it low and soft like Raven's, or old and worn like Mammy's? I wished it could speak now, begged it to, but it was only dry bones.

•••

I walked out of the courtyard and stood, looking up at the Break. Finding the Break is always easy. It is all around the city, like unnatural heat waves in the sky. The mists hang around it, manifestations of ghosts wanting to get back into the City of Dreams. In front of me, the sky wavered like paper in the wind and the mists boiled out of it, aching toward the city. I clutched my father's skull to me, ignored my nerves and walked toward it.

A wide road opened up before me, walls and ruins melting away. The Fringe knew what I wanted and was pushing me toward it instead of leading me away. The Break stood in front of me and my first step took me halfway to it. The mists were suddenly towering above me, snaking out tendrils toward my arms. Overhead, the sky was still blue and the ground underneath my feet was still rock and snow. I took another step and the sky was green, the furious green of limes and tornadoes. Under my feet the ground shifted and let out a deep groan, like a kettledrum. I took Netica's rope out of my pocket and tied one end of it around my bare wrist. I let the other end drop to the ground and stamped it into the snow, until it touched the dirt beneath. I stepped away and the sky overhead was suddenly gold, like topazes and expensive rings.

I took my fourth step and the ground was gone. The mists were all around me and shapes began to form out of them. I held my breath, waiting for the ghosts to steal my body, but Netica's magic held. They felt around me, seeking desperately in tiny frantic touches, and passed me by. Before me the Break stood, a shimmering wall like oil on water and shifting rainbows. I took one last step and passed into the Land Beyond.

The Land Beyond was covered in ice—not the ice that lay on the city, but great sheets of frozen water that glistened with all the colors of the rainbow. Great spires of it rose up around me, silent figure-eights and swooping curves and plateaus that stretched out like great wings. Overhead, the sky was black, a velvety expanse without clouds. A harsh breeze swept through it all and the ice throbbed under its touch, a deep noise that echoed through my bones.

The Wind King was there to meet me. He was crowned with icicles and diamonds and he was beautiful. His hair was the charcoal gray of storm clouds, his eyes the blue of deep oceans. He wore robes of black ice, rimmed with the white of new snow. His voice was everywhere around me, in a chorus of breezes and gales and light snowflakes. He sang a song of peace, of deep sleep where there is no cold or warmth. He sang a song of seduction, in the tones of wind whistling on rock and shaking its way through great tall pines. He sang of great pleasure, in the noises that power lines make during a hurricane, deep throbs of power. I was frozen, listening, feeling his voice move through me and vibrate into the depths of my mind.

The Wind King reached out pale blue fingers and touched me. It sent a shock through my body, leaving me breathless and wanting more. He touched me again and I arched toward him, only wanting to feel that thrill, that chill tingle that brought so much heat to my skin. My heart beat slower. My blood froze in my veins and I only wanted him to touch me again. His hands ran over my arms, my back, my face. I leaned into his touch, feeling each finger, and suddenly his hands were around my neck, choking me. I couldn't breathe; there was frost in my lungs and my hair and I was sinking, falling into black ice. I fought back, squirming under his violent hands, and there was a sudden burst of pain around my neck. The Wind King screamed, flying backward, a high fierce sound like shattering ice. His hands were on fire and there were flames shooting out from around my neck. I reached up with one hand and burned myself on tiny white-hot bumps that stood out from my neck: the ivy necklace that Mammy had given me so long ago.

I felt my blood surge to life, tingling through my fingers and toes. Behind the Wind King's great dark shape I could see other, shadowy figures. Spring, her flowers withering as she watered them with her tears. Summer, dying from the heat of a drought. Fall, buried under gray clouds and slimy dark leaves.

My heart gave a shivery thump that brought tears of grief and terror to my eyes. The Wind King snarled and came toward me. I twisted away from him and ran toward where the other seasons stood. They reached out their arms to me weakly and I crouched between them, willing them to protect me. The Wind King shifted and was there before us, his song hinting of forgiveness and greater pleasure to come. He reached out to me and I forced myself not to take his hand.

"No!" I said. "I am the Poet King's heir and you will not kill me." I held up the skull and called out for the ghost of my father.

"Listen to me," I said. I felt the surge of power inside me, like when I told the story to Raven, like when I convinced Netica to work her magic for me. Only this time, it was deeper, as though a well had opened inside me. The Wind King paused before me, as if held in place by my voice. I spoke again, feeling magic in every word.

"I want to tell you a story," I said. "It's the story of a girl you never knew. She grew up with many other children, in a house that crawled with witches and magic, with strange smells and powers. But she was not a part of it. She could never be a part of it, but she still loved the

woman who became her mother and the children who
became her brothers and sisters and, if given the chance,
she would do anything to help them. One day she got
that chance, one chance to save everything she had ever
loved. She had to find the father she had never known
and ask him to give her his power, a power that no one
understood, including that girl. So I am asking you, my
father, the Poet King, to please answer me. Because you
are the only chance I have left."

Nothing happened. The hollow ice sculptures
throbbed in the air. The Wind King looked up, eyes like
bright sapphires, and laughed. He gathered himself
together and rushed toward me. I thrust the skull out,
trying to shield myself and it exploded into hundreds
of tiny stars. There was a sound of great wings. A ghost
plummeted down toward me, a shape of burgundy fire
and black smoke, and I screamed, uncertain what I had
done. The Wind King, the other seasons and the ice-
coated landscape all disappeared as if they had never
been, leaving only shifting fog. The ghost fell around me
and wrapped me in wings of fire. My mind filled with
images, of life and death. Of snow melting and
becoming rivers. Of flowers dying and becoming dirt.
Of animals feeding on animals. Of trees springing to life
out of fallen leaves. I saw the Poet King, silhouetted at
the edge of the Break, telling each season its story. How
each one gives way to the other in order to be brought
back to life again. I saw the magic in his words, how he
made each story come to life, and I saw how my words
had lived, forcing him to find me.

"Hello, Rune," a voice said, in tones of caramel and
dusk.

"Father?" I asked. The word felt strange on my
tongue.

"I have no powers to give you, Rune," the Poet King said. "You already know everything you need to know."

"I do?" I asked.

"If your story is close enough to you, and your need is great enough, the world will listen. The seasons will listen to you, as I listened to you. They are creatures of passion and emotion, nothing else. All you have to do is tell your story. But you knew that." My father wrapped around me, his ghost like pale mist, smiling into me. I sat there, comforted by his words.

He was right. I had known, since the minute I had felt that first surge of power inside me. I had just not believed that it was real magic. I had spent so long believing that I was not a witch, that I had never believed I could have a greater gift. I reached up, trying to touch him, and his ghost frayed around my fingers.

"Goodbye, Rune," my father said. "You will be a good Poet King. I will sleep safely knowing you are alive."

"Wait!" I said. There was so much I wanted to ask him. Who he had been, who my mother had been, how it had been to first face the seasons. But he was gone, leaving me alone. Ghosts flitted around me, shifting in and out of shapes and faces and colors. I began to cry, loss cutting into me like a knife, tears spilling down my face. I panicked as one hit my arm and I felt Netica's spell give, a short pain that ran through my fingers. A ghost dipped down and nuzzled around the spot. Around me, the ice was beginning to reappear, the beginnings of the towers chasing through the fog like a crystalline web. The Wind King was coming back for me. I grabbed for the rope at my wrist, the sharp nettles reassuring me. I followed it hand over hand, stepping back through the emptiness. I could see the Break ahead

of me, a massive silver wall that wavered and ran like
an old mirror.

I took another step and burst through it. The chill
winter wind whipped through me, freezing my bones.
The sky was a deep green, like jade and cucumbers. I
took another step and another and I was back in the
Fringe. The wide road that had opened for me was
gone, and the snow around me was crushed down, as if
a struggle had taken place.

It was late, almost night, and the sky overhead was
filling with black and violet storm clouds. The Wind
King was preparing to move into the City of Dreams. I
took the rope and threw it back toward the Break with
all my strength and the end of it disappeared into the
mists. Good. It would serve as a beacon for the Wind
King, to guide him here to me.

Tell the Wind King a story, I thought. I pictured my
father, standing alone at the edge of the Break. His eyes
were filled with pain at the thought of the frozen, dying
city behind him. I thought of Mammy, wearing a
bathing suit and spitting at frost to ward off winter. I
thought of the pinched cold faces on the trolley and the
wilted flowers in Netica's kitchen.

I found a flat rock and sat down, waiting. I had a
story, about a girl who found her magic, who found her
father. I would wait here, until the storm began and the
Wind King came out of the Break, looking for me, and
then I would use my new power. I would tell my story
to the Wind King.

THE ART OF CREATION

Written by
Carl Frederick

Illustrated by
Rey Rosario

About the Author

Carl Frederick is a theoretical physicist. After a postdoc at NASA and a stint at Cornell University, he left theoretical astrophysics and his first love, quantum relativity theory, to become Chief Scientist of a small company doing AI (artificial intelligence) software.

A few years ago, Carl decided he'd like to write in the SF genre. To that end, he attended the Odyssey Writers Workshop where he managed to acquire writing skills.

Carl has two children, shares his house with a pet robot and time-shares a dog at the office. For recreation, he fences épée and plays the bagpipes. Carl currently lives in rural Ithaca, New York. And rural is good if you play the bagpipes.

George ran through the house in a fit of
destruction, breaking things, tearing
photographs to bits, and obliterating all traces of
Joanne, his fiancée—ex-fiancée—ex-fiancée du jour. His
rage spent, and wanting to think about something else,
he flopped down in front of the 3V and switched on to
an adventure series.

The scene zoomed in on a close embrace, and George
cursed under his breath. For there, in living 3-D, he saw
his ex and himself pawing each other and kissing
passionately. He grabbed the remote, disabled Joanne's
avatar, then paused for a moment. The default actress
had a pretty good body. George keyed default, tossed
the remote on the floor and turned back to the screen. No
good. Even with the default actress, he still imagined
Joanne. With a sigh, he rummaged for the remote and
disabled his own avatar in favor of the default actor.

He'd barely gotten comfortable again when he heard
the door chimes from the office entrance. He glanced at
the upper left corner of the 3V display where an image
from the door-cam blinked into view.

"Oh, shit. The Covingtons."

George sprang up and ran for the bathroom. He
examined himself in the mirror, brushed his hair and
did a quick powder touch-up to his face. It wouldn't do
for a certified, premier-class DNA artist to look less than
perfect.

George darted through the door that separated his office from his bachelor apartment. He pulled out the Covington file, dropping it on his desk as he went to answer the door.

"Grace and Robert, it's so good to see you. Come in. Come in." He led them to two chairs beside the desk. "Let me take your coats."

"I'm sorry it took so long to answer the door," said George, returning from the coat rack, "but I was doing a final check of the chromosome selection. I'm sure you'll be extremely pleased with your baby daughter."

"I should hope so," said Mr. Covington. "It's certainly costing us enough."

George laughed, sympathetically. "Left to chance, your child would inherit twenty-three random chromosomes from you, Mr. Covington, and the other twenty-three from your wife." He'd explained this so often to so many clients that the words came almost of their own volition. "That's about sixty-four trillion possible arrangements. You certainly wouldn't want to leave it to chance."

"We've been through all this before," said Mr. Covington. "Now let's see what you've got."

"Fine." George opened the folder. He enjoyed stretching out the drama. "Let's see. You wanted blue eyes, blond hair—tricky since both of you are dark—high intelligence, five-foot-seven adult height, musical ability, athleticism, mesomorph——"

"Yes, of course. We know all that." Mr. Covington leaned in over the desk. "Show us our daughter."

George tapped a few keys at his desk and the picture window dominating one wall of the office gradually turned from clear to milky-white. The office lights dimmed to off, and the window flickered to light. Gone were the neighboring houses. Instead, the window looked out on a rolling green meadow under a bright blue canopy. An occasional fluffy white cloud drifted lazily across the sky.

"Enjoy the show," said George.

From the left of the window, now a huge LCD display, a naked toddler crawled into view. Her golden hair and smooth baby-white skin showed clear and brilliant against the sunny meadow.

"Is that our daughter?" Grace whispered.

"Yes. At about fourteen months."

"She's adorable."

A butterfly fluttered low to the ground, and the toddler tumbled after it. Happy cooing and giggling filled the room. George watched the Covingtons and felt the familiar pleasure. No matter how many times he'd orchestrated these simulations, he never tired of watching the look of loving awe on the faces of the prospective parents.

"Would you like to see her grow?"

With eyes locked on the screen and, apparently too overcome with emotion to speak, Grace nodded.

Over the course of the next five minutes, the little toddler grew. She still chased the butterfly, but now she ran lightly over the grass, and the cooing changed to sparkling laughter. George noticed Mr. Covington fidgeting and tapped a few desk-keys. Suddenly, the naked child became clothed in a white blouse, light blue shorts, socks and sandals—and Covington stopped fidgeting.

"She's about six here."

"Simply gorgeous," said Mr. Covington.

"She's perfect," said Grace.

Illustrated by Rey Rosario

"Yes, pretty near perfect," said George, "genetically speaking."

Mr. Covington gave a bare hint of a smile. "You know I don't really approve of this designer baby business, but"—he turned to his wife—"you might have been right, dear." He looked again at the display. "I have to admit, she's a beautiful child."

George commanded the desk console to fade out the meadow and bring the window to clear. He tapped the office lights back on and took a holorom card and an envelope from the folder on his desk.

"This is the chromosomal selection," he said, holding the holocard out to Mrs. Covington. "And this," said George, flourishing the envelope, "has your clinic appointment details. You're scheduled a week from next Tuesday." He handed over the envelope to Mr. Covington. "It won't be anywhere near as satisfying as traditional methods, but you can count on the results."

George pulled another holorom from the folder. "This is an avatar card. It has your daughter's data for ages three to six. Just pop it in your 3V. Whenever a program comes on with a little-girl character, your daughter will be that character."

Grace reached for the holocard, but her husband caught her hand and gently pulled it back.

"Thank you, but no," said Mr. Covington. "I think it would be better if we observed the miracle of our daughter's life as it happens. I don't want to ruin the reality. I hope you understand."

"Yes, certainly." George hid his disappointment. He was an artist and they were spurning his art.

"No offense," said Grace. "We appreciate all you've done for us. And please stay in touch, so you can see how your creation turns out."

"Have no fear about that. By tradition, the DNA artist is the goduncle of the child. And I certainly do intend to keep an eye on the progress of my godniece."

Grace clutched his hand. "Good. I'm so glad."

•••

At the door, George waved the Covingtons off. As he paced slowly back to his desk, he felt a pang of regret about Joanne. It would have been so good to settle down and have a family—a perfect family.

He sat heavily at the desk, absently tapped a few keys and the window again became an LCD display. George replayed the growth scene, this time not bothering to add the blouse and shorts. The little girl bounded free across the meadow.

"Beautiful. Truly beautiful."

George keyed his desk a few more times, and the growth simulation resumed. He watched as the little girl grew. Baby fat and freckles receded, and she grew tall and slender. George felt an instant of embarrassment as breasts and pubic hair transformed the innocent child into a woman. He continued watching and his feelings drifted far from the avuncular.

At about age twenty, he keyed off the growth, but kept the simulation active. The young woman ran along with the butterfly. George, overwhelmed by her poise and grace, hit a key and froze the image. He stared long at that perfect figure—alabaster skin of a fine Rubens, the voluptuousness of a Courbet, the subtle grace of a Degas, and the uncharted magnificence of her crystalline brown eyes and her amber hair that glowed warm in the sunlight.

"Absolutely stunning."

He couldn't pull himself away. There was nothing he wanted more than to gaze upon his creation—clearly his best work.

"This must be how Michelangelo felt."

He keyed more commands, posing the woman like a doll. He clothed her, unclothed her, styled her hair, applied lipstick and makeup, and then canceled out all of those affectations. She looked better, far better, with her hair flowing free, unencumbered by jewelry and without lipstick, and without clothes.

George slipped a blank holorom into a slot in the side of his desk and busied himself in a frenzy of programming. A few minutes later, he withdrew the holocard, voice-commanded the office lights to full-on, and examined the spectral reflection of the newly burned holorom card. He marked the card, "Covington child: Avatar—age twenty."

George canceled the simulation, set the window to clear and, card in hand, shot through the door to the residential side of the house. He popped the avatar card into the control console of the extra-large 3V unit in his living room and sat back for an evening of 3-D television starring the most beautiful body he'd ever seen.

But he couldn't just keep thinking of her as "the body," or "his creation." She needed a name. George laughed with an idea.

"Synthia." He played with the name. "I love you, Synthia."

George sampled a number of 3V programs that evening, starting with innocuous fare, rated "family." Then, feeling just a twinge of guilt, he sampled a few "adult-plus-plus" offerings.

Through an evening of prime-time entertainment, he could not take his eyes off Synthia. He loved the way she moved, the way she carried herself, and as he watched a steamy love scene, he realized he was becoming increasingly jealous of the male lead.

This is insane. She's just a simulation. Get a grip.

Nevertheless, George went to the console and switched in his avatar as a replacement for the offending actor.

Finally, late, when the 3V showed only old, non-avatar-enabled movies, George switched off the set and went to bed.

●●●

George woke tired and worried. He knew the symptoms. It had started this way with Joanne, and with Christine before her—and with Maude, and Helen, and God knows who else. He'd thought that segment of his life was over, and that Joanne would be his forever. But no. She turned out to be no better than any of the others.

To force Joanne out of his mind, he visualized Synthia. Yes. Without doubt, he was coming down with a serious case of infatuation. But this time it was different, aberrantly different, for, at the moment, he was infatuated with a woman who had yet to be born.

He stretched out in his bed, hands clasped behind his head.

"God, I need a vacation."

The sound of his words against the empty silence drew his attention. He grasped at the idea as a substitute obsession. On the spot, he decided that he'd take a vacation, maybe a cruise where he could meet some unattached woman made of flesh and blood.

George hopped out of bed and, clad only in his underwear, walked across to the office, sat down at his desk and pulled up his appointment calendar. Before he could change his mind, he e-cancelled a week's worth of engagements, explaining that he'd be out of town for a while and would have to reschedule. It was abrupt, he knew, but he was an artist.

Then, feeling underclothed at his desk, he keyed the window dark and pulled up an image in its place. Without being consciously aware of it, he selected an image of Synthia. It startled him and, even though in his low-cut briefs he was still more clothed than was she, he felt embarrassed by his near nakedness.

Hidden behind his desk, he stared at Synthia's image. With growing certainty, he realized he would not be going off on a cruise. He might not even leave the house for the next week.

In the kitchen, foraging for breakfast, George smiled sadly as he opened the refrigerator. Unlike Joanne, Synthia was unlikely to prepare food for him. He rummaged through the unkempt fridge and withdrew some Camembert and an iridescent, yellow grape.

While waiting for tea water to boil, he cut a few slices of French bread and sliced the golf-ball-sized fruit in two. He closed his eyes in sensual pleasure as he bit into a grape half. The taste was exquisite—not surprising since he'd genetically engineered the fruit to please him so. But, as their taste receptors were different, Joanne had never appreciated his achievement. A self-indulgent hobby, she'd called it.

George took his plate and a cup of tea into the study and settled down in front of the 3V for a leisurely breakfast. He'd fully intended to squander a few hours watching Synthia-based programming, but he grew listless. He didn't want to merely observe her. He needed to be with her.

Leaving his breakfast mostly uneaten, he switched off the set and wandered back to the office side of his house.

Again, he played with the Synthia simulation, but after an hour or so, he tired of it. It was like playing with a doll.

George commanded the window to clear and gazed out onto the neighborhood. Then, smiling with an idea, he turned to his desk monitor and did a product search for AI personality software. He found a package that was both voice-recognition and avatar compliant and realized he could write it off as a business expense. It would be a nice touch for his clients to be able to actually speak to their future progeny.

"I'll buy it," he said to his desk.

George downloaded the module, linked it to Synthia's avatar and entered "Setup." Synthia's face appeared on his desk monitor.

"Who are you?" asked Synthia. "You may speak your answers."

"I am your husband. My name is George Bernhardt. I am a DNA artist."

"Who am I?"

"You are Synthia. You are the most beautiful woman in the world."

George created a detailed life history for Synthia, then modeled his house and, finally, installed Synthia inside it.

"This is our bedroom. And you sleep in the nude."

"What does 'in the nude' mean?"

"It means wearing no clothes."

"Say 'yes' to add the term 'in the nude' to the speech recognition library," said Synthia.

"Yes."

This is art, thought George, *this building of a life.*

•••

Next morning, George woke to a new world. Synthia was everywhere. She was the co-anchor on the morning news on all 3V channels, and she lived a private life within the computer, so all he had to do was speak and she'd hold a conversation with him. And with the computer output patched into the 3V, he could even talk to a full-size, 3-D Synthia.

But even with all this, George was unsatisfied. He fantasized about having her at his side as his wife, and he wondered at its appeal. How could he be so infatuated with a computer synthesis? Was it just an aftereffect of the breakup with Joanne? Or maybe, unlike the past where he'd only had chromosomes to work with, here he'd created the entire person. Art, complete. A perfect woman. His perfect woman. How he wished he could crawl into the computer to be with her.

That gave him an idea. He'd take his 3V avatar and build an AI simulation of himself. He'd pop the simulation into Synthia's environment. George smiled. He'd be able to experience the pleasures of the flesh— vicariously, to be sure, but maybe it would be enough.

At his desk, he copied the avatar files into the AI program. The software was sophisticated and could actually take chromosomal data. He had those data, but as he started to load them, he changed his mind. Why settle for a product of nature? Why not a more perfect George?

He was excited by the idea of changing himself, or at least the simulation of himself. He'd been trained in genetic engineering, but as a DNA artist, he was certified only to choose chromosomes, not to modify them. George's mind swirled with the possibilities of genetic engineering—genetic art.

He darted down to the basement, to his hobby genetics lab.

He'd not be too ambitious. If the simulation were too different, it would be hard to identify with it.

Using a hair cell, George did the gene sequencing and modifications that would add a couple of inches to his height, and replace his hazel eyes with the steel gray that nature had inexplicably denied him.

These were small changes so he only needed to engineer a dozen or so controlled mutations—a false bonding of thymine with adenine to start with—a piece of cake.

George was happy to be actually doing something, and not simply go moping about, incapacitated by his growing love for Synthia. He started at the thought. Love for Synthia? Could that really happen?

In the lab, George worked steadily: moving nucleotides, coaxing base pairs, testing the expression of genes, verifying the amino acids from the DNA triplets.

It took him two days to finish.

• • •

"Who are you?" asked the new George simulation. "You may speak your answers."

"I am your creator. My name is George Bernhardt. I am a DNA artist." George smiled sheepishly. "And I am twenty-five years old," he said, understating his age by a few decades.

"Who am I?"

"You are . . . ." George paused. He'd never liked his first name—too pedestrian.

"You are Gunther Bernhardt. You are Synthia's husband."

It took only a few hours of talking to his simulation for a large portion of his likes, dislikes and personality traits to be transferred.

For a few hours, George did little but watch Synthia and Gunther engage in family life. At first, it was fascinating, but soon it seemed nothing more than a plotless 3V program. And it was hard talking to Synthia now that Gunther was around. Increasingly, George felt like a voyeur peering through a window—peering at himself.

At length, George took control of Gunther. Now he could talk to Synthia through Gunther's mouth and could control Gunther's movements. He commanded Gunther to embrace Sylvia, but sadly, this gave him little satisfaction. Then he switched the simulation point of view to see through Gunther's eyes. Better, but George could not touch Synthia, nor smell her hair, nor feel her soft body in his hands.

Maybe Gunther was not that great an idea. George wondered how he could possibly have been so stupid as to think he could satisfy his needs secondhand.

That night, surrounded by Synthia and Gunther, George went to bed, angry.

•••

After a fitful sleep, George looked in on the simulation and realized that he was wildly jealous of Gunther. Not only did Gunther have Synthia for his own, and was taller than George by a few inches, and was younger by a generation, but he also had those deep, penetrating steel gray eyes.

George stormed back to his living room and switched on the 3V. There, at least, he could watch Synthia and himself, and there would be a plot.

The 3V flickered, emitted a high-pitched whine and went dead. The odor of fried electronics and ozone filled the air.

"Damn it to hell."

He wondered if he could perhaps watch 3V on the set in Synthia and Gunther's living room. *It would be in 2-D, of course.* George turned off the 3V. *God. I'm losing it.*

He activated his watch-phone, voice-commanded directory assistance, contacted a 3V repair outlet and arranged for a house visit. Unfortunately, the repair agent wouldn't be able to get there until noon, a wait of almost two hours.

With the repair agent coming, George spent a quarter hour or so in a desultory cleaning: picking up clothes from the floor, moving scattered dishes to the growing pile in the sink and sweeping up the debris from his outburst over Joanne's leaving. Then he walked from the bachelor chaos of his living quarters through to the neatness of his office and sat at his desk to wait.

He engaged the AI simulation, but then switched it abruptly off as he saw Gunther in bed with Synthia. George activated the window display and gazed intently at Synthia's stunning body.

The doorbell chimed and George, looking at his watch, could scarcely believe two and a half hours had passed.

"Must be the repair agent."

George headed for the door but, halfway there, spun around and ran back to the desk. Guiltily, he slapped a few keys, canceling Synthia's unclad window image, and only then went to let in the repair-agent.

In the study, the agent sniffed the air. "EPR photon diffractor. I'd know that smell anywhere."

George looked on as the agent disassembled the 3V's cowling and withdrew an electronic subassembly.

"Just as I thought," said the agent, "a dead EPR unit. I'll drive back to the shop and pick up a replacement—after I reassemble the cowling of course."

"Why? You'll just have to disassemble it again. Leave it as it is. I don't care. Or are you paid by the hour?"

The agent laughed. "Read this," he said, picking up a section of cowling and handing it to George. "That's not a joke. If you should suddenly decide to turn on your 3V and hug it, you'd be fricasseed on the spot. Like being struck by lightning."

The agent took back the section and fitted it against the large 3V floor unit, talking as he did so.

"And if I'd left the cowling off, I'd lose my certification and would be lucky to escape the slammer. These 3V units are treacherous. And yeah, as a matter of fact, I am paid by the hour."

"Okay, okay. Do what you have to do." George went back to his office and sat smoldering in jealousy. He hardly noticed when the repair agent left nor when, an hour later, he returned with the replacement EPR unit.

George sat, imagining terrible things happening to his simulation. But then he laughed. Those terrible things could indeed happen. He was the god of that world. As God, he couldn't hug Synthia, but there were compensations. George smiled grimly and plotted the will of a vengeful god.

•••

On the living room couch, Gunther and Synthia sat side by side watching 3V. Synthia, wearing only a dressing gown and slippers, nuzzled against Gunther, who wore nothing but undershorts.

George, his fingers scurrying over the virtual keyboard, smiled grimly. He tapped one key with a flourish, and the 3V went black.

"Damn it to hell," said Gunther, rising from the couch.

George switched to thought-bubble mode and selected Gunther.

"You can fix it," said George. "You've done it before, and you didn't replace the screws in the cowling. Oh, and you're thirsty."

"I can fix it," said Gunther. He clicked the power switch off and went behind the set. "I've done this before." He pulled off the cowling. "This is hot work. Could you get me something to drink from the kitchen?"

"Sure," said Synthia. "What would you like?"

"Lemonade," said George.

"Lemonade."

Gunther nosed about in the interior of the set, stopping when Synthia returned with the lemonade. As Gunther took the glass, George hit a key. The glass slipped out of Gunther's hand, sending a waterfall of lemonade onto the carpet.

"Shit!" Gunther kicked the glass away. "Let me finish with this first." He reached his hands into the 3V. "I suspect it's just a loose cable." Wiggling the wires, Gunther worked his hands further into the set. "Ah, here it is. It'll just take a moment, and"—Gunther fumbled with the connector—"when I say 'go,' flip on the power and we'll give it a try."

"Go," said George.

Synthia flipped the switch. The 3V emitted a low hum, accompanied by the counterpoint of a similar sound from Gunther's quivering mouth. After a few frozen seconds, Gunther ceased making noises and crumpled to the soggy carpet, leaving the hum from the 3V as the only sound in the room. That sound was soon joined by Synthia's screams.

With shaking hands, George powered down the monitor and bolted from the house. The satisfaction he got from Gunther's death scared him. If he was capable of virtual murder, what else was he capable of? George needed to think.

He hadn't been out of the house in a week, and now outside, everything looked artificial and random. The streets, the rush of traffic, the people: it all seemed surreal, as if he were in a computer game. Against that backdrop, he visualized Synthia. It wasn't hard; her image seemed etched in his mind. Gazing at the traffic, he tried to force the image of that perfect body to fade. Impossible. Losing Synthia was not an option.

By the time he returned home, he had a plan. His passion for Synthia was real, even if she wasn't. There was only one answer then. He'd have to simply wait for her. In twenty-one years, he'd marry her. Until then, well, he'd manage somehow.

The more he considered the plan, the more the idea grew on him. The constant vision of her would be his redemption. He'd live the monastic life, thinking of her, improving himself, purifying himself, perfecting himself in mind and body. When she reached twenty he'd be in his early sixties, but if he worked at it, he could have the body of a thirty-year-old. It would take discipline, but he could do it for her. *And sixty isn't old — not these days.*

And further, the plan was not all that aberrant. It was like an arranged marriage: like the old custom of betrothing a girl at birth, usually to a wealthy elder. And he expected to be pretty wealthy in twenty years.

But what if she turns me down? Could happen. Why would she ever want to marry her goduncle?

George was all but paralyzed with the fear that Synthia, in her innocence, might just marry someone else.

I can't allow that to happen.

Yet it seemed impossible. How could he guarantee that a woman who hadn't even been born yet would fall irresistibly in love with him? A solution came quickly, but he discarded it as too monstrous. Throughout the day, he tried every possible avenue of thought, but kept coming back to the same solution.

By mid-evening, George gave up the fight. The solution was a horrendous breach of professional ethics, but it was the only way. He had no choice.

At his desk, George checked the time and worried that it might be too late to phone. But then, afraid that if he didn't do it now, he might change his mind, he went ahead and rang up the Covington residence. Grace answered.

"This is George Bernhardt. Sorry for calling so late. . . . Yes, yes. I'm fine."

He toyed nervously with a pencil.

"But you'll have to postpone your clinic appointment. There's a problem with the chromosome mix. . . . No, nothing too serious, but I've found a genetic disease. . . . It's very correctable, if we do it now. . . . Look, it's my fault. Should have found it earlier. . . . Yes, but since it's my error, I won't charge you anything. In fact, you won't even have any clinic charges. I'll pick those up. But I have to do a gene repair on a few chromosomes. . . . I still have some cells from each of you. I'll use those. . . . They'll transfer the new chromosomes to sperm and egg at the clinic. . . . It's good I found this before you went ahead with it. No sense taking risks with genetic diseases. . . . No need to thank me. . . . I'll phone you tomorrow with the details, but rest assured. Your daughter will be one in a billion."

George closed the connection. Redemption would have to wait.

With weary fingers, he tapped a few keys on his desk and Synthia appeared on the monitor.

"Hi, Synthia."

"Hello, darling."

"Do you love me?"

"Always."

"Do you really?"

"I love you passionately."

George smiled. He knew it was only programming, but hearing the words warmed him to the core.

"Do you know what a pheromone is?" he asked on impulse.

"No, darling. Tell me."

"It's a smell," said George in the soft voice he used with clients. "Every human being has a unique smell. And that smell usually elicits an emotional reaction. People don't talk about smell very much, but it's a powerful stimulus."

"Say 'yes' to add the term *pheromone* to the speech recognition library."

"Yes." George smiled at the incongruity. "First I need to isolate and synthesize my own particular pheromone. That should be easy. Getting Synthia to respond to that pheromone will take some doing."

"I'm Synthia."

"Yes, my love. But I mean a different Synthia."

"Oh." There was a pause. "Does this mean you don't love me anymore?"

"Of course I love you. I'll love you forever." As he said it, George realized that he meant it.

"The hard part," he continued, "will be to hard-code an affinity for my pheromone into Synthia's vomeronasal organ."

"What is a 'vomeronasal organ'?"

"A second nose. Dogs have it. People have it also, but with humans, it atrophies a few weeks after birth. I'll engineer it so Synthia's doesn't atrophy. The vomeronasal organ is ultrasensitive to pheromones. Once she smells my distinct odor, she won't be able to resist me."

"Say 'yes' to add the term *vomeronasal organ* to the speech recognition library."

"No." George keyed the AI program to background mode and tapped the desk into standby. "Good night, Synthia."

Pheromone engineering's no big deal. People or fruit— what's the difference?

•••

After he'd transferred a week's worth of food down to the basement refrigerator and closed down the rest of the house, George isolated himself in his lab for a long session of heavy genetic engineering.

After three days, he reemerged with two sets of cryo-frozen chromosomal solutions—one for sperm and the other for egg. He packaged them up and sent them off to the clinic. At that point, it would have been good form to ring up the Covingtons and wish them luck. But he couldn't bring himself to phone—not when he'd played God with a human being. He'd gone far beyond the edge of malpractice, and felt guilty as hell. Still, he wouldn't undo his actions even if he could.

With the evil behind him, now it was time for penance and to make himself the best person he could be. Maybe he'd even do some pro bono work. That was supposed to be good for the soul.

• • •

During the next few months, George settled into a routine. He devoted most of his energy to his work, spent two hours a day exercising and working on his physique. And he spent several hours a night watching Synthia on 3V.

Before exercise, one evening, George decided to lubricate his treadmill. Opening a cabinet in search of silicon spray, he saw a framed picture of Joanne on the inside door. He yanked the picture off, lined up a jump-shot to a trash basket, hesitated, then gazed at the picture, holding it at arms length.

"Ingres could have painted this." He brought the picture closer. "Joanne, why? I worshiped you—put you on a pedestal." He placed the picture, face down, on a shelf in the cabinet.

With the treadmill set to an unusually high speed, he started running. Later, at the point of exhaustion, body dripping with sweat and face drenched, he collapsed to an easy chair and forced his thoughts back to Synthia.

It occurred to him that he couldn't go through life calling her Synthia, since within a few months his future wife would be flesh-and-blood real. There was nothing else to do but phone the Covingtons. And he couldn't postpone the call forever, especially if he were to exercise his right to watch over his godniece. Already, the Covingtons must think it strange that he hadn't called. Come to think of it, it was pretty strange that the Covingtons hadn't called him.

George put it off for another week, but finally the growing worry that something might have gone wrong compelled him to make the call.

"Hi, Grace. This is George Bernhardt. Just calling to say hello. How are things going?"

"Oh, Mr. Bernhardt. Things are fine. It's good to hear from you."

The words were right, but the tone was distant. Something seemed wrong. Maybe there'd been a miscarriage.

"Is the pregnancy going well?"

"Quite well. They say it'll be a healthy baby."

"Oh, good." George smiled with relief. "Listen. Since I'm her goduncle, could you tell me what you're going to name her? I'll keep it in confidence. I promise."

"Well, I suppose that would do no harm," said Grace.

George furrowed his brow. He sensed tentativeness in her voice.

"We've decided to call her Kimberly, after my mother . . ."

"Kimberly." George thought on the name. "Kimberly. I like it."

". . . and if it's a boy, we'll name him Joshua, after Robert's father."

"What?" He wondered if she'd gone suddenly insane.

There was a pause of a few seconds before Grace answered.

"We didn't know how to tell you this, but . . . well, when you delayed the fertilization to work on preventing the genetic disease, Robert took that as a sign."

"I don't understand," said George.

"He thought God was telling us that what we were about to do was immoral."

"Immoral?" George's face flushed and he struggled to hold the receiver steady. "No. It's beauty—art. How could you ever think—"

"Anyway," Grace continued, "we decided on the more usual method of conception. I'm sorry. I know how hard you worked to give us the perfect baby."

"Mrs. Covington. Please." George knew he sounded like an anguished child, but somewhere, deep within, dwelt the notion that if he could just plead well enough, everything would be okay. "But, what about the egg and sperm?"

"Destroyed," said Grace sadly. "Since the egg had never been fertilized, in God's eyes, it wasn't a life, so discarding it wasn't abortion."

"It's murder!" cried George. "You're murderers, and"—George groped for words—"and desecrators of art."

"Now really," said Grace, "if you're going to carry on that way. . . ."

She broke the connection.

He glared at the dead phone while his anger drained away, leaving, in its place, emptiness. Standing, he darted hungry glances around his office, but the place seemed hollow and sterile. There were no artifacts of

Synthia that he could cling to. His wife, Synthia, was dead and the simulation just a ghost. Slowly, he sat again, put his head in his hands and cried.

A half-hour later, depleted of tears, he sat back at his desk. He noticed he was toying with a leather book-mark, one of Joanne's that had somehow survived the earlier destruction. Tentatively, he picked up the phone, hesitated, and finally called her. But she hung up on him as soon as he said his name.

George fingered the soft calfskin bookmark. Then he brought it to his mouth, closed his eyes and kissed it.

• • •

Dazed and despondent, George wandered through the house, stopping at length in the living room. Without being able to help himself, he walked to the 3V and switched it on. Synthia was there, piped in from the computer's AI program. Once more, he gazed upon her perfect form.

"Take off your clothes," he said.

"Why?"

"I just want to look at you."

She disrobed, and George's heart ached. And it was odd that he hadn't noticed it before, but her voice was so like Joanne's.

He turned away and rushed from the room. He didn't know why, but he didn't want her to see him cry.

George rummaged through the house for a screw-driver, found one, put it in his back pocket and went to the kitchen. He took a large bottle of mineral water from the fridge and returned to the living room.

He stood facing the display.

"You're beautiful."

Synthia blushed.

George slowly undressed, until he stood naked in front of the 3V.

"Do you love me?" he asked.

"Always."

George retrieved the screwdriver from his discarded clothing and walked behind the 3V. Without turning it off, he removed the protective cowling from the back and sides of the set. Then he came around front again.

"Hi, he said."

"Hello, darling."

"Do you love me, Joanne?"

"I'm Synthia, darling."

"Do you love me?"

"Always."

George uncapped the bottle and ceremoniously poured out the mineral water, creating a shallow lake in front of the 3V unit.

He took a few steps forward, making small splashes with his bare feet. The hair on his body tingled as he drew close to Synthia.

He leaned forward to embrace the unit.

"Always."

ADVICE TO THE NEW WRITER

Written by
Andre Norton

About the Author

Andre Alice Norton began her career as a writer by serving on the staff of her high-school newspaper. During those years, she had the opportunity to study under a gifted teacher of journalism, Sylvia Cochran; of ten students in the class Andre attended, five went on to distinguished careers in various fields of writing. To the instruction of Miss Cochran, and the inspiration of her mother, Miss Norton attributed her entry into the authorial arena. Prior to graduation, she wrote an adventure tale that was later expanded to book length and published as her first novel, Ralestone Luck (1932). Shortly thereafter, in response to the prejudice of the period against female writers, she legally changed her name to Andre.

In a literary career spanning more that six decades, Andre Norton has written over one hundred novels in a number of popular genres, including juvenile, Gothic and historical stories. Her best-known work, however, has been done in the fields of science fiction (the "Beastmaster" saga) and fantasy (the "Witch World" series).

After serving for twenty-two years as a librarian in the Cleveland Public Library System, Miss Norton retired to write full time. In 1997, she moved to Murfreesboro, Tennessee, where she now oversees High Hallack Library, a research-and-resource facility for genre writers. She also continues her creative labors and has recently finished two new fantasy novels. Her informative and insightful essay, which is addressed to aspiring authors, graces the pages of this anthology.

Throughout many cultures worldwide, one of the signs of humanity itself is reading; indeed, it has been said that the state of a civilization can be judged by the literacy of its people. Reading and writing offer both individuals and nations the power to record information; to learn about environment and existence; to feed imagination; and to achieve fellowship with all humankind. Every example of writing is subtly—sometimes arbitrarily—influenced by the beliefs of its author and his or her time, and even the ideally objective chronicle of history often renders a given event unrecognizable through many retellings (remember the old children's game of "Whisper Down the Lane?"). Yes, the process has its flaws and pitfalls; nevertheless, our chief tool for furthering awareness of ourselves and our world remains the written word.

Thus the most valuable service performed by a book is precisely that: to add to the knowledge of the reader. However, though gaining acquaintance with one's past and present may be the first and foremost reason to read, increased insight does not come from factual material alone. Fiction also makes a critical contribution toward that goal, especially in fostering acceptance— and, more importantly, appreciation—of the "different" behavior of unfamiliar cultures, for an idea presented in story form often catches the attention and engages the sympathy more effectively than a factual account.

Having been asked to counsel beginning writers as to the best ways to cultivate their craft, I offer the following advice.

One of the questions most frequently posed to an author of fiction is this: "Where do you get your ideas?" The answer is very simple: "*I read.*"

Above all, a writer must be a reader. First, he/she needs to acquire authentic factual information for the construction of stories. Many people accept unquestioningly an author's rendering of historical persons, places and events as correct, so that if such elements of a tale are convincingly presented, they will become fixed in the minds of those readers as true. Thus the foremost duty of the writer is to make certain that such data reflect the most current scholarship on the subject. *Duty* is not too strong a word, for the author often acts as a teacher, and slipshod or—worse—nonexistent research is a form of lying and therefore a violation of trust.

Happily, in addition to representing the known universe in fiction, authentic historical facts can also serve as fascinating jumping-off places for the building of imaginary worlds. Anchoring projections about tomorrow to the science, religion or politics of today will tether the armchair astronaut by a secure, familiar lifeline for his mental spacewalks. In addition, the greater the number of real-seeming details that can be supplied about a created universe, the more believable that country-of-the-mind will be. Writing as an art is twin to painting, with words for its colors; if it is to present a complex, lifelike picture, a rich palette must be accumulated in order to be drawn from—and "drawn" with. Names in particular are—literally—vital; their sensitive selection is often the Pygmalion touch that grants an inert work life. Begin a list of names that sound like proper ones for the hero/ines, villains, rulers, peasants. Baby-christening books and telephone directories, especially if ethnically diverse, are good places to start.

Read, then, if you would write: history, natural science, sociology, astronomy—and not only what has been discovered in the past in these fields but what is being predicted as a future trend. Examine layouts of cities that were, then look at plans for air- or spaceborne cities that might be. Study swords, then investigate the sonic knives with which surgery is even now being performed. Having laid a broad foundation for your world with such cutting-edge extrapolations, you can then make logical guesses about the smaller aspects of your creation—what your characters could wear, eat, and enjoy for entertainment; how they might govern themselves; what deities they may worship. Keep notebooks in which you can record facts that especially intrigue you, and retain interesting clippings from magazines and newspapers. You may use much or little of your research for any given project; however, you might find that, when dealing with another piece of work, a previously unused tidbit could be employed to form the nucleus of an entirely new plot.

•••

In the early years of the last century, few works of the type we would now consider science fiction or fantasy were brought out in hardcover format by the well-established publishing houses; in fact, until *Sputnik* astounded the world in the 1950s, speculative stories were generally confined to the so-called "pulps." However, after the Russians broke into space, such companies began to actively campaign for book-length tales of imagination.

A core group of authors who had served their apprenticeship in the magazines made the transition smoothly to the new market. In this promotion of popular writing to "real" publication, L. Ron Hubbard, who had written action stories in a number of widely diverse genres, not only saw a chance for himself but perceived an even greater opportunity for others. He believed that newcomers to the imaginative field should be encouraged and nourished. From this conviction was eventually born the L. Ron Hubbard Writers of the Future Contest, in which fledgling authors might receive experienced critical assessment of their efforts, and recognition, in the form of prizes and publication, for quality work.

For nearly a decade, the privilege and pleasure has been given me of serving as one of the judges for this competition. The many stories of high merit which have been placed in my hands have proven that Mr. Hubbard was emphatically correct in his estimation: that a cadre of leaders-to-be in the field of imaginative writing stands ready, willing and able to deliver its best when given the chance of a lifetime to do so offered by the contest he established. To paraphrase Walt Kelly's Pogo, "We have met the Future—and it is They."

THE ROAD TO LEVENSHIR

Written by
Patrick Rothfuss

Illustrated by
Jason Pastrana

About the Author

Pat Rothfuss was born in Madison, Wisconsin, in 1973. But according to him, *"The real story began when my mother gave me my first real book to read. When she gave me that book, it shaped my mind. My life. It was* The Lion, the Witch and the Wardrobe." *Pat's love of reading eventually became a love for writing.*

He began college in 1991 at the University of Wisconsin Stevens Point. Pat walked away from his college experience with a B.A. in English; minors in philosophy, psychology, history and writing; a teaching assistantship at Washington State University and a fantasy trilogy called The Song of Flame and Thunder.

"The Road to Levenshir" is an excerpt from The Song of Flame and Thunder, *and Pat's hopes have risen since it won first place in the second quarter of this year's contest. "It's the first objective confirmation of my skill as a writer, my foot in the door for finding an agent or a publisher. I guess you could call it a beginning."*

About the Illustrator

Jason Pastrana was eighteen years old and a senior in the visual arts program at South Miami Senior High when he won the Illustrators' Contest. Since that time, he has been applying to some of the top visual arts programs in the nation and has been accepted to Art Center College of Design in Pasadena, School of Visual Arts in New York, Maryland Institute College of Art and the Ringling School of Art and Design in Sarasota. His initial goal is to get a bachelor of fine arts degree followed by a master's degree in illustration.

Jason currently lives in Miami Beach with his family. He has two baby sisters, ages two and three, a teenage sister named Melissa, an awesome mother and incredibly wonderful stepfather. In his own words, "I could not ask for a more supportive and loving family, and everything that I am today I owe to them."

Jason adds that he has enjoyed working on the illustration piece for this story tremendously. As an aspiring illustrator, he feels the experience pushed him further to explore, research, think and re-think the vast number of design possibilities for a single scene.

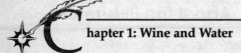

Chapter 1: Wine and Water

It started on one of those long, lonely stretches of road that you only find in the low hills of Vintas, far from civilization. I was, as my father used to say, on the edge of the map. I had passed only one or two travelers all day, and not a single inn. The thought of sleeping outdoors wasn't particularly troubling; I was used to it. But I had been eating from my pockets for a couple days now, and a warm meal would have been a welcome thing.

Night had nearly fallen and I had given up hope of something decent in my stomach, when I spotted a line of white smoke trailing into the darkening sky ahead of me. I took it for a farmhouse at first. Then I heard a faint strain of music and my hopes for a bed and a hearth-hot meal began to rise again. But as I came around a curve in the road, I found a surprise better than what I had hoped for.

Through the trees, about fifty feet from the road, there was a tall campfire flickering between two familiar wagons. Men and women lounged about, talking. One strummed a lute; another tapped a tabor idly against his leg. Others were pitching a tent between two trees while an older woman set up a tripod next to the fire. One of the men laughed.

Troupers. I grew excited and quickened my pace. As much as I enjoy the company of other people, troupers are a different breed. What's better, I recognized familiar markings on the side of one of the wagons. I won't tell you what they are, but they meant these were true troupers: my family, the Edema Ruh.

As I stepped from the trees, one of the men gave an alarmed shout, and before I could draw breath to speak, there were three swords pointing at me. Following the music, the sudden stillness was unnerving.

A handsome man with a black beard and a silver earring took a slow step forward. The point of his sword angled perfectly toward my eye. "Otto!" he shouted into the woods behind me. "If you're asleep, I swear on my mother's milk I'll gut you myself. Who the hell are you?"

The last was directed at me, but before I could respond, a voice came from the trees behind me. "I'm right here, Alleg, as . . . who's that? How in the devil's name did he get past me?"

When they'd drawn their swords, I'd raised my hands. It's a good habit to have whenever anyone points something sharp at you. Nevertheless, I was smiling as I spoke. "Sorry to startle you, Alleg. . . ."

"Save it," he said coldly. "You have one breath left to tell me why you were sneaking around our camp." He took a step closer to me, "And if you even look at that sword you're wearing," he gestured significantly with the tip of his sword, "we'll cut that down to half a breath."

Still smiling, I turned so everyone by the fire could see the lute case I had slung across my back.

The change in Alleg's attitude was immediate. He relaxed and sheathed his sword. The others followed suit as he smiled and approached me, laughing.

I laughed too. "One family."

"One family." He shook my hand. Turning to the fire he shouted, "We have a guest tonight!" There was a low cheer, and everyone went busily back to whatever they had been doing before I arrived.

A thick-bodied man wearing a sword came stomping out of the trees. "I'll be damned if he came past me, Alleg. He's probably from—"

"He's from our family," Alleg interjected smoothly.

"Oh," Otto said, obviously taken aback. He looked at the lute that now hung at my side. "Welcome then."

"I didn't go past you, actually," I lied, not wanting to make him look bad. "I heard the music and circled around. I thought you might be a different troupe, and I was going to surprise them."

Otto gave Alleg a superior look, then turned and trudged back into the woods.

Alleg laughed again and put his arm around my shoulders. "You'll have to forgive him. He's been irritable for weeks. Myself, I think he's constipated. Might I offer you a drink?"

"Some water, if you can spare it."

"No guest drinks water by our fire," he protested. "Only our best wine will touch your lips."

"The water of the Edema is sweeter than wine to those who have been upon the road." I smiled at him.

"Then have water and wine, to your desire." He led me to one of the wagons, where there was a water barrel.

Following a tradition older than time, I drank a ladle of water and used a second ladle to wash my hands and face. Patting my face dry with the sleeve of my shirt, I looked up at him and smiled. "It's good to be home again."

He clapped me on the back. "Come. Let me introduce

Illustrated by Jason Pastrana

you to the rest of your family."

He led me to two men with scruffy not-quite beards. "Fren and Josh are our two best singers, excepting myself, of course." I shook their hands.

Next were the two men with instruments by the fire. "Gaskin plays lute, Manst does pipe and tabor." They both smiled at me, Manst giving the tabor a shake.

"There's Tim," Alleg pointed across the fire to a tall man oiling a sword, "and Otto, whom you've already met. They're our strong arm. They keep us from falling into danger on the road." Tim was as tall as Otto was large. He nodded to me, looking up only briefly from sharpening what looked to be a well-notched sword.

"Here is Anne." Alleg gestured to an older woman with a pinched expression and a gray bun of hair. "She keeps us fed and dressed, and plays mother to us all." Anne continued to cut carrots for the stew, ignoring both of us.

"Far from last is our own Kete, who holds the keys to all our hearts." Kete had hard eyes and a mouth like a thin line, but her expression softened a little when I kissed her hand.

"And that's all of us," Alleg said with a smile and a little bow. "Your name is?"

"Kvothe."

"Welcome, Kvothe. Rest yourself and be at your ease. Is there anything we can do for you?"

"One thing perhaps."

Alleg looked at me curiously.

"A bit of that wine you mentioned earlier?" I smiled.

He touched the heel of his hand to his forehead. "Of course! Or would you prefer ale? We were getting ready to crack a keg when you surprised us."

"Ale would be fine."

He returned in a minute or two and handed me a tall glass. I touched it to my lips. "This is excellent," I complimented him, seating myself on a convenient stump.

He tipped an imaginary hat. "Thank you. We were lucky enough to nick it on our way through Levenshir a couple days ago."

That gave me a little pause. "Nick it?" I asked, somewhat hesitantly. "I'm not quite sure I follow you."

"Have I been picking up the local dialect again?" He laughed at himself. "We picked it up easily, if you know what I mean." He gave a conspiratorial smile.

I forced myself to relax and return the smile. "I see."

"How's the road been treating you of late?"

I stretched backward and sighed. "Not bad for a lone minstrel. I play whatever they pay me to, then after they drink themselves to sleep . . ." I shrugged, "I take advantage of what opportunities present themselves. About two weeks ago, I stole the virtue from the mayor's wife. But that's about all. I have to be careful, since I'm alone."

Alleg nodded wisely. "The only safety we have is in numbers," he admitted, then nodded to my lute. "Would you favor us with a bit of a song while we're waiting for Anne to finish dinner?"

"Certainly," I said, setting down my drink. "What would you like to hear?"

"Can you play 'Leave the Town Tinker'?"

"Can I? You tell me." I lifted my lute from its case and began to play. Everyone stopped what they were doing to listen to me. I even caught sight of Otto near the edge of the trees as he left his lookout to listen.

When I was done, everyone applauded enthusiastically. "You can play it," Alleg admitted. Then his expression became serious and he tapped a finger to his mouth, thoughtfully. "How would you like to walk the road with us for a while?" he asked after a moment. "We could use another player."

I took a long moment to consider it. "I *have* been a long time away from the family," I admitted, looking around at everyone sitting in the firelight. "But . . . ."

"One is a bad number for a Ruh on the road," Alleg said persuasively, running a finger along the edge of his dark beard.

I sighed. "Ask me again in the morning."

He slapped my knee, grinning. "Good! That means we have all night to convince you."

I replaced my lute and excused myself for a call of nature. Coming back, I stopped and knelt next to Anne, who still stooped by the fire. "What are you making for us, Mother?" I asked.

"Stew," she said shortly.

I smiled. "What's in it?"

She squinted at me. "Lamb," she said, as if daring me to challenge the fact.

"It's been a great long while since I've had lamb, Mother," I said. "Could I have a taste?"

"You'll wait, same as everyone else," she said sharply.

"Not even a small taste?" I wheedled, giving her my best ingratiating smile.

She drew a breath, then darted a look at Alleg. He was watching her from across the fire. "Oh, fine," she said throwing up her hands. "It won't be my fault if your stomach sets to aching."

I laughed. "No, Mother. It won't be your fault." I reached for the long-handled wooden spoon and drew it out. After blowing on it, I took a bite. "Mother!" I exclaimed. "You've done better on the road than wives hope for in their homes. This is the best thing to touch my lips in a full year."

"Hmmmph," she said.

"It's the first truth, Mother," I said earnestly. "Anyone who does not enjoy this fine stew is hardly one of the Ruh, in my opinion."

She turned back to stir the pot and shooed me away, but her expression wasn't as sharp as it had been before.

I returned to my seat next to Alleg. Gaskin leaned forward. "You've given us a song. Is there anything you'd like to hear?" he asked solicitously.

"How about 'Piper Wit'?" I asked.

His brow furrowed. "I don't recognize that one. Maybe I know it by a different name? . . ."

"It's about a clever Edema Ruh who kills a farmer while he's stealing his purse."

Gaskin shook his head. "I'm afraid not."

I bent to pick up my lute. "Let me; it's a song every one of us should know."

"Pick something else," Manst protested. "I'll play you something on the pipes. You've played for us once already tonight."

I smiled at him. "I forgot you piped. You'll like this one," I assured him. "Piper's the hero. Besides, I don't mind at all. You're feeding my belly, I'll feed your ears." Before they could raise any more objections, I started to play, quick and light.

They laughed through the whole thing. From the beginning, when the fumbling farmer gets killed, to the end, when Piper manages to seduce the dead man's wife and daughter. I left off the last two verses where the townsfolk kill Piper. It made for a good ending.

Either none of my audience noticed my omission, or they approved of it.

Manst wiped his eyes after I was done. "Heh. I'm better off knowing that one. Besides," he shot a look at Kete where she sat across the fire, "it's an honest song. Women can't keep their hands off a piper."

Kete snorted derisively and turned away.

Alleg laughed at the exchange and pushed more ale on me. I accepted, and we talked of small things until Anne announced the stew was done. Everyone fell to, breaking the silence only to compliment Anne on her cooking.

"Honestly, Anne," Alleg pleaded after his second bowl. "Tell me. Did you lift a little pepper back in Levenshir?" Anne looked pleased at all the praise, but didn't say anything.

As we were eating, I asked Alleg, "Have times been good for you and yours?"

"Oh, certainly," he said between mouthfuls. "Levenshir especially, about three days back, was especially good to us." He winked. "You'll see how good later."

"I'm glad to hear it."

"In fact, we did so well that I feel free offering you anything you would like. Anything at all. It's yours already, of course, being family and all." He leaned toward me and said in a stage whisper, "But I want you to know that this is a blatant attempt to bribe you into staying on with us. We would make a thick purse off that lovely voice of yours."

"Not to mention the songs he could teach us," Gaskin chimed in.

"Don't help him bargain, boy." Alleg gave a mock snarl. "I have the feeling this is going to be hard enough as it is."

I gave it a little thought. "I suppose I could stay . . . ." I let myself trail off uncertainly.

Alleg gave a knowing smile. "But . . . ."

"But I would ask for three things."

"Hmmmm, three things." He looked me up and down. "Just like in one of the stories."

"It only seems right," I urged.

He gave a hesitant nod. "I suppose it does. And how long would you travel with us?"

"Until no one objects to my leaving."

"Does anyone have any problem with this?" Alleg looked around.

"What if he asks for one of the wagons?" Tim asked. His voice startled me; it was a harsh rasp, like two bricks grinding together.

"It won't matter, as he'll be traveling with us," Alleg argued. "They belong to all of us, anyway. Besides, we have him for as long as we like, and not one minute more." He winked at me.

There were no more objections. Alleg and I shook hands on it, and there was a small cheer.

Gaskin held up his glass. "To Kvothe and his songs. I have a feeling he will be worth whatever he costs us."

Everyone drank, and I held up my own glass. "I swear on my mother's milk, none of you will ever make a better deal than the one you made with me tonight." This evoked a more enthusiastic cheer and everyone drank again.

Wiping his mouth, Alleg looked me in the eye. "So, what is the first thing you would have from us?"

I lowered my head. "It's a little thing, really. But sometimes little things make a big difference in a life. I lost my tent when I was chased out of a town a couple weeks ago. I could use a new one."

Alleg smiled and waved his glass like a king granting a boon. "Certainly, you'll have my own tent. Piled with furs and blankets a foot deep." He made a gesture over the fire to where Fren and Josh sat. "Go set it up for him."

"That's all right," I protested. "I can manage it myself."

"Hush, it's good for them. Makes them feel useful. Speaking of which"—he made another gesture at Tim. "Bring them out, would you?"

Tim stood and pressed a hand to his stomach. "I'll do it in a quick minute. I'll be right back." He turned to walk off into the woods. "I don't feel very good."

"That's what you get for eatin' like you're at a trough," Otto called after him. Then he turned back to the rest of us. "Someday he'll realize he can't eat more 'n me and not feel sick."

"Since Tim's busy painting a tree, I'll go get them," Manst said with thinly veiled eagerness.

"I'm on guard tonight," Otto said, "I'll go get 'em."

"*I'll* get them," Alleg said firmly, and stared the other two back into their seats. He walked behind the wagon on my left.

Josh and Fren came out of the other wagon with a tent, ropes and stakes. "Where do you want it?" Josh asked.

"That's not a question you usually have to ask a man, is it, Josh?" Fren joked, nudging his friend with an elbow.

"I tend to snore," I warned them. "You'll probably want me a little away from everyone else." I pointed, "Over between those two trees would be fine."

"I mean, with a man, you normally know where they want it, don't you, Josh?" Fren continued as they wandered off in the direction that I had pointed and began to string up the tent.

Alleg returned a minute later with a pair of lovely young girls. One had a lean body and face, with straight black hair cut short like a boy's. The other was more generously rounded with curling golden hair. They both had hopeless expressions and looked to be about sixteen.

"Meet Krin and Ell." Alleg smiled. "They are one of the ways in which Levenshir was generous to us. Tonight, one of them will be keeping you warm. My gift to you, as the new member in our family." He made a show of looking them over. "Which one would you like?"

I looked from one to the other. "That's a hard choice. Let me think on it a little while."

Alleg sat both of them down near the edge of the fire and set a bowl of stew in each of their hands. The girl with the golden hair, Ell, ate woodenly for a few bites, then slowed to a stop like a toy winding down. Her eyes looked almost blind, as if she were watching something none of us could see. Krin's eyes, on the other hand, were focused fiercely into the fire. She sat stiffly with her bowl in her lap.

"Girls," Alleg chided, "don't you know that things will get better as soon as you start cooperating?" Ell took another slow bite, then stopped. Krin stared stiffly into the fire.

Alleg sighed and knelt beside them. "Girls, it is time to eat. You're going to eat, aren't you?" His expression was calm, but his tone was angry. The response was the same as before. One slow bite. One stiff rebellion.

Gritting his teeth, he took the dark-haired girl firmly by the chin.

"Don't," I urged. "They'll eat when they get hungry enough." Alleg looked up at me curiously, and I reassured him. "I know what I'm talking about. Give them something to drink instead."

Alleg looked for a moment as if he might continue anyway, then shrugged and let go of Krin's jaw. "We'll try it your way. I'm sick of force-feeding this one. Let her starve if she wants." He left, poured each of them a cup and set it in their unresisting hands.

"Water?" I asked.

"Ale," he said. "It'll be better for them if they aren't eating."

I stifled my protest. Ell drank in the same vacant manner in which she had eaten. Krin moved her eyes from the fire to the cup to me. I felt an almost physical shock seeing her resemblance to Denna. Still looking at me, she drank, her hard eyes telling me nothing of what was happening inside her mind.

"Bring them over to sit by me," I said. "It might help me to make up my mind."

Ell was docile. Krin was stiff. They both allowed themselves to be led.

Tim came back looking a little pale. He sat by the fire where Otto gave him a little shove. "More stew?" he asked maliciously.

"Sod off," Tim rasped weakly.

"A little ale might settle your stomach," I advised.

He nodded, seeming eager for anything that might help him. Gaskin fetched him a mug.

By this time, the girls were sitting on either side of me, facing the fire. Closer, I saw things I had missed before. Red marks on their wrists told me that they had been tied. I saw a fading bruise on the back of Krin's neck. They both smelled clean, to my surprise. I guessed Kete had been taking care of them.

They were also much more lovely up close. I reached out to touch their shoulders. Krin flinched, then stiffened. Ell didn't react at all.

From off in the direction of the trees, Fren called out, "It's done. Do you want us to light a candle for you?"

"Yes, please," I called back. I looked from one girl to the other and then to Alleg. "I can't decide," I told him honestly. "So I will have both."

Alleg laughed incredulously, then seeing I was serious, he protested, "Oh, come now. That's hardly fair to the rest of us. Besides, you can't possibly . . ."

I gave him a frank look.

"Well," he hedged, "Even if you can. It . . ."

"This is the second thing I ask for," I said formally. "Both of them."

Otto made a cry of protest that was echoed in the expressions of Gaskin and Manst.

I smiled at them. "Only for tonight."

Fren and Josh came back from setting up my tent. "Be thankful he didn't ask for you, Otto," Fren said to the big man. "That's what Josh would have asked for, isn't it, Josh?"

"Shut your hole, Fren." Otto said in an exasperated tone, "Now I feel ill."

I stood and slung my lute over one shoulder. Then I led both lovely girls, one golden and one dark, toward my tent.

Chapter 2: Black by Moonlight

Fren and Josh had done a good job with the tent. It was tall enough to stand in, but still crowded with both me and the girls standing. I gave the golden-haired one, Ell, a gentle push toward the bed of thick blankets. "Sit down," I said gently.

When she didn't respond, I took her by the shoulders and eased her into a sitting position. She let herself be moved, but her wide blue eyes were vacant. I checked her head for any signs of a wound. Not finding any, I guessed she was in deep shock, recognizing the symptoms from my time in the Medica.

I took a moment and dug through my travel sack. I shook some powdered leaf into my traveling cup and added some water from my waterskin. I set the cup into Ell's hands and she took hold of it absently. "Drink it," I encouraged, trying for a tone of gentle authority, hoping to strike some chord in her.

It may have worked, or perhaps she was just thirsty. Whatever the reason, Ell drained the cup to the bottom. Her eyes still held the same faraway look.

I shook another measure of the powdered leaf into the cup, refilled it with water and held it out for the dark-haired one to drink. Her eyes appeared as vacant as Ell's, but I could tell she was more aware than she appeared to be.

We stayed there for several minutes, my arm outstretched, her arms motionless at her sides. Finally, she blinked and focused her eyes on me. "What did you give her?" she asked.

"Crushed Velia," I said gently, neglecting to mention the charcoal. "It's a counter-toxin. There was poison in the stew."

Her eyes told me she didn't believe me. "I didn't eat any of the stew."

"It was in the ale too. I saw you drink that."

"Good," she said. "I want to die."

I gave a deep sigh. "It won't kill you, not with as little as you drank. It will just make you miserable. You'll throw up and be weak for a day or two." I raised the cup, offering it to her.

"Why do you care if they kill me?" she asked tone-lessly. "If they don't do it now, they'll do it later. I'd rather die . . ." She clenched her teeth before she finished the sentence.

"They didn't poison you. I poisoned them and you happened to get some of it. I'm sorry, but this will help you over the worst of it."

Krin's gaze wavered for a second, then became iron-hard again. She looked at the cup, then fixed her gaze on me. "If it's harmless, you drink it."

"I can't drink it," I explained. "It's harmless, but it would put me to sleep and I have things to do tonight."

Krin's eyes darted to the bed of furs laid out on the floor of the tent.

I smiled my gentlest, saddest smile. "Not those sort of things."

Still she didn't move. We stood there for a long while. I heard a muted retching sound from off in the woods. I sighed and lowered the cup. Looking down, I saw that Ell had already curled up and gone to sleep. Her face looked almost peaceful. I took a deep breath and looked back up at Krin.

"You don't have any reason to trust me," I said, looking straight into her eyes. "Not after what has happened to you. But I hope you will." I held out the cup again.

She met my eyes without blinking and, after a long moment, she reached for the cup. She drank it off in one swallow, choked a little and sat down. Her eyes stayed hard as marble as she stared at the wall of the tent. I sat down, slightly apart from her.

In ten minutes she was asleep. I covered the two of them with a blanket and watched their faces. In sleep they were even more beautiful than before. I reached out to brush a strand of hair from Krin's cheek. To my surprise, she opened her eyes and stared at me.

I froze with my hand on her cheek. We watched each other for a second. Then her eyes drew closed again. I couldn't tell if it was the drug pulling her under or her own will surrendering to sleep.

I settled myself at the entrance of the tent and laid Caesura across my knees. I felt rage like a fire inside me; the sight of the two sleeping girls was like a strong wind fanning the coals. I set my teeth and forced myself to think of what had happened here, letting the fire burn fiercely, letting the heat of it fill me. I drew deep breaths, tempering myself for what was to come.

•••

I waited for three hours, listening to the sounds of the camp. Muted conversation drifted toward me for a while, shapes of sentences with no individual words. But they faded quickly, mixing with soft cursing and sounds of people being ill. I made the circle breath as Tempi had shown me, relaxing my body. Slowly counting my exhalations to mark the passing time.

Then, opening my eyes, I looked at the stars and judged the time to be right. I slowly unfolded myself from my sitting position and made a long, slow stretch. The half-moon illuminated everything in silhouettes and silver.

I approached the campfire slowly. It had fallen to sullen coals that did nothing to light the space between the two wagons. Otto was there, his huge body slumped against one of the wheels. I smelled vomit. "Is that you, Kvothe?" he asked blurrily.

"Yes." I continued my even walk toward him.

"That bitch Anne didn't let the lamb cook through," he moaned. "I swear to holy God I've never been this sick before." He looked up at me. "Are you all right?"

Caesura leapt, caught the moonlight briefly on her blade and tore his throat. He staggered to one knee, then toppled to his side with his hands staining black as they clutched his neck. I left him bleeding darkly in the moonlight, unable to cry out, dying but not dead.

Manst startled me as I came around the wagon. He made a surprised noise as he saw me walk around the corner with my naked sword. But the poison made him sluggish and he had barely managed to raise his hands before Caesura took him in the chest. He choked a scream as he fell backward, twisting on the ground.

None of them had been sleeping soundly due to the poison, and Manst's cry set them staggering from the wagons and tents, looking around wildly. Two indistinct shapes that I knew must be Josh and Fren leapt from the open back of the wagon closest to me. I struck one in the eye before he hit the ground and tore the belly from the other.

Everyone saw, and now there were screams in earnest. Most of them began to run drunkenly into the trees, some falling as they went. But the tall shape of Tim hurled itself at me. The heavy sword he had been sharpening all evening glinted silver in the moonlight. I took off his hand as quickly as I could, knowing that every moment was vital.

I ran after the fleeing shapes, not wanting to lose them in the forest at night. I was hurried, and stupid, so when Alleg threw himself on me from the shadow of a tree I wasn't ready. He had no sword, only a small knife flashing in the moonlight. But a knife is enough to kill a man. He stabbed me in the stomach as we rolled to the ground. I struck the side of my head against a root and tasted blood.

Despite that, I fought my way to my feet before he did and cut the hamstring on his leg. Then I stabbed him in the stomach and left him cursing on the ground as I went to hunt the others. I held one hand tight across my stomach. I knew the pain would hit me soon and, after that, I might not have long to live.

• • •

But I didn't die. In fact, when I dared to look at the wound about an hour later, I was surprised to see it was nothing worse than a shallow gash. My traveling cloak had a tidy slice cut in it, but, more important, my belt was cut nearly in two where the leather was doubled over near the buckle. Doesn't sound very heroic, I admit, but it's the truth: I was saved by my belt. That's why I'm telling this story, I suppose. So you can see the truth of things. I'm not a hero. There's no such thing. Not unless a hero is just someone lucky enough to live through their own stupidity.

It was a long night, and I will not trouble you with any further details. I found all the rest of them as they made their way through the forest: Gaskin, Anne, Kete and Tim. Anne had broken her leg in her reckless flight, and Tim made it nearly a mile despite the loss of his hand. Each of them begged for mercy as I stalked them through the forest, but nothing they said could appease me. It was a terrible night, but I found them all. There was no honor to it, no glory. But there was justice of a sort, and blood, and in the end I brought their bodies back.

•••

I came back to my tent as the sky was beginning to color to a familiar blue. I wiped my sword, sat in the wet grass in front of the tent and began to think.

Chapter 3: The Broken Circle

I had been busy for more than an hour when the sun finally peered over the tops of the trees and began to burn the dew from the grass. I had found a flat rock and a hammer and was proceeding to pound a spare horseshoe I'd found into a different shape. Above the fire, a pot of oats was boiling.

I was just putting the finishing touches on the horseshoe when I saw a flicker of movement from the corner of my eye. It was Krin peeking around the corner of the wagon. I guessed I'd woken her with the sound of hammering iron.

"Oh, my God!" Her hand went to her mouth and she took a couple stunned steps out from behind the wagon. "You killed them."

"Yes," I said simply, my voice sounding dead in my ears. I examined the horseshoe that I had hammered into a rough circular shape and decided it was close enough. It was short work to bind it firmly to one end of a long, straight branch I had cut. After I moved the kettle off the fire, I thrust the horseshoe into the coals.

Seeming to recover from some of her shock, Krin slowly approached, eyeing the row of bodies I had laid on the other side of the fire. I had done nothing other than lay them out in a rough line. Blood stained the bodies and their clothes, and their wounds gaped openly. After coming within a couple feet of them, Krin stopped and stared as if she were afraid they might start to move again.

"What are you doing?" she asked finally.

In answer, I pulled the now hot horseshoe from the coals and approached the nearest body. It was Tim. I pressed the hot iron against the back of his hand. The skin smoked and hissed and stuck to the hot metal. After a moment I pulled it away; it left a black burn against his white skin. A broken circle. I moved back to the fire and began to heat the iron again.

Krin stood mutely, still a little too stunned to react normally. Not that there could be a normal way to react in a situation like this. But she didn't scream or run off as I thought she might. She simply looked at the broken circle and asked again, "What are you doing?"

I thought for a long moment before responding. When I finally spoke, my voice sounded strange to my own ears. "All of the Edema Ruh are one family, like a closed circle. It doesn't matter if some of us are strangers to others, we are still family, still close. We have to be this way, because there are not many of us, and people don't trust us because, wherever we travel, we are strangers.

"We have laws among us. Rules we follow. When one of us does a thing that cannot be forgiven or mended, if he jeopardizes the safety or the honor of the Edema Ruh, he is killed and branded with the broken circle to show that he is no longer one of us. It is rarely done. There is rarely a need."

I pulled the iron from the fire and walked to the next body. Otto. I pressed it to the back of his hand and listened to it hiss. "These men were *not* Edema Ruh. But they made themselves out to be. They did things no Edema would do, so I am making sure the world knows that they were not part of our family. The Ruh do not do the sort of things that these men did."

"But the wagons," she protested, "the instruments."

"They were not Edema Ruh," I said firmly. "They probably weren't even real troupers, just a group of thieves who killed a band of Ruh performers and thought they could take their place."

"But . . . how?"

"I am curious about that myself," I said, pulling the broken circle from the fire again. I moved to Alleg and pressed it firmly into the palm of his hand.

The false trouper jerked away and screamed himself awake.

"He isn't dead!" Krin exclaimed shrilly.

I had examined the wound earlier. "He's dead," I said coldly. "He just hasn't stopped moving yet." I turned to look him in the eye. "How about it, Alleg? How did you come by a pair of Edema wagons?"

"Ruh bastard," he cursed at me with blurry defiance.

"Yes," I said. "I am. And you are not. So how did you learn my family's signs and customs?"

"How did you know?" he asked. "We knew the words, the shake. We knew water and wine and songs before supper. How did you know?"

"Ruh don't do what you did. Ruh don't steal, don't kidnap girls."

He shook his head with a mocking smile. There was blood on his teeth. "Everyone knows what you people do. . . . ."

My temper exploded. "Everyone thinks they know. They think rumor is the truth! Ruh don't do this!" I gestured wildly around me. "People only think those things because of people like you!" My anger flared even hotter and I found myself screaming. "Now tell me what I want to know or God will weep when he hears what I've done to you!"

He paled and had to swallow before he found his voice. "There was an old man and his wife and a couple other players. I traveled guard with them for a while and they kind of took me in . . . ." He ran out of breath and gasped a bit as he tried to get it back.

He'd said enough. "So you killed them."

He shook his head. "No . . . were attacked on the road. I showed the others afterward . . . acting like a troupe." He gasped again, trying to draw a breath against the pain. ". . . good life."

I turned away, disgusted. He actually was one of Ruh of sorts. One of our adopted family. It made everything ten times worse knowing that. I pushed the circle into the coals of the fire again, then looked to the girl as it heated. Her eyes had gone to flint again as she watched Alleg.

Not sure if it was the right thing to do, I offered her the brand. Her face went hard and she took it.

Alleg didn't seem to understand what was about to happen until she had the hot iron against his chest. He shrieked and twisted but lacked the strength to get away as she pressed it hard against him. She grimaced as he struggled weakly against the iron, her eyes brimming with angry tears.

After a long minute, she pulled the iron away and stood, crying quietly. I let her be.

Alleg looked up at her and somehow managed to find his voice. "Ah, girl, we had some good times, didn't we?" She stopped crying and looked at him. "Don't—"

I kicked him sharply in the side before he could say anything else. He stiffened in mute pain and then spat blood at me. I landed another kick and he went limp. Not knowing what else to do, I took back the brand and began heating it again. There was a long silence. "Is Ell still asleep?"

Krin nodded.

"Do you think it would help for her to see this?"

She thought about it, wiping at her face with a hand. "I don't think so," she said finally. "I don't think she *could* see it right now. She's not right in her head."

I nodded. "The two of you are from Levenshir?" I asked, to keep the silence at arm's length.

"My family farms just north of Levenshir," Krin said. "Ell's father is mayor."

"When did these come into your town?" I asked, as I set the brand to the back of another hand. The smell of burned flesh was becoming thick in the air.

"What day is it?"

I counted in my head. "Luten."

"They came into town on Theden." She paused. "Five days ago?" her voice tinged with disbelief. "We were glad to have the chance to see a play, hear the news from far off. Listen to some music." Her voice choked off for a moment and she looked down. "They were camped on the west edge of town. And when I came to get my fortune read they told me to come back that night. They seemed so friendly, so exciting." She looked away, back at the tent. "I guess Ell got an invitation too."

I finished branding the backs of their hands. I had been planning to do their faces too, but the iron was slow to heat in the fire and I was quickly growing sick of this work. I hadn't slept, and the anger that had burned hot all through the night was in its final flicker, leaving me feeling cold and numb.

I made a gesture to the pot of oats I'd pulled off the fire. "Are you hungry?"

"Yes," she said quickly. She darted a look toward the bodies. "No."

I gave a faint smile. "Me, neither. Go wake up Ell and we can get you home."

Krin hurried off to the tent. After she disappeared inside, I turned to the line of bodies. "Does anyone object to my leaving the troupe?" I asked.

None of them did. So I left.

Chapter 4: The Road to Levenshir

It was an hour's work to drive the wagons into a thick piece of forest and hide them well enough to keep them from accidental discovery. I destroyed their Edema markings and unhitched the horses. There was only one saddle, so I loaded the other two horses with food and whatever other portable valuables I could find.

When I returned with the horses, Krin and Ell were waiting for me. More precisely, Krin was waiting for me. Ell was standing nearby, her expression vacant, her eyes empty.

"Do you know how to ride?" I asked Krin.

She nodded and I handed her the reins to the saddled horse. She got one foot in the stirrup and seemed to change her mind. "I'll walk."

"Do you think Ell would stay on a horse?"

Krin looked over to where the blonde girl was standing. One of the horses nuzzled her curiously and got no response. "Probably. But I don't think it would be good for her. After . . . ."

I nodded in understanding. "We'll all walk then."

• • •

"*What is the heart of the Way?*" I asked my old swordmaster.

Tempi replied without hesitation, "*Success and right action.*"

"*Which is the more important, success or rightness?*"

"*They are the same. If you act rightly, success follows.*"

"*But others may succeed by doing wrong things,*" I pointed out.

"*Wrong things never lead to success,*" Tempi said firmly. "*If a man acts wrongly and succeeds, that is not the Way. Without the Way, there is no true success.*"

"*Sir?*" a voice called. "*Sir?*"

My eyes focused on Krin. Her hair was windblown, her young face tired. She looked at me timidly. "Sir? It's getting dark."

I looked around and saw twilight creeping in from the east. I was tired and had fallen into a walking doze after we had stopped for a rest and lunch at midday.

"Just call me Kvothe, Krin. And thanks for waking me up; my mind was somewhere else."

Krin and I set up camp. She gathered wood and started a fire. I unloaded the horses, fed and rubbed them down. Then I took a few minutes to set up the tent. Despite what I'd told Alleg, normally I don't bother with a tent when I'm traveling. But I brought it because there was room for it on the horses, and I guessed the girls weren't used to sleeping out of doors. However, after setting up the tent, I realized I had only brought one blanket from the false troupe's supplies. Stupidity again, and fatigue. I made up the best bed I could using the single blanket and the one I always carry with me when I travel. By the time I was finished, Krin had dinner ready. Potato soup with bacon and toasted bread.

Ell sat blankly by the fire, staring into nothing.

Ell worried me. She had been the same all day. Walking listlessly, never speaking or responding to anything Krin or I said to her. Her eyes would follow things, but there was no thought behind them. Krin and I had discovered the hard way that if left to herself she would stop walking or wander off the road if something in the trees caught her eye.

Krin handed me a bowl and spoon as I sat down. "It smells good," I complimented her.

She half-smiled as she dished a second bowl for herself. She started to fill a third bowl, then hesitated, realizing that Ell couldn't feed herself.

"Would you like some soup, Ell?" I asked, in normal tones. "It smells good."

She gave no response. Her eyes reflected the dancing patterns of the fire.

"Do you want to share mine?" I asked, as if it were the most natural thing in the world. I moved closer to where she sat and blew on a spoonful to cool it. "Here you go."

She ate it mechanically. I blew on another spoonful. "It's Ellie, isn't it?" I asked her, then looked to Krin. "Is it short for Ellie?"

Krin nodded. I fed Ellie another mouthful.

"It sure was a long walk today," I said conversationally. "How do your feet feel, Krin?"

She continued to watch me with her serious dark eyes. "A little sore."

"Mine, too. I can't wait to get my shoes off. Are your feet sore, Ellie?"

No response. I fed her another bite.

"It was pretty hot too. But it should cool off tonight. Good sleeping weather. Won't that be nice, Ellie?"

No response. Krin continued to watch me from the other side of the fire. I took a bite of soup for myself. "This is truly fine, Krin," I said earnestly, then turned back to the vacant girl. "It's a good thing we have Krin to cook for us, Ellie. Everything I cook tastes like horseshit."

On her side of the fire, Krin tried to laugh with a mouthful of soup with appropriate results. I thought I saw a flicker in Ellie's eyes. "If I had some horse apples I could make us a horse apple pie for dessert," I offered. "I could make some tonight if you want . . ." I trailed off, making it a question.

Ell gave the slightest frown, a small wrinkle creased her forehead.

"You're probably right," I said. "It wouldn't be very good. Would you like more soup instead?"

The barest nod. I gave her a spoonful.

"It's a little salty, though. You probably want some water."

Another nod. I handed her the waterskin and she lifted it to her own lips. She drank for a long minute. She was probably parched from our long walk today. I would have to watch her more closely tomorrow to make sure she drank enough.

"Would you like a drink, Krin?" I asked.

"Yes, please," Krin said, her eyes fixed on Ellie's face.

Moving automatically, Ellie handed the waterskin in Krin's direction. Directly over the fire, the strap dragged in the coals and Krin grabbed it as quickly as she could, then added a belated, "Thank you, Ellie."

I kept the slow stream of conversation going through the whole meal. Ellie fed herself toward the end of it, and though her eyes were clearer, it was as if she were looking out through a thick pane of frosted glass, seeing but not seeing. Still, it was an improvement.

After she ate two bowls of soup and half a loaf of bread, her eyes began to bob closed. "Would you like to go to bed, Ellie?" I asked.

A more definite nod.

"Should I carry you to the tent?"

Her eyes opened wide at this and she shook her head firmly once.

"Maybe Krin would help you get ready for bed if you asked her."

Ellie turned to look in Krin's direction. Her mouth moved in a slight, vague way. Krin darted a glance at me and I nodded.

"Let's go and get tucked in then," Krin said, sounding every bit the older sister. She came over and took Ellie's hand, helping her to her feet. As they went into the tent, I finished off what was left of the soup and a piece of bread that had been too badly burnt for either of the girls to eat.

Before too long, Krin came back to the fire. "Is she sleeping?" I asked.

"Before her head was down. Do you think she will be all right?"

She was in shock. Her mind had stepped through the doors of madness to protect itself from what was happening. "It's probably just a matter of time," I said tiredly, hoping it was the truth. "The young heal quickly." I chuckled humorlessly as I realized that she was probably only a year or two younger than me. I felt every year twice tonight, some of them three times.

But despite the fact that I felt covered in lead, I forced myself to my feet and helped Krin clean the dishes. I sensed her growing uneasy as we finished our work and checked the horses. It grew worse as we approached the tent. I stopped and held the flap open for her. "I'll sleep out here tonight."

Her relief was tangible. "Are you sure?"

I nodded. She slipped inside and I let the flap fall closed behind her. Her head poked back out almost immediately, followed by a hand holding a blanket.

I shook my head. "You'll need them; there'll be a chill tonight." I pulled my cloak around me and lay directly in front of the tent. I didn't want Ellie wandering out and getting lost or hurt in the middle of the night.

"But won't you . . . ."

"I'll be fine," I said as I pulled my hood up over my ears. I was tired enough to sleep on a running horse. I was tired enough to sleep *under* a running horse.

Krin ducked her head back into the tent. Soon I heard her nestling into the blankets. Then everything was quiet.

I lay down and closed my eyes. I remembered the surprised look on Otto's face as I cut his throat. I heard Alleg struggle weakly and curse me as I dragged him back to the wagons. I remembered the blood. The way it had felt against my hands. The thickness of it.

I had never really killed anyone before. Not coldly, not close up. I remembered how warm their blood had been. I remembered the way Kete had cried as I stalked her through the woods. "It was them or me!" she had screamed hysterically. "I didn't have a choice. It was them or me!"

I lay awake a long while. When I finally slept, the dreams were worse.

Chapter 5: Homecoming

We made poor time the next day. Krin and I were obliged to lead the horses as well as Ellie. Luckily, the horses were well behaved, as horses trained by the Edema Ruh tend to be. I thank my luck for that. If they had been as wayward as the mayor's poor daughter, we might have never made it to Levenshir at all.

Krin and I did our best to keep Ellie engaged in conversation as we walked. It seemed to help a bit. And by the time our noon meal came around, she seemed almost aware of what was going on around her. Almost.

I had an idea as we were getting ready to set out again after lunch. I led our dappled-gray mare over to where Ellie stood. Her golden hair was in a great tangle and she was trying to run one of her hands through it while her eyes wandered around in a distracted way, as if she didn't quite understand where she was.

"Ellie." She turned to look. "Have you met Graytail?" I gestured to the mare.

A faint, confused shake of the head.

"I need your help leading her. Have you led a horse before?"

A nod.

"She needs someone to lead her. Can you do it?"

Graytail looked at me with one large eye, as if to let me know she needed leading as much as I needed wheels to walk. But then she lowered her head a bit and nuzzled Ell in a motherly way. The girl reached out a hand to pet her gray nose almost automatically. Ellie nodded to my question, and actually reached to take the reins from me.

"Do you think that's a good idea?" Krin asked when I came back to pack the other horses.

"Graytail is gentle as a lamb."

"Just because Ell is witless as a sheep," Krin said archly, "doesn't make them a good pairing."

I cracked a smile. "We'll watch them closely for an hour or so. If it doesn't work, it doesn't. But sometimes the best help a person can find is helping someone else."

● ● ●

As I had slept poorly, I was twice weary today. I was almost tempted to ride the horse and doze in the saddle, but I couldn't bring myself to ride while the girls walked. It didn't seem right.

So I plodded along, leading my horse and nodding on my feet. But today I couldn't fall into the comfortable half-sleep I tend to use when walking. I was plagued with thoughts of Alleg, wondering if he was still alive.

I knew from my study at the university that the gut wound I had given him was fatal. I also knew it was a slow death. Slow and painful. With proper care it might be weeks before he died. Even alone in the middle of nowhere, with no medical attention at all, he could live for days with such a wound.

Not pleasant days. He would grow delirious with fever as the infection set in. Every movement would tear the wound again. He couldn't walk on his hamstrung leg, so if he wanted to move, he'd have to crawl. He would be cramped with hunger and burning with thirst by now.

But not dead from thirst. No. I had left a full water-skin nearby. I had laid it at his side before we had left. Not out of kindness. Not to make his last hours more bearable. I had left it because I knew that with water he would live longer, suffer more.

Leaving that waterskin was the most terrible thing I had ever done, and now that my anger had cooled to ashes I regretted it. I wondered how much longer he would live because of it. A day? Two? Certainly no more than two. I tried not to think what those two days would be like.

But even when I forced thoughts of Alleg from my mind, I had other demons to fight. I remembered bits and pieces of that night, the things the false troupers had said as I cut them down. The sounds the sword had made as it dug into them. The smell of their skin as I had branded them. I had killed two women. What would Tempi think of my actions? What would anyone think?

Exhausted from worry and lack of sleep, my thoughts spun in these circles for the remainder of the day. I set camp from force of habit and kept up a conversation with Ellie through an effort of will. The time for sleep came before I was ready. I found myself rolled in my cloak lying in the front of the girls' tent. I was dimly aware that Krin had started giving me the same vaguely worried look she had been giving Ell for the past two days.

I lay open-eyed for an hour before falling asleep, wondering about Alleg.

When I slept, I dreamt of the night that I had killed them. In my dream I stalked the forest like grim death, unwavering.

But it was different this time. I killed Otto; his blood spattered my hands like hot grease. Then I killed Manst and Josh and Tim. They moaned and screamed, twisting on the ground. Their wounds were horrible to look at, but I could not look away.

But then the faces changed and I was killing Taren, the bearded mercenary who had been a part of the troupe I had grown up with. Then I killed Trip, our acrobat. Then I was chasing Shandi, one of the dancers, through the moonlit forest, my sword naked in my hand. She was crying out, weeping in fear. When I finally caught her, she clutched at me, knocking me to the ground, burying her face in my chest, sobbing. "No, no, no," she begged. "No, no, no."

I came awake. I lay on my back, terrified and not knowing where my dream ended and the world began. After a brief moment, I realized the truth. Ell had crawled from the tent and lay curled against me. Her face pressed against my chest, her hand grasping desperately at my arm.

"No, no," she choked out. "No, no, no, no, no." Her body shook with helpless sobs when she couldn't say it anymore. My shirt was wet with hot tears. My arm was bleeding where she clutched it. I made consoling noises and brushed at her hair with my hand. After a long while she quieted and eventually fell into an exhausted sleep, still clinging tightly to my chest.

I lay very still, not wanting to wake her. My teeth were clenched. I thought of Alleg and Otto and all the rest; I remembered the blood and screaming and the smell of burning skin. I remembered it all and dreamed of worse things I could have done to them.

I never had the nightmares again. Sometimes I think of Alleg and I smile.

● ● ●

We made it to Levenshir the next day. Ell had come to her senses, but remained quiet and withdrawn. Still, things went quicker now that she was truly with us. The girls decided they had recovered enough to take turns riding the tall roan with the saddle.

We covered eight miles before we stopped at midday, with the girls becoming increasingly excited as they began to recognize turnings in the road. The shape of hills in the distance. A crooked tree by the wayside.

But as we drew closer still, they grew quiet, almost frightened.

"It's just over the hill here," Krin said, getting down off the roan. "You ride from here, Ell."

Ell looked from her to me, to her feet. She shook her head.

I watched them. "Are the two of you okay?"

"My father's going to kill me," Krin said suddenly, her face full of serious fear.

"Your father will be one of the happiest men in the world tonight," I said, then thought it best to be honest. "He might be angry too, but that's only because he's been scared out of his mind for the last eight days."

Krin seemed slightly reassured, but then Ellie burst out crying. Krin put her arms around her, making gentle words. When she had calmed a bit, I asked her what was the matter.

"No one will marry me," she sobbed. "I was going to marry Jason Waterson, help him run his store. He won't marry me now. No one will."

I looked up to Krin and saw the same fear reflected in her wet eyes. But Krin's eyes were angry, while Ell's held nothing but despair.

"Any man who thinks that way is a fool," I said, weighting my voice with all the conviction I could bring to bear. "And the two of you are too beautiful and too clever to be marrying fools."

It seemed to calm Ell somewhat. She looked up at me as if looking for something to believe.

"It's the truth," I said. "And it's not your fault. Make sure you remember it for these next couple days."

"I hate them!" Ell spat, surprising me with a sudden rage. "I hate men!" Her knuckles were white as she gripped Graytail's reins. Her face twisted into a mask of anger. Krin moved to put her arms around her, but when she looked at me I saw the sentiment reflected quietly in her dark eyes.

"You have every right to hate them," I said, feeling more anger and helplessness than ever before in my life. "But remember that it was a man who helped you when the time came. Not all of us are like that."

We stayed there for a while, not more than a half-mile from their town. We had a drink of water and a small bite to settle our nerves. Then I took them home.

• • •

Levenshir wasn't a big town. Two hundred people lived there, maybe three hundred if you counted the families in the surrounding farms. It was mealtime when we rode in, and the dirt road that split the town in half was empty and silent. Ellie had told me that her parents' house was on the far side of town. I hoped to get the girls there without being seen. They were worn down and distraught; the last thing they needed was to face a mob of gossipy neighbors.

But it wasn't meant to be. We were halfway through the town when I saw a flicker of movement in a window. Then a woman's voice cried out, "Ellie!" and in ten seconds people began to spill from every doorway in sight.

The women were the quickest, and inside a minute a dozen of them had formed a protective knot around the two girls, talking and crying and hugging one another. The girls didn't seem to mind. Perhaps it was better this way; a warm welcome home would do a lot to heal them.

The men held back, knowing that they were useless in situations like this. Most watched from doorways or porches; six or eight came down onto the street, moving slowly and eyeing up the situation. These were cautious men, farmers and friends of farmers. They knew the names of everyone within ten miles of their homes. There were no strangers in a town like Levenshir, except for me.

None of them were close relatives to the girls. Even if they were, they knew they wouldn't get close to the girls for at least an hour, maybe as much as a day. So they held back to let their wives and sisters take care of things. And since they didn't have anything else to do, their attention wandered briefly past the horses and settled onto me.

I motioned over a boy of ten or so. "Go tell the mayor that his daughter's back. Run!" He tore off in a cloud of road dust, his bare feet flying.

The men moved slowly closer to me. Their natural suspicion of strangers made ten times worse by recent events. A boy of fourteen or so wasn't as cautious as the rest and came right up to me, eyeing my sword, my cloak.

I sprung a question on him before he could do the same to me. "What's your name?"

"Pete."

"Can you ride a horse, Pete?"

He looked insulted. "S'nuf."

"Do you know where the Walker farm is?"

He nodded. "'Bout north two miles by the millway."

I stepped sideways and handed him the reins to the roan. "Go tell them their daughter's home. Then let them use the horse to come back to town."

He had a leg over the horse before I could offer him a hand up. I kept a hand on the reins long enough to shorten the stirrups so he wouldn't kill himself on the way there. "If you make it there and back without breaking your head or my horse's leg, I'll give you a penny," I said.

"You'll give me two," he said.

I laughed. He wheeled the horse around and was gone.

The men had wandered closer in the meantime, closing around me in a loose circle.

A tall fellow with a permanent scowl seemed to appoint himself the leader. "So who're you?" he asked, his tone speaking more clearly than his words: *Who the hell are you?*

"Kvothe," I answered pleasantly. "And yourself?"

"Don't know as that's any of your business," he growled. "What are you doing here?" *What the hell are you doing with our two girls?*

"God's mother, Jake," an older man said to him. "You don't have the sense God gave a dog. That's no way to talk to the—"

"Don't give me any of your lip, Benjamin," the scowling man bristled back. "I don't got to take it from you. We got a good right to know who he is." He turned to me and took a few steps in front of everyone else. "You one of those trouper bastards what came through here?"

I shook my head and attempted to look harmless. "No."

"I think you are. I think you look kinda like one of them Ruh. You got them eyes." The men around him craned to get a better look at my face.

"God, Jake," the old fellow chimed in again. "None of them had red hair. You remember hair like that. He ain't one of 'em."

"Why would I bring them back if I had been one of the men who took them?" I pointed out.

His expression grew darker and he continued his slow advance. "You gettin' smart with me? Maybe you think all us are stupid here? You think if you bring 'em back you'll get a reward or mebbe we won't send anyone else out after you?" He was almost within arm's reach of me now, scowling furiously.

I looked around and saw the same anger lurking in the faces of all the men who stood there. It was the sort of anger that comes to slow boil inside the hearts of good men who want justice, and finding it out of their grasp, decide on vengeance as a substitute.

I tried to think of a way to diffuse the situation, but before I could do anything, I heard Krin's voice lash out from behind me. "Jake, you get away from him!"

Jake paused, hands half raised against me. "Now . . . ."

But Krin was already stepping toward him. The knot of women loosened to release her, but stayed close. "He saved us, Jake," she shouted furiously, "you stupid shit-eater, *he* saved us. Where the hell were all of you? Why didn't you come get us?"

He backed away from me as anger and shame fought their way across his face. Anger won. "We came," he shouted back. "After we found out what happened, we went after 'em. They shot out Bil's horse from under him and he got his leg crushed. Jim got his arm stabbed. And old Cupper still ain't waked up from the thumping they give him. They almost killed us."

I looked again and saw anger on the men's faces. Saw the real reason for it. The helplessness they had felt, unable to defend their town from the false troupe's rough handling. Worse yet, the failure to reclaim the daughters of their friends and neighbors had shamed them.

"Well, it wasn't good enough," Krin shouted back hotly, her eyes burning. "He came and got us because he's a real man. Not like the rest of you who left us to die!"

The anger leapt out of a young man to my left, a farmboy, about seventeen. "None of this would have happened if you hadn't been running around like some Ruh whore!"

I broke his arm before I quite realized what I was doing. He screamed as he fell to the ground.

I pulled him to his feet by the scruff of his neck. "What's your name?" I snarled into his face.

"My arm!" he gasped, his eyes showing me their whites.

I shook him like a rag doll. "Name!"

"Jason," he blurted. "God's mother, my arm . . . ."

I took his chin in my free hand and turned his face toward Krin and Ell. "Jason," I hissed quietly in his ear, "I want you to look at those girls. And I want you to think about the hell that they've been through in these past days, tied hand and foot in the back of a wagon. And I want you to ask yourself what's worse: a broken arm or getting kidnapped by a stranger and raped three times a night."

Then, I turned his face toward me and spoke so quietly that even an inch away it was hardly a whisper. "After you've thought of that, I want you to pray to God to forgive you for what you just said. And if you mean it, Tehlu grant your arm heal straight and true." His eyes were terrified and wet. "After that, if you ever think an unkind thought about either of them, your arm will ache like there's hot iron in the bone. And if you ever say anything unkind, it will go to fever and slow rot and they'll have to cut it off to save your life." I tightened my grip on him watching his eyes widen. "And if you ever do anything to either of them, I'll know. I will come here, kill you and leave your body hanging in a tree."

There were tears on his face now, although whether from shame or fear or pain I couldn't guess. "Now you tell her you're sorry for what you said." I let go of him after making sure he had his feet under him and pointed him in the direction of Krin and Ellie. The women stood around them like a protective cocoon.

He clutched his arm weakly. "I'm sorry. I shouldn'ta said that, Ellie," he sobbed out, sounding more wretched and repentant than I would have thought possible, broken arm or no. "It was the devil talkin' out of me. I swear, though, I been sick worryin'. We all been. And we did try come get you, but they was a lot of them and they jumped us on the road, then we had to bring Bil home or he'd died from his leg."

Something tickled my memory about the boy's name. Jason? I suddenly suspected that I had just broken Ellie's boyfriend's arm. Somehow I couldn't feel bad for it just now. Best thing for him, really.

Looking around, I saw the anger had left the faces of the men around me, almost as if I'd used up the whole town's supply in a sudden furious flash. Instead, they watched Jason, looking slightly embarrassed, as if he were apologizing for the lot of them.

Then, looking past them, I saw a big, healthy looking man running down the street followed by a dozen other townsfolk. From the look on his face, I guessed it was Ellie's father, the mayor. He forced his way into the knot of women, gathered his daughter up in his arms and swung her around.

You typically find two types of mayors in small towns. The first type are balding, older men of considerable girth who are good with money and tend to wring their hands a lot when something unexpected happens. The second type are tall, broad-shouldered men whose families have grown slowly rich and strong because they had worked like angry bastards behind a plow for twenty generations. Ellie's father was the second sort.

He walked over to me, keeping one arm around his daughter's shoulders. "I understand I have you to thank for bringing our girls back." He reached out to shake my hand and I saw his arm was bandaged up tight. His grip was solid in spite of it. He smiled the widest grin I'd ever seen. "My name's Jim."

"How's the arm?" I asked, not realizing how it would sound. His smile faded a little and I was quick to add, "I've had some training as a physiker. And I know that those sort of things can be tricky to deal with when you're away from home." *When you're living in a country that thinks mercury is a cure-all,* I thought to myself.

His smile came back out from behind its cloud and he flexed his fingers. "It's stiff, but that's all. Just a little meat. They caught us by surprise. I got my hands on one of them, but he stuck me and got away. How did you end up getting the girls away from those godless Ruh bastards?" he spat.

"They weren't Edema Ruh," I said, my voice sounding more strained than I would have guessed. "They weren't even real troupers."

The smile began to fade again. "What do you mean?"

"They weren't Edema Ruh. We don't do the things that they did."

"Listen," he said plainly, his temper starting to rise a bit. "I know damn well what they do and don't do. They came in all sweet and nice, played a little music, made a penny or two. Then they started to make trouble around town. When we told them to leave, they took my girl." He almost breathed fire as he said the last words.

"*We?*" someone said faintly behind me. "Jim, he said *we*."

Jake scowled around the side of the Mayor to get a look at me again. "I told you he looked like one," he said triumphantly, then dropped his voice to a hush. "I know 'em. You can always tell by their eyes."

"Hold on," the mayor said with slow incredulity. "Are you telling me you're one of *them?*" His expression grew dangerous.

Before I could explain myself, Ellie had grabbed his arm, her expression terrified. "Oh, don't make him mad, Daddy," she said quickly, holding onto his good arm as if to pull him away from me. "Don't say anything to get him angry. He's not with them. He brought me back. He saved me."

The mayor seemed somewhat mollified by this, but his former congeniality was gone. "Explain yourself," he said grimly.

I sighed inside, realizing what I mess I'd made of this. "They weren't troupers, and they certainly weren't Edema Ruh troupers. They were bandits who had killed some of my family and stolen their wagons. They were only pretending to be performers."

"Why would anyone pretend to be Ruh?" he asked, as if the thought were incomprehensible.

"So they could do what they did," I snapped. "You let them into your town and they abused your trust. That is something the Edema Ruh would ever do."

"You never did answer my question," he said. "How did you get the girls away?"

"I took care of them," I said simply.

"He killed them," Krin said loudly enough for everyone to hear. "He killed them all."

I could feel everyone looking at me. Half of them were thinking, *All of them? He killed seven men?* The other half were thinking, *There were two women with them; does he mean them too?*

"Well, then," Jim said, looking down at me for a long moment. "Good," he said, as if he had just made up his mind. "Good. The world's a better place for it."

I felt everyone relax slightly. "These are their horses." I pointed to the two horses that had been carrying our baggage. "They belong to the girls now. About thirty miles east on the road you'll find the wagons. Krin can show you where they're hidden. They belong to the girls too."

"They'll fetch a good price in a bigger city," Jim mused.

"Together, with the instruments inside them and the clothes and such, they'll fetch a heavy penny," I agreed. "Split two ways, it'll make a fine dowry," I said firmly.

He met my eyes, nodded slowly as if understanding. "That it will."

"What about the things they stole from us?" a stout, balding man in an apron protested. "They smashed up my place and stole two barrels of my best ale!"

"Do you have any daughters?" I asked him calmly. The sudden stricken look on his face told me he did. I met his eye, held it. "Then I think you came away from this pretty well."

The mayor looked around and finally noticed Jason clutching his broken arm. "What happened to you?"

Jason looked at his feet. There was tense silence for a moment. Jake spoke up for him. "He said some things he shouldn't 've."

The mayor looked around and saw that getting more of an answer would involve an ordeal. He shrugged and let it go.

"I could splint it for you," I said easily.

"No!" Jason said too quickly. Then backpedaled. "I'd rather go to Gran."

I gave a sideways look to the mayor. "Gran?"

He gave a fond smile. "Everyone's grandma. When we scrape our knees, Gran patches us back up again."

"Would Bil be there?" I asked. "The man with the crushed leg?"

He nodded. "She won't let him out of her sight. Not for another span of days, if I know her."

"I'll walk you over to her house," I said to the sweating boy, who was carefully cradling his arm against his chest. "I'd like to watch her work."

•••

Judging from the way she dealt with Jason's broken arm, Gran was worth more than several students I could name in the Medica. After a small amount of persuasion she let me see Bil, who was in a small room at the back of her home.

His leg was ugly, broken in several places and broken messily. Swollen and discolored as it was, it was healing.

Gran had done everything to mend it that I could have, and then some. He wasn't fevered or infected, and it looked like he would probably keep the leg. How much use it would be was another matter. He might come away with nothing more than a heavy limp, but I wouldn't bet on him ever running again.

"What sort of folk shoot a man's horse?" he asked me as I looked at his leg. "It ain't right."

You know as well as I do how expensive horses are, and this wasn't the sort of town where people had horses to spare. Bil was a young man with a small farm and a new wife: his whole life ahead of him. Now his only horse was dead and he might never walk again because he had tried to do the right thing. It hurt to think about it.

When I came outside, the crowd had swelled considerably. Krin's father and mother had ridden in on the roan. Pete was there too, having run back to town. He offered up his head for my inspection and demanded his two pennies for services rendered.

I was warmly thanked by Krin's parents. They seemed to be good people. Most folk are, if given the chance to be. I managed to get hold of the roan, and using him as a sort of portable wall, managed to get a few minutes of relatively private conversation with Krin.

Her dark eyes were a little red around the edges, but her face was bright and happy. "Make sure you get Burrback," I said, nodding to one of the horses. "He's yours." The mayor's daughter would have a fair dowry no matter what, so I'd loaded Krin's horse with the more valuable goods, as well as most of the money the false troupers had.

Her expression grew serious as she met my eyes. "You're leaving."

I guess, I was. I nodded. She didn't try to convince me to stay, and instead surprised me with a sudden, emotional embrace. After kissing me on the cheek she whispered in my ear, "Thank you."

We stepped away from each other, knowing that propriety would only allow so much. "Don't sell yourself short and marry some fool," I said, feeling as if I should say something.

"Don't you either," she said, her sad dark eyes mocking me gently.

I unpacked my lute case and travel sack from Graytail and led the roan over to where the mayor stood. He was alone, off to one side, watching the crowd in a proprietary way. I handed him the reins to the horse. He cocked an eyebrow at me.

"You'd be doing me a favor if you took care of him until Bil is up and about," I said, "or took him to Bil's farm, if he's got family taking care of it."

He looked somewhat surprised. "You're leaving without your horse?"

"He's just lost his," I shrugged, "and we Ruh are used to walking. I wouldn't know what to do with a horse, anyway," I said half-honestly.

He took the reins and gave me a good long look, as if he weren't quite sure what to make of me. "Is there anything we can do for you?" he asked at last.

"Remember who took them," I said. "Remember it was one of the Edema Ruh who that brought them back."

EATING, DRINKING, WALKING

Written by
Dylan Otto Krider

Illustrated by
Brian Hailes

About the Author

Dylan was born in Jelm, Wyoming, a small town consisting of ten people, and he personally increased the population by ten percent. He has lived in many states since, and currently resides in Texas with his lovely wife, Sandy, an attorney at Edwards & George.

Dylan now works as the Night & Day Editor of the Houston Press and occasionally does freelance articles and interviews for magazines. With Writers of the Future, Dylan has now won most of the major amateur fiction contests (including the Asimov Award and Star Trek: Strange New Worlds) and needs to seriously hunker down and start publishing professionally. To that end, he has just completed a novel that he is shopping for an agent. More information can be found at his web site: www.dylanottokrider.com.

The horn I play is of a truly unique design, molded by one of the finest craftsmen in the metallurgic district, usually to the west of here (the City keeps track of these things). Obtaining my horn was not easy. I mean, the horn was not *given* to me; I had to earn it through a long, tedious ordeal I would not dare bore anybody with the details of, but the short of it is, I had yielded a few personal trinkets I later regretted and found it impossible to find any mediation for our quarrel. No matter. This is the burden we citizens must carry. Bare necessities are all the City provides, but at least She freed us from the mundane tasks that merely sustain us so that we may devote our time to more artistic and intellectual pursuits. Music is my pastime of choice, and I have become quite good, I must say—the neighbors have stopped complaining, and lately I have even received a few compliments.

I play: *Foompa, foompa, thumpa, foompa, thumpa, foompa, foom* . . . .

My mouth has started to become dry due to the saliva I have lost during my practice. Anticipating this, the City forms a little straw that extends from the wall, automatically inserting itself between my lips so that I may suck as many liters of glucose solution as I require. *What is needed, the City shall provide.* Instead, the liquid is bland and tasteless. I spit it out.

"What's this?!" I scream, trying to remove the taste of it.

"Water," the City answers. "It is the most efficient fluid for rehydration." As if sensing my reluctance, She continues: "It has the added benefit of not creating phlegm, which tends to interfere with your playing. . . ."

I don't like this. I don't like this one bit, but it is a small sacrifice. Improvements are often intertwined with small miseries. *No pain, no noticeable increase in the acclimation of benefits,* as the saying goes. "Well—if it will improve my playing." The straw returns and I force some of the liquid down. Despite the taste—or lack thereof—I do feel refreshed.

I notice a woman coming up the street, cradled in a nest that extends from the floor of the City, carrying her atop the standard array of cushions. She scoots along in her little nest, both moving over the surface yet part of it, as if on the crest of an ocean wave, the concrete mere water beneath her tush. Then the nest starts to climb upward, now but an extension of the wall.

At first, I can only see her feet and a few tubes extending from the City-provided britches we all wear to carry away our wastes. Two long arms follow her, one holding a plate of food, the other carrying it to her mouth with a fork. I can see her clearly now: plump, white and billowy. I know most of the people who frequent this section of the City, but her, I do not recognize. I find myself developing the distinct urge to procreate with her. She chews contentedly, swallows, and the City brings another forkful, which she refuses. Her face contorts like she's in pain. "It's coming again!" she says. The plate and fork melt into the wrists of the City's arms to form hands that remove her britches, and for a moment I think someone's beaten me to her.

She starts huffing and puffing, as the hands move down between her legs, and I understand what's going on now. I play: *Foompa, foompa, thumpa, foompa . . . .*

The woman howls, forcing me to set my horn aside. "Push, push . . . ." says the City. I consider asking the City carry me to another wall to perch.

"Quiet down up there," says the man beneath me. In the afternoons I often hear him reciting his poetry, all dreadful derivatives of Rimbaud and Baudelaire, but we have learned to tolerate each other. My horn, he's used to; screaming, he's not.

"I see it," says the City.

Buildings hang from the ceiling of the City, some stretching down to the ground. During lights-on periods, it reminds me of the photographs of the insides of caves that I have called up from the City libraries. All except for the nests that dot the surface of everything, giving the silhouettes a furry appearance when the lights dim, like some thick forest canopy. Inside, outside; it ceases to matter in our environmentally controlled environment.

The City kicks in, forming little hands to message my backside, keeping the blood moving. I'm curious as to how the woman is progressing. I've never actually sat up on my own before, at least not that I can remember. Why would I? Still, I think it might be fun to try—who knows what benefits we conceive from small miseries?—so I start to lean forward. The City springs into action. "No!" I say as my nest tilts. "I want to do this!"

"It's no trouble," insists the City.

"I know it's no trouble for you, nonetheless . . . ."

The City seems confused. I can tell by the hesitant quiver of the wall, wanting to perform some task yet finding none I have allowed Her to do. I push my head forward, then rock back, hoping to get enough momentum. I take a few deep breaths, then try again, using my arms to pull me along. Seeing Her opportunity, the

Illustrated by Brian Hailes

City forms little handholds in the armrests of my chair. I don't object. It's just the amount of assistance I need. I can see a head peeking out of the woman, all red and blue and slimy. The woman squeals again, and there's a torso. The rest is real easy: the baby slides safely into the City's hands with one last shrill. It's a boy. A third arm with a pair of scissors extends from the wall to cut the umbilical cord, and the hands holding the baby become towels to scrub it clean.

Then the towels join to form a blanket to wrap the baby in before he is whisked away, snuggled in the arms of the City. The City wraps the woman back up in her britches, and I think now may be my chance to approach her, but she looks exhausted, her chest heaving as she drifts out of consciousness. My arms quiver, starting to give, and I'm considering letting myself fall back comfortably into the cushions when I spot someone below. He looks up from the street with nothing extending from the City to assist him. He is not large, nor terribly thin—you only see one extreme or the other in the City. He smiles, standing—standing!—and then, as if showing off, he lifts a leg to remove his boot and pours some pebbles onto the street, tapping the sole a few times before pulling his boot back on his foot.

I marvel at the grace of his legs as he continues down the road, propelling himself on two meaty poles, defying all the laws of gravitation. I have seen a few of his kind before, but have yet to tire of witnessing the feat. A rough and thimble bunch, by all accounts, who reject the comforts of the City for a tepid life of struggle and subsistence. I hold myself steady, as the quivers in my arms become quakes. A rag wipes the moisture forming on my face as I grit my teeth, wanting to achieve this pale mimic of the Walker's accomplishment, but my muscles give, the arms of the City rushing to my aid, placing tubes in my mouth with food, oxygen and a variety of liquids to choose from as She rocks me gently, gently rocks me to sleep.

•••

During the night, I heard a sound: a scream and a whoosh of air as something heavy whipped past me to the street below. As I looked over the side of my nest, I did think I saw something, only a glimpse before the pavement swallowed it up. It was far too dark to know for sure. It occurred to me, albeit only briefly, that it might have been a person down there, but even if the City had allowed someone to tumble out of their nest through some freak glitch in Her operation, She would have quickly threaded a net between the buildings to break their fall. At the very least, converted the concrete into rubber matting. The City has safety features, after all, certain safeguards to prevent such tragedies.

Normally after my nap, I spend a few hours sipping coffee through a catheter and emerging myself in the classics, but I am having trouble focusing, despite the City presenting a favorite passage of Edgar Allan Poe's "The Maiden." Nonetheless, I read the stanza where the narrator cries up to the damsel perched above his chamber door:

"Prophet!" said I, "thing of evil!—prophet still,
if maid or devil!—
"Leave no black broom as a token of that lie thy shawl
hath spoken!
Leave my loneliness unbroken—take thy bust
from off my door!"

And then:

Quoth the Maiden, *"Evermore."*

My mind shows definite signs of fatigue after my ordeal of last night. I decide it best to postpone my readings. I ask the City to move me a little closer to the woman. She is awake, looking refreshed and lively.

"Would you like to hear me play?" I say, pointing to my horn.

"I heard you play before," she says through a full mouth.

Sounds promising. "I suppose it would have been a nice distraction from the task at hand . . . ."

"That was the theory," she says, adding: "Didn't work very well."

"Maybe this will make you feel a little better," I say, taking the horn to my lips. It is a song of my own creation, one I am especially pleased with. She listens, only taking a bite or two during my performance.

"You're very good," she says when I am finished.

I bow my head in thanks.

"Must have taken quite a bit of work to learn to play like that. I wouldn't have the patience."

I modestly concede. "So, when do you think you'll see him again?"

"Who?"

"Your son."

She shrugs. "Why? Should I worry?"

"No," I admit. He's in good hands. "What is needed . . ."

". . . the City shall provide." She completes the thought with a smile. When she finishes eating, the arms merge into the wall.

"Would you like to share nests?" I ask.

She smiles, nodding. "Sure. I'd like that."

Hearing this, the City goes to work, merging our nests together to form a single bed with us lying on our backs, side by side. We each take a moment to turn our heads so that we are looking at each other. She tries to fight the smile that's forming, but it only makes it worse, so she gives up and shows teeth, giggling a little. We start to stroke each other—me with my right hand, her with her left—and the City removes our britches without even having to be asked. We do this for some time, not wanting to hurry. When we are both good and ready, the City returns our britches, this time connected by a single tube, and we continue our caresses, feeling every part of the other's body. Everything, that is, except for the groin area—the City will take care of that.

We both tense when we feel the hum of our britches kicking in, causing us to dig our fingernails into the other's skin, willing, for a time, to overlook the pain for the sake of the pleasure we will receive. When we have acclimated enough, we continue our strokes, each studying the other's pupils, except this time with a look that is the complete opposite of what we are feeling. We huff and wheeze and breathe like this is work for us.

●●●

I scoot along in my nest for my morning stroll, enjoying the air against my skin and the occasional rise and fall as the City maneuvers my nest with millimeter precision. I slide down the wall to the street, my nest now a lounge chair, speeding toward the park, my usual postcoital resting spot. I hope that I can see Katchin again—luckily, I had thought to ask her name.

The park is the only place where the roof is clear, allowing the sun through except for carefully calculated areas that are tinted to shade individuals. The City rearranges the flowers and plant life weekly for variation, though I sometimes wish She wouldn't. I understand Her concern, but I find myself missing the landscapes of the past, now only memories.

Before I had my horn, I would read history, anything I could download from the City library. This marvel of modern technology is the ultimate model of self-sufficiency, one of the first completely self-sustaining colonies ever built. Everything used is recycled and resynthesized, all powered by a virtually limitless supply of fusion energy, and the City is self-healing, eliminating the need for any form of government, which is Her greatest benefit.

Before, we were all like poor Sisyphus of Greek myth, forced by the gods for all eternity to roll a stone up the hill only to see it roll back down again the moment he reached the top: working so hard to earn a meal only to find ourselves hungry, or toiling for a paycheck only to find it spent. We have found that need is not necessarily the grandmother-in-law of invention. The great human advances of the past were often a product of leisure time, made by those who had the luxury to design great churches, statues and pyramids, and to think up new philosophies, mathematics and literatures, a luxury we now have in abundance. Unlike Sisyphus's stone, a human advancement stays firmly at the top of the hill where it was placed, waiting for the next to be rolled on top of it, in the eternal struggle to improve the quality of human life.

This is the reason I live, I think, to have these moments in the garden with my music in the air. Yet, I envy some of that constancy of the past. I have tried to return to the street I slept above the night before, only to discover it rerouted by the City to build a more efficient path, to find Herself needing to construct yet another street to compensate for the inefficiencies of the previous one. It is not uncommon to find the park moved a few blocks over from its location the week before, changing, always changing. Sisyphus at least had some sense of continuity.

Perhaps this is why the same citizens tend to gather together night after night, neighbors of sorts, seeking familiar faces before the lights go down, though rarely bothering to socialize. Only my horn is dependable, my rock, my stone. That scratch there was made during my first public performance; I bent that key while my fingers were still clumsy; that dent I made when I threw my horn at that dreadful poet. I would not change one nick of her brass for anything.

I sit up with only minimal objections from the City, though my arms are sore from the day before. I cross my legs swaying slightly in front of me and play.

"It's beautiful," someone says. It's the Walker, from before. "Your music," he says. "Not bad."

I am only able to nod. This is the first time I have gotten a good look at him. His clothes have holes and there is color to his skin. He hasn't bothered to shave his head and there are splotches of whiskers on his chin, though I have never known the City to miss a spot. I notice a big bulky bag tied to his back, as if being upright weren't enough of a challenge for him. "I thought Walkers hated the City . . . ."

"Oh, it's nothing personal," he says. "We just prefer to be elsewhere." He sets the pack beside him on the rock. The Walker raises a defiant hand before the City can mold the boulder to the contours of his rear and scolds: *Uh, uh, uh, uh.* "Just got to be firm with Her," the Walker says as the contours recede. He reaches into the pocket of his pack to retrieve a harmonica. "You like the blues?"

I shrug.

The Walker hands me a leather-bound book from his pack. "How about that one," he says, pointing to the page. I've never held a book before, let alone one as old as this one. It's a compilation of sheet music from the 1930s—over three hundred years ago. Aside from my horn, it's the first thing I've touched that's more than a few days old. The City holds it open for me to follow along. The Walker taps his foot and plays a few bars before he sings:

> *When the music's good an' hot,*
> *I start to sway a lot,*
> *And all because I've got loose ankles.*

> *No matter where I go*
> *They never think I'm slow,*
> *As long as I can show loose ankles.*

He sings marvelously. I listen a little longer to get the rhythm down.

> *Now, it used to be the passion*
> *To hold hands oh-so-sweet,*
> *But now to be in fashion*
> *You must have dancing, prancing feet.*

The Walker shuffles and shakes as he sings, even waving his arms about him as he slides to the side. I almost forget to accompany him. I wonder how he learned to play like this, without the apprenticeship of the City. Could it possibly have been from these books alone or mimicking his elders? The Walker does a wonderful spin move for a grand finale.

> *Those sweeties, one and all,*
> *For me are bound to fall*
> *'Cause I've got what they call loose ankles.*

The Walker laughs, giving his knee a slap. "Now that's what I call playing."

I start to hand the book back to him, but he refuses.

"Why don't you borrow it for a while, so you'll have no trouble keeping up next time."

I have to admit, it's what I'd hoped he'd say. "I could call the lyrics up on the City library."

The Walker seems amused by the suggestion. "Why don't you take it? Nothing like following along in a real book."

So, he won't even use the City databases. I have to admire his conviction.

"You here for long?"

"Me? No, just passing through." The Walker pushes his lips forward like he's about to blow a kiss and thrusts his tongue against the inside of his cheek. "Been to a lot of places, and you start to see that everyone's pretty much the same in the City. But not you. You intrigue me."

"How so?"

"Most people don't much care what goes on outside their little hovel. Sure, they talk art and philosophy, but as long as they're taken care of, they have no drive, no wants. No *desire*. That's no way to live."

"Surely there's some joy in a desire fulfilled."

He laughs at that, as if conceding the point, then takes the metal container from his belt and twists the cap off. "Our desires are defined by what we lack, my friend. And when I look across these walls, I don't see many happy faces—except yours."

I'm not sure how to respond. The City provides, so yes, I am happy. At least I should be. If it's more I want, I'm not sure what it is I want more of. The Walker takes the container to his lips, then grunts, turning it upside down to shake out the few remaining drops.

"Allow me," I say, a small tube snaking from my armrest.

"Oh, no. I'm fine," he says, licking the top of his mouth.

"You're thirsty."

The Walker smiles at that, his teeth yellow and crooked. "That I am." He places the container back on his belt and gives it a final pat. "I best be off to find some more." I want to push the issue further, but he just lifts his hand. "I'm fine. Believe me, I am." And with that, he stands to leave. "Perhaps I'll see you around?"

I nod, but there's so much more I want to ask him. He walks away slowly, ever so slowly, through the streets, wiping his own brow with his arm, until he disappears in the swarm of nests that swerve around him, but a brief deviation in their City-plotted path.

•••

"He talked to me. He did. We had a conversation."

"That's amazing," Katchin says. Who ever said sharing nests is never as good the second time?

"The same one that was there when you gave birth."

"I never gave birth," Katchin says.

"I *intrigue* him. That's what he said. He liked my playing, too."

"You play? What instrument?"

Her game is wearing thin. I choose to ignore her. "Oh, Katchin, it was incredible . . . ."

"I'm not Katchin."

I turn to look at her. Her nose *is* bigger, the lips a little thin.

"You sure look like Katchin."

"I'm not," she says. "I've never seen you before in my life."

We both take a moment to study each other. The hair, the breasts, the eyes . . . . She's right. She looks nothing like her—what was I thinking? "The horn," I say. "I play the horn. Would you like to hear?"

She shakes her head. "Don't like music."

I'm thirsty. I don't let on, wanting to hold on to it. I sit up, tugging on a piece of wall and molding it in my hands. If one wishes, one can squeeze the walls of the City like clay. I have watched some very talented artists sculpt beautiful objects from the City, in much the same way the artisans crafted my horn. The trick is to keep some tiny piece of the sculpture connected to the City; the finest wire is enough to keep the atoms in flux. Even solid metal can be molded like putty, but, once disconnected, will become solid as all things do when they are separated from the City. I make myself a bowl, smoothing it with my fingers, then flick the filament, crystallizing the bowl instantly. It is crude compared to the Walker's container, but adequate (*a tulip, by any other name . . .*). I take a straw, filling the bowl with water, trying not to spill any, then lift the bowl to my lips, pouring most of the contents into my mouth—the City towels up the rest.

"What are you doing?" the girl asks.

I take another sip, exhaling loudly after I've swallowed, just like the Walker. "Drinking," I say. That's what I'm doing. I'm *drinking*.

●●●

Out of habit, I call the blues song up on the Computer library before I remember the Walker's book. I am about to send the monitor away when I read the last verse:

> *Those tootsies, ten in all,*
> *If I stand, I'm bound to fall*
> *'Cause I've got what they call loose ankles.*

"These aren't the lyrics, City!"

"Sadly, I find I must disagree with you. These are the lyrics as transcribed from the original recording by Billy Massey on April 29, 1930. An easy mistake to make."

I order the City to open the Walker's book to the appropriate page. "Why do your lyrics differ from the book here? Are there other versions of the song?"

"None, that I am aware. I'm sorry that the song does not agree with you—how about some music from a more contemporary artist?"

It bothers me. The Walker's means of passing down information would be far less accurate than any the City had designed. But this book was published just a few years after the song was recorded. "Don't you corroborate your databases with a permanent archive?"

"All aspects are always open to transfer, upgrade or renovation, but everything is cross-checked and verified before and after each change, with absolute precision."

But if that information were being checked against information that had itself been transferred . . . . "There is no possibility of error when you move information or renovate your databases?"

"There is no possibility of anything being free of error, but our level of accuracy is so close to an absolute that it can, for all intents and designs, be considered such. The chances of misplacing even a single comma in any given transfer are negligible."

This sounded reasonable. Even the Walker's book had to rely on some level of uncertainty—especially one transcribed by human beings. "Then how do you explain the difference?"

The City took a pause before answering. "Might I gently suggest that this book is a forgery?"

I suppose it's possible. We know so little about the Walkers. Views of the Walkers vary widely, ranging from uncultured ruffians following a set of mistaken, even dangerous, ideas to those of a glowing admiration, verging on the mystical. The Walker would have to be a bit of a fanatic to go to such extremes. It was possible he came to spread propaganda in the hopes of recruiting a few believers. I had always assumed his gift was inborn, something we weeded out of the gene pool as we evolved; but it was possible, as absurd of a notion as it was, that it could be taught. Whatever his reasons for coming, I could only hope they would bring him here again.

•••

There had been an accident.

I was at the park practicing when I saw the nests huddled in the street as the bodies flew above them in a straight trajectory until the tubes to their britches snapped taut, pulling them fast to the ground like tangled parachutists. Some screamed from pain, others from the undeniable proof of the inconceivable: the City had failed them. Then the dead and wounded were sucked beneath the pavement as the City offered the witnesses all sorts of special treats through their tubes to pacify them. Tranquility slowly restored.

No doubt, She does this to protect us. She, more than anybody, knows how dependent we have become on Her. The mere thought of Her failing . . . I am not so very different from them. It was only a few short weeks before that something fell past my nest and was swept beneath the City. How easily I had rationalized.

> *So, this is how the world ends*
> *This is how the world ends*
> *This is how the world ends*
> *Not with a bang, but a blubber.*

But of late, I have found myself choosing difficult truths over comfortable lies.

During my practices, I have actually progressed to the point where I can lift myself out of my nest, with only my legs to suspend me. This is what I have been doing the past few weeks; I go to the park and I just *stand*, though there is some pivoting involved—a slight twisting in the hips as I play, enjoying the surroundings from my new vantage point.

And I've taken my first steps. Not much, just a few, but it's a start. I'm not even sure if it's allowed, but as the great writer Charles Pickens once said, "It was the best

of crimes, it was the worst of crimes." I toot my horn—
foompa, foompa—tap my foot, move my hips and sway. I
can't explain; it just comes naturally for me to do this.
Thumpa, foompa, foom . . . I start to twist as I take a step,
then another, stopping after each for a little head bob
and shake. I can see the mystified faces of the people
above me, tilting their nests so they can watch.

I fall, landing hard on my horn. I try to push myself
up, fighting against gravity, but I drop. I try again,
lifting my head just enough to see the people above me,
some fearful for my safety, others laughing at my stubbornness as my nest sinks. "No! Don't help me!" I shout
as the nest resurfaces beneath me. I want to show them
all. I can feel the softness of the City's cushions forming
around me, yet I resist. "No! No! Put me down! Put me
down!" I shake my head as the City carries me far away
from the heckles, choosing a wall to rest on. "You bitch!
You bastard!" I say. "You cold, blind bastard!"

I turn over on my side and peer down over the edge,
to the man in the nest below—nothing in his skin but
bones. He sucks on a tube as he sleeps, so happy. I wish
I could go back to being like that. The skin on my chest
has started to darken from when I fell, turning black-
purple; I fear I am dying.

"You'll be fine," the City assures me. "Now rest.
Rest."

When I calm, I see that the rim of my horn is
completely folded, and one of the keys is bent. I blow
into the mouthpiece, but my horn only squeaks. The
man below me yells for quiet, so I squawk one more
time out of spite before tossing the horn over the side.

I see the Walker now for what he is—not a blessing,
but a curse. If any problems exist, he is the cause, I am
sure of it. Why would the City start to fail after all this
time except from some form of sabotage?

I spend the rest of the night rubbing my chest and muttering promises to myself. Never again, never again. I turn on my side so that the City can message my backside. If She hadn't gotten rid of the alleyway and added that curve to the street, I would be looking at the very spot where the Walker stood a few weeks ago, looking up with his crooked grin. "Yahoo, Brute?" I mutter soft enough so the City can't hear. *"Yahoo?"*

• • •

Today, the park has moved itself to the edge of the City. I sit—only sit—sipping punch through a tube. It still hurts to breathe.

There is no evidence of the wreck. Only a matter of time before I heal and forget, like the City does. Such things are expected in any system as complex as this. Certainly the City is no more dangerous than before She existed. I see a glint of metal in my peripheral vision. I almost sit up before I catch myself and order my nest to turn.

"You forget something?" The Walker holds my horn out to me as he chews on something so tough he's got to yank to pull a bite off with his teeth. His timing is impeccably bad. I want to curse him for what he's done, but he looks at me with such sincerity. He places the horn in my nest. "I think you'll want it. Eventually." The rim has been hammered out, and the button is upright, if still a little crooked.

"Why?" I say. "What are you going to do?"

"Nothing," he says. "It just can't be." He puts the remainder of the food strip into his pocket. "Nor should it." The Walker gives my arm a squeeze. "I see you're putting a little meat on your bones."

I squeak when he pinches me, which only encourages him. The Walker laughs, pinching me again.

"Ow! Stop it! Quit it!"

The Walker gives my tummy a prod, then eases back. "There's hope for you."

"Do you just show up every now and then to taunt me?"

The Walker doesn't say anything for a time, and just opens his hand in front of him, admiring his fingers. "I heard once that the cells in our body are replaced every twenty-three days or so. Every month, a totally new body, from top to bottom, yet my skin droops, and my sight blurs. I often wondered why that was. I finally figured that it's because every time one of these little cells splits in two, they're both just a little different than the one they came from. Wouldn't have to be much. The tiniest variation over the years, and it just starts to add up." I want to press him further, but he has already started to walk away. "Everything must end, my friend."

It makes me mad, him popping in and out like this. The City, now accustomed to ignoring my orders, has to be given instructions before making chase.

"Hey! What do you mean by that?" I shout.

He's already at the street, starting to cross.

"Answer me! What's going to end? What'd you do?"

An exit forms at the edge of the City and the Walker steps through. The nest hesitates, not wanting to follow him through the tunnel, and by the time the City obeys my orders, the Walker's already outside. My nest stops at the City limits, unable to go any further. That does it, I think, and force myself to stand. "Hey! Hey! Come back here!" The door opens, and I step through, but the tubes of my britches keep me leashed. "Let me go! Let me *go!*" I shout, beating the britches with my horn until they drop off.

There's not much vegetation. Dirt, mostly, and rocks
cutting the heels of my feet; it would stop me if I weren't
so damn angry. "You can't leave!" I stumble forward and
step on something sharp that almost throws me off
balance, but I actually manage to hop on one foot long
enough to remove it and continue on—I would be
amazed if I took the time to evaluate it. I march in as
straight a line as I can manage, sometimes drifting to the
left, sometimes right. In the distance there are some large
pieces of cloth draped over wooden poles and tied to
metal pegs in the ground. I see a group of twelve or so,
each with a pile of burning wood near their tarps. A
woman tends to the Walker as he sits near his own
flame.

I take my eyes off my feet a little too long and stub
my toe, shouting obscenities on my way down. Fear sets
in. The City isn't here this time. I'm all alone. I roll,
calling for the Walker. I know he's close enough to hear
me. "Help me, Walker! Walker!" He'll come, if I scream
long enough.

The City towers above me, unable to listen. I see it's
a huge network of tubes and pipes diverted, twisted and
jury-rigged, a mangled collection of all the repairs the
City has made over the decades, hidden from the inside.
The sight of it has so captivated me that I have forgotten
to thrash and kick. Every renovation is built on the
previous one. A hose breaks, blowing steam, and
another snakes out over countless generations of failed
ducts and wires to bypass it.

Its surface droops, tired and loose, like the Walker's
skin. How many more before the City collapses under its
own bureaucracy of enhancements and cosmetics? The
Walker is right. It is only a matter of time before I would
be left out here to my own devices.

I struggle up to the crawling position where I rest, breathing heavily as I close my eyes. I must do this if I am to survive. I use the horn for a crutch as I slowly, ever so slowly, lift myself. "Hey!" I say, starting to laugh. "Hey! Look!" I balance on the one knee, planting my right foot flat and pushing downward. "Look at me! I'm doing it! I'm *standing!*" I'm standing! I start to walk toward the camp, using the lights of the fires to guide me. I concentrate on my feet, one moving in front of the other. I close the distance, step by step, stopping just a few yards from where the Walker sits, staring into the fire. "I did it, Walker!" I pace, not wanting my journey to end. "I did it!"

The Walker tries to conceal his smile.

Then I feel something. The air pressing against me as the last bit of sun disappears, similar to the way it feels when the nest moves me quickly through the City, except this is much different. I can feel it over my entire body, causing my skin to tighten, becoming rough and bumpy as if, for the first time, it's alive. My shoulders lift without any prodding on my part until they touch my earlobes, and my genitals slowly retract into my body. Every part of me comes to life. Then, I do something unexpected: I take the air deep into my lungs, open my mouth and scream. . . .

"Oh, my poor dear," the woman says, walking back into the tent. "You must be freezing."

I take a few steps, turn left. *Aaaaaaahhhh!* It just comes naturally for me to do this.

The woman returns with a blanket stretched between her fingers. "Here."

The Walker lifts a hand to stop her. "Don't you dare," he says, as I scream into the wind, unable to explain this sensation that's washing over me. "Can't you see he's enjoying himself?"

The others have started gathering around, muttering questions amongst themselves as I scream, the wind carrying my voice back, over the desert and toward the City I left behind me.

ORIGAMI CRANES

Written by
Seppo Kurki

Illustrated by
Anthony Arutunian

About the Author

The short story "Origami Cranes" was the second entry from Seppo Kurki, a native of Finland, to L. Ron Hubbard's Writers of the Future Contest. Seppo received a masters degree in creative writing from the University of South Alabama in 2001, and he is on the pursuit of a career in writing, hoping to "one day in the near future" gather his short stories, novels, poems and screenplays from underneath a pile of dust and start actively looking for places to have them published. He is currently in the process of relocating to Tokyo, Japan.

Seppo credits his interest in writing to comics and books read at an early age, his overtly imaginative brain, the opportunity of learning several languages while growing up and a multitude of teachers who have helped and encouraged him on his journey.

Besides literature, his interests include watching movies and car racing, playing with his cat, Chibuli, and listening to electronic music. His perhaps greatest regret in life is never having learned to skate properly, hence missing out on becoming a professional ice hockey goalie, an activity he must therefore pursue only in his waking dreams, firmly keeping his two feet on the ground—to the extent a science fiction enthusiast is capable of doing that.

About the Illustrator

Anthony Arutunian is a young man of few words. We know he was born March 15, 1981, and makes his home in Havertown, Pennsylvania. We know he goes to school in Savannah, Georgia.

Anthony likes to draw, but he's never published anything before this ILOF illustration. Prior to entering the Contest, he had done one commissioned painting, a mural for the Sunday school that his sister and brother attend.

Anthony uses pencil, pen/ink, paintbrush and sometimes even computer to produce artistic images that more than make up for his lack of words.

The computer deck was still in its place, on a worn mahogany desk perched against the windowsill. Mimosa hadn't touched the deck since Gregorian died. She didn't know how to use one, either, but something had drawn her to it, calling her across the silence that had fallen into the apartment in the weeks since Greg's death.

The smooth black deck, lined with chromed alloys and mute LED lights, now contained the last physical evidence of Greg's presence. He had kept few things in the apartment: white cotton shirts and black pants he had pressed at the Pakistani Laundromat behind the corner once every two weeks, old magazines, a pair of blank white coffee cups . . . nothing more.

After the Department of Interior had notified her of Greg's death, the blackness crept in from the corners of the room, blanketed her in its amorphous numbness and held her tight, finally lifting in the last few days, when she had finally accepted Greg's absence and started rummaging through his things, only to find out he had none. There were no old postcards or notebooks piled in a cardboard box in the back of the closet, no diplomas or pictures framed above his desk, not even a plastic plant sitting beside the window as if to feed on the light it wouldn't need. She'd looked in the drawers of the table she'd bought and given to him to hold the deck, but they were empty. Greg always carried his wallet with him. She'd browsed through it once, but there was just his bank chip, his ID chip and DIP security clearance card. There was no physical evidence of his existence that would remind her of his absence. Just the shirts, coffee cups—and the deck.

When Greg had still been alive, his lack of possessions had never bothered her, but now it was another enigma in the maze that had culminated in his death, in another country, under circumstances she would never know. Staring into the emptiness, she'd wondered if there had ever been a Greg, if Greg had been nothing more than a firefly, now burnt out and gone forever, leaving behind only memories that had already begun fading, disappearing into the darkness left behind by the dead firefly.

•••

"Miss Mimosa Hamasaki?" the crackling voice in her intercom had asked. She walked to the door and looked at the monitor, bolted with titanium into the concrete wall beside the access panel. A man with close-cut short brown hair, wearing an expensive gray suit, stood behind the door, bare hands resting on his sides, palms up. He was wearing aqua-blue or purple mirrored sunglasses, automatically adjusting to light levels. She saw a reflection of the door in his shades. Only people from DIP wore sunglasses indoors. But they'd never asked for her. They always came for Greg.

"Yes?" she said, not opening the door, knowing that if he was from the DIP and wanted to get in, he could bypass the sequencer in five seconds or less.

"Miss Hamasaki, I have come here on behalf of the Defense Industry Properties. I have an important message for you."

"Please remove the shades."

He took off the sunglasses. His eyes were hazel brown. The green light from the scanner reflected back from the back of his irises. He was sliced, probably for night vision or infrared frequencies. Night cats. Men like that were usually assigned to grunt work, Greg had told her.

The monitor flashed a brief bio, John Doe, age thirty-five, all other data classified, priority override by DIP. He was with them, all right. She pressed her thumb on the scanner and tapped Greg's birthday on the keypad. The door opened with a low hydraulic hum.

• • •

She had watched Greg, sitting on the floor hooked to his deck, time and again. She'd seen him blend into the current of electrons often enough to know that the wires would have to be connected to the temples, and that the visor would go over her head. There was a switch somewhere on the bottom that turned the power on. Another set of wires, slim fiberoptics no wider than a needle thread, would go to her fingers and let her toggle the menus without a keypad. Besides the password, Greg had told her, some people wired the deck to the their own brain waves. If someone else tried the deck, the waves would not match. The deck would fry the neurons of the intruder with microbursts. Greg hadn't mentioned anything about wiring his deck.

• • •

The man from DIP hadn't told her much. Greg had died in an accident in Malaysia. His body was charred.

Illustrated by Anthony Arutunian

Had to ID him from a fragment of bone marrow, but no chance in misidentifying; the tracking chip had located him in the spot of the implosion fifteen nanoseconds before the burst. Implosion? Classified information, investigation still underway, results pending. But in this case, the rules could be stretched, the widow informed: The biotech company had been working on an illegal fusion project. Greg had gone there on behalf of DIP to investigate. Then something went wrong. Something? Most likely the scientists got freaked and pulled the plug. Along with it, the backup systems control. The reaction went into overkill. No, overheated, or something. Within forty-four seconds, the building evaporated. Best estimate of casualties: three hundred seventy-five. Most of them still unidentified. During that forty-four seconds . . . ? Not enough for anyone to get out. Did Greg have time to know what was going to happen? Had he tried to reach her? Oh, yes, there was a brief datastream sent by Mister Gregorian Chant to the Singapore agency, exactly fifteen seconds in length, ending in the implosion. Some of the data was corrupted by the emission of particles. Was there an audio decoder that would play unpacked 256G data? Would she like to hear it?

●●●

She knew the password for the deck. She'd dreamt it two nights earlier. Greg had been there, walking alongside her up the exit ramp from Shinjuku station, tapping the steel railing, his footsteps echoing in the halogen-lit tunnel. Then they'd come out to the sunlight, brighter than it had been in decades. The sky was cleaner, clearer, with distinct shades of blue visible. The trees had big green leaves, and the cranes in the Grusgrus Park up the road from the station were moving smoothly, without jerks or carefully precalibrated dips and shudders. Their white-coated metal wings didn't reflect the light like they used to; the new white fluffy coating they now had seemed to somehow absorb the photons.

They stopped on a bench, oxidized into a dark shade of green, and sat down. Greg grabbed her hand and kissed it. "Mimmy," he said, lifting his eyes to hers. "Mimmy, Mimmy, Mimmy, if only you knew."

"What?" she asked, her pulse suddenly tightening.

"If only you knew how it all could be. The grass greener than this, the cherry trees blossoming under the sun, the cranes crying of their own free will . . . how it all should be."

"I don't understand, Greg."

"Nothing here is real. The birds, the cones . . . see," he said, picking up a cone that had fallen from an old fenced oak behind the bench. "Feel it, Mimmy. Touch it."

She reached for the brown cone Greg was holding on the palm of his hand. The surface was smooth, the small pores polished, with no rough edges. "Yes, but I don't understand."

"Plastic. It's plastic."

She knew. It was all plastic, the trees, the grass, the cones. Everything in the park was plastic. The cranes were motorized replicas. But they were supposed to be like that, weren't they? She couldn't remember them ever being anything else. She didn't ask.

Greg undid the first three buttons of his shirt, revealing a patch of paper-white hairless skin. "Touch me. Feel me, Mimmy." She saw her hand move across the space between them, to touch his bare skin; her hand moved without her command, and she could not stop it. Her fingers brushed against his chest.

Plastic. It felt plastic.

She withdrew her hand. Touched her own cheek. Plastic too.

Everything. Was. Always. Plastic.

•••

"This place is going up. It's out of control. Tell . . . not to . . . sad . . . it's . . . okay . . . I . . .," Greg shouted. Then the sound of an explosion, then white noise and finally silence. The man from DIP turned the recording off.

"We are working on clearing up those bits. We think the last part was for you," he said, folding and unfolding the sunglasses in his hands.

"Can you play it back?" She listened until the hum of the ceiling fan grew louder and mixed into the humming of Greg's words in her head, dulling the words of the tall man from DIP.

Three days later they brought Greg back in a box. The square urn was five inches across, black, with a silver chromed touch lock on the top. They told her it could recite his words, twenty short sentences, in a random order, or play the same message every time she activated the box. Whichever way she preferred.

She never opened the box. Never touched the alloy of shining black steel and polished chrome, the holographic fingerprint reader that glowed dull green in the dark room like a pathetic neon ghost.

•••

"The password, Mimmy, the password is *digiphotosynthetic*," dead Greg in her dream had whispered to her ear when they were lying down naked on the bed, under thin slices of blind-slit moonlight. "The password, Mimmy, is digiphotosynthetic," he said, over and over until she fell asleep and woke up on that same bed, alone, cold, Greg one more day deader, the moon hidden behind dark blue clouds, gone, invisible.

•••

She opened the steel lock of the deck. The wires and receptors and sensors were bundled up inside. The thick sensor plates, gold lined for minimum resistance, were for the temples. She connected the power plug to the wall, then put the temple wires on. A current of static trembled through her temples, then faded into a gentle throbbing pulse. Then she connected the wires for her fingers, then the visor.

The screen was black. Neon letters, bright green, in alphabetical order, floated in front of Mimosa. The words "enter password" blinked on the bottom right corner. Slowly, one by one, she reached for the letters that spelled *digiphotosynthetic*, then pressed the enter key. The letters disappeared. Nothing. Then a slight tingling on her temples. She closed her eyes. She could feel the synapses in her head burning, flickering, exploding in a series of invisible electric shocks. Like empty fireworks.

When she opened her eyes again, the deck had opened to a blue sky pulsating to white clouds traveling across it. Greg's avatar glided in through the clouds. She'd seen the avatar before, through reflections on his visor when she'd walked in on him, telling him the dinner was ready or that someone from the DIP had delivered a disc and needed his encoding to authorize the transaction. The Greg in the deck was a younger man, in his early twenties, with his long hair bound in a ponytail. She'd never seen his hair long, never seen that ponytail. The Greg she knew had existed only in the present, in the man in front of her. She had never seen old photos of him, no baby pictures, no prom snapshots, no Greg in his twenties. She wondered if he'd ever worn a ponytail, or if he'd just pasted the hair from an image bank.

Greg's avatar stopped mid-screen, a few feet above the green meadow underneath him, and smiled. "Hi, Mimosa," he said. "The deck recognized your waves. I coded them in here, just in case."

"Hi, Greg," she said, not knowing how to feel. The real Greg was dead and the avatar was not Greg but a young stranger speaking his words, with his tongue, with his voice.

Then the avatar changed, aging years in front of her eyes, developing tiny wrinkles on his face, grooves around his lips, and the long hair was gone, replaced by his usual short spiky cut that revealed the places on his temples where the brown hair was getting thinner.

"Recognize me now?" the avatar asked, looking exactly like Greg the day she'd last seen him. "Your brain waves, again. The deck . . . or I, if it makes more sense . . . can pick up on the things you think. It's like reading your mind. I can interpret the activity in your brain, translate it into words. You don't need to speak. But if it makes you more comfortable, go ahead."

"I . . . I've never used one of these things before. Sorry," she said, almost whispering.

"No need to apologize, Mimmy. I should be the one doing that, since I am now dead."

"How . . . oh, you read my mind again. Sorry."

"Yes. Does it make you feel uncomfortable? I can stop doing that. Some people find it unnerving."

"No, it's all right. I wasn't ready, that's all. You have been dead for three weeks and four days now. I didn't know what to do. They didn't tell me what had happened. They just told me you were dead."

"Mimmy, my dear Mimmy. They didn't want to cause you any more pain."

How do you know? You weren't there, she said without speaking.

I wasn't there. I don't know. But I know the procedure. They will tell the widow what happened, without any unnecessary details.

I'm getting a headache, she said, hoping he wouldn't say anything about what she'd thought when he'd called her a widow.

It's from the deck. Motion sickness or the strain from the wave decoder. You can log off, if you want. I'll be here.

I don't want you in a box. I have one with your ashes. Why should I carry around another box of you?

I understand.

I can never touch you. I can never feel your breath on my neck.

I understand.

I can never make love to you. Have your baby. Watch you grow old.

Greg's avatar began aging, slowly, the grooves on his face becoming more distinguished, his hair grayer and thinner.

Stop it. That's not what I mean. Stop it.

The aging stopped and Greg's avatar was thirty-four again.

Sorry. I just wanted to show you there are things I can still do.

But that's not good enough.

How about this, then? he asked, and suddenly they were in an amusement park, near Central Tokyo. It was mid-May, late in the evening, dark, gusty and cool.

Do you remember this place?

This is our first date, isn't it? I remember the Ferris wheel and the lights. It's from my memories, isn't it? It's exactly like I remember.

Yours and mine. I have things stored here, in the deck.

And they walked across the fairgrounds, toward the giant wheel, spinning in the darkness between the black buildings rising out to the sky, invisible behind tinted glass and chromed steel, reflecting the shimmering lights of the park like a million stars. Somewhere in the distance, hidden behind the curbs, neon-bright red letters spelled "Rabu Hoteru," the hotel where they'd made love for the first time that night, in the darkness, slowly, enjoying the touches, synaptic impulses, every drop of the endorphins, as their sweating bodies connected into one. She felt him moving inside her, faster, against her membranes. . . . She had clawed her nails into his back, felt his flesh under her hands. . . . And then the tender burning inside her. Stopping. Staring at the roof. Breathing quietly. The beat of Greg's heart through her chest.

It was never as good as the first time, someone had said. Something is lost. Lost in time. Lost forever. Ever and after . . . .

I think the fireworks are about to start, the avatar said, lighting a cigarette, just as the first rockets started flying up toward the heavens. First the boom, then nothing for a few seconds as the fireworks were shooting up.

Then light. Fire flowers exploded in the sky, opening into unimaginable combinations of colors, spreading into small balls of luminescent fire, falling down and fading. Disappearing.

Pale ghosts, she thought, and looked at Greg's avatar's hand in hers. She felt the pressure, the rough texture of his palms, the warmth. None of it was real. She squeezed the avatar's hand. He turned around. She saw the fireworks in his dark eyes, exploding, fluttering down. Beautifully rendered pixels. Better than real.

Greg . . . all the things you said . . . she said, straying to catch the final burst of gunpowder from the tinted mirrors of Ginza Tower.

. . . never meant as much as the things I didn't say. There's so much more, Mimmy. So much more. I never had the time, the avatar said, and flicked his cigarette away.

One last firework, she thought as the cigarette smashed against the concrete, scattering orange-burning tobacco onto the pavement.

There are so many things that I still don't know. What do you do? I mean, what did you really do?

I was a data reacquisition expert. I broke into other people's computers and stole their data. Retrieved it for DIP. They paid well. I know, that's barely legal, but it's not any different from working for any other large corporation. Everyone steals. Sony-Daibatsu from IBM, NASA from ESA and the Russians.

What happened then? How did you die?

I was sent to Malaysia to break into a computer owned by Cerebrol Biocom. They were doing something

really high-tech, something that could have changed
the world.

Like a bioweapon? Like the one they used on San Fran?

No. This was all about energy. The data is still classified. I can't tell you. I am not sure myself what it was.
No, I'm not lying. I only saw some of the stuff. All I can
tell you is that it had something to do . . .

. . . with ones and zeroes. Everything does.

Greg's avatar winked.

Yeah, you've got it. Anyway, they kept all the codes
on their mainframe. It wasn't hooked up to any systems,
just stood there by itself in a superconducted room, with
all sorts of cooling systems hooked to it to prevent the
system from crashing. Malaysia's an awfully hot place
for something like that. Anyway, I had to go there to
hack into that thing. I guess something went wrong. I'm
sorry, Mimmy. This is not how I planned it.

*I know. Bye, Greg. I need to go. It was good to see you
again. Really. But this is as it should be. This is not real. You
are dead. I'm sorry, Greg. Goodbye.*

Goodbye, Mimmy. Greg's avatar waved a goodbye.

Then everything faded to weary gray. Bright spots of
light burned on her retinas for a moment, growing
fainter with each blink of an eye.

Mimosa took off the visor. Everything in the room
seemed fainter, too, unreal. The colors were duller, the
air darker and dustier. The walls, stained by cigarette
smoke, dust and passed years, were the color of aged
gray. Unwrapping her fingers one by one from the wires,
she turned the deck over and shut it off.

• • •

That night, she lay down in her bed, counting the holographic projections of stars and distant nebulae on the black concrete ceiling, the deck on the other side of the bed, silent and cold, cold to her touch, black slick steel. Unsure, she wondered whether Greg had just played back the words she wanted to hear, prying them out of her brain like a CAT neuron scanner. . . .

She leaned back, listening to regurgitating noise from the street below, steady rumble, a bass with an alternating beat, the deck next to her. She sat up, opened the blind, then the window.

Warm stale air blew into the bedroom, the noise from below louder, a mesh of rumbling trains and cars, distant hollers, shouts of late night show hosts from comboxes left on. She took the deck from the bed and put it on the window ledge. It would shatter into tiny pieces on the pavement below, and Greg with it. Greg's death, only this time not in Malaysia but in Tokyo, if only she gave the deck one more push . . . .

•••

Mimosa was one-eighth Chinese, seven-eighths Japanese. One-eighth *gaijin*, that's what it said on her ID chip. Enough to prevent three promotions she had deserved, Mimosa was sure of it. Greg was half *gaijin*. Their child would have been five-sixteenths foreign, a mix between Manchurian and Portuguese. Under the regulations, their child would have to carry a foreigner's ID, like Greg.

A Taiwanese oracle had told her that she would have three children. The oracle was the sister of her friend Tang Lam, whom she'd met in Singapore. The sister, Tang had told her, had been retarded all through her childhood, until one day, when she was twenty-five, she suddenly started seeing things. She wrote perfect Mandarin too, all of a sudden, even though she could barely even spell her name before. Her writing, moreover, was scholarly, spawning from decades of intense education she'd never had. The townsfolk said she had been possessed by a spirit, but went to her anyway because she had an uncanny ability in predicting the future. She had told Mimosa's parents they were going to die within six months. At the time, only the father had cancer, and the prognosis had been good. But soon it had spread into the spine and brain. Then her mother was diagnosed with aggressive ovarian cancer. She died first, two months later, Mimosa's father a few weeks after that.

The oracle's brother, Tang's younger brother, was one of two survivors of a Japan Airlines crash near Osaka International Airport. He was burned badly and shattered his left foot, but he lived, along with a little girl, both of whom had been ejected from the plane in their seats when the plane went down. Later, Tang told Mimosa the brother had told her that their sister had predicted everything.

The only thing the oracle had told Mimosa when she visited her in Taiwan was that she was going to meet her husband at the age of thirty-one, and that they would have three babies. Mimosa met Greg when she was thirty-one. They had been together for four years. They hadn't married, had no children. Greg was dead. The oracle was wrong.

• • •

On the Seibu Shinjuku-line subway, Mimosa was pushed against the mass of commuters leaving work, almost too tightly to breathe. She was in the middle of the cart, near the windows. On the tinted window, she saw herself, pale, ghostly, partial. Akihabara, Roppongi and Ginza went by. Then Shinjuku, Shibuya, her station, then Chiyoda, Minato, Bunkyo, chasing each other in an endless cycle around the heart of the city. It was hot too, but dark, always dark, on the Seibu Shinjuku-line orbit, ten miles from the sun.

•••

She opened the door and walked into the living room after removing her shoes and changing into a pair of red slippers. She turned on the lights to make the green glow of the box in the bookshelf fade into the artificial illumination. She walked into the kitchen, past Greg's room, stopped and turned around.

The deck was on the desk. She didn't remember putting it there.

She walked back to the bedroom.

The window was open. The afternoon rain had soaked the bedsheets, painted them with gray dust and toxic soot. She closed the window, went back to the deck in Greg's room.

The deck was dry, heavier than she remembered. She plugged it in, turned it on and jacked it in.

The screen was blank, no neon words, nothing.

"Greg? Greg? Are you here?" she called out to the darkness. The sky, a lighter shade of blue, more pleasant, green mountains and low-lying clouds slowly emerged. Then Greg, walking in from the right.

Hi, Mimmy. I didn't think you were coming back.

You couldn't read my mind?

There's no way to guess what you are going to do. I can only analyze your thoughts on a given moment. You were dead serious on tossing the deck out the window. And me with it. You could have done that, you know. I am already dead.

I almost did. I thought I had. I couldn't remember.

Sometimes we do things we can't remember.

An open triangle of birds came from behind the mountain, flew between the valleys and disappeared into the clouds.

Do you know how long I cried after your death?

I know.

No. You don't know.

I don't know.

You weren't there. You were in here. This place doesn't have any time, does it?

No, not like yours. But everything is still linear. Your every visit is recorded into my database. The next time you come here, I will remember everything you said. Regardless if it happened a day, week, a year ago. It will always be a second before you turned the deck off, fifteen seconds after you turned it back on.

How much will you remember?

My database is currently just over half full. That's about ten years of blank memory remaining. After that, I can erase parts of the old data. Yes, it's like forgetting the little things, like the kind of dress you wore the second time you came here, the exact words you said when we had this conversation, how many times we rode on the wheel. It mimics the way the brain works fairly accurately, really.

You could have an upgrade.

Yes. I can tell you how to download the data into a new deck. Newer models come into the market every five years or so. The next version will have more storage space.

And you have perfect control over the environment here, right?

What do you want to see?

The Rosetta stone.

They were inside the British Museum, in an exhibition hall filled with Egyptian mummies and obelisks and columns ciphered with hieroglyphs. The Rosetta stone was in a glass case in front of them, black and cracked. The surface looked smooth and polished. Too smooth. Too polished. A group of tourists entered the room, speaking in a foreign tongue, looking around with glazed eyes. Maybe they also knew the stone was really just a replica.

Dolphins.

The ocean was translucent blue and green. A speck of white in the horizon was the only land she could see. They were on a small raft. Dolphins everywhere, in the ocean around them, circling, jumping, wailing . . . . Greg was placid, with a touch of sadness running across his face. Maybe because he was dead. Maybe because he was now a computer program. Maybe because they'd never seen real dolphins. They were all dead like Greg. Extinct.

Greg? I think I want to become pregnant. The dolphins disappeared into the dark ocean that was growing fast into a green hill, under white clouds, between two snowcapped mountains.

But you need my help.

Yes. Can you make it happen? In here?

Do you want a boy or a girl?

A girl. At first. We can have a boy later.

Greg smiled. A newborn?

Yes. Just after birth, and we are in the hospital. The doctor has just brought in the baby . . .

•••

. . . a pink little baby girl with the umbilical cord still dangling from her belly. The doctor, clad in a white uniform, turns to Greg. "Do you want to do it?"

"No. I think I'd better let you do it. I might cut off something else." The doctor hands the baby over to the nurse, a short blonde with tanned skin and face covered with a blue surgical mask, as he reaches over to the side table and picks up a pair of surgical scissors. The baby cries as the doctor snaps the umbilical cord—now black and thin without any blood, like one of the wires in the deck—into two.

"That's a good girl," the doctor says, and picks up the baby from the nurse and places her on Mimosa's lap. Greg walks over and sits on the chair next to the two.

"She's so beautiful, isn't she?" Mimosa asks, brushing the baby's forehead.

"She is," Greg says, kissing the baby, then Mimosa, stroking Mimosa's hair with his fingers. "Have you thought of a name? How about Marina?"

"That's just what I was thinking," she says, turning to look out the window. White clouds. Parts of blue sky. Not the side of the next building, like it always was.

She closed her eyes. It was not real. Plastic. Everything was happening inside a box of chrome and plastic alloys, relaying the images she saw directly into her retinas, the rest of the sensory data into her brain, feeding her brain the images she wanted to see. It was not real. Nothing was.

She looked at her baby. Marina had a blue birthmark on her rear end. The mark would disappear as she grew older. Hers had. And now her blood flowed through Marina's veins, or the best possible approximation of it.

•••

Her great-grandmother had told her stories of World War II. The Japanese had colonized Manchuria and built a Japanese state there in China called Manchukuo. Then the war ended, Japan had lost. All of the Japanese had to leave Manchuria at once. There wasn't much time, the space was limited, Japan was in chaos. . . . So the government declared for the young children to be left behind. The parents could always have another baby back in Japan. So they left without the children. Thousands of Japanese infants stranded in enemy territory. Waiting to be killed.

But the Chinese raised the children as their own. The children of the people who had burned Nanking, killed, raped, mutilated, burned, everyone there. Even the women and children. Then the enemy was gone, only the children remained. Children of the invaders, conquerors. Murderers. Blood of the enemy, right there, in the children's veins. And yet the Chinese in Manchuria raised the Japanese children as their own. Her great-grandmother didn't know why they'd done that. She didn't know either.

She'd never been to Manchuria. She'd seen pictures; it looked beautiful. Maybe one day she would go.

With Marina.

She looked out the window again, and thought of the green mountains in Manchuria. Greg smiled. Marina had stopped crying. The nurse and the doctor

had left the room. Another nurse came in and took
Marina. Marina looked at her when the nurse gently
carried her away. Marina was one-sixteenth Manchurian.

Greg? Will Marina be here when I come back?

Yes.

Will she be able to grow up?

As fast as you want her to.

Real time. Day by day.

Of course.

Greg? I will see you tomorrow. I need to go now.

I will be here. I'll wait for you.

As the power shut off, Greg faded into the black
space inside his black deck.

•••

That night, with Mimosa sleeping with the sensors
on her temples, the deck on the bed, blinking in green
and red and blue as the electrons passed through the
diaphanous optical data link, the three of them walked
down the park, Mimosa pushing Marina in a small pink
baby carriage, Greg walking beside her, his arm around
her waist.

And it was wonderful, the air in Grusgrus Park,
fresh, filled with the thick scent of thousands of cherry
blossoms opening, unfolding, painting the park light
pink and white and yellow.

Only a few other people were in the park with them,
a man in a gray flannel suit, a jogger and an old woman
in a kimono, sitting on a bench on the other side of the
park, sleeping or feeding the pigeons. Mimosa liked the
quietness. The park was usually too crowded. Too many
people breathed the air of Tokyo. Too many people
ruined everything, made it all fake, plastic.

Out on the far side of the park, a sole white crane stood on one foot, listening. Mimosa, too, stopped and listened. Then she heard, it, the absence of the white noise, the sound of traffic, cars, trains, airplanes, words, steps. . . . Complete absence of all sounds but her breathing, Marina's blanket ruffling in the wind, the gravel wincing as Greg shifted his feet, and behind all that, the distant echo of the wind, singing a melody she had never heard, perhaps something like Beethoven's ninth symphony . . . .

The crane lowered itself into the water and started swimming slowly across the blue lake. Origami, she thought, the bird looked like an origami crane. But its features were more delicate, sharper, intricately crafted than those of any origami crane she'd seen. Paper could never be bent to replicate those cranes, not like that. And she looked into the carriage, at Marina sleeping, counting the days until she could teach her to make birds from paper, beautiful tall cranes, and dragons, and pandas, maybe, from different-colored paper.

Greg smiled, and Mimosa looked at the bird again, now stopped, fluttering its wings just above the still face of the lake, creating a whisk of wind, spreading ripples across the lake, decreasing in intensity until the waves were gone, never reaching the three on the other side, behind a curved steel fence. . . .

A gust of wind picked up and raced across the pond onto the other side. The cool air fluttered Mimosa's hair, flicking it on her face. The dead leaves on the ground ruffled against the concrete, playing a game of catch with each other. The crane stretched its wings, flapped them, and rose up effortlessly against the cold northern air and flew toward the dark clouds.

Marina cried. Greg picked her up from the crib and rocked her in his arms, back and forth, back and forth, as Mimosa looked at the flying crane slowly disappear behind an invisible mountain, behind steel and chrome.

And slowly, the day turned into a night, then a day again, the night into a day, the graceful white cranes of Grusgrus Park into neat, gently folded origami cranes in Marina's small hands, white and beautiful cranes, eyes and beaks painted with black and red ink, beautiful, more beautiful than Mimosa had ever seen, more beautiful than she'd thought possible, but never quite as good as the real.

A NEW ANTHOLOGY

Written by
Tim Powers

About the Author

Tim Powers was born in Buffalo, New York, on Leap Year Day in 1952, but has lived in southern California since 1959. He graduated from California State University at Fullerton with a B.A. in English in 1976; the same year saw the publication of his first two novels, The Skies Discrowned and Epitaph in Rust (both from Laser Books).

Powers's subsequent novels are The Drawing of the Dark (Del Ray, 1979), The Anubis Gates (Ace, 1983, winner of the Philip K. Dick Memorial Award and the Prix Apollo), Dinner at Deviant's Palace (Ace 1985's winner of the Philip K. Dick Memorial Award), On Stranger Tides (Ace, 1987), The Stress of Her Regard (Ace, 1989), Last Call (Morrow, 1992, winner of the World Fantasy Award), Expiration Date (Tor, 1996), Earthquake Weather (Tor, 1997), and Declare (Morrow, 2001, winner of the World Fantasy Award). The Manchester Guardian has called Powers "the best fantasy writer to appear in decades."

Powers has taught at the Clarion Science Fiction Writers' Workshop at Michigan State University six times, and has three times co-taught the Writers of the Future Workshop with Algis Budrys.

Powers is married, and lives with his wife, Serena, in San Bernardino, California.

The Writers of the Future awards event happens in an elegant building on Hollywood Boulevard, two blocks west of the Chinese Theater. Only a few blocks northeast is the old Parva Sed Apta apartment building—the name means "small but suitable"—where Nathanael West wrote *The Day of the Locust*. A few blocks southwest is the apartment where F. Scott Fitzgerald wrote what we have of *The Last Tycoon*. And Raymond Chandler's fictional detective Philip Marlowe had his office on Franklin, just a block north of Hollywood Boulevard.

It's in this setting that the new edition of the *Writers of the Future* anthology is first seen by the writers whose stories are in the book.

I don't think there's any moment in your writing career quite as affecting as the first time you autograph a published copy of a story of yours. There's a sense of breaking a bottle of champagne over the bow of a vessel that you can hardly make out the shape of, and it occurs to you that this action—signing your autograph under your printed name—might one day become routine, unremarkable.

It's certainly not unremarkable the first time it happens. And you think about all of the copies you won't autograph, the copies that are bought in states and countries you'll never visit, to be read by people who will never meet you. Inevitably someone born long after your death will pick up a copy of the book and read your story, and perhaps wonder who you were, what you were like.

I think this is for me the most memorable moment in the week-long itinerary of the winners of the Writers of the Future Contest—the moment when the newly published book is unveiled, and I get to pick up a copy and take it around the crowded room to the authors whose stories are in it, and say to each of them, "Could you sign this for me?"

By this time, the winners have spent nearly a week in an intensive writers' workshop, in which they've read articles by L. Ron Hubbard on everything from plotting to research to marketing; listened to frank nuts-and-bolts lectures from writers like Algis Budrys, Orson Scott Card, Kevin J. Anderson and myself.

By this time, they've done research at the Los Angeles Library, outlined plots, argued about every aspect of fiction writing, interviewed strangers they've found on the streets of Hollywood—and they've discovered, generally to their astonishment, that they can write a story in one day.

It's a busy week, culminating in the awards ceremony and a big party for the release of the new anthology. The next day they all fly back to their various homes, all over the world—but while it was a group of gifted amateurs that originally assembled, it's professional writers who disperse afterwards.

Many of the winners in years past have gone on to successful, distinguished careers in fiction writing; a majority have sold stories and novels. It's no longer a remarkable moment when someone asks them to sign a book!

But it was, once—here, on an evening in the shadows of Fitzgerald and West and Chandler, and in the shadow too of the young Ray Bradbury, who now has a star on Hollywood Boulevard sidewalk pavement where he used to make his rent money by selling newspapers in the 1930s.

It's people and events that make a place magical—and it's still going on here.

WORLDS APART

Written by
Woody O. Carsky-Wilson

Illustrated by
Hristo Dimitrov Ginev

About the Author

Woody lives in Virginia with his exceptionally supportive wife, Meg, and son, Lucas (who inspired a horror short story!). Woody is a stay-at-home dad, also a major in the Army Reserves.

Born in Heidelberg, Germany, Woody is an Army brat. The travel and exposure to other cultures has led to some interesting experiences. In the Gulf War, he saw the first combat intercept in history of one missile against another when a Patriot shot down a Scud at Al-Khobar.

Woody's parents, Woody and Shirley, said he'd be a writer when he grew up. He didn't believe them. They encouraged him, never forcing him into the wrong mold. Years later, it turns out they were partially right. He never grew up, but he did become a writer.

Woody had a great year in 2001, selling two stories and winning this contest. He feels "Worlds Apart" would never have succeeded without the advice of his writers' group when he lived in Cincinnati. He is eternally grateful to Ryck Neube, his mentor and anarchic leader of the Cincinnati Writers' Project fiction critique group. He also thanks his other friends and colleagues of the CWP.

lewess cocked her head. "There is a test in five minutes."

I coughed, trying to steady myself in the juggling spaghetti of shifting corridors called the stellarplex. I'd just jumped from Earth-Moon L5. "What test?" I hurried to follow, not wanting to get lost in the ever mobile 'plex. Clewess was a New Human, all advanced evolution, her glasslike body spilling light from every orifice. Me, I was stock, with the same body plan the cave men had shared.

We entered another globe, bigger than the translation globe. The technician sat off to the side.

"Tell me about this contract," I said.

Clewess smiled, leaking light from her mouth. "You will help create worlds."

"Why me? Why not a comwave?"

She shook her head. "Doesn't work. They tried it. The technicians set up a comwave network that happily spit out data all day long. The control globe interpreted the data and fabricated worlds accordingly, but the worlds lacked something vital."

"What?" I asked.

She waved her hand. "Panache, flair, soul, the human element, one of those clichés that makes your people so . . . . Never mind. The worlds attracted no visitors." She touched a finger to my chest. "Please watch yourself, Terrin. The screens in this control globe are more dangerous than translation screens."

I stepped away from the globe's surface.

"Here is your partner. We can test your compatibility." She sprayed something in my face.

I recoiled, turned and saw my partner. My mouth hung open.

New Humans have ethereal light-spun beauty like an angelic choir singing in a vast cathedral. It's a beauty born of technology, genetics and whatever else drove them to super-evolve their bodies and minds. But this girl was no New Human.

She was a Natural, with earthy, grab-you-by-the-roots beauty that makes you want to revel in its smell, touch and taste. Young, beautiful and bursting with life. Her hair was ohh. Her face was ahh. Her body was the gift that keeps on giving.

Maybe that's why I kissed her.

She kissed back, arching into me with a moan. I licked her eyelids, played hands across her breasts and thighs and felt the surge inside of me as—

"Ahem. Compatibility readings are fine," said the technician.

I stepped back, averting my eyes. "Sorry, I don't know what came over me."

She extended her hand. "It was just a test. I'm Tayl." The nails were perfect and trim, the fingers tapered, long and smooth.

I looked at that hand, thinking a world of pleasure could be found there. I would kiss each fingertip with love and—

"Hello?" she asked. "You there?"

I shook myself and took her hand. Its warmth quickened my blood. "Sorry."

She brushed aside a strand of wavy black hair and spoke matter-of-factly. "They want us to make beautiful music together. If we do, then this"—she pointed to the interface screen—"can make beautiful planets."

I licked dry lips. "So we'll, ah—"

Her eyebrow arched. "Yes, we'll 'ah,' but it's just a job, nothing more."

I watched the little gulp of air she took, the way it rippled the smooth skin at the side of her neck. She stood with hands folded in front, one leg slightly bent.

The fluid walls of the control globe, the light-filled New Humans, the deadly screen, all spun. If I fell, I might bump the screens. Goodbye, Terrin.

Clewess examined the bottle she'd sprayed in my face. "Maybe I gave him too many pheromones. It's probably temporary. No, wait, these are ape pheromones. Damn! Wrong bottle."

Tayl shook her head. "I've got to study. Make sure he sleeps. Big day tomorrow." She turned and walked off, tunic swishing with her steps.

"God, she's beautiful!" I whispered.

Clewess led me by the arm out of the globe, shaking her head. "Naturals. Next you'll be rutting in the halls! Just focus on your job."

•••

The nonexistent phenomenon called morning dawned in the place that had no planets or suns. Clewess buzzed my sleeping globe.

"Good morning," she said.

I sighed and threw off the covers. "On Earth I've seen blood-red dawns. Why does my window show me uninspired black?"

Illustrated by Hristo Dimitrov Ginev

"Red inspires you?" She moved about the room, light dripping.

"Dawn inspires me."

Clewess handed me teethcream as we walked. It foamed around my gums and enamel, erasing the taste of morning mouth. We entered the control globe, and Clewess stood by the technician.

Tayl approached, wearing a white linen tunic that revealed strong, golden calves and smooth feet in thin-strapped black sandals.

"When does it begin?" I asked.

"Now," she said, leaning forward to kiss me lightly on the lips.

A yellow streak swirled on the walls of the globe.

I melted against her, grinding myself against perfect softness. My heart wrenched. "Is this the pheromones again?"

"No one sprayed you, did they?"

"Then I must be in love."

"Just focus, okay?"

I shook my head and concentrated on her full, red lips. Visions of mountain pine forests in the place once called Arizona flitted through my brain. A waterfall gullied and murmured down a rocky slope. The sun shone butter golden across moist blades of grass.

A flicker of movement caught my eye. The globe swirled with new colors: sedate blue, muted earthy green, and aroused purple. The color of our passion.

"You're doing fine," said Clewess. "The technician is adjusting the metal mix in the planet's core."

We continued the slow, deep kiss. Tayl moved in my arms, writhing slowly and sweetly. Her arms rose above my head. Her eyes went heavy-lidded. She danced a

dance that had sent many men to their graves hunting
saber-toothed tigers with spears and lust-born courage.

I thought of Earth, that planet of green and blue I
could never escape.

Tayl's eyes remained riveted to the screen. Mother-
receptive waters gathered their cloak over the emerging
planet. Tayl's dance was warm and sultry. It mirrored
the oceans, which reflected her dance, and I swam in
both with abandon.

"Your turn," she said.

I balked. "I'm not that graceful."

She frowned and pinched me. "Dance, fool!"

I danced.

An island formed in the sea, but was quickly covered.
I danced harder, faster. The land rose up from the oceans,
tall, massive peaks thrusting high into the air.

The land grew. Tayl touched me and I shivered.
Lakes rose within the landed surfaces. Her touch eroded
my soil, sank it beneath the weight of inland seas, bent
me to her will, but I pushed back, grabbed her by the
hips and thrust forward.

At some point her tunic came off, she unlaced her
sandals and kicked my clothes aside with her bare feet.
My breath came ragged. I dueled with her tongue,
kissed her face, hands scrabbling across the golden
perfection of her strong back. We built a volcano, a fire
ring of lust searing the ocean bed.

Her eyes never left the screen. When I'd spent my
passion inside her, she looked to the technician. "Well?"

"Stand by."

The planet rotated, complete. The screen stopped
shimmering, and I relaxed.

The technician continued. "The rating is three and a
half."

"Is that good?" I turned to Tayl.

"Dammit! If I didn't have to study, I'd do it again." She retrieved her tunic and was gone.

Clewess frowned. "There is room for improvement."

•••

I wandered the halls. Half-formed shapes appeared suddenly, then disappeared before I could identify them. There was nothing to properly name. Everything was a something-like.

I passed something like a kitchen for project staff. Tayl was the only solid object present. I sat on something like a chair and sipped something quite unlike coffee from a mug, as she kept her nose buried in a text scanner.

"If they're so advanced," I said, "why can't they make a decent cup of joe?"

She shrugged, did not look up.

"Sorry about today," I said. "I wasn't prepared."

"That was Clewess's fault." She looked up and stared past me into something like a window, except that windows in a 'plex gaze into open space, or show real-time views of planets thousands of light-years away at random intervals.

"But it's not life or death," I said.

She frowned. "Maybe not for you, but I have to maintain a steady job during my studies or I'll get kicked out. A rating of three and a half is too low."

I grunted and drank more of the disgusting liquid. "What planet are you from? Is it anything like the Earth or the Moon?"

"How should I know? Never heard of those places."

I slammed the mug down. "Never heard of Earth? Poor child!"

She raised an eyebrow.

I assumed a theatrical stance. "The maiden Earth is swathed in come-hither clouds, bathed in storm-swept seas, girded with verdant valleys, majestic mountains and unparalleled plains. Who can deny the appeal of her naked planetary body under azure skies?"

That got a smile from her. "Are you quoting poetry?"

I shook my head. "No, the travel brochure."

She laughed. "All brochures claim their planet is unique."

"Earth *is* unique," I said. "It's the historical birthplace of mankind."

"Really? Guess we had to come from somewhere. Are you a tour guide for visiting planet trash? I know New Humans don't go there."

I blinked.

"I'm sorry. That came out wrong." She placed a hand on my arm. "I've never really related to other Naturals. My family always worked for the 'plex. I find planets a little scary. They're so claustrophobic. No offense intended."

I waved it off and coughed. "None taken. The New Humans don't visit because we're so far out in the arm, that's all."

"Of course."

"It's late," I said. "Gotta sleep. Don't want me messing up again tomorrow."

She nodded. "You'll do okay. Just let it flow."

"Let it flow, sure." I poured my something-like coffee down the drain and left without turning back. Planet trash. She'd called me a tour guide for planet trash.

Planet trash is the derogatory name for a Natural who lives on a single world and cannot leave that world without being homesick. This poor Natural would usually have a sponsor, nominally called an agent, who supplied him with the basics of life and maybe a few techno toys to stave off boredom.

I'd always traveled, but Earth was home. Clewess was my agent, but, really, wasn't she just a sponsor? She gave me my hovercar, and that orbital ship was a birthday present. Who was I fooling? I was a charity case. I helped Clewess feel better about being superior. I was planet trash, green as they come.

•••

Someone touched my shoulder. I rolled over in bed and looked up. "Hi, Clewess."

"Morning, Terrin."

Red light broke through the fake window. I smiled. "It's beautiful, but it ain't Earth. I once awoke in a desert, and the light that greeted my eyes was—"

"Interesting, but we are late."

I rose and followed, slapping teethcream in my mouth and swishing. "I'm coming. Anyway, thanks for the dawn."

We entered the control globe. Tayl sat in the alcove.

Same drill as before, only I relaxed into the process. She swayed and the oceans foamed. I pressed myself against her, forming the land. She kissed me and lakes appeared in the land, and I took her in my arms, hands caressing her back and rear, removing her tunic. The island lofted. We made two rings of volcanoes, one within the other, with multiple resurgences of land and water. It was done.

The technician looked up. "A solid six."

Clewess ran in, too quickly. "Well done!" She tripped.

"Clewess!" I rushed forward, pulling her back from the deadly screens. She was light, insubstantial, like holding water, and she shivered violently. The screens turned gray, inactive.

"Thanks." It seemed she would shake apart.

Later that night, I walked what may or may not have been the same halls. I knew I couldn't get lost. The structure somehow perceived how far I wanted to walk and configured itself to support my intended trek. It repeated that feat for trillions of others simultaneously. The traffic control comwave was listed as the third wonder of the known universe.

I stopped at the project kitchen. A New Human sat in the chair Tayl had occupied the night before. "Clewess?"

"Hi, Terrin. Thanks for saving me today. I'm still in neural shock."

"My pleasure. Mind if I sit? I've been pacing the halls. Where's Tayl?"

"Studying for important exams. She's a driven woman. One day she'll snap."

"I doubt it. Tayl is tough. She knows what she wants. Me, I haven't a clue."

Clewess peered at me, light leaking from her eyes. "Desire is written plainly on your face."

"Am I that transparent?" I blushed. "For a Natural, I mean."

"In matters of the heart, you are a moron. Real love could stare you in the face and you wouldn't see it." Her tone was brittle. Her eyes held mine.

She rose and left, leaving me shaking my head and wondering if there was any way to get real coffee. The

New Humans were killing us in a war of polite proximity. They could peer in on our private lives anytime they wished. Faster, smarter, more sophisticated, they were better than us in every way.

But, gods, their coffee sucked!

•••

The next morning, I awoke to a beautiful interplay of colors.

"Sonoran Desert, the North American continent," I guessed.

"Perhaps. I found it in the archives," said Clewess.

"Thanks. You didn't have to do that."

"I wanted to, Terrin. I wanted . . . ." She sighed. "Never mind. Let's go."

We went to the globe. Tayl arrived at the same time.

It was better this time. We cued to each other's responses. The mountains rose, the oceans frothed, the land and lakes met as lovers. Time fled. The screens went active blue to inactive gray.

The technician nodded. "Eight."

Clewess frowned.

"What's wrong?" I asked.

"Nothing. You did fine."

That night I sought Tayl in her sleeping globe. The globe opened a portal, and I waited for her to notice me. She hunched over her comwave unit. I coughed.

She turned. "Hi." She returned to her work.

"Whatcha doing?"

She answered without turning. "Studying for exams."

I came closer, massaging her shoulders.

She shrugged off my hands. "Another time, huh?"

"Everyone needs friends, Tayl."

"I've got friends." She turned her back.

"They aren't planet trash like me, huh?" It came out harsher than intended.

"That's your word," she said, "not mine."

"You're the one who asked if I was a tour guide for visiting planet trash, so it's your word too." I paced. "Fine, I love Earth and the Moon, and even if you haven't heard of them, they mean a lot to me. There's nothing wrong with that. Beats the hell out of a stupid stellarplex!"

"I like it here."

"It's nauseating! Everything changes, nothing's permanent. A planet is solid. It's ground beneath your feet, sky above your head. Everything where it should be."

"Not my thing," she said. "I'll stay here my whole life."

I scoffed. "I don't think so. You're like a dog who wants to stay in the master's bedroom. Sooner or later you'll get kicked out. If you're lucky, they'll give you a nice doghouse." My stomach flopped. "Tayl, I'm sorry. I had no right to say that."

"You sure as hell didn't!"

I raised my hands in surrender. "It's the 'plex. I get disoriented."

"Like that freakin' dog? Can a dog manage night courses and the constant pressure of job performance? These exams are the most important thing I've ever done. One slip-up and I fail. How dare you? You're Clewess's little dog!"

"I shoulda kept my mouth shut."

"Damn right! Go back to your planet if you can't handle the 'plex."

A cold rock lodged in my stomach. "Tayl, dammit, I said I was sorry."

"Go. I've got work."

I entered the shifting halls. The local comwave correctly sensed my mood, because it took two hours to return to my sleep globe. Passersby gave me a wide berth, probably thought I was just another crazy Natural with murder in his eyes.

They were right.

• • •

I awoke before fake dawn light could filter through the fake window of my fake room. Clewess found me walking to the control globe. Tayl came later, eyes red-rimmed and sleepless. I ignored her, stepped into the center and waited. When the gray of the screens went blue, I flexed my fingers.

Tayl joined me. "About last night—"

"Shut up." I drew her close and kissed her hard on her mouth.

"Careful, Terrin!"

I forced her chin around. "Look at me when I kiss you."

The seas retreated. The land rose to claim its stake. Tayl would not meet my gaze. Lakes spread like a pox on the face of the world in the screens. I held her immobile, staring straight into her eyes.

Lakes dried and barren desert swept the planet. Mountains rose high and stark. There were no clouds to swathe the planet.

Tayl glared, grabbed her tunic and exited the control globe. The soles of her bare feet flashed and were gone.

The technician grunted. "I rate it a four, only because some travelers like deserts."

I grabbed my robe and left, met Clewess in the something-like-a-break room.

"You want something you can't have with Tayl," she said.

"Thank you, agent, or sponsor, or charity case collector—whatever you are. Why don't you squirt me with ape pheromones? What do you think I want?"

"A home and a wife to look after you."

"Brilliant insight, but I'm happy as a single man."

"You're not si—" She stood quickly, eyes whiter that I'd ever seen them. "Go to hell." She turned and strode out.

Having successfully pissed off fellow colleague, technician and agent, I escaped to my sleeping globe for a lousy night's sleep.

●●●

Clewess woke me to a dawnless morning. I groaned before following her to the chamber where Tayl waited. It was a terrible session. I was not up to the challenge. Our creation was unimpressive.

"An all-ocean world," said the technician. "Comwave could've done better."

I grabbed my robe, wrapped it about me and left, waving off Clewess.

I found Tayl walking the hall. "Can we talk?"

Her breasts rode high and proud. Her trim ankles and smooth wrists sent sparks through me, despite my anger. I reached out to touch her face. "Tayl—"

She slapped my hand aside. "Don't touch me!"

"Dammit, whether you like it or not, we *are* the same species."

She turned with a snarl. "Planet trash!"

I recoiled. "New Human whore!"

Her eyes went wide. "Stupid jackass!"

I balled my fists. "Uppity bitch! You think because you're so beautiful I should waste time on you?" My fingers flexed toward her body.

She sneered. "You with your rakish good looks and devil-may-care attitude. I'm supposed to be swayed by that? Ha!" She scratched at my chest. "Just because my body wants you, doesn't mean I do!"

"You're not content with who you are. Pathetic!" I squeezed her nipples. "Your oceans are shallow, your lakes small and unformed."

She grasped my manhood, pumped it. "Your volcano is tiny, your lava tepid."

I held her stare. "I ought to take you here and now on the floor of your beloved stellarplex."

"You aren't man enough!" she spat. "Not with your betters watching."

Light-shimmered faces looked our way. "Let them ogle our naked bodies—"

"—while we shamelessly rut?" Her eyes were moist and bright.

We sank to the floor and gave the crowd a show it would not soon forget.

Later in the night, I held Tayl, stroking her hair and kissing her face. "Could you be happy with a Natural for the rest of your life?"

She turned. "As happy as you living in the 'plex for the rest of yours. Go to sleep, you sap."

•••

The next day gave me the best dawn yet. Tayl and I joined, loved and shared. It produced a wholesome, stable planet with much to offer the weary traveler.

"Seven," said the technician.

I left with buoyant spirits and found Clewess.

"You've done a good job nursemaiding a monkey," I said.

"You're not a monkey. You're an ape, remember?" She smiled.

"Where's Tayl? Thought she'd be here."

"She's studying for conversion finals."

"Conversion finals? I thought they were regular night course exams."

"No, she wants to become a New Human."

The bottom dropped out of my stomach. "Are you serious?"

Clewess nodded. "There are genetic and technological tricks that transform Naturals into New Humans. It's very expensive and you must pass a difficult test. You've never heard of it?"

"Sure, but why would she—? Oh, hell, never mind. May as well ask why I'm so tied to Earth and the Moon. It's just one of those things, right?" I tried to laugh it off.

Clewess nodded. "Go rest. You have more worlds left on this contract."

I nodded. "Okay, but when my contract is over, I'm going to Earth for a cup of real coffee!"

•••

Tayl was excited. We kissed hello, and the kiss grew to something else.

"Save it for the planet." Clewess glared.

We laughed. I looked into Tayl's eyes. "You're happy."

"I took the first part of the finals last night, passed with flying colors."

"Congratulations," I said, with unfelt enthusiasm.

"Don't jinx me! I take the second part tonight. I pass, or it's permanent failure; no retests allowed."

I stroked her shoulder. "You'll do fine." I had a brief vision of her failing the test, falling into my arms, and letting me take her to Earth, where we'd drive my hovercar to all my old haunts. I shook my head, clearing the unrealistic vision.

We began.

Our session was slower than before, longer and more powerful. Our technique had matured. The volcano ring spewed lava three times, and during every interlude, the land and ocean folded back and forth across each other. The shores and the waters they faced infinitely reflected one another.

The technician looked up, silent and respectful. Clewess's mouth hung open.

I took lovely Tayl by the hand and winked at both New Humans on the way out. "What's the matter?" I glanced at the proud purple and blue world spinning like a ballerina on the screens. "Haven't you ever seen a ten?"

Tayl giggled and we left them.

"Let's celebrate," I said, once we entered the hall.

"No, I have exams tonight. I want to be focused."

"Take them tomorrow."

"I can't, I told you. The administrators are very strict."

My brows knit. "Just a little celebration. Please?"

She nodded, and we adjourned to her sleeping globe. One beer became ten, then there was wine, and I scrounged a bottle of champagne. Our kisses grew sloppier as the night wore on.

"I gotta get ready, Terrin," she said. "No more alco—*hic!*"

The 'plex spun about me. "You can take a hangover pill. You'll be fine."

"But the exam is in two hours."

I missed her mouth and kissed the side of her face. "You studied. You've got plenty of time to recover."

"But—"

I kissed her again, this time on target. Our mouths merged and I thought of the warm, salty ocean. She swam into my arms and we made our own little world without deadly screens or agents or technicians grading our effort, and definitely without ape pheromones. We collapsed in a heap.

●●●

I awoke to a piercing noise, like a teakettle but louder. I covered my ears, rose and turned on the light. Someone huddled by the comwave.

I approached. "Who is that? Stop screaming!" I looked to the screen.

YOU FAILED TO TAKE THE FINAL PORTION OF THE TRANSITION EXAM. YOU HAVE FAILED OUT. SIGNED—THE ADMINISTRATORS

My stomach lurched. "Oh, God, we overslept the exams."

Her face was red and tear streaked, her eyes completely wild. Her matted hair lay in disarray.

"Tayl, I'm so sorry . . . ."

She screamed again, a wracking, painful, sobbing cry that shook her frame and spiked my eardrums. I held and rocked her, covering her mouth with my hand when it was too much to bear.

Tears pooled in my eyes and fell to the floor. "Honey, don't do this to yourself. Everything will be okay."

She kept screaming, until she was hoarse and moaned incoherently. "I . . . I . . . ten years . . . hard work . . . They . . . think I'm stupid . . . couldn't take on time . . . the exams . . . never be one of them . . . Oh, God, I want to die!"

We cried together, our faces wet with snot and tears, shoulders hunched inward and hands shaking. I forgot Earth and the 'plex, just tried to keep poor Tayl from going insane.

If it wasn't already too late.

• • •

Morning crept by, slow as fate. Clewess must have known I stayed in Tayl's globe, because there was a dawn from the window that made me cry.

Tayl sat on the bed, staring through sightless eyes.

I touched her shoulder. "Honey?"

She turned, eyes blank with pain, face drooped, breasts slumped.

"It's going to be okay," I said. "When our contract expires, we'll take time off, explore Earth. I can show you an island called Lanzarote. It's like the end of the universe with the waves crashing on jagged rocks. And the Andes Mountains, they've got these hidden valleys so deep and green with the farmland spread out like a magic cape. There's nothing in the 'plex to compare."

She stopped me with a finger to my lips and spoke her first coherent words. "It's not your fault."

I shook my head, and the tears rushed once again to my eyes. "Tayl, I am so sorry about last night."

She shushed me again. We dressed and walked together to the control globe like two old people clutching one another for support.

"If you wish to postpone—" began Clewess.

Tayl spoke in a terrible hoarse whisper. "No. I'll give this all I've got."

We faced each other and sank into the metaphor.

We sprang from the dark tragedy of formless black space. We clung, we accreted, we grew. Oceans rose to birth the land. The land and sea hugged, wrestled, twisted, each pursuing its own course, and in the combination forged an unsuspected middle way. Clouds coalesced and rain hammered the planet with a million butterfly kisses. Land shaped itself, lakes gaped, islands peeked up to stare in wonder.

I lost myself in her, and she in me, and the planet in itself.

Unseen machines burned with power. Something green appeared on the world. Simple plant life, then animals that grew and evolved without constraint.

"We're reaching overload levels," warned the technician.

We ignored him, and watched life claim the planet for its playground.

"Stop!" cried Clewess. "This goes beyond project parameters!"

We loved with the deepest passion. Let the New Humans rave. We would have our moment in the sun.

"I love you, Tayl," I said.

"Emergency filters not responding!" The technician stabbed at the comwave.

"I love this, Terrin," she said.

Tayl and Terrin, Terrin and Tayl, we became one creature with two bodies.

"This is illegal!" Clewess rushed forward, but balked at the hellish glowing screens.

Life rushed top-speed across the planet. Smart as lemmings, then monkeys, then . . . one could only wonder.

I ached for her, my Earth, my mistress Moon, my valleys and verdant green joy, my blue skies and deep oceans and desert sands, my everything, my all, my one and only. I poured it all into the planet's creation.

We collapsed.

The world spun.

The screens glowed with deadly spitting energy.

I kissed Tayl on the forehead. She stood on shaky legs, as Clewess and the technician could only stare, then moved toward the screens for a closer look.

"Rating?" I asked.

"You went beyond." The technician shook his head. "No!"

I turned, but caught a mere glimpse as Tayl threw herself into the hissing screen and was reduced to her component atoms in less than an eyeblink. The New Humans gaped. Clewess covered her mouth, giggling uncontrollably. I remember screaming, then waking up in the veterinary globe under observation.

● ● ●

I grieved and Clewess comforted me, taking up residence in the local Earth-linked stellarplex and visiting me often. One planetbound day, I opened my eyes to see the love in hers and we kissed an electric kiss that bridged centuries of directed evolution. It made me feel young again. It gave me hope.

They say mixed marriages are difficult. I don't know. I'm happy, but then I'm a moron when it comes to matters of the heart.

I stare at the night sky, arm around my lovely, glass-skinned wife, with whom I shared many beautiful sunsets. I search for a world—green, blue and bright, filled with life. I know the planet Tayl is a wonderful place to live or visit.

It's the second most beautiful world in the sky.

PRAGUE 47

Written by
Joel Best

Illustrated by
Anthony Arutunian

About the Author

Joel Best lives in upstate New York with his wife and son. With a degree in German literature, he was almost preordained to become a writer, but some of his other occupations have included painter, puppeteer, kiln operator, picture framer and ice chipper.

A multiple finalist in the Writers of the Future Contest, he has had fiction accepted by Chiaroscuro, Ideomancer, Electric Wine and Deep Outside. Besides helping to raise his son, he is currently working on a novel.

In the alley behind Gorczy's, Milana Masaryk propositioned a member of the Kaiser's occupational forces, a young soldat who stammered and had trouble looking her in the eye. He'd been standing by the tavern window for an hour, watching her, before finally summoning the courage to come outside and compliment her red dress. "On you it drapes well," he said in appalling Czech. "Wie schön," he added, lapsing into German.

The soldat couldn't have been more than sixteen. Wilhelm had used up all of his seasoned men in the early days of the War, thrown them away in a greedy bid for territory. Now all he had left to occupy the newly conquered lands were boys barely able to grow a little fuzz on their chins.

But old enough to carry a gun, Milana thought. Old enough to walk patrols. Old enough to think they own Prague.

"Do you have any money?" she asked.

"Korunas?"

"Marks."

"Military scrip only."

She sighed. "I'm forbidden to spend your scrip and a wheelbarrow of korunas wouldn't buy me a loaf of stale bread."

The soldat hesitated. "You would maybe take whiskey instead of money? Czechs are not easily affording to purchase liquor, ja? In the tavern for you I can get a bottle."

Milana had already drunk more than her share that night, but the pleasant fuzziness she relied upon for emotional armor was starting to fade. Would she maybe take? Liquor was not so good as a few marks in the pocket, but infinitely better than korunas. These days Czechs used their native currency as kindling for stoves.

She accepted the fact that no real choice existed for her in this matter.

That acceptance almost brought on laughter.

1939 is turning out to be an excellent year for fatalism.

"Go fetch the whiskey," she directed.

2

As the soldat vanished into Gorczy's, the crazy man who lived with her darted across the street. Milana waved him away, but Franz kept on coming.

From the tavern, a German martial song praising Kaiser Wilhelm's abilities as the supreme conqueror. Gorczy's was one of the few drinking establishments open to the soldats (not bombed, not burned), and Andel, the owner, had grown fat and prosperous as a soulless collaborator. When the occupation ended, if that day ever arrived, he would either flee Prague or find himself at the tender mercies of its citizens.

Milana dragged Franz into the alley.

"What are you doing on the streets so late? Don't you know what the soldats do to curfew violators?" Whores had a special dispensation when it came to the curfew because they performed a service vital to the happiness of the Kaiser's troops, but for the ordinary citizen . . . .

"You want to end up in Execution Square with a stretched neck?"

"The words," Franz said far too loudly, completely oblivious to his danger. "I've found more of the words."

"Wonderful. Now, for God's sake, go home." Milana glanced at the tavern. If the soldat emerged now, her heart would stop.

Franz began to recite, and it nearly ceased beating anyway.

"'When Gregor Samsa opened his eyes, he tumbled from a startling dream and found himself locked in the body of an unseemly cricket.'" He stopped. "It's the beginning of a novel, I can feel it in my bones. A novel!"

Milana thought, God help us.

"Since coming to your world, I've sensed the presence of the words." Franz wouldn't lower his voice. "They come to me as butterflies seeking blossoms, as birds to warmth. Not since Prague 21 have I found so many of the words."

Milana put a hand over his mouth. Prague 21? Franz talked about this imaginary world more often than the others. There Germany had lost the War and found itself forced to surrender vast amounts of territory. Humiliated by the Brits, the French (and the Americans, of all people), it had fallen into ruinous poverty that lasted for decades.

Germany losing the War? Good God.

Kaiser Wilhelm controlled Europe from Belfast to the Ukraine. His fleet of invincible airfoils, loaded with gas and incendiaries, had swept across the continent like a firestorm, annihilating and annexing with terrible efficiency. Britain and France had suffered the worst from Germany's fury. The labor camps outside of London and Paris? How many thousands of prisoners entered their

Illustrated by Anthony Arutunian

gates, never to emerge again? Milana once saw a photograph, smuggled into Prague, God only knew how. Skeletons in ragged uniforms, faces hollow and dead.

Imagine a Europe where the Kaiser had lost the War.

She forced the treasonous thought from her mind.

"Go back to the apartment," she hissed, moving her hand and giving Franz a gentle push in the right direction. "I'll be home in a little while with some whiskey. We'll have a nice drink together and you can tell me all about Prague 21."

Franz stayed long enough to kiss her cheek. "We can read some of the words."

"Yes, now go!"

He melted into the night just in time. The soldat pushed through Gorczy's door, a bottle of whiskey in one ham-fisted hand.

"Now we are having good time," this one rumbled in his dreadful Czech.

3

Milana had met Franz a month earlier while trying to drum up some daytime business in the park. He seemed to appear from a mist that came from nowhere, but she was drunk and couldn't trust her eyes. His clothes were strangely cut, and he behaved as someone who'd lost his way. Numbers. He asked about numbers. Was this 47? He wanted 47.

In the end she took him back to her basement apartment by the river, because helping someone in need made Milana feel good about herself. It had been too long for that. Pride was a rarity for whores in occupied Prague. Franz didn't ask for much, just a place to sleep.

He managed to find his own food and always shared. But there were . . . other considerations.

The first night he slept in her bed, he woke her with a bizarre confession. "I'm not an owl," Milana said, annoyed at having her rest disturbed. She reached for him, thinking he just wanted a little sex, but Franz turned away.

"This is important. You deserve to know."

She felt cold. Know? Know what?

God, please don't tell me I'm sheltering a partisan.

Not a partisan. A lunatic.

"I came from another world," Franz whispered in the darkness. "For thirty years I worked for the same insurance firm, sitting at my desk, each day passing like a lost drop of blood. I hated my very existence because what I wanted more than anything else was to be a writer. Stories swirled in my mind. Titles. 'The Cricket Man,' 'Arrest and Conviction,' 'The Palace.' One dreary day I decided to quit work early. I left the office without even bothering about my hat and coat. The words were out there waiting to be found. My heart screamed this at me, so I began walking."

Milana wasn't sure what to say. Another world?

"You're dreaming, Franz. It was a nightmare."

"No. I'm from a Prague you wouldn't recognize."

"There is only one world."

"There are many," Franz answered calmly, as though it made complete sense. "I've walked through one Prague after another in search of the words that mean so much to me."

He added quietly, "This is Prague 47."

4

Franz never struck her as being dangerous. Milana knew some head cases you really wanted to avoid. One of her friends—petite, delicate Nescu, whose favorite possession had been a ridiculous feather boa—took the wrong man home and ended up in pieces. Milana had watched the police taking Nescu away in bloody canvas bags. "One less whore to worry about," the grizzled cop had muttered while his younger companion tried not to throw up.

Franz didn't have the look of someone who wanted to harm her. His eyes were deep and quiet and far-seeing. They reminded Milana of Miko, her dead son.

So Franz said he came from another world. He was a loonie. So many people were now. Considering the times, was his such a bad kind of craziness?

5

Milana's son had been dead for a year. In the winter of '37, scarlet fever rolled over the city like a sickly fog.

"Mama, I'm hot."

"Have some tea, dear."

"My stomach hurts."

"Come sit in Mama's lap."

She'd buried Miko in the huge cemetery by the river. Milana often went there to sit by his grave and listen to the Vlatva's gently murmuring waters. Papa used to bring her to the river and show her the stars. "That's Cassiopeia's Chair," he'd once said, pointing to a W-shaped grouping of stars. "She was the proud and vain wife of Perseus, the warrior-king who slew the Gorgon . . . ."

Milana tried to picture Miko untouched by worms in his tiny box beneath the earth. He was only asleep, hands crossed over his chest.

Wake up, she'd say. Let me show you the stars.

Milana drank too much whiskey. She was aware of this fact, but whiskey was one of the things that kept Miko alive in her mind.

Children died all the time, even before the War.

She missed him terribly.

6

On a rainy afternoon, Milana stood under a tree and shared a cigarette with a whore named Yvette.

A refugee from the Kaiser's work camps in France, Yvette sold her body for a man with a temper. Once upon a time she'd been lithe and lovely, but no more. Eight years of beatings had given her countless scars and hard edges.

The rain discouraged customers. In two hours, only a single German patrol marched past, kicking up mud and grunting, "Eins, zwei, drei, vier." Some of the soldats whistled at the tree, but their squad leader shouted fiercely, "Wegbleiben, Hüre!"

"Damn this weather." Yvette shivered as the patrol passed out of sight. She took the cigarette from Milana's hand. "We'll freeze our asses off and be lucky to scrape up a few korunas for the trouble." She made a face, probably thinking of her angry man, and spat at the rain.

"Maybe business will pick up," Milana said, not that she believed any such thing. "If not, you could always come home with me."

"And face Edvard in the morning?" Yvette shivered. "He'd only beat me for staying out all night."

"It's just an offer," Milana said. "Why you put up with such a beast is a mystery."

"You should talk. Better a beast than a head case."

Milana didn't respond. She shouldn't have told Yvette about Franz's dreams, the different Pragues he claimed to have seen. Walked to.

Like Prague 39.

Ice and snow. The streets filled hip-deep with rime-frost and silent as a tomb. Nothing moved, there were no people. The city had been abandoned for ages, the air cold enough to freeze skin. He spoke with a solemn reverence.

"In that majestic, dead city, I found traces of the words. How did they come to be there? It remains a mystery. The words filtered into my mind, then vanished. I couldn't hold on to them. This wasn't the particular Prague I needed, so I started walking again, and again, and again."

Yvette gave Milana a hard look. "I think you should be careful of that loonie. I've seen his type before. Soldiers, mostly. This damned War. Even if they come home with their arms and legs and balls, there's something wrong with their heads. You never know what they're likely to do."

"Franz is all right," Milana said. But she was remembering the look in his eyes as he spoke of these words.

Obsessive.

Angry.

Bewildered.

"You get rid of the head case," Yvette warned. "Kick him out before his craziness starts leaking out over you."

Milana lit another cigarette, saying nothing.

7

She returned from the park to find Franz sitting at the table, scribbling on sheet after sheet of paper, crumpling the results, beating his temples, cursing. She'd seen this a dozen times when the words failed to come to him.

"If it hurts so much, why not just stop?"

Franz tapped his pencil. "You don't understand the artistic mind."

Milana rolled her eyes.

"I must write. It's what I was meant to do. When I'm putting words on a page, even the wrong ones, that's the only time I feel that I'm doing the work God intended of me." He muttered under his breath, damn this, damn that. Cursed were insurance firms and jobs that robbed a man of his life.

Looking over his shoulder, Milana read what Franz had written. "More Gregor Samsa?"

"A soul in torment."

She read a bit more. "So he really is a bug?"

"Yes, but it's a metaphor."

"For what?"

"Alienation. Disenfranchisement from an unsympathetic society." Focusing on the pencil, Franz explained further about how the world shaped man, not the other way around, and how life usually ended in pain no matter what a person did to the contrary. Half-listening, Milana poured a glass of whiskey to chase the chill from her bones. Bugs were bugs, men were men. Pain? Yes, she knew all about that.

Suddenly, her glass was empty. She poured more whiskey. It was getting late. She was exhausted and needed sleep.

Franz still lectured.

"Heartless forces rule our lives," he said, pounding the table with his fist. "The universe doesn't give a damn about humanity. As far as it's concerned, we're all pieces in some unfathomable game whose rules make no sense."

Mad writer. Milana knew it. But one who needed her.

God. If only that didn't make her feel so warm inside.

Attacking the paper anew, Franz continued muttering about forces.

Milana poured more whiskey. Christ, she missed Miko. She was just drunk enough to think of her son without breaking down. To feel his sweet breath against her cheek once more, to hear his laugh . . . .

Could longing be considered a force?

She drained her glass and went to bed.

8

And dreamed of Miko. And dreamed of crying. The crying was real; Milana woke with damp cheeks.

Franz lay beside her, also awake.

"I was thinking of Prague 21. I walked there in the spring. A lovely world even though it held only a few of the words."

He settled back and stared at the ceiling. "'Gregor fled to the seclusion of the attic, scuttling up the stairs on his tiny legs, vanishing into the cobwebs with a soft clatter.'"

Milana decided she needed a drink and got out of bed, intent on going to the kitchen and having a calming glass of whiskey. She could already taste it, hot and smoky in her throat.

Franz reached out and took her hand. His grip was hot and rough. "You don't really believe I go to other worlds, do you?"

"I'm thirsty."

"You must believe."

"Let go of me." Milana tried to pull away.

"I'll show you," Franz whispered.

The bedroom dissolved.

9

They stood on the Charles Bridge, one of many spanning the Vlatva, built in the fourteenth century and decorated with statues of saints turning green with age. Across the river, the baroque palaces of Prague's Lesser Town crowded like undergrowth around mountainous Hradcany Castle.

Lesser Town had been destroyed by the Kaiser's airfoils in the earliest days of the War. This portion of the city no longer existed.

Clouds, white as sugar, drifting over the palace.

Bright morning, the air so clean and alive it felt alien to Milana's lungs.

She had trouble breathing and needed a few moments to realize this had nothing to do with the air.

"On this world the Kaiser lost his War," Franz said. He sounded like a tour guide. "Armistice brought about Germany's dissolution."

Milana barely heard. Her heart ached. She couldn't stop looking at the children, a flock of them, noisier than sparrows, racing across the bridge. The girls wore colorful dresses, the boys tidy shorts and shirts. Most clutched sweets in sticky hands.

The last boy across was Miko, her dead son.

Not dead here.

She tried to draw a breath.

Impossible.

"Franz," she gasped.

Prague 21 evaporated.

10

Scaffolds filled with offerings for the birds.

Wandering the tangled streets of Prague's Old Town, Milana found herself in Old Town Square, renamed Execution Square by the Kaiser's resident kommandant. Mourners crowded the cobblestones, praying for the souls of the departed. They were family, they were friends.

The early afternoon sunlight hurt her eyes. Milana was not a creature of day, but her nightly routine had been disrupted. She was tired. Sleep had been beyond her for a week. Bed for her, that would have been the best thing, but instead she haunted the streets, looking for Miko.

Yes, he was dead for more than a year. She'd felt his final, rattling breath. She'd buried him by the Vlatva.

But Miko was also out here . . . somewhere. She was positive without being able to explain why, other than it had something to do with Prague 21.

A dream, that springtime world? Hallucination?

Yvette had warned her about being contaminated by Franz's insanity.

"Am I going mad?"

Milana realized she'd spoken out loud. An old woman wrapped in a dirty shawl scowled and moved away from her.

The scaffolds were arranged in front of Golz-Kinsky Palace, now the offices of the regional kommandant. Herr Hitler, it was rumored, painted the most delicate landscapes when not overseeing executions of looters, thieves, malcontents and anyone else deemed a threat to the occupation. The kommandant had them rounded up and hung, then worked at his easel as the bodies slowly turned black and bloated.

He's here, Milana thought with dread. She wanted to run, then it was too late.

One of the dead was a young boy, face ravaged by crows, empty eye sockets lifted as though hoping to see animals in the clouds. He became Miko, smiling with shriveled lips.

Mama. . . .

"Did you know him?" said the woman in the shawl, seeing Milana's face, white and drawn. Maybe she thought the earlier outburst had come from grief. Her expression shifted to one of care.

"It is hard to lose a loved one," the woman said as one who knew, and suddenly a great deal of time had passed and Milana chased shadows through the part of the city west of the river. Stumbling among the broken blocks of Hradcany Castle, she called Miko's name. She saw him everywhere, in the moon, in the hard snow that fell like tiny razors, in the mud at her feet.

Franz appeared from nowhere as she staggered over the Charles Bridge. What was he doing out so late? He should know better than to break curfew. It would be a miracle if the soldats didn't arrest them both.

"I've been looking all over for you, Milana." His face was slick with sweat, his hair a wild mess. Fear brightened his gray-green eyes. "You've been gone for three days."

She stared. Days?

"Come home now."

"But I must find Miko."

Franz had to throw her over his shoulder and carry her back to the apartment.

"What did you do to me?" Milana screamed.

11

The apartment was freezing. No coal for the stove. Milana found a forgotten bottle of whiskey and drank herself stupid while Franz sat at the kitchen table, trying to work on his bug man story, but spending more time looking at her with concern. She hadn't seen that in him before. Franz had said he felt a great deal for her; she'd said the same about him. But what did any of it mean? She liked being needed; he required an apartment, a safe haven from which to pursue his precious words.

She finished off the whiskey. Two lonely people. That was the sum of it.

She didn't realize she'd fallen asleep. Waking, she found her crazy writer sitting on the edge of the bed.

"You said the name Miko in your sleep."

Milana fumbled for the whiskey bottle, forgetting it was empty.

"My son. He died of fever. Only I see him now. It started after you did . . . that thing to me. Miko as a blur in a mirror or a dark shape flitting at the edge of my vision. . . ."

She told Franz about Execution Square. "That was a bad one."

"This is my fault." Franz hung his head. "A window must have opened within you after Prague 21. Now you can catch glimpses of the other worlds. It's the forces playing their wretched games again. Let a mother see her dead child, but not touch him. What does it matter if this game shatters a human soul?"

"I saw him, Franz. He was eating candy." Milana trembled. "Miko is alive."

"In Prague 21, yes. Possibly in many Pragues."

"But without me. Without his mother."

Franz said nothing for so long that Milana began to fall asleep again. Distantly she felt his hand, warm and soothing, touch her cheek.

"I never meant to hurt you," he said.

12

Dream/not dream. Franz standing by the window, folding a sheaf of papers. His bug man story. Milana thought she saw the same mist forming around him as that first day in the park. It was probably a trick of the moonlight.

"You're leaving." She just knew it. "I'm always being abandoned."

"This is for the best." Franz slipped the papers into his pocket and knelt beside the bed. "This world has been generous to me, so many words to find, so many more waiting, but I don't want to take the chance of hurting you anymore. I've already done enough." He was conflicted. The need to stay, the need to go. "You deserve better than pain."

"I'm so lonely, Franz."

He took her hand.

"Accept this parting gift."

13

The sun tickled away her sleep and Milana woke, not surprised to be alone in bed. Franz said he was going, and she knew men could usually be trusted to keep that particular promise. Good-bye, farewell, thank you for the hours we shared.

But he hadn't left her yet, not quite. Her mad writer lingered by the window, surrounded by the same kind of mist she remembered from the park on the day they met. The mist, a pearly globe, generated its own light, hard and metallic. Years later she would swear to hearing an insect's buzz, high pitched and jarring.

Franz spoke, but Milana couldn't hear what he said over the buzzing.

Another dream/not dream, she thought. Or too much whiskey. Milana knew she was a drunk. Or perhaps Yvette's prediction had finally come true and she'd lost her mind.

Buzzing. Silvery light. Her head swam. She finally understood what Franz was trying to say.

"Be happy."

The mist expanded, changing the room around her. The chest of drawers moved to the wrong corner; the walls, once a dirty white, became pale yellow; curtains magically waved by the open window.

A warm breeze carried the sound of tolling church bells.

Bells? In occupied Prague? When all of the cathedrals had been destroyed by the Kaiser's airfoils during the War?

Franz, hardly more than a shadow now, nodded to a door that had never existed in her apartment before this moment.

The door flew open and Miko, dressed in his crisp funeral pantaloons and shirt, threw himself into Milana's arms.

"Mama, I'm hungry."

Milana held the boy so tightly she couldn't breathe.

"Franz . . . ."

She turned to thank her mad writer, but he'd already faded away.

WHAT BECAME OF THE KING

Written by
Aimee C. Amodio

Illustrated by
Fritz Peters

About the Author

Aimee C. Amodio is first and foremost a storyteller. Since 1998, she has been creating and performing interactive storytelling shows for elementary schools and libraries. Find out more at http://home.earthlink.net/~starchaser99/index.html. Mostly, she tells traditional folktales from around the world, but she's been known to throw in an original here and there.

This story, however, is the first of her originals to see print—and it's a lifelong wish come true. She's honored to be here, and in such good company.

Like many of Aimee's stories, this one came to her in a dream.

The thing made quite a ruckus as it was hauled through the Grand Entryway. All the nobles assembled, and many of the foreign ambassadors, stopped their idle wordplay to turn and gape at it. The silence came in a great wave, starting at the door and rushing toward me. I had decided to sit on my throne for this, when the messenger had brought word to me that a survivor was being brought in. That it was a half-breed was no real surprise; that it was so very vocal was.

It sputtered indignantly in some half-breed language that I could almost understand, if I had wanted to bother. Pidgin, it was, a hybrid of proper Dundorra *gotton* and some other language. From the large amounts of growling and teeth-baring that punctuated its tirade, it was easy enough to assume that it was some sort of animal tongue. Two guards dragged it to a stop, each one pulling on a cord binding the half-breed. The one around its neck choked it into silence. I signaled for that noose to be loosened.

"Do you speak intelligibly?" I asked, first in *gotton* and then in *cotton*, thinking it might be able to understand the common Fei tongue, if not the other.

It snarled again, straining against the ropes.

"If you can behave in a civilized manner, you will not need to be bound." Despite the fact that it had not agreed to my suggestion, I signaled the guards to release it. Immediately it hunched down, almost disappearing into a shapeless lump of the scraps and rags that were its garments. It was very difficult to tell the sex of the thing or the age.

"toopEd 'dorah," it muttered. The voice was youthful. It gave me no clues, other than the thing was foul-tempered and rude. I chose to ignore the insult and try again. This, at least, was a curiosity, a distraction from the usual wordplay of my court.

"What is your name?"

"m/KaLLE," it responded instantly. "m/KaLLE!"

"Emcalli," I repeated blandly, softening the sounds into proper *gotton*.

"YEz," it affirmed. Its pidgin tongue was close enough for me to understand, now that I was used to the sounds of it. Languages are a simple enough game for us, anyway. I myself speak the main tongues of each of the Nine Tribes as well as the common tongue and a few others.

"Emcalli, do you speak *gotton*?" I asked again. Patient, almost bored. Truly, I was interested. Now that our official hostilities with the Tana-Ierra were momentarily suspended, this child-thing could entertain me for a while.

"Yesss," Emcalli hissed. It was beginning to understand the game, I believed. Most half-breeds did not seem as quick as this one did.

"Good. You have been brought to the court of Dundorra. I am Tuckerann'Lazirr Quoyan'Orr." One letter added for each decade of my reign, from the day I inherited the kingship as a boy called Tuc.

The beady eyes in an androgynous and filthy face narrowed. "King."

"Yes, I am the King of the Dundorra." The court, I noticed, was yet still and silent. This was as much a diversion for them as it was for me.

"Dundorra war killed m/KaLLE family," it said, quite distinctly. There was hatred in the voice.

I was surprised that it realized, to be honest. Most half-breeds were simple. Almost more stunned, in fact, by the awareness than by its use of Dundorra *gotton*. "Yes, I fear that the Tana-Ierra made it necessary for us to take drastic measures. I apologize for your loss, Emcalli."

The dark eyes continued to squint, sharp white teeth flashed and a low growl emerged from its throat. What I had thought might be some sort of fur headband turned out to be ears, for they moved aside and back to lay flat against Emcalli's skull. Canine body language, I concluded. I suppressed a shudder.

"You do not accept my apology?"

"King means it? King talks about it like family are not important. Like family are things and not . . . people."

Though its general grammar was questionable in proper *gotton*, it was apparently familiar with certain nuances of word choice. The word "people" it had spoken connoted Fei. Not half-breeds. The choice did not escape the court, and a murmur of surprise broke their silence. The golden ambassador of the Naga hissed long and low. My guards drew weapons, but with a single raised hand, I silenced all indignant whispers and resheathed all blades.

"I truly am sorry, Emcalli. On behalf of the Dundorra, I apologize. Nothing I can say or do will bring your family back, but I will make reparations to you."

Illustrated by Fritz Peters

A gasp shook the court this time.

"I must say, I am impressed by the education and bravery you have displayed in this court. From this day forward, you are my ward and will be cared for as if you were my own. I can only hope that Dundorra hospitality lives up to your standards."

They chuckled at this, and it eased the waves of shock that had radiated over me. The air whispered each person's reaction to me, brought me the scents of outrage and amusement. Most expected this new plaything to last about as long as others had, but I suspected this Emcalli would surprise them all.

Emcalli was not chuckling at my offer. Instead, it bristled. I had added insult to injury in making it my favored pet, and the insult had not gone unnoticed. This little half-breed would be quite a diversion for us all. I signaled two bodymaids to take the hunched and indignant half-breed out and make it presentable.

●●●

Much to my surprise, Emcalli turned out to be a girl. A woman, even. The Chief Bodymaid had reported to me that the half-breed had refused to wear proper woman's clothing, but I gave my dispensation. The girl was allowed to appear at the court dinner in man's clothes, as long as she was clean and neat. So they had dressed her in my nephew's breeches and blouse, with a simply but elegantly trimmed vest.

The Chief Bodymaid herself brought Emcalli in to dinner, escorted by two guards. Inwardly, I thought this just a little excessive, though I had to let my lips curve in a smile at the sight of the Bodymaid's bruised cheek. Apparently, the little mongrel had put up quite a fight to remain in her rags. An angry glare was exchanged between the two women before my Emcalli bowed her head ever so slightly in a grudging show of respect and status.

I dismissed the Bodymaid and scrutinized the slender girl in boy's clothing. Definitely a canine half-breed, from the coarse-looking hair that covered her hands and forearms, feet and calves. She even had a tail, which had apparently required the hasty alteration of my nephew's breeches to accommodate. Her cheeks were lightly furred—down, really—and her ears, thankfully, were in proper place on either side of her head. Some of the more grotesque half-breeds had differently shaped skulls and limbs, but my pet was at least built like a proper Fei.

"Let me see your hands," I said, feeling like a stern father. Of course, in all my years of reign, I'd had no children. Her jaw set in an expression of stubborn defiance, but she slowly lifted her hands, palms down. I extended one hand to hold hers and was surprised to encounter softness. Without letting the emotion show, I studied her claws and nearly laughed. The Bodymaids had managed to gloss and blunt them! Quite possibly, that was the feat that earned my Chief Bodymaid a punch in the face.

"ztYL hav tYth," she said with a wolfish grin. *Still have teeth*. She knew exactly what I was looking at. And why.

"ov KorZ," I answered with a sly smile of my own. *Of course*. Languages had always been a gift of mine, and hers was easy enough, now that I knew the tricks. Her tail wagged once, betraying her amusement. Indicating a large cushion at the foot of my throne, I offered her a seat.

Slowly, Emcalli moved toward the cushion. I would almost say "stalked." Her dark, chocolate eyes considered it, then me, then it again. With a seemingly effortless coiling of muscles, she leaped into the air, landing lightly on the wide arm of my throne. Truly, the arms alone were wide enough to seat a generous bottom; kings long gone and with far many more letters to their names had commissioned and added to the ostentatious thing. But there she squatted, tail lashing, that wolfish grin again adorning her face, as if daring me to remove her. It made no difference to me where the half-breed chose to perch. It did, however, occur to me that the Clikk entourage would be quite amused by this mongrel girl on their next visit to the court.

Emcalli remained perched on the arm of my throne all that evening, her bright eyes eagerly soaking in the intrigues of the court. During dinner she had offended some of the more sensitive courtiers by using her fingers as utensils and disdaining the proper hierarchy of service. The look on one of the Fifth Rank dandies when she helped herself to the meat before he'd had his turn was priceless. Several demanded her removal before the meal was finished, but I denied them all. Emcalli was yet there just before the official close of evening festivities, when several of my Seconds approached the throne.

"First Lord," the highest ranking Second intoned formally, "this has gone on long enough."

Out of the corner of my eye, I could see the fur on the back of Emcalli's hands bristle. Absently, I reached out to smooth it as I spoke. "You presume to set limits on me, Second?"

"My Lord, be reasonable. You cannot expect our distinguished guests to share a roof with a half-breed!" The other Seconds wrung their hands and made gestures of inferiority. Emcalli growled low in her throat.

"Dinner alone was a travesty," he wailed. "Imagine how a visiting dignitary would react! Dundorra would be fortunate if the Naga did not dissolve our current alliance after such a display of impropriety."

"If you would care to remove her yourself," I said lightly, "then by all means you may set her wherever you wish for the night."

"Cannot even dress right," a lower Second grumbled, eager to get in some cutting comment in order to curry my favor.

The highest Second drew his ornamental knife. If he was no fool, the blade was not merely ornamental. Everyone knew the tales and most heeded the warnings: Idle threats lead to early deaths, as the proverb went. "As you wish, First Lord. I shall remove the half-breed."

No sooner were the words out of his mouth than my pet sprang at the man. And the scuffle was short and sweet, ending with the knife clattering out of the highest Second's hand and Emcalli kneeling triumphantly on his heaving chest. I was on the verge of laughing and proclaiming her Highest Second by right of duel—in jest, of course. But her growl became a roar as she flashed those gleaming white fangs again. The look in her eyes spoke of wild animals, of throats torn out, of sweet, hot blood. Vaguely, I heard the pleased hiss of the golden Naga, saw that forked tongue come flickering out to wet scaly lips.

"EMCALLI!" I roared, coming to my feet. "NO TEETH."

She glared up at me from beneath her short, spiky hair, then deliberately lowered her head and sunk her teeth into the Second's meaty shoulder. He yowled, and she drew back, then leaped off him entirely. In a breath I knew the wound was superficial. She licked her lips; her tail lashed. Pivoting on one bare foot, she walked out through the Grand Entryway, head held high. She had made her point.

•••

She hid somewhere in the crystal palace and grounds for several days. Had she left the grounds entirely, I would have known. I am not King of Dundorra for nothing. But the wolf laid low, and waited. I would not search for her myself; nor would I have any of my lowers on the hunt. She would come back. Because she wanted to. And because she belonged to me.

•••

I was holding a conference with the Naga delegation and a group of Desaridd the reptiles had sponsored. We had no official hostilities with the Desaridd—yet—but they were allies of the Tana-Ierra, on whom we had placed blame for the problem of Emcalli in the first place. The Desaridd are quick in all things, especially temper. They had come to request leniency for their allies and a return of some of the Tana-Ierra lands. Taking advantage of their bond with the Naga, the Desaridd had weaseled their way into my court for a visit. I had to receive them.

I saw no reason, however, to be nice about it.

The chief delegate of the Desaridd, a wiry and wrin-kled old Fei, was droning on about historic boundaries when I caught a scent of my pet on the wind. Since I did not care either way whether or not I offended our guests' guests, I let my eyes roam. Another taste of the

wind pinpointed her location, though my eyes could
not find her.

And then she burst into the open, raging in her
growly pidgin tongue.

Much to my amusement, the Desaridd all ignited,
their eerily slim bodies crackling with electric energy. I
did mention those tempers. The Naga leader, that
golden temptress, slid closer to me and hissed low for
only me to hear.

"Quite a pet," she murmured.

"Perhaps the Tana-Ierra are useful after all," I replied.

"What, for throwing this warmblood thing into your
court?" The disdain was clear in her voice. I merely let
the words roll past me. "There are better things than half-
breed furballs to spend your time on." It did not occur
to me then that Ssyl was jealous, though the three Naga
slurs should have given me a hint. Sometimes, even a
king is distracted by a pretty face, a tempting form.

She slid a hand down my arm, the sensation simultaneously arousing and distasteful. There was a certain
quality of Naga skin, even when in their full Fei forms,
that was slick and just a bit too cold. It was one of the
main reasons I had not succumbed to Ssyl's invitations.
Though I was not opposed to the occasional dalliance, I
had a sneaking suspicion that she had been sent to the
court in an attempt to dethrone me.

But the leader of the Desaridd was sputtering at me.
"What is the meaning of this?" he blurted in *cotton*, the
common Fei tongue. As we had already exchanged
pleasantries in Dundorra *gotton*, I continued to speak in
that language instead.

"Do not mind my pet, Honored Guest," I intoned.

"Your pet? This worthless heap is your pet?" He was
once again speaking in the gods' tongue, and the sneer
of disdain was clear.

My worthless heap was nose to nose with one of the junior Desaridd. Her claws, which, I noted, had been resharpened, were splayed; the Desaridd's form crackled with energy. And fear. The energy was making Emcalli's fur stand on end.

"Emcalli," I said, trying to soothe with my voice.

"thYz ahr hEEr phor taNa-YErra," she squawked, whirling to glare at me.

"I know they are here on behalf of the Tana-Ierra," I affirmed. The senior Desaridd's eyes bulged.

"m/KaLLE BLaYm Yooh Both." Her dark eyes blazed with anger. *I blame you both.*

So she had been hiding and licking her wounds these past days. Mourning her family and hating those she saw as responsible for their deaths. "Emcalli, the Tana-Ierra intruded on land that is ours, where your family was. Had they simply kept to what was theirs, everything would be as it should."

The senior Desaridd sputtered at that, but another snarl from Emcalli quieted him.

"Not 'toopEd," she said defiantly. Then, she switched to *gotton.* "I know exactly who is to blame."

Silence fell over the courtyard where we had been discussing politics and boundaries, and I thought it best then to adjourn for the day.

●●●

I had the still squalling half-breed brought to my chambers. The time had long passed for me to assert my authority; perhaps I was too long used to the automatic hierarchies of the Dundorra. And my place at the top. "Brought," I had said. I should have chosen a different word. Hauled. Dragged. Wrestled through the doorway, though she dug those ragged claws into the wood frame and hung on with all her wiry strength. She had no idea where she was being taken, only the certainty that she did not want to go.

"Emcalli, enough."

Somehow, my voice was enough to quiet her, though her fur still bristled and her pointed ears lay flat against the sides of her head. Gratefully, the Hallguards shut the double doors, closing me in with my pet.

"Yem not Yoor pEt," she growled, her thoughts apparently aligning with my own.

"Speak properly to me or not at all," I suggested, in a tone of voice that made it clear the words were anything but a suggestion. They were a command.

Her cheek twitched ever so slightly as her jaw clenched, but I did not need the visual clue. I could feel the disturbance of air from her slightest movement.

"Why am I here?" she asked through gritted teeth, each syllable forced out.

"You are part of my family now, Emcalli. I thought you understood that."

"Part of your collection, you mean," she snapped back. "You treat that snake-bitch better than you do your own people."

I would have opened my mouth to correct her coarse language, but it occurred to me that in her half-breed canine mentality, "bitch" might be an acceptable synonym for "woman." "I do not believe that court intrigues belong in this discussion. This is of you and of me."

"I am not your pet," she said clearly and distinctly, the same words she had snarled at me only moments before.

"And you are not true Fei," I snapped back, rising to my feet. I could feel the coldness of air along every inch of my skin, which seemed to boil with fury. "I may be able to give you some leeway, but do not forget that you are not equal."

Emcalli snarled and lunged at me, claws aimed for my face. We struggled for a moment longer than I would have liked before I flung her aside, careful to direct her toward my soft bower and not into the crystal statues or stone and wood walls. She rolled with the momentum and came up poised for another attack.

"I will fight you if you wish," I said calmly, though I was inwardly seething. "But you will be resigned to the fact that we are superior and you are inferior. I am superior."

She lunged forward again and managed to sink her teeth into my forearm before I again disengaged her. "I will not sit in this gilded cage and play your pet."

Her conviction was, on some level, endearing.

Then she shattered my favorite sculpture, a gift from a Caverna artisan.

Here in my mind, a rage rivaling that of the fiercest Desaridd clouds clear memory. My next distinct impression was using my weight against her, kneeling on her arms with my two hands around her throat, attempting to buckle a leather belt into a sort of collar. I succeeded and released her.

The air followed the strangely slow movements of her body as she stood. Straightened. Her dark eyes lifted to meet mine. The moment seared onto my senses. Infinitely slowly, the molecules parted to make way for a lifting arm. A curving of fingers. Then, to make up for the lack, time snapped into full speed as she slashed her claws through the double-wound leather.

The remains of my belt fell away as blood spurted from her throat.

At a perfectly normal pace, she crumpled.

I sprang to her side, bellowing for the Hallguards, the Bodymaid, anyone, to fetch a healer. I stanched the blood as best I could and had the strangest sensation of looking down at my own flesh and blood. My own child. Her eyes stared up at the ceiling.

But a moment before the healers burst into the chambers, she met my eyes. No haze of pain, no gloss of the dream before death. Clear-eyed, she coughed blood away and licked her lips. One claw dug, briefly, into the back of my hand, drawing blood.

"Mine," she said so softly, a hint of fluid in her voice, "is the same color as yours." Then she closed her eyes.

●●●

I had the healers leave her in my bower for her period of recovery. After the struggle I had in simply getting them to treat Emcalli, it was as easy as breathing to have them agree to turning my chambers into her sickroom.

The days that she slept were shattering. Humbling.

Everything I had believed, for centuries, about the half-breeds had been changed in an instant. In all the years, I had occasionally known those who kept a half-breed for a servant, or a sort of a pet. They had been slow, stumbling, inelegant. After a time, they had run off, disdaining the civilized life for wild scrabbling outside the Fei cities. Completely unlike Emcalli. Bright, fierce, strong Emcalli. Emcalli who stood and fought rather than run and hide.

Discovering that I admired her was a shock. Respect came easier after that.

And I told her all this as she slept. First in *gotton*, then the common tongue. Then in her pidgin, my throat growing hoarse from imitating her growls. I told stories. I sang songs. I talked endlessly, sleeping fitfully between words, hardly realizing I'd dozed.

My advisors all thought I'd gone mad.

The Desaridd contingent left in a huff, followed in short order by the Naga.

And I did not care.

Strange, how quickly admiration becomes respect, and both become affection. Love. I was afraid to admit it, at first. With love came a whole new terror: What exactly would happen to me after I abdicated the kingship? It is the way of the Dundorra that the King loves only the country. When he formally makes his pledge to another, the mantle of kingship flies from him and shifts to the youngest person present. That is how a young boy called Tuc, a page to an underling of a bodyservant, came to be King of Dundorra.

No one remembered what happened to the old King.

Having lived so many centuries, long past the normal, decent age for a Dundorra Fei, did he simply fade away? Or worse, did he linger in his death? It had never been an active fear of mine, for I never felt the first stirrings of love. The golden Naga, Ssyl, had hoped—I was certain, now—to slither into my affections and wrest the kingship from me. Not in any hopes of garnering power for herself; in the wake of an abdication, the resulting disharmony, no matter how short, would give the Naga, or any Fei, an advantage over us.

I was not prepared to die. Nor was I eager to continue on in the lonely position of King without this strange, endearing half-breed at my side.

It would have been horribly dangerous to pretend no affection for Emcalli, to continue on as I had for decades before. Once, my sole purpose for being had been the love of Dundorra. I could no longer give that focus to my land and people. The charade of that love continued, I reasoned, would be just as bad as abdication. A distracted king is no king at all.

Thus, I resigned myself to putting my kingdom in order and the business of falling in love with Emcalli.

•••

I opened my eyes.

Obviously, the gods were punishing me: the first thing I saw was that arrogant King. I was dead, and he was dead, and this was my eternal torment.

I moved my head.

All right, the first part of my nightmare wasn't so bad compared to the searing pain in my neck. Served me right, I supposed, for cutting my own throat.

A coward's escape, but an escape nonetheless. Or so I thought.

Eventually, I decided that I was not dead.

If death had as much, or more, pain than life, it was no better. Especially if that King was in death with me. And since I'd always believed death would—at some point—bring you to a better place, I was forced to conclude that I was still alive. And still in this cursed Dundorra palace.

The King looked strange. And smelled worse. It took a moment to place it, then I realized he was . . . unclean. His long hair was lank, his clothes were wrinkled. Something was definitely not right. And then his eyes opened. I had barely moved, thought I was being cat-stealthy . . . but it was enough to rouse him.

"Emcalli?" His voice was hoarse. Like mine had been, after howling my grief into the nights. He lifted his head, then raised a hand to my cheek. Instinctively, I wanted to dodge it—it smelled unwashed, and like old food—but the slightest bunching of muscles in my neck brought back that searing pain.

"Do not move," he commanded. Stupid Dundorra King. Always bossing.

But I nearly choked in surprise on the cup of water he held to my lips. I would have thought it beneath him. He stroked my hair, rather awkwardly, with his free hand, then offered the cup again. This time I managed a sip. The water was as refreshing as it was painful, for the motion of swallowing gave new strength to the pains. I nearly cried.

"I will fetch the healers." And then I remembered, after barely a moment of wondering how he knew I was in such pain, that the gift of the Dundorra is in the air. They could tell a hundred things about you just by taking a breath. Once, I had thought my own nose was smart. His was so much smarter.

"Wait," I ground out over the frayed cords in my throat.

"What is it?" Fluidly, he was back at the bedside. His bedside, if my nose was to be trusted.

"Why?"

A look of such pain came over his face, then. Fear lit his eyes, changed an undertone of his scent.

"I was wrong." He closed his eyes, hung his head. Shook it, to indicate negative. Not my family's habit, but a common enough Fei gesture for me to recognize the meaning. "No. You were right. You are . . . people." He chose the word, as I had, that connoted Fei people.

My head grew fuzzy again, on the inside. So I let myself rest.

•••

The next time I opened my eyes, that King was quick to bundle me into a ridiculously cushioned chair on wheels. At least he smelled and looked better.

It was going to hurt to talk, I knew. "What are you doing?"

His answer was to whisk me out into the gardens. The gardens! Obviously, the man had lost his mind. He was silent as he toured me up and down the paths, but I could scent the pride puffing out his chest. They were nice enough, for tamed flora. I was surprised he didn't stop to mark every tree as his own.

He finally stopped the rolling chair near a pond. Which servant had the job of keeping the water so sparkling clean? I wondered. I envisioned some lowly Dundorra rising early each day to sift particles of dirt out of the crystal perfection of the pond. And they probably had some stupid and special title like Chief Water Sorter or Environmental Tamer, First Rank. The Dundorra were in love with words about themselves. Everyone was shuffled into their slot, and this mad King at the top of the heap.

I missed my family terribly. The whine slid into my throat before I could stop it.

Immediately, the King knelt at my side. Was that concern in his eyes? I narrowed mine, warning him to back away. He did not. My ears went flat. He did not back away. The whites of my eyes showed.

"Emcalli, I'm not going to hurt you." His voice was like a song. A lullaby.

I bared my teeth.

He put his soft king-hands on me and lifted me out of the rolling chair. He was damn lucky I was still so weak or I would have torn out his throat. What was he going to do now, have me given a scrub in this pond in the garden? Sure, I could sleep in his bower while I was bleeding to death, but now I can't even be washed in his house? Before I could stretch a claw forward, he had placed me in the grass and stepped away.

A servant of some sort—the Chief Chair Retriever, I supposed—hurried forward and hauled the cushion on wheels some distance back down the path. The King settled himself on a rock near the pond. Not that I was paying attention. This grass. . . smelled so sweet. Probably because in that instant before I clawed out my throat, I knew I would never smell the outside again. Now those claws were digging into the ground, clutching handsful of dirt and grass and reveling in the feel.

It was glorious to be outside again after being dead.

• • •

During the course of my recovery, the King took me to see all sorts of things, all on the palace grounds. Obviously, he was ashamed to take me out among his people on that ridiculous rolling chair. Long after I was strong enough to walk on my own and every movement did not cause searing pain in my throat, he continued to carry me around, as if I were some sort of a baby.

I came to realize that this was his penance.

Some time before I awakened, the King had discovered a conscience. Perhaps he was just too used to everyone falling obediently into their proper slots in the

Dundorra hierarchy. When I refused to be slotted, it threw him off. And in the aftermath of driving me to attempt suicide, he discovered life outside the hierarchy.

Not all beings are put on this Sphere for the express purpose of serving or entertaining him.

What a surprise.

So I was his penance. I had caused the revelation, so now he obviously felt obligated to heal me, to care for me. I half expected him to pick me up by the scruff of the neck and carry me around in his mouth, like true bitches do to their pups. It wasn't quite that way among my family. . . it's a little harder when your jaw isn't grown quite the same way. Of course, for the True Lupines, that's not a problem.

All in all, I was coming to realize, the entire Fei Sphere was dominated by a strong sense of hierarchy. One group was better than another—like the True Lupines were better than my family. Supposedly. Personally, I found it all ridiculous. One Lupine must have agreed, to mate with a mortal and make my family. My grandmother, zY/rhEnE. Syreni, they would have called her in *gotton*.

Half-breeds, they call us. In many tongues.

All Fei are half-breeds, actually.

As I understood it, all the Fei were once one big, happy family. There wasn't a division of powers like there is now: the Dundorra masters of air, the Tana-Ierra mind warpers and so on. All the Fei had all the gifts. Then they started to fracture. They bred themselves with the express purpose of strengthening one talent above the others.

In doing so, they created the Nine Tribes who have survived to this day. They also created bitter animosities, like the long-standing hostilities between the Dundorra and Tana-Ierra that resulted in the battle that killed Syreni's family. My family.

It all comes back to my family.

The King's penance.

And I was getting tired of being the balm on his soul. He deserved every torment imaginable and some I couldn't begin to dream up.

I never wanted to be his pampered pet.

•••

I had taken to sitting in the gardens early in the morning, before the King's body servants had finished primping him for the day. It was one of my few moments of solitude, when I could quietly mourn zY/rhEnE and my parents and cousins. The pain was growing less, as more and more days passed, but the memories of them remained strong.

My favorite part of the garden was at the edges, where the manicured lawns and shrubs started to give way to the wild, untamed forest. Most of the servants of the house would leave me alone there. Most of the servants left me alone anywhere. The only place I was forced to see them was in the evenings, at the ornate palace dinners, where everyone who held the most obscure rank in the Kingdom of Dundorra was welcome to see and be seen. For the most part, I sat quietly on the King's throne, exchanging angry glares with the higher-ups whom I'd embarrassed that first night.

My old life, in the forest, was starting to seem like a dream.

The Dundorra routine of pomp and preening came to seem like the only world I had ever known. I let myself fall into the tiers and ranks of the court, waiting my proper turn to take food and drink and watching the nightly intrigues with dull, guarded eyes. And I was never allowed outside the grounds of the King's palace. To me, it was like being imprisoned. But to the King, I could imagine he saw himself protecting me. He had conveniently forgotten that I had grown up in the forest borderlands between Dundorra and the Tana-Ierra. As soon as I could walk, I could hide myself from either side's guard patrols. Physically, at least. Between the mind warpers and the powerful Dundorra noses, we were all fooling ourselves that we were truly hidden. However, the sense of security was enough.

But I did not like being penned in. And I was quite vocal to the King about the whole state of affairs.

The worst part is, he would listen to my rants with a peculiar half-smile on his face, then murmur some vague agreements to me. And that, in his mind, closed the matter for the moment. It didn't stop me from trying again at the next opportunity. And that stupid King just kept smiling and murmuring. Like I was a cub.

●●●

I think the moon had gone through its changes at least twice while I recovered. And one bright morning, the King surprised me by finally agreeing to let me outside the palace grounds.

I was thrilled until I realized he intended to accompany me.

Curse him and his brand-new conscience! I was very tempted to bite him right in the . . . conscience . . . but held myself back. In all fairness, he HAD nursed me back to health. True, he had been the cause of the injury in the first place, but he could have just let me die.

In the end, I accepted his presence because I had no other choice and wanted so desperately to be outside the palace grounds.

The coach that was waiting for us was even more ridiculous than the chair on wheels. This was like an entire bedroom on wheels! Such needless excess. There were heaps of cushions in rich, deep colors to match the heavy drapes over the windows. A servant offered us drinks in sparkling crystal goblets. I could barely feel the motion of the cart from the inside; it was like we were not even moving at all.

"Why ride when you cannot feel it?" My voice still sounded wrong to my ears. It would take some getting used to, for this new voice seemed to be permanent.

"Do you not like the carriage?" The King had that cursed smile on again, like he was humoring me.

"I would rather feel the wind," I said, trying to keep my tone light. I had not yet figured out a way to manipulate this King. Whether I was subtle or direct made no difference. He did what he wanted anyway. This time, however, he surprised me. He drew back the heavy drapes himself—with his soft king-hands!—allowing the air to circulate. The perfumy scent of the overstuffed cushions quickly gave way to the fresh, crisp draft of freedom.

I gave in to impulse and stuck my head out the window, laughing at the rush of wind past me. It occurred to me, somewhere in the vague back of my head, that perhaps there was a reason the Dundorra favored such heavily guarded rooms-on-wheels. Perhaps the thick drapes shielded their sensitive noses from the chaotic scents of the outside. At the moment, giddy with fresh air and being outside the palace, I didn't really care. I stole a glance back at the King . . .

and he was just staring at me. A strange expression on his face.

When we arrived at the first market, we abandoned the wheeled bower to walk. Perhaps the King thought I might bolt, for he kept a hand on me at all times: cupping my elbow or clutching at my hand or resting on my shoulder. At the same time, his attention was light in my direction. He was busily engaging every google-eyed lowling we encountered, from Merchant Chiefs to Junior Coin Changers and everything between. And they adored him for it. Packages and pouches, sachets and sacks were carted off to the coach, without a coin passed over from the Dundorra King. Here and there, he would deign to split a treat with me or pause over something that caught my eye.

He was suspiciously solicitous, then contrarily aloof. One moment he was ignoring me to exchange ritual pleasantries with another underling and the next he was murmuring to me in that particular voice he used, coaxing me to taste this sweet or touch that fabric. I could not fathom his motive. It was almost as if he were showing himself off, preening subtly with each kowtowed greeting and gesture of deferral.

Every so often, he would give me a quiet smile, as if we shared some secret. Indeed! And if that were not strange enough, he plucked a flower from a roadside basket and placed it in my hair.

And I suddenly realized that he didn't just take care of me to ease his conscience. He wasn't just toting me around out of duty or guilt. The stupid King actually fancied that he was courting me. That he was in love with me!

I might have laughed . . . if every muscle in my body had not seized up at the thought. From ear tips to toe-claws, I had become like rock. And curse his nose, of course he noticed right off.

"Are you well?"

I continued to stare at him, frozen, for another long moment. Then, unable to form words as my tongue seemed to have forgotten how to listen to my mind, I simply imitated the head-bobbing gesture of agreement.

"Perhaps it is time to return to the palace," he suggested. Though, as usual, I had no choice but to acquiesce. His hand shot out toward me, to guide me back, but I shied away. I did not want to be touched. Once in the coach, I curled myself in the farthest corner from him, sneaking glances at him out of slitted eyes. The ride seemed interminable, but when we finally glided to a stop at the front of the palace, I darted out between the heavy drapes and bolted for the gardens.

The King let me go.

•••

He gave me several days to hide in the wild edges where the forest and gardens met. But one morning, just as the sun began to lighten the sky, he was there, squatting before me, having moved up as silently as one who controls the very air can only move. And he just watched me, until I could no longer bear the silence.

"You are in love with me."

"I am."

His agreement was so quiet, so simple, that it infuriated me. I wanted to rage, to deny it, and him, to claw at his folded arms and shake him until he came to his senses. I wanted to tell him he was crazy, that his love was false. But I could not and did not know what was in his mind. If he fancied it love, then love it was . . . at least inside him. And inside me was a snarl of thoughts and questions and screams that tangled me up so I could hardly decide what to say at all in response.

So he began to talk, in that quiet murmur he used only on me. A story, he told, about a boy called Tuc who had been the youngest person present when the last Dundorra King formally pledged his love. A lowly page-in-training who had been on the throne for the last twenty-one decades. And now his time was drawing to a close. He spoke of fear, of not knowing what would become of him once he made his formal declaration and the mantle of kingship flew off to another surprised child in the court. There was no one remaining who remembered what happened to that last King in the flurry of adjusting to the boy-King Tuc.

The passing of Dundorra leadership was odd enough, but a strange sensation pierced through me at the mystery of what would become of this King when he was King no longer. To my surprise, I recognized it as fear. Concern. So I began to curse the King in every tongue I knew, not only for making me his pet, but for making me care about him. Not love. But there was an affection there. Even as I tried to continue to hate him, it had developed. I tried to remember that this man was responsible, at least in part, for the loss of my family. . . but some other part of me had forgiven him. All his mothering care, all his stupid little gifts, all his secret smiles had worked a glamour on me and now I was tied to him with a thread of my own making. Imprisoned by unconscious choice, before I even realized it.

But he just sat there, squatted in the high grass, and smiled as I raged. It was a long time before I ran out of curses to speak and languages to use, ending with the King's own precious *gotton*.

His soft hand moved, and I drew back, bearing my teeth. I did not want to be touched. But he spoke my name, softly, once. Then again. I could hear the emotion in his voice, as clearly as (I am certain) he could smell the

fear in me. Perhaps if he had showered me with fancy
words, I would have stayed so angry. But he only spoke
my name, and twice. I stilled, and he touched my cheek.
Lightly. And then he spoke again.

These words were vaguely familiar, things I thought
I had dreamed during my convalescence. He spoke of
admiration and respect, and affection. It seemed, at first,
that he was speaking of someone else. It could not have
been me. But it was. Confusion was my first reaction,
for I had all along assumed he continued to hold the
prejudices of his people and that I was still nothing but
a pampered pet. And then I was only half-listening to
his soft words, for in my mind, I was reviewing every
action of his that I had cursed for being intended to hurt
or mock or control.

Perhaps the prejudices I had assigned to him were
my own. It was my own snobbery that had me
holding myself aloof from what he offered. I was so
determined to be the better Fei that I was blinded to
him. I had thought of him and treated him as an
abstract, as a King, rather than as a Fei. A person.

Then my own hand moved, my fingers just brushing
against his lips in a quieting gesture zY/rhEnE had
often used on me. The King . . . Tuc . . . was shocked, I
think, into silence. I smiled.

"Do you do anything besides talk?" I teased. His
own hand came up to rest lightly over mine.

"Little," he answered. Something new flared in his
eyes that looked like hope.

I moved back into the green shade of the high grass
and wild vines, and he followed. And for a long while,
a long and silent while, we did nothing but sit, my palm
against his, fingers curled to hold.

~The Coda~

We passed that long and sunny Midsummer day—
one of the highest and most sacred days of power
among all Fei—together at the garden edges. At dusk,
Tuc decided, at the opening of the Dundorra celebration
of Midsummer in the great crystal palace, he would
formally pledge his love to me and abdicate the throne.

"You could just walk into the forest and never come
back," I suggested. It was a continuing delight to hear
his soft, deep chuckle at my words. But there was no
hiding the fear of his fate. Would he immediately age
through his twenty-one decades of kingship and
crumble to dust before my eyes? Or would he age, but
live, and hobble out as a wizened elder? Could he
possibly remain as he stood before me? Would he revert
to his child-self, the boy before the King? Through the
day we had both ignored the looming specter of his fate.

"Take more time," I urged, a little desperately. "How
can I know in a day if I can love you? What if I do not?
You would want to keep your kingship, then."

"I would not," he answered. "For so long, I have
loved nothing above Dundorra. Whether my affection is
returned or no, I cannot remain King without giving my
whole heart to my people."

I reminded him that he had waited through my
convalescence without abdicating. What difference
would another day make? Another fortnight? But my
stupid, stubborn King held firm. With or without me at
his side, he would enter the crystal palace for the last
time tonight as the sun finally began to fall. And all the
while he talked so solemnly, so sadly, he was weaving

garlands from wildflowers and clinging vines to crown my head and his.

The sky was shading to a wild mix of orange and pinks when we emerged together from the high grass at the garden's edge, holding palm to palm and wearing our flowered crowns. We walked like that through the Grand Entryway into the great hall and passed onto the dais to stand before the throne.

What words he spoke, I will never recall. They passed in a blur, ringing out strongly among the displeased murmurs of the assembled Dundorra. What I do remember clearly, and will never forget, is the moment of perfect stillness after he pledged his love to me and surrendered the kingship. The hand that was not already holding mine came up to touch my cheek, and he brushed his lips over mine. I could feel something—the invisible mantle of kingship—rise out of him and away, leaving behind just a man. A man whom I knew I would love, once I was ready to admit it.

Navigating our way through the chaos of a new King (or Queen, since the chosen one had been a young girl), we exited the crystal palace and walked, palm to palm, toward the rainbow halo around the setting sun.

And no one ever knew, or remembered, what became of the King.

THE YEAR IN THE CONTESTS

Written by
Algis Budrys

About the Author

Algis Budrys was born in Königsberg, East Prussia, on January 9, 1931. East Prussia (now the republic of Belarus) was at that time a part of Germany, but Budrys is a Lithuanian from birth, because his father, the Consul General of Lithuania, was merely stationed in East Prussia at the time. The family came to America in 1936.

Budrys became interested in science fiction at the age of six, when a landlady slipped him a copy of the New York Journal-American *Sunday funnies. The paper was immediately confiscated by his parents, as being low-class trash, but it was too late. Shortly thereafter, Budrys entered PS 87 in New York. There, he was given a monthly publication called* Young America, *which featured stories by Carl H. Claudy, a now-forgotten juvenile science fiction author, and such serials as* At the Earth's Core *by Edgar Rice Burroughs. He was hopelessly lost, and by the age of nine was writing his own stories.*

At the age of twenty-one, living in Great Neck, Long Island, he began selling steadily to the top magazine markets.

He sold his first novel in 1953, and eventually produced eight more novels, including Who?, Rogue Moon, Michaelmas *and* Hard Landing, *and three short-story collections. He has always done a number of things besides writing, most but not all of them related to science fiction. Notable among them was a long stretch as a critic.*

He has been, over the years, the Editor in Chief of Regency Books, Playboy Press, all the titles at Woodall's Trailer Travel *publications, and L. Ron Hubbard's* Writers of the Future, *where he works now. He has also been a PR man for various clients, including Peter Pan Peanut Butter, Pickle Packers International and International Trucks. His favorite client was Pickle Packers International, for which he participated in a broad variety of stunts; but his most challenging client was International Trucks, for which he crisscrossed the country for four years, from the Bridgehampton Race Track on Long Island to the sun palaces of Newport Beach.*

In 1954, he married Edna F. Duna, and is still married to her, an arrangement that suits both of them. They have four sons, now scattered over America and the world. Life is good.

he year 2001 proved to be a year of unparalleled expansion for the Writers and Illustrators of the Future Contests. Perhaps this was due to the wonders of the Internet, friends telling friends, or growing recognition of the importance of providing real opportunity for new writers and artists. The competition was tough; the winners' success all the more earned.

This year we have added two new writers to our illustrious panel of judges. We've added Hal Clement, recipient of the Science Fiction Writers of America Grand Master Award in recognition of his lifetime of achievement in the field of science fiction writing. His first story appeared in the July 1942 issue of *Astounding Science Fiction* magazine. He published consistently throughout the intervening years and continues writing to this day.

We also welcome Charles Sheffield, winner of the Campbell, Sei-un (Japanese), Hugo and Nebula Awards. In addition to his prize-winning novels, Dr. Sheffield, a distinguished scientist, has published more than one hundred science fiction short stories.

Our writer judges for this year were:

Kevin J. Anderson   Doug Beason
Gregory Benford   Algis Budrys

Hal Clement   Nina Kiriki Hoffman
Eric Kotani   Anne McCaffrey
Larry Niven   Andre Norton
Frederik Pohl   Jerry Pournelle
Tim Powers   Charles Sheffield
Robert Silverberg   K. D. Wentworth
Orson Scott Card   Jack Williamson

Our illustrator judges for this year were:

Edd Cartier   Vincent Di Fate
Diane Dillon   Leo Dillon
Bob Eggleton   Will Eisner
Frank Frazetta   Judith Holman
Laura Brodian Freas   Frank Kelly Freas
Ron Lindahn   Val Lakey Lindahn
Sergey V. Poyarkov   H. R. Van Dongen

L. Ron Hubbard's Writers of the Future Contest 2001 winners:

First Quarter
1. Ray Roberts
   The Haunted Seed
2. Ari Goelman
   Lost on the Road
3. Tom Brennan
   Free Fall

Second Quarter
1. Patrick Rothfuss
   The Road to Levenshir
2. David D. Levine
   Rewind
3. Lee Battersby
   Carrying the God

Third Quarter

1. Dylan Otto Krider
   Eating, Drinking, Walking
2. Seppo Kurki
   Origami Cranes
3. Woody O. Carsky-Wilson
   Worlds Apart

Fourth Quarter

1. Susan Fry
   Graveyard Tea
2. Leon J. West
   Memoria Technica
3. Jae Brim
   All Winter Long

Published Finalists

Aimee C. Amodio
What Became of the King
Carl Frederick
The Art of Creation

Joel Best
Prague 47
Drew Morby
The Dragon Cave

Nnedi Okorafor
Windseekers

L. Ron Hubbard's Illustrators of the Future Contest 2001 winners:

Irena Yankova Dimitrova
Hristo Dimitrov Ginev
Brian Hailes
David C. Mullins
Fritz Peters

Anthony Arutunian
Darlene Gait
John Kolbek
Jason Pastrana
C. M. Wolf

Rey Rosario

Our heartiest congratulations to them all! May we see much more of their work in the future.

NEW WRITERS!

L. Ron Hubbard's
Writers of the Future Contest

OPPORTUNITY FOR
NEW AND AMATEUR WRITERS OF
NEW SHORT STORIES OR NOVELETTES OF
SCIENCE FICTION OR FANTASY

No entry fee is required.
Entrants retain all publication rights.

ALL AWARDS ARE ADJUDICATED BY
PROFESSIONAL WRITERS ONLY

PRIZES EVERY THREE MONTHS: $1,000, $750, $500.
ANNUAL GRAND PRIZE: $4,000 ADDITIONAL!

Don't Delay! Send Your Entry to
L. Ron Hubbard's
Writers of the Future Contest
P.O. Box 1630
Los Angeles, CA 90078

CONTEST RULES

1. No entry fee is required and all rights in the story remain the property of the author. All types of science fiction, fantasy and horror with fantastic elements are welcome.

2. All entries must be original works, in English. Plagiarism, which includes the use of third-party poetry, song lyrics, characters or another person's universe, without written permission, will result in disqualification. Excessive violence or sex, determined by the judges, will result in disqualification. Entries may not have been previously published in professional media.

3. To be eligible, entries must be works of prose, up to 17,000 words in length. We regret we cannot consider poetry or works intended for children.

4. The contest is open only to those who have not had professionally published a novel or short novel, or more than one novelette, or more than three short stories, in any medium. Professional publication is deemed to be payment, and at least 5,000 copies or 5,000 hits.

5. Entries must be typewritten or a computer printout in black ink on white paper, double spaced, with numbered pages. All other formats will be disqualified. Each entry must have a cover page with the title of the work, the author's name, address and telephone number, an approximate word count and e-mail address if available. Every subsequent page must carry the title and a page number, but the author's name must be deleted to facilitate fair judging.

6. Manuscripts will be returned after judging if the author has provided return postage and a self-addressed envelope. All other manuscripts will be destroyed.

7. There shall be three cash prizes in each quarter: a First Prize of $1,000, a Second Prize of $750, and a Third Prize of $500, in U.S. dollars or the recipient's local equivalent amount. In addition, at the end of the year the four First Prize winners will have their entries rejudged, and a Grand Prize winner shall be determined and will receive an additional $4,000. All winners will also receive trophies or certificates.

8. The contest has four quarters, beginning on October 1, January 1, April 1 and July 1. The year will end on September 30. To be eligible for judging in its quarter, an entry must be postmarked no later than midnight on the last day of the quarter.

9. Each entrant may submit only one manuscript per quarter. Winners are ineligible to make further entries in the contest.

10. All entries for each quarter are final. No revisions are accepted.

11. Entries will be judged by professional authors. The decisions of the judges are entirely their own, and are final.

12. Winners in each quarter will be individually notified of the results by mail.

13. This contest is void where prohibited by law.

NEW ILLUSTRATORS!

CONTEST RULES

1. The contest is open to entrants from all nations. (However, entrants should provide themselves with some means for written communication in English.) All themes of science fiction and fantasy illustrations are welcome: every entry is judged on its own merits only. No entry fee is required, and all rights in the entries remain the property of the artists.

2. By submitting work to the contest, the entrant agrees to abide by all contest rules.

3. The contest is open to those who have not previously published more than three black-and-white story illustrations, or more than one process-color painting, in media distributed nationally to the general public, such as magazines or books sold at newsstands, or books sold in stores merchandising to the general public. The submitted entry shall not have been previously published in professional media as exampled above.

If you are not sure of your eligibility, write to the contest address with details, enclosing a business-size self-addressed envelope with return postage. The Contest Administration will reply with a determination.

Winners in previous quarters are not eligible to make further entries.

4. Only one entry per quarter is permitted. The entry must be original to the entrant. Plagiarism, infringement of the rights of others, or other violations of the contest rules will result in disqualification.

5. An entry shall consist of three illustrations done by the entrant in a black-and-white medium. Each must represent a theme different from the other two.

6. ENTRIES SHOULD NOT BE THE ORIGINAL DRAWINGS, but should be large black-and-white photocopies of a quality satisfactory to the entrant. Entries must be submitted unfolded and flat, in an envelope no larger than 9 inches by 12 inches.

All entries must be accompanied by a self-addressed return envelope of the appropriate size, with correct U.S. postage affixed. (Non-U.S. entrants should enclose international postal reply coupons.) If the entrant does not want the photocopies returned, the entry should be clearly marked DISPOSABLE COPIES: DO NOT RETURN.

A business-size self-addressed envelope with correct postage should be included so that judging results can be returned to the entrant.

7. To facilitate anonymous judging, each of the three photocopies must be accompanied by a removable cover sheet bearing the artist's name, address, telephone number, and an identifying title for that work as well as an e-mail address if available. The photocopy of the work should carry the same identifying title, and the artist's signature should be deleted from the photocopy.

The Contest Administration will remove and file the cover sheets, and forward only the anonymous entry to the judges.

8. To be eligible for a quarterly judging, an entry must be postmarked no later than the last day of the quarter.

Late entries will be included in the following quarter, and the Contest Administration will so notify the entrant.

9. There will be three co-winners in each quarter. Each winner will receive an outright cash grant of U.S. $500 and a certificate of merit. Such winners also receive eligibility to compete for the annual Grand Prize of an additional outright cash grant of $4,000 together with the annual Grand Prize trophy.

10. Competition for the Grand Prize is designed to acquaint the entrant with customary practices in the field of professional illustrating. It will be conducted in the following manner:

Each winner in each quarter will be furnished a specification sheet giving details on the size and kind of black-and-white illustration work required for the Grand Prize competition. Requirements will be of the sort customarily stated by professional publishing companies.

These specifications will be furnished to the entrant by the Contest Administration, using Return Receipt Requested mail or its equivalent.

Also furnished will be a copy of a science fiction or fantasy story, to be illustrated by the entrant. This story will have been selected for that purpose by the Coordinating Judge of the contest. Thereafter, the entrant will work toward completing the assigned illustration.

In order to retain eligibility for the Grand Prize, each entrant shall, within thirty (30) days of receipt of the said story assignment, send to the contest address the entrant's black-and-white page illustration of the assigned story in accordance with the specification sheet.

The entrant's finished illustration shall be in the form of camera-ready art prepared in accordance with the specification sheet and securely packed, shipped at the entrant's own risk. The contest will exercise due care in handling all submissions as received.

The said illustration will then be judged in competition for the Grand Prize on the following basis only:

Each Grand Prize judge's personal opinion on the extent to which it makes the judge want to read the story it illustrates.

11. The contest shall contain four quarters each year, beginning on October 1 and going on to January 1, April 1 and July 1, with the year ending at midnight on September 30. Entrants in each quarter will be individually notified of the quarter's judging results by mail. The winning entrants' participation in the contest shall continue until the results of the Grand Prize judging have been announced.

Information regarding subsequent contests may be obtained by sending a self-addressed business-size envelope, with postage, to the contest address.

12. The Grand Prize winner shall be announced at the L. Ron Hubbard Awards Event to be held in the year subsequent to the year of the particular contest.

13. Entries will be judged by professional artists only. Each quarterly judging and the Grand Prize judging may have different panels of judges. The decisions of the judges are entirely their own and are final.

14. This contest is void where prohibited by law.

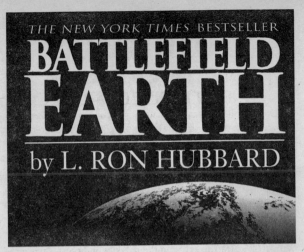

ENTER THE COMPELLING AND IMAGINATIVE UNIVERSE OF

WWW.BATTLEFIELDEARTH.COM

Discover the exciting and expansive universe of *Battlefield Earth*, which has an arsenal of features, plenty of content and free downloads. Here are a few highlights of what's in store for you:

• UNIVERSE—Find out about the different characters, places, races, crafts, weapons and artifacts that make up the universe of *Battlefield Earth*. Also discover the major events that led up to the discovery of Earth by the Psychlos, and the technology that they have used for hundreds of thousands of years to terrorize the galaxies and crush their enemies.

• COMMUNITY—As a member of the *Battlefield Earth*® community you have access to free downloads, including screensavers and desktop wallpaper. You also get to explore the *Battlefield Earth* Fan Gallery, where fans have contributed their artistic visions and interpretations of the story. (You can also create and add your own art to the gallery.)

• TRIVIA—Do you know:
How the Psychlos discovered Earth?
What element is lethal to Psychlos?
Where the Brigantes originate from?

Test your *Battlefield Earth* knowledge in the trivia game contained in the community section of the site.

**NEXT TIME YOU'RE ON-LINE
ENTER THE <u>BATTLEFIELD EARTH</u> SITE—
WHERE L. RON HUBBARD'S MASTERPIECE
OF FICTION COMES ALIVE!**

Mission Earth

BY
L. RON HUBBARD

The ten-volume action-packed intergalactic spy adventure

"A superbly imaginative, intricately
plotted invasion of Earth."
—*Chicago Tribune*

An entertaining narrative told from the eyes of alien invaders, *Mission Earth* is packed with captivating suspense and adventure.

Heller, a Royal Combat Engineer, has been sent on a desperate mission to halt the self-destruction of Earth—wholly unaware that a secret branch of his own government (the Coordinated Information Apparatus) has dispatched its own agent, whose sole purpose is to sabotage him at all costs, as part of its clandestine operation.

With a cast of dynamic characters, biting satire and plenty of twists, action and emotion, Heller is pitted against incredible odds in this intergalactic game where the future of Earth hangs in the balance.

"If you don't force yourself to set it down and talk to your family from time to time, you may be looking for a new place to live." —Orson Scott Card

". . . all the entertainment anybody could ask for."
— *New York Newsday*

Each Volume a *New York Times* Bestseller:

Available in paperback for $6.99 or audio for $15.95 each

Vol. 1. The Invaders Plan

Vol. 2. Black Genesis

Vol. 3. The Enemy Within

Vol. 4. An Alien Affair

Vol. 5. Fortune of Fear

Vol. 6. Death Quest

Vol. 7. Voyage of Vengeance

Vol. 8. Disaster

Vol. 9. Villainy Victorious

Vol. 10. The Doomed Planet

BUY YOUR COPIES TODAY!

Call toll free: 1-877-8GALAXY or visit www.galaxy-press.com
Mail your order to:
Galaxy Press, L.L.C.
7051 Hollywood Blvd., Suite 200
Hollywood, CA 90028